PRAISE FOR NEAL STEPHENSON AND

SNOW CRASH

$2.50

"Stephenson has not stepped, he has ~~~~ onto the literary stage with this novel."

—*Los Angeles Reader*

"Brilliantly realized ... Stephenson turns out to be an engaging guide to an onrushing tomorrow."

—*The New York Times Book Review*

"Fast-forward free-style mall mythology for the 21st century."

—William Gibson

"Stylish noir extrapolation becomes gloriously witty social satire ... savor Stephenson's delicious prose and cheerfully impudent wit. Cyberpunk isn't dead—it has just (belatedly) developed a sense of humor."

—*Locus*

"The all-too-near future masterfully conceived."

—*San Francisco Bay Guardian*

Zodiac

THE ECO-THRILLER

Neal Stephenson

BANTAM BOOKS

New York   Toronto   London   Sydney   Auckland

This edition contains the complete text
of the original trade paperback edition.
NOT ONE WORD HAS BEEN OMITTED.

ZODIAC
A Bantam Book/published by arrangement
with Atlantic Monthly Press

PUBLISHING HISTORY
Atlantic Monthly Press published 1988
Bantam edition/July 1995

ISBN 0-553-57386-1

Published simultaneously in the United States and Canada

Bantam Books are published by Bantam Books, a division of Bantam Doubleday Dell
Publishing Group, Inc. Its trademark, consisting of the words "Bantam Books" and the
portrayal of a rooster, is Registered in U.S. Patent and Trademark Office and in other
countries. Marca Registrada. Bantam Books, 1540 Broadway, New York, New York
10036.

PRINTED IN THE UNITED STATES OF AMERICA
OPM 0 9 8 7 6 5

ACKNOWLEDGMENTS

A mere acknowledgment doesn't fully reflect the contribution made by Marco Paul Johann Kaltofen; a spot on the title page would be more fitting.

In the category of plain old, but deserved, acknowledgments, it should be mentioned that the hard-boiled fiction of James Crumley got me going on this project; people who like this one should buy his books. Joe King put me on the hard-boiled trail with a well-timed recommendation. Jackson Schmidt read and corrected the manuscript with an attention to fine detail I would not have expected even if I had been paying him. My agents, Liz Darhansoff, Abby Thomas, and Lynn Pleshette, gave useful suggestions and then scorched the earth with their zeal, despite blaming me for a sudden aversion to eating lobsters and swimming in the Hudson. Gary Fisketjon edited it closely and intelligently, once again proving his more-than-casual acquaintance with the novel—a 250-year-old art form.

Jon Owens, Jon Halper, Jackson Schmidt, Steve Horst, and Chris Doolan all said or did things that got blended in. My wife, Dr. Ellen Lackermann, helped with the medical research, and refrains from becoming too despondent over my spending eight to sixteen hours a day welded to a Macintosh. Finally, Heather Matheson read the manuscript and told me that the main character was an asshole—confirming that I was on the right track.

TO ELLEN

Down by the river,
Down by the banks of the River Charles
That's where you'll find me
Along with lovers, muggers and thieves
Well I love that dirty water,
Oh Boston, you're my home.

—THE INMATES

1

ROSCOMMON CAME and laid waste to the garden an hour after dawn, about the time I usually get out of bed and he usually passes out on the shoulder of some freeway. My landlord and I have an arrangement. He charges me and my housemates little rent—by Boston standards, none at all—and in return we let him play fast and loose with our ecosystem. Every year at about this time he destroys my garden. He's been known to send workmen into the house without warning, knock out walls in the middle of the night, shut off the water while we shower, fill the basement with unidentified fumes, cut down elms and maples for firewood, and redecorate our rooms. Then he claims he's showing the dump to prospective tenants and we'd better clean it up. Pronto.

This morning I woke to the sound of little green pumpkins exploding under the tires of his station wagon. Then Roscommon stumbled out and tore down our badminton net. After he left, I got up and went out to buy a *Globe*. Wade Boggs had just twisted his ankle and some PCB-contaminated waste oil was on fire in Southie.

When I got back, bacon was smoldering on the range, filling the house with gas-phase polycyclic aromatics—my favorite carcinogen by a long shot. Bartholomew was standing in front of the stove. With the level, cross-eyed stare of the involuntarily awake, he was watching a heavy-metal video on the TV. He was clenching an inflated Hefty bag that took up half the kitchen. Once again, my roommate was using nitrous oxide around an open flame; no wonder he didn't have any eyebrows. When I came in, he raised the bag invitingly. Normally I never do nitrous before breakfast, but I couldn't refuse Bart a thing in the world, so I took the bag and inhaled as deep as I could. My mouth tasted sweet and five seconds later about half of an orgasm backfired in the middle of my brain.

On the screen, poodle-headed rockers were strapping a cheerleader to a sheet of particle board decorated with a pentagram. Far away, Bartholomew was saying: "Pöyzen Böyzen, man. Very hot."

It was too early for social criticism. I grabbed the channel selector.

"No Stooges on at this hour," Bart warned, "I checked." But I'd already moved us way up into Deep Cable, where a pair of chaw-munching geezers were floating on a nontoxic river in Dixie, demonstrating how to push-start a comatose fish.

Tess emerged from the part of the house where women lived and bathrooms were clean. She frowned against the light, scowling at our bubbling animal flesh, our cubic yard of nitrous. She rummaged in the fridge for some homemade yogurt. "Don't you guys ever lay off that stuff?"

"Meat or gas?"

"You tell me. Which one's more toxic?"

"Sangamon's Principle," I said. "The simpler the molecule, the better the drug. So the best drug is oxygen. Only two atoms. The second-best, nitrous oxide—a mere three atoms. The third-best, ethanol—nine. Past that, you're talking lots of atoms."

"So?"

"Atoms are like people. Get lots of them together, never know what they'll do. It is my understanding, Tess, that you've been referring to me, about town, as a 'Granola James Bond'."

Tess didn't give a fuck. "Who told you about that?"

"You come up with a cute phrase, it gets around."

"I thought you'd enjoy it."

"Even a horse's ass like me can detect sarcasm."

"So what would you rather be called?"

"Toxic Spiderman. Because he's broke and he never gets laid."

Tess squinted at me, implying that there was a reason for both problems. Bart broke the silence. "Shit, man, Spiderman's got his health. James Bond probably has AIDS."

I went outside and followed Roscommon's tire tracks through the backyard. All the pumpkins were destroyed, but I didn't care about these decoys. What could you do with a pumpkin? Get orange shit all over the house? The important stuff—corn and tomatoes—were planted up against fences or behind piles of rubble, where his station wagon couldn't reach.

We'd never asked Roscommon if we could plant a garden out here in the Largest Yard in Boston. Which, because it wasn't supposed to exist, gave him the right to drive over it. Gardens have to be watered, you see, and water bills are included in our nominal rent, so by having a garden we're actually ripping him off.

There was at least an acre back here, tucked away in kind of a space warp caused by Brighton's irrational street pattern. Not even weeds knew how to grow in this field of concrete and brick rubble. When we started the garden, Bartholomew and Ike and I spent two days sifting through it, putting the soil into our plot, piling the rest in cairns. Other piles were scattered randomly around the Largest Back Yard in Boston. Every so often Roscommon would dynamite another one of his holdings, show up with a rented dump truck, back across the garden, through the badminton net, and over some lawn furniture, and make a new pile.

I just hoped he didn't try to stash any toxic waste back there. I hoped that wasn't the reason for the low rent. Because if he did that, I would be forced to call down a plague upon his house. I would evacuate his bank accounts, burn his villages, rape his horses, sell his children into slavery. The whole Toxic Spiderman bit. And then I'd have to become the penniless alter ego, the Toxic Peter Parker. I'd have to pay real Boston rent, a thousand a month, with no space for badminton.

Peter Parker is the guy who got bit by the radioactive spider, the toxic bug if you will, and became Spiderman. Normally he's a nebbish. No money, no prestige, no future. But if you try to mug him in a dark alley, you're meat. The question he keeps asking himself is: "Do those moments of satisfaction I get as Spiderman make up for all the crap I have to take as Peter Parker?" In my case, the answer is yes.

In the dark ages of my life, when I worked at Massachusetts Analytical Chemical Systems, or Mass Anal for short, I owned your basic VW van. But a Peter Parker type can't afford car insurance in this town, so now I transport myself on a bicycle. So once I'd fueled myself up on coffee and Bart's baco-cinders—nothing beats an all-black breakfast—and read all the comics, I threw one leg over my battle-scarred all-terrain stump-jumper and rode several miles to work.

Hurricane Alison had blown through the day before yesterday, trailed by hellacious rainfall. Tree branches and lakes of rainwater were in the streets. We call it rainwater; actually it's raw sewage. The traffic signal at Comm Ave and Charlesgate West was fried. In Boston, this doesn't lead to heartwarming stories in the tabloids about ordinary citizens who get out of their cars to direct traffic. Instead, it gives us the excuse to drive like the Chadian army. Here we had two lanes of traffic crossing with four, and the two were losing out in a big way. Comm Ave was backed up all the way into B.U. So I rode between the lanes for half a mile to the head of the class.

The problem is, if the two drivers at the front of the line aren't sufficiently aggressive, it doesn't matter how tough the people behind them are. The whole avenue will just sit there until it collectively boils over. And horn honking wasn't helping, though a hundred or so motorists were giving it a try.

When I got to Charlesgate West, where Comm Ave was cut off by the torrent pouring down that one-way four-laner, I found an underpowered station wagon from Maine at the head of one lane, driven by a mom who was trying to look after four children, and a vintage Mercedes in the other, driven by an old lady who looked like she'd just forgotten her own address. And half a dozen bicyclists, standing there waiting for a real asshole to take charge.

What you have to do is take it one lane at a time. I waited for a twenty-foot gap in traffic on the first lane of Charlesgate and just eased out into it.

The approaching BMW made an abortive swerve toward the next lane, causing a ripple to spread across Charlesgate as everyone for ten cars back tried to head east. Then he throbbed to a halt (computerized antilock braking system) and slumped over on his horn button. The next lane was easy: some Camaro-driving freshman from Jersey made the mistake of slowing down and I seized his lane. The asshole in the BMW tried to cut behind me but half the bicyclists, and the biddy in the Benz, had the presence of mind to lurch out and block his path.

Within ten seconds a huge gap showed up in the third lane, and I ate it up before Camaro could serve over. I ate it up so aggressively that some Clerk Typist II in a Civic slowed down in the fourth lane long enough for me to grab that one. And then the dam broke as the Chadian army mounted a charge and reamed out the intersection. I figured BMW, Camaro, and Civic could shut their engines off and go for a walk.

Pedestrians and winos applauded. A young six-digit lawyer, hardly old enough to shave, cruised up from ten cars back and shouted out his electric sunroof that I really had balls.

I said, "Tell me something I didn't know, you fucking android from Hell."

The Mass Ave Bridge took me over the Charles. I stopped halfway across to look it over. The river, that is. The river and the Harbor, they're my stock in trade. Not much wind today and I took a big whoof of river air in my nostrils, wondering what kind of crap had been dumped into it, upstream, the night before. Which might sound kind of primitive, but the human nose happens to be an exquisitely sensitive analytical device. There are certain compounds for which your schnozz is the best detector ever made. No machine can beat it. For example, I can tell a lot about a car by smelling its exhaust: how well the engine is tuned, whether it's got a catalytic converter, what kind of gas it burns.

So every so often I smell the Charles, just to see if I'm missing anything. For a river that's only thirty miles long, it has the width and the toxic burdens of the Ohio or the Cuyahoga.

Then through the MIT campus, through the milling geeks with the fifty-dollar textbooks under their arms. College students look so damn young these days. Not long ago I was going to school on the other side of the river, thinking of these trolls as peers and rivals. Now I just felt sorry for them. They probably felt sorry for me. By visual standards, I'm the scum of the earth. The other week I was at a party full of Boston yuppies, the originals, and they were all complaining about the panhandlers on the Common, how aggressive they'd become. I hadn't noticed, myself, since they never panhandled me. Then I figured out why: because I looked like one of them. Blue jeans with holes in the knees. Tennis shoes with holes over the big toes, where my uncut toenails rub against the toeclips on my bicycle. Several layers of t-shirts, long underwear tops, and flannel shirts, easily adjustable to regulate my core temperature. Shaggy blond hair, cut maybe once a year. Formless red beard, trimmed or lopped off maybe twice a year. Not exactly fat, but blessed with the mature, convex body typical of those who live on Thunderbird and Ding-Dongs. No briefcase, aimless way of looking around, tendency to sniff the river.

Though I rode through MIT on a nice bike, I'd sprayed it with some cheap gold paint so it wouldn't look nice. Even the lock looked like a piece of shit: a Kryptonite lock all scarred up by boltcutters. We'd used it to padlock a gate on a toxic site last year and the owners had tried to get through using the wrong tools.

In California I could have passed for a hacker, heading for some high-tech company, but in Massachusetts even the hackers wore shirts with buttons. I pedalled through hacker territory, through the strip of little high-tech shops that feed off MIT, and into the square where my outfit has its regional office.

GEE, the Group of Environmental Extremists. Excuse me: GEE *International*. They employ me as a professional asshole, an innate talent I've enjoyed ever since second grade, when I learned how to give my teacher migraine headaches with a penlight. I could cite other examples, give you a tour down the gallery of the broken and infuriated authority figures who have tried to teach, steer, counsel, reform, or suppress me over the years, but that would sound like boasting. I'm not that proud of being a congenital pain in the ass. But I will take money for it.

I carried my bike up four flights of stairs, doing my bit for physical fitness. GEE stickers were plastered on the risers of the stairs, so there was always a catch phrase six feet in front of your eyes: SAVE THE WHALES and something about the BABY SEALS. By the time you made it up to the fourth floor, you were out of breath, and fully indoctrinated. Locked my bike to a radiator, because you never knew, and went in.

Tricia was running the front desk. Flaky but nice, has a few strange ideas about phone etiquette, thinks I'm all right. "Oh, shit," she said.

"What?"

"You won't believe it."

"What?"

"The other car."

"The van?"

"Yeah. Wyman."

"How bad?"

"We don't know yet. It's still sitting out on the shoulder."

I just assumed it was totalled, and that Wyman would have to be fired, or at least busted down to a position where he couldn't so much as sit in a GEE car. A mere three days ago he had taken our Subaru out to buy duct tape, and in a parking lot no larger than a tennis court, had managed to ram a concrete light-pole pedestal hard enough to total the vehicle. His fifteen-minute explanation was earnest but impossible to follow; when I asked him to just start from the beginning, he accused me of being too linear.

Now he'd trashed our one remaining shitbox van. The national office would probably hear of it. I almost felt sorry for him.

"How?"

"He thinks he shifted into reverse on the freeway."

"Why? It's got an automatic transmission."

"He likes to think for himself."

"Where is he now?"

"Who knows? I think he's afraid to come in."

"No. You'd be afraid to come in. I might be afraid. Wyman won't be afraid. You know what he'll do? He'll come in fresh as a daisy and ask for the keys to the Omni."

Fortunately I'd taken all the keys to the Omni, other than my own, and hammered them into slag. And whenever I parked it, I opened the hood and yanked out the coil wire and put it in my pocket.

You might think that the lack of coil wire or even keys would not stop members of the GEE strike force, Masters of Stealth, Scourge of Industry, from starting a car for very long. Aren't these the people who staged their own invasion of the Soviet Union? Didn't they sneak a supposedly disabled, heavily guarded ship out of Amsterdam? Don't they skim across the oceans in high-powered Zodiacs held together with bubble gum and bobby pins, coming to the rescue of innocent marine mammals?

Well sometimes they do, but only a handful have those kinds of talents, and I'm the only one in the Northeast office. The others, like Wyman, tend to be ex-English majors who affect a hysterical helplessness in the face of things with moving parts. Talk to them about cams or gaskets and they'll sing you a protest song. To them, yanking out the Omni's coil wire was black magic.

"And you got three calls from Fotex. They really want to talk to you."

"What about?"

"The guy wants to know if they should shut their plant down today."

The day before, talking to some geek at Fotex, I'd mumbled something about closing them down. But in fact I was going to New Jersey tomorrow to close someone else down, so Fotex could keep dumping phenols, acetone, phthalates, various solvents, copper, silver, lead, mercury, and zinc into Boston Harbor to their heart's content, at least until I got back.

"Tell them I'm in Jersey." That would keep them guessing; Fotex had some plants down there also.

I went back to my office, cutting across a barnlike room where most of the other GEE people sat among half-completed banners and broken Zodiac parts, drinking herbal teas and talking into phones:

"500 ppm sounds good to me."

"Don't put us on the back page of the Food section."

"Do those breed in estuaries?"

I wasn't one of those GEE veterans who got his start spraying orange dye on baby seals in Newfie, or getting beat senseless by Frog commandos in the South Pacific. I slipped into it, moonlighting for them while I held down my job at Mass Anal. Partly by luck, I broke a big case for GEE, right before my boss figured out what an enormous pain in the ass I could be. Mass Anal fired, GEE hired. My salary was cut in half and my ulcer vanished: I could eat onion rings at IHOP again, but I couldn't afford to.

My function at Mass Anal had been to handle whatever walked in the door. Sometimes it was genuine industrial espionage—peeling apart a running shoe to see what kinds of adhesives it used—but usually it amounted to analyzing tap water for the anxious yuppies moving into the center of Boston, closet environmentalists who didn't want to pour aromatic hydrocarbons into their babies any more than they'd burn 7-Eleven gasoline in their Saabs. But once upon a time, this guy in a running suit walked in and got routed to me; anyone who wasn't in pinstripes got routed to me. He was brandishing an empty Doritos bag and for a minute I was afraid he wanted me to check it for dioxins or some other granola nightmare. But he read my expression. I probably looked skeptical and irritated. I probably looked like an asshole.

"Sorry about the bag. It was the only container I could find on the trail."

"What's in it?"

"I'm not sure."

Predictable answer. "*Approximately* what's in it?"

"Dirt. But really strange dirt."

I took the Doritos bag and emptied it out all over the

comics page of the *Globe*. I love the comics, laughing out loud when I read them, and everyone thinks I'm a simpleton. The runner let out kind of a little snort, like he couldn't believe this was how I did chemistry. It looks impressive to pour the sample into a fresh Pyrex beaker, but it's faster to spread it out over Spiderman and Bloom County. I pulled the toothpick out of my mouth and began to pop the little clods apart.

But that was just for the hell of it, because I already knew what was wrong with this dirt. It was green—and purple and red and blue. The runner knew that, he just didn't know why. But I had a pretty good idea: heavy-metal contamination, the kind of really nasty stuff that goes into pigments.

"You jogging in hazardous waste dumps, or what?" I asked.

"You're saying this stuff's hazardous?"

"Fuck, yes. Heavy metals. See this yellow clump here? Gotta be cadmium. Now, cadmium they tested once as a poison gas, in World War I. It vaporizes at a real low temperature, six or seven hundred degrees. They had some people breathe that vapor."

"What does it do?"

"Gangrene of the testicles."

The jogger inhaled and shifted his pair away from my desk. One of the problems, hanging out with me, is that I can turn any topic into a toxic horror story. I've lost two girlfriends and a job by reading an ingredients label out loud, with annotations, at the wrong time.

"Where?"

"Sweetvale College. Right on campus. There's a wooded area there with a pond and a running trail."

I, a B.U. graduate, was trying to imagine this: a college campus that had trees and ponds on it.

"This is what it looks like," the guy continued, "the dirt, the pond, everything."

"Colored like this?"

"It's psychedelic."

Despite being a chemist, I refuse psychedelics these days on the grounds that they violate Sangamon's Principle. But I understood what he was getting at.

So the next day I got on my bike and rode out there and damned if he wasn't right. At one end of the campus was this weedy patch of forest, sticking out into a triangle formed by some of the Commonwealth's more expensive suburbs. It wasn't used much. That was probably just as well because the area around the pond was a heavy-metal sewer, and I ain't talking about rock and roll. Rainbow-colored, a little like water with gasoline floating on it, but this wasn't superficial. The colors went all the way down. They matched the dirt. All the colors were different and—forgive me if I repeat myself on this point—they all caused cancer.

From my freshman gut course in physical geography at Boston University, I knew damn well this wasn't a natural pond. So the only question was: what was here before?

Finding out was my first gig as a toxic detective, and the only thing that made it difficult was my own jerk-ass fumbling in the public library. I threw myself on the mercy of Esmerelda, a black librarian of somewhere between ninety and a hundred who contained within her bionic hairdo all knowledge, or the ability to find it. She got me some old civic documents. Sure enough, a paint factory had flourished there around the turn of the century. When it folded, the owner donated the land to the university. Nice gift: a square mile of poison.

I called GEE and the rest was history. Newspaper articles, video bites on the TV news, which didn't look that great on my black-and-white; state and federal clean-up efforts, and a web of lawsuits. Two weeks later GEE asked me to analyze some water for them. Within a month I was chained to a drum of toxic waste on the State house steps, and within six, I was Northeast Toxics Coordinator for GEE International.

My office was the size of a piano crate, but mine nonetheless. I wanted a computer on my desk, and none of the other GEE honchos would risk sharing a room with one. Computers need electrical transformers, some of which are made with PCBs that like to vaporize and ooze out of a computer's ventilation slots, causing miscarriages and other foul omens. The boss gave me his office and moved into the big barnlike room.

The same people barely noticed when Gomez, our "office manager," started painting the walls of that office. By doing so he exposed them to toxic fumes millions of times more concentrated than what I was getting from my computer. But they didn't notice because they're used to paint. They paint things all the time. Same deal with the stuff they spray on their underarms and put into their gas tanks. Gomez wanted to paint my office now, but I wouldn't let him.

Esmerelda, ever vigilant, had shot me a bunch of greasy xeroxes from the microfilm archives. They were articles from the *Lighthouse-Republican* of Blue Kills, N.J., a small city half-way down the Jersey Shore which was shortly to feel my wrath. It was the kind of newspaper that was still running Dennis the Menace in the largest available size. A Gasoline Alley, Apartment 3-G, and Nancy kind of paper.

The articles were all from the sports section. Sports, as in hunting and fishing, which take place outdoors, which is where the environment is. That's why environmental news is in the sports section.

Esmerelda had found me four different articles, all written by different reporters (no specialist on the staff; not considered an important issue) on vaguely environmental subjects. A local dump leaching crap into an estuary; a freeway project that would trash some swamp land; mysterious films of gunk on the river; and concerns about toxic waste that could be coming from a plant just outside of town, operated by a large corporation we shall refer to as the Swiss Bastards. Along with the Boston Bastards, the Napalm Droids, the Plutonium Lords, the Hindu Killers, the Lung Assassins, the Ones in Buffalo, and the Rhine-Rapers, they were among the largest chemical corporations of a certain planet, third one out from a certain mediocre star in an average spiral galaxy named after a candy bar.

Each of the articles was 2500 words long and written in the same style. Clearly, the editor of the *Lighthouse-Republican* ruled with an iron hand. Local residents were referred to as Blukers. Compound sentences were discouraged and the inverted-pyramid structure rigorously followed. The PR flacks who worked for the Swiss Bastards were referred to by the old-fashioned term "authorities," rather than the newer and sexier "sources."

My only worry was that maybe this editor was so fucking old and decrepit that he was already dead, or even retired. On the other hand, it seemed he was a dyed-in-the-wool "sportsman," a type traditionally long-lived, unless he'd spent too much time sloshing around in a particular toxic swamp. Esmerelda, accustomed to my ways, had sent a xerox of the most recent masthead, which didn't show any changes. The senior sports editor was Everett "Red" Grooten and the sports-page editor was Alvin Goldberg.

Raucous laughter probably sounded from my office. Tricia hung up on Fotex's PR director and shouted "S.T., what are you doing in there?" Called the florist and had them send the usual to Esmerelda. Cranked up my old PCB-spitter and searched my files. "Fish, marine, sport, Mid-Atlantic, effects of organic solvents on." "Estuaries, waterfowl populations of, effects of organic solvents on." These were old boilerplate paragraphs I'd written long ago. Mostly they referred to EPA studies or recent research. Every so often they quoted a "source" at GEE International, the well-known environmental group, usually me. I directed the word processor to do a search-and-replace to change "source" to "authority."

Then I pulled up my press release about what the Swiss Bastards were pumping into the waters off Blue Kills, which my gas chromatograph and I had discovered during my last trip down there. Threw it into the center of the piece and then composed a hard-hitting topic sentence in basic Dick-and-Jane dialect, no compound sentences, announcing that Bluker sportsmen might be the first ones to feel the effects of the "growing toxic waste problems" centered on the Swiss Bastards' illegal dumping. Hacked it all into an inverted-pyramid shape, and ended up with 2350 words. Put on a final paragraph, the lowly capstone of the pyramid, mentioning that some people from GEE International, the well-known environmental group, might be dropping by Blue Kills any day now.

Opened up my printer and put in a daisy wheel that produced a typeface that went out of style in the Thirties. Printed the article up on some unpretentious paper, stuck it in an envelope along with some standard GEE photos of dead flounder and two-headed ducks, suitable for the *Lighthouse-Republican*'s column width. Federal Expressed it to one Red Grooten at his home address, because I had this idea that maybe he didn't stop by the office all that often.

2

WYMAN CALLED. Wyman, the Scourge of Cars. He wanted the keys to the Omni so that he could drive to Erie, Pennsylvania to see his girlfriend, who was about to leave for Nicaragua. For God's sake, she could be bayoneted by contras and he'd never see her again.

"Where's the van, Wyman?"

"I'm not telling you until I get the keys to the Omni."

So I hung up and called the Metro Police, who told me: on the shoulder, westbound lanes, Revere Beach Parkway, near the bridge over the Everett River. Due to be towed at any moment. I hung up when they asked for my name, grabbed my toolbox and headed out.

Gomez heard the wrenches crashing against the insides of the toolbox, fired the last half of his whole-wheat croissant into the "noncompostable nonrecyclables" wastebasket, where it belonged, and intercepted me at the top of the stairs. "Got a job?"

"Sure. What the fuck, come on."

A lot of people out there simply adore GEE. One of them had donated this car to us—in fact, she'd done better. In Massachusetts, the insurance can run way over a thousand bucks a year, so this fine lady was lending us the Omni, no strings attached, and paying the insurance as well. We didn't even know who she was.

Normally an Omni is a piece of shit, an econobox with a 1.6-liter engine. But for a higher sticker price you can get an Omni GLH, which has aerodynamic trim and 2.2 liters and, for a few hundred more, an Omni GLH Turbo, which has all of that plus a turbocharger. GLH, by the way, stands for Goes Like Hell. Honest. When the blower is singing, the engine puts out as much power as a small V8. Add big fat racing tires and alloy wheels and you have yourself a poor man's Porsche, the most lethal weapon ever developed for the Boston traffic wars. Sure, spend three times as much and you could get a car that goes a little faster, but who is seriously going to thrash a vehicle that costs that much? Who'll risk denting it? But if it's an Omni, who cares?

I popped in the coil wire, a detail that Gomez richly appreciated—he made sure I knew it too—and we blew out of there. First we had to unload a lot of junk from out of the back to make room for what we were going to strip off the van: the two containers of hydraulic cement had to go. If I felt the urge to plug a pipe between here and Everett, I'd have to fulfill it later. The big, long roll of nylon banner material, the rappelling harness and climbing ropes, an extra outboard-motor gas tank, a Zodiac inflation pump, and the traveling chemistry lab we jettisoned. The laptop computer for tapping into the GEE International databases. The $5000 gas chromatograph. My big magnets. The Darth Vader Suit. We packed it all into the trunk of Gomez's Impala so we wouldn't have to haul it up to the fourth floor.

We'd hired Gomez after I'd inadvertently gotten him canned from his previous job as a minimum-wage rent-a-cop at one of the state office buildings. Unfortunately for his breed, I make my living by making people like him look like jerks. For weeks we'd been trying to make an appointment with a honcho in the state environmental agency, and he wouldn't even answer our letters.

Shortly before Christmas, I dressed up in a Santa Claus outfit and had Tricia and Debbie (one of our interns) dress up as elves. I forged an ID card, complete with a mug shot of Saint Nick and an address at the North Pole, stuffed my Santa sack full of GEE leaflets, and we blew right past Gomez; he was really in the Christmas spirit. We hit on an *Untergruppen*-secretary who passed us on up to an *Übergruppen*-secretary, then three floors up to a *Sturmband*-secretary, then ten more floors on up to Thelma, the *Übersturmgruppenführer*-secretary, and that poor lady didn't even blink. She led us right into Corrigan's office, the place we'd been trying to penetrate for three months, without even the courtesy of a nasty letter.

"Ho ho ho," I said, and I was sincere.

"Well, Santy Claus!" said Corrigan, that poor jackass. "What you got there?"

"I've got a surprise for you, you naughty boy! Ho ho ho!" In the corner of my eye I could see beams of high-energy light sweeping down the hall as the Channel 5 minicam crew stormed past Thelma's vacant desk.

"What kind of surprise," he said. I upended my pillowcase and treated him to a propaganda blizzard just as the cameraman centered his crosshairs on Corrigan's forehead. We not only got him to agree to a meeting, but also got the agreement broadcast throughout the Commonwealth—just about the only way to make an environmental appointee keep his word. Corrigan hasn't been very nice to me since then, but I did make Thelma's Christmas card list.

Anyway, Gomez got fired for accepting my fake ID. We ended up hiring him to do jobs here and there around the office. Nothing illegal. When it came to finding things that needed fixing or painting he was an enterprising guy. To watch him find loose stair treads and peeling paint was to see free enterprise in action. Not unlike my own job.

The van was right where Wyman had left it, in the dirtiest, the most dangerous, the most crime-ridden neighborhood in Boston. I'm not talking about crack dealers, tenements, or minority groups here. The neighborhood isn't Roxbury. It's the zone around the Mystic River where most of New England's heavy industry is located. It's split fifty-fifty between Everett and Charlestown. I spend a lot of my time up here. Most of the "rivers" feeding into the Mystic are drainage ditches, no more than a couple of miles long. The nation's poisoners congregate along these rivers and piss into them. In my Zodiac I have visited them personally, smelled their yellow, brown, white, and red waters, and figured out what they're made of.

We could see Wyman's footprints wandering out across the mud flats next to the Everett River, heading for a side street that might lead him to a telephone. I already knew the name of the street: Alkali Lane. We could see the place where he got a whiff of something, maybe, or got close enough to read the name of the street, then spun around the loped back to the nontoxic shoulder, obsessively wiping his Reeboks on the dead ragweed. From there, he'd hitchhiked.

Gomez stripped the van in much the same way that a Sioux would dismantle a buffalo. I just concentrated on getting the wheels off, with their brand-new, six-hundred-dollar set of radials that Wyman was going to abandon—a free gift from GEE to a randomly chosen junkyard. I also made sure we got our manhole-lifting tool, which is to me what a keychain is to a janitor. Gomez got the battery, electronic ignition box, cassette player, sheepskin, jack, lug wrenches, tire chains, half case of Ray-Lube, spare fan belt, alternator, and three gallons of gasoline. He was going after the starter when I officially pronounced the van dead.

We took the license plates so we could prove to the insurance company that we weren't driving it anymore, and then I removed the Thermite from the glove compartment. It's wise to keep some handy in case you need to weld some railroad rails together. The van's serial number was stamped on its parts and body in three places, all of which I'd noted down, so I put Thermite on each and ignited them with my cigar. Instant slag. Like a Mafia hitter chopping the fingertips off a corpse.

The identification numbers were still smoking as we climbed back into the Omni. But immediately a vehicle pulled up behind us, a Bronco II with too many antennas and a flashing light on the roof.

"Fucking rent-a-cop," Gomez said. From being one himself, he'd become sensitized to the whole absurd concept.

I walked back so I could read the sign on the Bronco's door: BASCO SECURITY. I knew them well. They owned everything on Alkali Lane and most of the Everett River. In fact, if you stepped off the shoulder of the parkway, you were on their property. Then your shoes would dissolve.

"Morning," said the rent-a-cop, who, like Gomez, was young and skinny. They never had the authority belly of a true Boston cop.

"Morning," I said, sounding like a man in a hurry, "Can I help you?"

He was looking at a picture of me from what looked startlingly like a dossier. Also included were photographic representations of my boss, and of a jerk named Dan Smirnoff, and one I hadn't seen in a while, a fugitive named Boone.

"Sangamon Taylor?"

"You got a warrant somewhere? Hey! You aren't a real cop at all, are you?"

"We got some witnesses. A bunch of us security guards been over there on the main building, watching you here. Now, we know this van."

"I know, we're old pals."

"Right. So we recognized it when it stopped here last night. And we watched you stripping it. And maybe fucking with the VIN?"

"Look. If you want to hassle me, just go to your boss and say, 'pH'. Just tell him that."

"P-H? Isn't that something they put in shampoo?"

"Close enough. Tell him 'pH thirteen'. And for your sake, get a different job. Don't go out there, into those flats, patrolling around. You understand? It's dangerous."

"Oh, yeah," he said, highly amused. "Big criminal element down there."

"Exactly. The board of directors of Basco. The Pleshy family. Don't let them kill again."

Back at the Omni, Gomez said, "What'd you tell him?"

"pH. Went here last week and tested their pH and it was thirteen."

"So?"

"So they're licensed for eight. That means they're putting shit into the river that's more than two times the legal limit."

"Shit, man," Gomez said, scandalized. That was another good thing about Gomez. He never got jaded.

And I hadn't even told him the truth. Actually, the shit coming out of Basco's pipe was a *hundred thousand times* more concentrated than was legally allowed. The difference between pH 13 and pH 8 was five, which meant that pH 13 was ten to the fifth power—a hundred thousand times—more alkaline than pH 8. That kind of thing goes on all the time. But no matter how many diplomas are tacked to your wall, give people a figure like that and they'll pass you off as a flake. You can't get most people to believe how wildly the eco-laws get broken. But if I say "More than twice the legal limit," they get comfortably outraged.

3

I HAD GOMEZ DROP ME OFF in Harvard Square so I could eat birdseed and tofu with a reporter from *The Weekly*. Ditched my cigar. Then I went in to this blond-wood extravaganza, just off the square, allowed the manager to show me her nostrils, and finally picked out Rebecca sitting back in the corner.

"How's the Granola James Bond?"

I nearly unleashed my Toxic Spiderman rap but then remembered that some people actually admired me, Rebecca among them, and it was through admiration and James Bond legends that we got things like free cars and anonymous toxic tips. So I let it drop. Rebecca had picked the sunniest corner of the room and the light was making her green eyes glow like traffic lights and her perfume volatilize off the skin. She and I had been in the sack a few times. The fact that we weren't going to be there in the near future made her a hundred thousand time—oops—more than twice as beautiful. To distract myself, I growled something about beer to a waiter and sat down.

"We have—" the waiter said, and drew a tremendously deep breath.

"Genesee Cream Ale."

"Don't have that, sir."

"Beck's." Because I figured Rebecca was paying.

"The specialty is sparkling water with a twist," Rebecca said.

"I need something to wash the Everett out of my mouth."

"Been out on your Zode?"

"Zodiac to you," I said. "And no, I haven't."

We always began our conversations with this smart-assed crap. Rebecca was a political reporter and spent her life talking to mushmouths and blarney slingers. Talking to someone who would say "fuck" into a tape recorder was like benzedrine to her. There was also an underlying theme of flirtation—"Hey, remember?" "Yeah, I remember." "It was all right, wasn't it?" "Sure was."

"How's Project Lobster?"

"Wow, you prepared for this interview. It's fine. How's the paper?"

"The usual. Civil war, insurrection, financial crisis. But everyone reads the movie reviews."

"Instead of your stuff?"

"Depends on what I'm digging up."

"And what's that?"

She smiled, leaned forward and observed me with cunning eyes. "Pleshy's running," she said.

"Which Pleshy? Running from what?"

"The big Pleshy."

"The Groveler?"

"He's running for president."

"Shit. End of lunch. Now I'm not hungry."

"I knew you'd be delighted."

"What about Basco? Doesn't he have to put all that crap into a blind trust?"

"It's done. That's how I know he's running. I have this friend at the bank."

The Pleshy family ran Basco—they'd founded the company—and that made them the number one polluters of Boston Harbor. The poisoners of Vietnam. The avant-garde of the toxic waste movement. For years I'd been trying to tell them how deep in shit they were, sometimes pouring hydraulic cement into their pipes to drive the point home.

This year, the Pleshy-in-charge was Alvin, a.k.a. the Groveler, an important member of the team of management experts and foreign policy geniuses that brought us victory in Vietnam.

Rebecca showed me samples of his flacks' work: "Many environmentalists have overreacted to the presence of these compounds ..." not chemicals, not toxic waste, but compounds " ... but what exactly is a part per million?" This was followed by a graphic showing an eyedropper-ful of "compounds" going into a railway tank car of pure water.

"Yeah. They're using the PATEOTS measuring system on you. A drop in a tank car. Sounds pretty minor. But you can twist it the other way: a football field has an area of, what, forty-five thousand square feet. A banana peel has an area of maybe a tenth of a square foot. So the area of the banana peel thrown on the football field is only a couple of parts per million. But if your field-goal kicker steps on the peel just as time is expiring, and you're two points down ..."

"PATEOTS?"

"Haven't I told you about that?"

"Explain."

"Stands for Period At The End Of This Sentence. Remember, back in high school the hygiene pamphlets would say, 'a city the size of Dallas could get stoned on a drop of LSD no larger than the period at the end of this sentence.' A lot easier to visualize than, say, micrograms."

"What does that have to do with football?"

"I'm in the business of trying to explain technical things to Joe Six-pack, right? Joe may have the NFL rulebook memorized but he doesn't understand PCBs and he doesn't know a microgram from cunnilingus. So a microgram is about equal to one PATEOTS. A part per million is a drop in a railway tank car—that's what the chemical companies always say, to make it sound less dangerous. If all the baby seals killed last year were laid end to end, they would span a hundred football fields. The tears shed by the mommy seals would fill a tank car. The volume of raw sewage going into the Harbor could fill a football stadium every week."

"Dan Smirnoff says you're working together now."

Some beer found its way into my sinuses. I had to give it to Rebecca: she knew her shit.

Smirnoff was the whole reason for this conversation. All this crap about Pleshy and tank cars was just to get me loosened up. And when I went into my PATEOTS rap, she knew I was ready to be goosed in the 'nads. How many times had I given her my patented PATEOTS rap? Two or three at least. I like a good story. I like to tell it many times. By now she knew: talk to S.T. about eyedroppers and tank cars and he'll fly off the handle. Once I got flying on any toxic theme, she could slip in one tough question while my guard was down, watch my hairy and highly expressive face for a reaction, and glimpse the truth. Or find a basis for all her darkest suspicions.

"Smirnoff's one of these people I have to have contact with. Like a prison guard has to have contact with a certain number of child molesters."

"You'd put him in that category?"

"No, he's not crafty enough. He's just pissed off and very full of himself."

"Sounds familiar."

"Yeah, but I have a reason to be arrogant. He doesn't."

"Patti Bowen at NEST says . . ."

"Don't tell me. Smirnoff went to her and said, 'Hey, I'm putting a group together, a direct-action group, more hardhitting than GEE, and Sangamon Taylor is working with me.'"

"That's what Patti Bowen said."

"Yeah, well Smirnoff got ahold of me the other day—you understand, I just hung up on the bastard, because I don't want the FBI to even imagine him and me on the same line—so he tracked me down in the food co-op when I was cutting fish. And he said, 'Patti Bowen and me are working together on a hard-hitting direct-action group, nudge nudge wink wink.' So I waved my boning knife at him and said, 'Listen, pusswad, you are toxic, and if you ever call me, ever call GEE, ever come within ten feet of me again, I'll take this and gut you like a tuna.' Haven't heard from him since."

"Is that your position? That he's a terrorist?"

"Yeah."

Rebecca started writing that down, so I added slowly and distinctly, "And we're not."

"So he's the same as Hank Boone, in your opinion."

I had to squirm. "Morally, yes. But no one's really like Boone."

Boone had this thing about whaling ships. He liked to sink them. He was a founder of GEE and hero of the Soviet invasion, but he'd been kicked out seven years ago. Off the coast of South Africa he had filled a Zodiac full of C-4, lit the fuse, pointed it at a pirate whaler, and jumped off at the last minute. The whaler went to the bottom and he went to hide out in some weepy European social democracy. But he kept dropping out of sight and whaling ships kept digging craters on the floors of the seven seas.

"Boone's effective. Smirnoff is just pathetic."

"You admire Boone."

"You know I can't say that. I sincerely don't like violence. Honest to God."

"That's why you threatened Smirnoff with a knife."

"Second-degree. It's premeditated violence I can't stand. Look. Boone isn't even necessary. The corporations have already planted their own bombs. All we have to do is light the fuses."

Rebecca sat back with those green eyes narrowed to slits, and I knew some sort of profound observation was coming down the pipeline. "I didn't think you were scared of anything, but Smirnoff scares you, doesn't he?"

"Sure. Look, GEE rarely does illegal things and we *never* do violent things. The worst we do is a little property damage now and then—and only to prevent worse things. But even so, we're bugged and tapped and tailed. The FBI thinks I'm Carlos the fucking Jackal. And we never talk about anything over the phone. Regular professionals. But that clown Smirnoff is trying to organize an openly terroristic group— over the fucking telephone! He's about as shrewd as your brain-damaged Lhasa Apso. Shit! I wonder if we could sue him for defamation, just for mentioning our name."

"I'm not a lawyer."

"I could definitely see a defamation suit, though, if a news organization tried to connect us in any way."

She was more amused than furious. I knew she would be; she thinks I'm cute when I'm angry. After you've fucked a man on a Zodiac in the middle of Boston Harbor on your lunch hour, it's hard to distance yourself from him, say what you want about objectivity and ethics.

"S.T., I am stunned. Did you really just threaten *The Weekly?*"

"No, no, not at all. I'm just trying to express how important it is that we are kept separate from him and Boone in the public mind. And as soon as we're done I'm going to drop a dime on one of our earnest young ecolawyers and see if we can sue the crap out of him."

She smiled. "I don't want to connect you. There is no real connection. But I am interested in the topic. I mean, the Ike Walton League fades into the Sierra Club fades into GEE fades into NEST. . . . "

"Right, and then Smirnoff, then Boone, then al-Fatah. And I think Basco and Fotex are down there somewhere. It's a dangerous premise, babe. You have to draw a definite line between us and Smirnoff. Or even NEST."

"You're not allowed to call me babe."

"It's a deal. You can call me anything but a terrorist."

4

I took the T into the middle of Boston and cut across the North End to a particular yacht club. Mostly it was run by lifestyle slaves who were studying to be Brahmins, but there were a couple of old vomit-stained tour boats that ran out of there, one fishing boat, and it was the home base for GEE Northeast's nautical forces. They'd donated a small odd-shaped berth, a little trapezoid of greasy water caught between a couple of piers, for the same reason that someone else gave us the Omni. Upstairs we had a locker for our gear, and that's where I headed, driving up the blood pressures of all the deck-shoed, horn-rimmed twits waiting to be let into the dining room. I cruised past and didn't even turn around when some high-pitched jerk issued his challenge.

"Say! Excuse me? Sir? Are you a member of this club?"

It happens every so often, mostly with people who've just spent their Christmas bonuses on memberships. I don't even react. Sooner or later they learn the ropes.

But something was familiar about that goddamn voice. I couldn't keep myself from turning around. And there he was, standing out from that suntanned crowd like a dead guppy in a tropical aquarium, tall and slack-faced and not at all sure of himself. Dolmacher. When he recognized me, it was his nightmare come to life. Which was only fair since he was one of my favorite bad dreams.

"Taylor," he sneered, ill-advisedly making the first move.

"Lumpy!" I shouted. Dolmacher looked down at his fly as his companions mouthed the word behind his back. Grinning yuppie hyenas that they were, I knew that I had renamed Dolmacher for his career.

The implications did not penetrate and he sauntered forward a step. "How are things, Taylor?"

"I'm having the time of my life. How about you, Dolmacher? Pick up a new accent since we left B.U.?"

His soon-to-be ex-associates began to file their teeth.

"What's on the agenda for today, Sangamon? Come to plant a magnetic limpet mine on an industrialist's yacht?"

This was vintage Dolmacher. Not "blow up" but "plant a magnetic limpet mine on." He cruised bookstores and bought those big picture books of international weapons systems, the ones always remaindered for $3.98. He had a whole shelf of them. He went up on weekends and played the Survival Game in New Hampshire, running around in the woods shooting paint pellets at other frustrated elements.

"Yachts are made out of fiberglass, Dolmacher. A magnetic mine wouldn't stick."

"Still sarcastic, huh, S.T.?" He pronounced the word as if it were a mental illness. "Except now you're doing it professionally."

"Can I help it if the Groveler lacks a sense of humor?"

"I don't work for Basco any more."

"Okay, I'm stunned. Whom are you working for?"

"Whom? I'm working for Biotronics, that's whom."

Big deal. Biotronics was a wholly owned subsidiary of Basco. But the work was impressive.

"Genetic engineering. Not bad. You work with the actual bugs?"

"Sometimes."

Dolmacher dropped his guard the minute I started asking him about his job. No change at all since our days at B.U. He was so astounded by the coolness of Science that it acted on him like an endorphin.

"Well," I said, "remember not to pick your nose after you've had your hands in the tank, and enjoy your lunch. I've got samples to take." I turned around.

"You should come to work for Biotronics, S.T. You're far too intelligent for what you're doing."

I turned back around because I was pissed off. He had no idea how difficult . . . but then I noticed him looking sincere. He actually wanted me to work with him.

The old school ties, the old dormitory ties, they're resilient. We'd spent four years at B.U. talking at each other like this, and a couple years more on opposite sides of the toxic barricades. Now he wanted me to rearrange genes with him. I guess when you've come as far as he had, you feel a little lonely. Way out there on the frontiers of science, it hurts when a former classmate keeps firing rock salt into your butt.

"We're working on a process you'd be very interested in," he continued. "It's like the Holy Grail, as far as you're concerned."

"Dolmacher, party of four?" demanded the maitre d'.

"If you ever want to talk about it, I'm in the book. North Suburban. Living in Medford now." Dolmacher backed away from me and into the dining room. I just stared at him.

Up at our locker I picked up an empty picnic cooler. My deal with the cook was that he'd fill it up with free ice if I told him a dirty joke, a transaction that went smoothly. Then out and across the docks to our little grease pit.

The tide was out so I had to use the rope ladder to get down into the Zodiac. As soon as you drop below the level of the pier, the city and the sun disappear and you're dangling in a jungle of algae-covered pilings, like Tarzan sliding down a vine into a swamp.

It's not doing a Zodiac justice to call it an inflatable raft. A Zodiac has design. It has hydrodynamics. It's made to go places. The inflatable part is horseshoe-shaped. The bend of the horseshoe is in front, and it's pointed; the prongs point backwards, tapering to cones. The floor of the craft is made of heavy interlocking planks and there's a transom in back, to keep the water out and to hold the motor. If you look at the bottom of a Zodiac, it's not just flat. It's got a hint of a keel on it for maneuverability.

Not a proper hull, though. Hull design is an advanced science. In the days of sail it was as important to national security as aerodynamics are now. A hull was a necessary evil: all that ship down under the water gave you lots of drag but without it the rest of the ship wouldn't float.

Then we invented outboard motors and all that science was made irrelevant by raw power. You could turn a bathtub into a high-performance speedboat by bolting a big enough motor on it. When the throttle's up high, the impact of the water against the bottom of the hull lifts it right up out of the water. It skims like a skipping rock and who gives a fuck about hydrodynamics. When you throttle it down, the vessel sinks into the water again and wallows like a hog.

This is the principle behind the Zodiac, as far as I can tell. You take a vessel that probably weighs less than its own motor, you radio the control tower at Logan Airport and you take off.

We had a forty-horse on this puppy—a donation—and I'd never dared to throttle it up past about twenty-five percent of maximum. Remember that a VW Bug has an engine with less than thirty horsepower. When you hit running speed in this Zode, if the water's not too rough, the entire boat rises from the water. The only wet part is the screw.

It's the ultimate Boston transportation. On land, there's the Omni, but all these slow cars get in the way. There's public transit—the T—but if you're in good shape, it's usually faster to walk. Bicycles aren't bad. But on water nothing stops you, and there isn't anything important in Boston that isn't within two blocks of being wet. The Harbor and the city are interlocked like wrestling squid, tentacles of water and land snaking off everywhere, slashed with bridges or canals.

Contrary to what every bonehead believes, the land surface has been stretched out and expanded by civilization. Look at any downtown city: what would be a tiny distance on a backpacking trip becomes a transcontinental journey. You spend hours traveling just a few miles. Your mental map of the city grows and stretches until things seem far away. But get on a Zodiac, and the map snaps back into place like a rubber sheet that has been pulled out of shape. Want to go to the airport? Zip. It's right over there. Want to cross the river? Okay, here we are. Want to get from the Common to B.U., two miles away, during rush hour, right before a playoff game at Fenway Park? Most people wouldn't even try. On a Zodiac, it's just two miles. Five minutes. The real distance, the distance of Nature. I'm no stoned-out naturehead with a twelve-string guitar, but that's a fact.

The Mercury was brand-new, not even broken in. Some devious flack at the outboard motor company had noticed that our Zodiacs spent a lot of time in front of TV cameras. So we get all our motors free now, in exchange for being our extroverted selves. We wear them out, sink, burn and break them; new ones materialize. I hooked up the fuel line, pumped it up, and the motor caught on the first try. The stench of the piers was sliced by exhaust. I dropped it to a tubercular idle, shifted into forward, and started snaking out between the pilings. If I wanted to commit suicide here, I could just twitch my hand and I'd be slammed into a barnacled tree trunk at Mach 1.

Then out into a finger of water that ran between piers. The piers were actually little piers attached to big piers, so out into a bigger finger of water that ran between the big piers, then into the channel, and from there to a tentacle of the Harbor that fed the channel.

At some point I was entitled to say that I had entered Boston Harbor, the toilet of the Northeast. By shoving the motor over to one side I could spin the Zode in tight rings and look up into the many shit-greased sphincters of the Fair Lady on the Hill, Hub of the Universe, Cradle of Crap, my hometown. Boston Harbor is my baby. There are biologists who know more about its fish and geographers who have statistics on its shipping, but I know more about its dark, carcinogenic side than anyone. In four years of work, I've idled my Zodiac down every one of its thousands of inlets, looked at every inch of its fractal coastline and found every single goddamn pipe that empties into it. Some of the pipes are big enough to park a car in and some are the size of your finger, but all of them have told their secrets to my gas chromatograph. And often it's the littlest pipes that cause the most damage. When I see a big huge pipe coming right out of a factory, I'm betting that the pumpers have at least read the

EPA regs. But when I find a tiny one, hidden below the waterline, sprouting from a mile-wide industrial carnival, I put on gloves before taking my sample. And sometimes the gloves melt.

In a waterproof chest I keep a number of big yellow stickers: NOTICE. THIS OUTFALL IS BEING MONITORED ON A REGULAR BASIS BY GEE INTERNATIONAL. IF IN VIOLATION OF EPA REGULATIONS, IT MAY BE PLUGGED AT ANY TIME. FOR INFORMATION CALL: (then, scribbled into a blank space, and always the same), SANGAMON TAYLOR (and our phone number).

Even I can't believe how many violators I catch with these stickers. Whenever I find a pipe that's deliberately unmarked, whose owners don't want to be found, I slap one of these stickers up nearby. Within two weeks the phone rings.

"GEE," I say.

"Sangamon Taylor there?"

"He's in the john right now, can I have him call you back?"

"Uh, okay, yeah, I guess so."

"What did you want to talk to him about?"

"I'm calling about your sticker."

"Which one?"

"The one on the Island End River, about halfway up?"

"Okay." And I dutifully take their number, hang up, and dial right back.

Ring. Ring. Click. "Hello, Chelsea Electroplating, may I help you?"

Case closed.

A few years of that and I owned this Harbor. The EPA and the DEQE called me irresponsible on odd-numbered days and phoned me for vital information on even-numbered ones. Every once in a while some agency or politician would announce a million-dollar study to track down all the crap going into the Harbor and I'd mail in a copy of my report. Every year *The Weekly* published my list of the ten worst polluters:

(1)   Bostonians (feces)
(2-3) Basco and Fotex, always fighting it out for
       number two, (you name it)

  (4-7)   Whopping defense contractors (various solvents)

  (8-10)   Small but nasty heavy-metal dumpers like Derinsov Tanning and various electroplaters.

The Boston sewage treatment system is pure Dark Ages. Most of the items flushed down metropolitan toilets are quickly shot into the Harbor, dead raw. If you go for a jog on Wollaston Beach, south of town, when the currents are flavorful, you will find it glistening with human turds. But usually they sink to the bottom and merge.

Today I was out on the Zodiac for two reasons. One: to get away from the city and my job, just to sit out on the water. Two: Project Lobster. Number one doesn't have to be explained to anyone. Number two has been my work for the last six months or so.

Usually I do my sampling straight out of pipes. But no one's ever satisfied. I tell them what's going in and they say, okay, where does it end up? Because currents and tides can scatter it, while living things can concentrate it.

Ideally I'd like to take a chart of the Harbor and draw a grid over it, with points spaced about a hundred yards apart, then get a sample of what's on the sea floor at each one of those points. Analysis of each sample would show how much bad shit there was, then I'd know how things were distributed.

In practice I can't do that. We just don't have the resources to get sampling equipment down to the floor of the Harbor and back up again, over and over.

But there's a way around any problem. Lobstermen work the Harbor. Their whole business is putting sampling devices—lobster traps—on the floor of the sea and then hauling them back up again carrying samples—lobsters. I've got a deal with a few different boats. They give me the least desirable parts of their catch, and I record where they came from. Lobsters are somewhat mobile, more so than oysters but less than fish. They pretty much stay in one zone of the

Harbor. And while they're there, they do a very convenient thing for me called bioconcentration. They eat food and shit it out the other end, but part of it stays with them, usually the worst part. A trace amount of, say, PCBs in their environment will show up as a much higher concentration in their livers. So when I get a lobster and figure out what toxins it's carrying, I have a pretty good idea of what's on the floor of the Harbor in its neighborhood.

Once I get my data into the computer, I can persuade it to draw contour maps showing the dispersion pattern of each type of toxin. For example, if I'm twisting Basco's dick at the moment, I'll probably look at PCBs. So the computer draws all the land areas and blacks them out. Then it begins to shade in the water areas, starting out in the Atlantic, which is drawn in a beautiful electric blue. You don't have to look at the legend to know that this water is pure. As we approach Boston, the colors get warmer, and warmer. Most of the harbor is yellow. In places we see rings of orange, deepening toward the center until they form angry red boils clustered against the shore. Next to each boil I write a caption: "Basco Primary Outfall." "Basco Temporary Storage Facility." "Basco-owned Parcel (under EPA Investigation)." "Parcel Owned by Basco Subsidiary (under EPA Investigation)." Translate this into a 35-mm slide, take it to a public hearing, draw the curtains and splash it up on a twenty-foot screen—*voilà*, an instant lynch mob. Then the lights come up and a brand-new Basco flack comes out, fresh from B.U. or Northeastern, and begins talking about eyedroppers in railway tank cars. Then his company gets lacerated by the media.

This is the kind of thing I think about when buzzing around, looking for Gallagher the lobsterman.

Sometimes I had this daydream where a big-time coke runner from Miami got environmentally conscious and donated one of his Cigarette boats. It wasn't going to happen— not even coke dealers were that rich. But I thought about it, read the boating magazines, dreamed up ways to use one. And right now on the channel between Charlestown and Eastie, two miles north, I could see a thirty-one foot Cigarette just sitting there on the water. It's kind of like what my Zodiac would look like if it had been built by defense contractors: way too big, way too fast, a hundred times too expensive. The larger models have a cabin in front, but this didn't even have that comfort. It was open-cockpit, made for nothing in the world but dangerous speed. I'd seen it yesterday, too, sitting there doing nothing. I wondered if it would be terribly self-important if I attributed its presence to mine. The worst Fotex plant was up that way, and maybe they were anticipating a sneak attack.

Implausible. If their security was that good, they'd know that our assault ketch, the *Blowfish*, was off the coast of New Jersey, homing in on poor unsuspecting Blue Kills. Without it we didn't have enough Zodiacs, or divers, to stage a pipe-plugging raid on Fotex. So maybe this was some rich person working on a suntan. But if he owned a boat that could do seventy miles an hour, why didn't he take it off that syphilitic channel? He was on the Mystic, for God's sake.

I caught up with the *Scoundrel* off the coast of Eastie, not far from the artificial plateau that made up the airport. These guys were the first to join Project Lobster, and hence my favorites. Initially none of the lobstermen trusted me, afraid that I'd ruin their business with my statements of doom. But when the Harbor got really bad, and people started talking about banning all fish from the area, they started to see I was on their side. A clean Harbor was in their own best interests.

Gallagher should have been extra tough, because I had a tendency to rag on the subject of Spectacle Island. This was not a true island but a mound of garbage dumped in the Harbor by an ancestor of his, a tugboat operator who'd been lucky enough to get the city's garbage-hauling concession in the 1890s. But, as Rory explained many times and loudly, those were the Charlestown Gallaghers, the rich, arrogant, semi-Anglicized branch. Sometime back in the Twenties, some Gallagher's nose had gotten splintered in a wedding brawl or something, thus creating the rift between that branch and Rory's—the Southie Gallaghers, the humble farmers of the sea.

"Attention all crew, we have a long-haired invironmintl at ten o'clock, prepare to be boarded," Rory called, his Southie accent thick as mustard gas. All these guys talked that way. Their "ar" sounds could shatter reinforced concrete.

I'd been to a couple of games with them; we'd sit up there in the bleachers and inhale watery beer and throw cigars to the late, lamented Dave Henderson. They couldn't not be loud and boisterous, so they gave me shit about my hair, which didn't even come down to my collar. I could take a few minutes of this, but then I needed to go to a nice sterile shopping mall and decompress.

"Aaaay, we got some beauties for you today, Cap'n Taylor, some real skinny oily ones."

"Going to the game tonight, Rory?"

"A bunch of us are, yeah. Why, you wanna go?"

"Can't. Going to Jersey tomorrow."

"Jersey! Sheesh!" All the buys on the boat went "sheesh!" They couldn't believe anyone would be stupid enough to go to that place.

They tossed me a couple of half-dead lobsters and showed me where they'd trapped them on the chart. I jotted the locations down and put the bugs on ice. Later, when I got back, I'd have to dismantle them and run the analysis.

We traded speculation on what Sam Horn might do against the Yanks. These guys were Negro-haters all, and their heros were gigantic black men with clubs, a contradiction I wasn't brave enough to point out.

I went to handle the most depressing part of my job. Poor people get tired of welfare cheese after a while and start looking for other sources of protein. For example, fish. But poor people can't charter a boat to go out and catch swordfish, so they fish off docks. That means they're looking for bottom fish. Anyone who knows about Boston Harbor gets queasy just at the mention of bottom fish, but these people were worried about kwashiorkor, not cancer. Three-quarters of them were Southeast Asian.

So a month ago I'd typed up a highly alarming paragraph about what these particular bottom fish would do to your health, especially to the health of unborn children. Tried to make it simple: no chemical terms, no words like "carcinogenicity." Took it to the Pearl, which is my hangout, and persuaded Hoa to translate it to Vietnamese for me. Took it to an interpreter at City Hospital and got her to translate it into Cambodian. Had a friend do it in Spanish. Put them all together on a sign, sort of a toxic Rosetta Stone, made numerous copies and then made a few midnight trips to the piers where they like to do this fishing. We put the signs up in prominent places, bolted them down with lag screws, epoxied those screws into place and then chopped the heads off.

And when I came around the curve of the North End, bypassing a few hundred stalled cars on Commercial Street, riding the throttle high because I had miles to go before I'd sleep, I saw the same old pier, all hairy with fishing poles. It looked like one of those shadows you see under a microscope, with cilia sticking out all over to gather in food, healthy or otherwise.

Somehow I didn't figure these guys were sportsmen. They weren't of the catch-and-release school, like those geezers on TV. They were survivalists in a toxic wilderness.

The old etiquette dies hard. I grew up in a family that liked to fish, and I couldn't bring myself to break up the party. I backed off on the throttle when I was far away, and coasted to a safe distance where I wouldn't scare off any of those precious shit-eaters under the pier. Circled it slowly, looking at the fishermen, and they looked back at me. The name of my organization was writ large in orange tape on the side of the Zodiac. I wondered if they were reading it, and making the connection with those threatening signs just above their heads.

They were Vietnamese and black, with a few Hispanics. The blacks I wasn't as worried about. Not because they were black but because they seemed to fish for recreation. They'd been fishing here forever. You saw old black guys everywhere in Boston where there was water, sitting there in their old fedoras, staring at the water, waiting. Never saw them catch anything. But the Vietnamese went at it with a passion born of long-term protein deficiency.

There was kind of a ripple of interest up there on a corner of the pier and the crowd parted, leaving one Vietnamese in the middle. They were getting their lines and poles out of his way so he could reel one in. A flopping, good-sized flounder emerged, seeming to levitate because you couldn't see the line. Headed for a family wok in Boston. It wouldn't yield much meat, but the concentration of PCBs and heavy metals in that flesh would be thousands of times what it was in the water around us.

I glumly watched it ascend, thinking, these guys must use heavy-duty lines, because they had to support the whole weight of the fish. You didn't have a chance to net it in the water. The lucky angler made a grab for his prize and our eyes snagged each other for a second. I'd seen this guy before; he was a busboy at the Pearl.

What the fuck. Cranked up the Zode, twisted it, blew a crater in the Harbor and wheeled it around. Flounder be damned. When it came to this issue, GEE was fucked both ways. Try to stop them from poisoning themselves, and you look like you're interfering with a band of spunky immigrants. But now I had a face, at least. There wasn't any reason to hound this particular busboy, but I had good relations with Hoa and maybe I could get in touch with these people through him. Maybe GEE could run a free fishing charter out into the Atlantic, take these people out where they could catch some real fish. But pause to consider what the liability insurance would cost on that sucker.

Then, out of nowhere, it hit me: what I needed was some bitterly cold beer and really loud, brain-crushing rock and roll. Maybe some nitrous to go with that. I lit a cigar, cranked the Mercury up into one loud, long power chord, and headed for our naval base.

5

Bartholomew was lurking in his van in front of GEE when I got back. He started leaning on the horn as soon as he spotted me climbing up out of the T. All around the square, defense contractors flocked to their metallized windows to see if their BMWs were being violated, then drifted back, unable to localize the sound. I sauntered on purpose, pretended to ignore him, climbed the stairs to get my bike. I should have known that if I wanted recreation, my roommate would be thinking along the same lines. That is why, despite many kinds of incompatibility, we lived together: our minds ran in parallel ruts.

"Hey, you!" Tricia shouted, as I unlocked my bike. "That ain't yours."

"I'm fuckin' out of here," I said.

"Jim called," she said coyly, so I stepped just barely inside the door.

"What?"

"They're ready and waiting."

"He found a beachhead?"

"Yeah." Reading from a note, now: "Dutch Marshes State Park, ten miles north of Blue Kills. Take Garden State Parkway south to the Route 88 exit ... well, this goes on for a while. Here you go."

"Don't want it."

"Sangamon," she said in her flirtatious whine, which had been known to put men in the mind of taking their clothes off. "I spent ten minutes taking this down. And I don't like taking dictation."

"I'll never understand why people give out directions, or ask for them. That's what fucking road maps are for."

Outside, Bart blew a few licks on his horn.

"Find it on the map, you can always get to it. Try to follow someone's half-assed directions, and once you lose the trail, you're sunk. I've got maps of that fucking state an inch thick."

"Okay." Tricia was getting into some serious pouting; I bit the inside of my cheek, hard.

"Just tell me what time."

"He didn't say. You know, tomorrow afternoon sometime. Just follow the barbecue smoke."

"Ten-four on that. And now I truly am gone."

"Here's some mail."

"Thanks. But it's all junk."

"Don't I get to kiss the departing warrior?"

"Feels too weird, in a room that's bugged."

Threw my bike into Bartholomew's big black van and we headed west. Before going to work this morning, he'd had enough foresight to stop by our living-room canister and fill a couple of Hefty bags with nitrous, so I moved back behind the curtain and jackhammered my brain. Bart bragged that he could pass out on the stuff, but when that happens you let go of the Hefty and it all escapes.

He turned down the stereo a hair and screamed, "Hey, pop those suckers and we can have another Halloween party."

Last Halloween we had rigged up nitrous and oxygen tanks in one of our rooms, sealed the doors and windows, and created, shall we say, a marvelous party atmosphere. That was the first night I ever slept with a nonprint journalist. But it was an expensive way to seduce someone.

By the time we'd poked through Harvard Square, I was up in the front seat again, watching the colonial houses roll by.

"Yankees," Bart said.

Translation: "The Yankees are playing the Red Sox on TV tonight; let's stay at the Arsenal for the entire duration of the game."

"Can't," I said. "Have to do dinner with this frogman at the Pearl."

"French guy?"

"Frogman. A scuba diver. He's going on the Blue Kills thing. Don't worry, you hold down the fort and I'll ride over on my bike."

"You got a light on that thing?"

I laughed. "Since when are you the type to worry about that?"

"It's dangerous, man. You're invisible."

"I just assume I'm not invisible. I assume I'm wearing fluorescent clothes, and there's a million-dollar bounty going to the first driver who manages to hit me. And I ride on that assumption."

Sometimes it's nice to get away from the East Beirut ethnic atmosphere of the city and hang out in a bar where all the toilets flush on the first try and no one has ever died. We go to a place in Watertown, right across the river from our house, where there's a bar called the Arsenal. Character-free, as you'd expect in a shopping mall. But it's possible for a bar to have too much character, and there were a lot of bars like that in Boston. Right across the mall was a games arcade, which made the Arsenal even better. Into the bar for a beer, across the mall for a few games of ski-ball, back for another beer, and so on. You could eat up a pretty happy, stupid evening that way.

We ate up a couple of hours. I won about three dozen ski-ball tickets. Checked through the junk mail. I get a lot of junk mail because I own stock in hundreds of corporations—usually one share apiece. That puts me on the shareholder mailing lists, which can be useful. It's a hassle; I have to do it under as assumed name, through a P.O. box, paid for with money orders, so people can't ambush me on TV for some kind of conflict of interest.

I leafed through Fotex's annual report; a lot about their shiny new cameras, but nothing at all about toxic waste.

Also picked up some corporate news from a newsletter: it seemed that Dolmacher had a new boss. The founder/ president of Biotronics had "resigned" and been replaced by a transplant from the Basco ranks. There were photos of the founder—young, skinny, facial hair—and the new guy, a Joe Palooka type in yuppie glasses. Typical story. The people who founded Biotronics, bright kids from MIT and B.U., were chucked out to make room for some chip-off-the-old- monolith.

Bartholomew started a long-distance flirtation with some pert little sociology-major type who'd probably driven her Sprint over here from Sweetvale College, looking for Har- vard students or chip designers, but that romance died as soon as she noticed he was covered with something that looked remarkably like dirt. Bart worked in a retread busi- ness. All day long he picked up tires and flung them onto heaps, and by five o'clock he was vulcanized.

When it was time, I hauled my bike out of Bart's van and crossed the river into Brighton—a kind of small Irish pan- handle that sticks way out to the west of Boston proper— then followed back streets and sidewalks due east until I was in Allston, part of the same panhandle, but scruffier and more complicated. For example, here lived many of the Asian persuasion. If you judged from restaurants alone, you'd conclude that the Chinese dominated, that the Thais were catching up fast and that the Vietnamese ran a distant third. But I don't think that's true at all. The Vietnamese are just more discriminating when it comes to starting restaurants. The Chinese and the Thais, and for that matter the Greeks, print up menus automatically as soon as they get into the city limits; it's like a brainstem function. But the Vietnamese tend to be hard-luck cases to begin with, and they have a fas- tidious, catlike attitude about their chow. Maybe they got it from the French. To them, Chinese is gooey and greasy while Thai is monotonous—all that lemon grass and coconut milk. The Vietnamese cook for keeps.

Hoa's location was awful. In Boston, where landlords are as likely to carry gasoline cans as paint cans, all other build- ings like this had long ago been reduced to smoking holes. It was a solo Italianate monster that rose like a tombstone beside the Mass Pike, facing Harvard Street. Parking was no problem, though there was some question as to whether your car would still be there when you got out. The inside was bare and bright as a gymnasium, containing a dozen mismatched tables with orange oilcloth thumbtacked onto them. The decor was beer signs, depressing photographs of old Saigon and framed restaurant reviews from various newspapers, favoring phrases like "this Pearl is a diamond in the rough" and "surprising discovery by the Pike" and "worth the trip out of your way."

For the first couple months I had the feeling I was supporting this place singlehandedly by insisting that we hold large GEE luncheon meetings here. Then, after those reviews came out, it was "discovered" by Harvard Biz hopefuls who came to worship at the shrine of Hoa's entrepreneurial spirit. So I no longer felt like Hoa's kids would go hungry if I didn't eat there three times a week. But when people hemmed and hawed about where to eat, the Pearl was still my choice.

I carried my bike inside the front door, a privilege earned by steady patronage. Hoa and his brother thought it was outlandish that I, a relatively well-to-do American, rode around on a bike. I might as well have insisted on wearing a conical hat and black pajamas. They drove cars exclusively, scabrous beaters that got stolen or burned several times a year.

Once through the vestibule, I checked out my fellow diners. The man in circular glasses, with a one-inch-thick alligator briefcase? No, this was not the GEE frogman. Nor the five Asians, efficiently snarfing down something that wasn't on the menu. The three blue-haired Brighton Irish ladies, still flabbergasted by the lack of handles on the teacups? Not likely. But the mid-thirties unit, seated under a blurry photo of the statue of the marine, hair to his shoulders, Nicaraguan peasant necklace, bicycle helmet on the table, now this was a GEE frogman. Though at the moment he was interrogating Hoa's brother, in half-forgotten Vietnamese, about what kind of tea this was.

"Hey, man," he said when he saw me, "I recognize you from the '60 Minutes' thing. How you doing?"

"Tom Akers, right?" I sat down and moved his bike helmet to the floor.

"Yeah, that's right. Hey, this is a great place. You hang out here?"

"Constantly."

"What's good?"

"All of it. But start with the Imperial Rolls."

"Kind of pricey."

"They're the best. All the other Vietnamese places wrap their rolls in egg-roll dough. So it's just like a Chinese roll. Here they use rice paper."

"Outstanding!"

"It's so delicate that most restaurants won't fuck with it. But Hoa's wife has the touch, man, she can do it with her toes."

"How's their fish stuff? I don't eat red meat."

My recommendation—Ginger Fish—got stuck on the way out. It was a mound of unidentifiable white fish in sauce.

I was ashamed to be thinking this. Hoa, the man who barely broke even on his egg rolls because of the rice paper, wouldn't serve bottom fish to his customers. I *am*, I reconsidered, *an asshole*.

"It's all good," I said. "It's all good food."

Tom Akers was a freelance diver, working out of Seattle, who did GEE jobs whenever he had a chance. When I needed some extra scuba divers, the national office got hold of him and flew him out. That's standard practice. We avoid taking volunteers, since anyone who volunteers for a gig is likely to be overzealous. We prefer to send out invitations.

Normally we'd have flown him straight to Jersey, but he wanted to visit some friends in Boston anyway. He'd been hanging out with them for a few days, and tonight he was going to crash at my place so we could get a fast start in the morning.

"Good to see you again," Hoa was saying, having snuck up on me while I was feeling guilty. He moved soundlessly, without displacing any air. He was in his forties, tall for a Vietnamese, but gaunt. His brother was shorter and rounder, but his English was poor and I couldn't pronounce his name. And I can't remember a name I can't pronounce.

"How are you doing, Hoa?"

"You both ride your bike?" He held his hands out and grabbed imaginary handlebars, grinning indulgently, eyeing Tom's helmet. Double disbelief: not one, but two grown Americans riding bicycles.

As it turned out, he wanted to encourage Tom to move his bike inside where it wouldn't get ripped off. There wasn't room in the vestibule so Tom put it around back just inside the kitchen door.

"Lot of activity out in the alley, man."

"Vietnamese?"

"I guess so."

"They're always coming to the back door for steamed rice. Hoa gives it out free, or for whatever they can pay."

"All right!"

We had a five-star meal for about a buck per star. I had a Bud and Tom had a Singha beer from Thailand. I used to do that—order Mexican beers in Mexican places, Asian beers in Asian joints. Then Debbie and Bart and I sat down one hot afternoon and she administered a controlled taste-test of about twelve different imported brands. It was a double-blind test—when we were done, both of us were blind—but we concluded that there wasn't any difference. Cheap beer was cheap beer. No need to pay an extra buck for authenticity. Furthermore, a lot of those cheap importeds got strafed in the taste test. We hated them.

Hoa's brother was our waiter. That was unusual, but Hoa had his hands full babysitting the three biddies. Also, he had to chew out an employee in the back room; fierce twanging Vietnamese cut through the hiss of the dishwashers. Tom liked the food, but got full in a hurry.

"You want doggy bag for that?" Hoa's brother said.

"Aw, sure, why not."

"Good." He eyed us for a minute, fighting with his shyness. "I hate when people come, eat little, then I got throw food in dumpster. Make me very mad. Lot of people could use. Like the blacks. They could use. So I get mad sometime, you know, and talk to them. Sometime, I talk about Ethiopia."

He left us to be astounded. "Man," Tom said, "that guy's really into it."

The busboy, emerging from the back, had obviously been at the quiet end of Hoa's tantrum. I guessed he'd spent most of his life in this country; he had an openly sullen look on his face, and loped and sauntered and jived between the tables. When he came out of the kitchen, we locked eyes again, for the second time that day. Then he glanced away and his lip curled.

There's a certain look people give me when they've decided I'm just an overanxious duck-squeezer. That was the look. To get through to this guy I'd somehow have to prove my manhood. I'd have to retain my cool in some kind of life-threatening crisis. Unfortunately such events are hard to stage.

We were staging one in Blue Kills, but it wouldn't make the Boston news. That was part of the GEE image: to take chances, to be tough and brave, so that people wouldn't give us the look that Hoa's busboy was giving me.

He didn't know that he was getting fucked coming and going. Basco and a couple of other companies had rained toxic waste on his native land for years. Now, here in America, he was eating the same chemicals, from the same company, off the floor of the Harbor. And Basco was making money on both ends of the deal.

"What're you thinking about?" Tom asked.

"I hate it when people ask me that fucking question," I said. But I said it nicely.

"You look real intense."

"I'm thinking about goddamn Agent Orange," I said.

"Wow," he said, softly. "That's what I was thinking about."

Tom followed me back across Allston-Brighton and home. I had to ride slow because I was taking my guerrilla route, the one I follow when I assume that everyone in a car is out to get me. My nighttime attitude is, anyone can run you down and get away with it. Why give some drunk the chance to plaster me against a car? That's why I don't even own a bike light, or one of those godawful reflective suits. Because if you've put yourself in a position where someone has to see you in order for you to be safe—to see you, and to give a fuck—you've already blown it.

Tom mumbled a few things about paranoia, and then I was too far ahead to hear him. We had a nice ride through the darkness. On those bikes we were weak and vulnerable, but invisible, elusive, aware of everything within a two-block radius. A couple of environmental extremists in a toxic world, headed for a Hefty bag and a warm berth in the mother ship.

6

WE INVADED the territory of the Swiss Bastards shortly before dawn. At sea we had three Zodiacs, two frogmen, a guy in a moon suit, and our mother ship, the *Blowfish*. We had a few people on land, working out of the Omni and a couple of rented vehicles. Our numbers were swelled by members of the news media, mostly from Blue Kills and environs but with two crews from New York City.

At about three in the morning, Debbie had to shake a tail put on us by the Swiss Bastards' private detectives. There was nothing subtle about the tail, they were just trying to intimidate. Tanya, our other Boston participant, was driving the car and Debbie was lying down in the back seat. Tanya led the tail onto a twisting road that wasn't sympathetic to the Lincoln Town Car following them. She thrashed the Omni for five minutes or so, putting half a mile between herself and the private dicks, then threw a 180 in the middle of the road—a skill she'd learned on snowy Maine roads last February while we were driving up to Montreal to get some French fries. Debbie jumped out and crouched in the ditch. Tanya took off and soon passed the Lincoln going the other way. The private dicks in the Lincoln were forced to make an eleven-point turn across the road, then peeled out trying to catch up with her.

Debbie walked a couple hundred yards and located the all-terrain bicycle we'd stashed there previously. It was loaded with half a dozen Kryptonite bicycle locks, the big U-shaped, impervious things. She rode a couple of miles, partly on the road and partly cross-country, until she came to a heavy gate across a private access road. On the other side of the gate was a toxic waste dump owned by the Swiss Bastards, a soggy piece of ground that ran downhill into an estuary that in turn ran two miles out to the Atlantic. The entire dump was surrounded by two layers of chainlink fence, and this gate was a big, heavy, metal sucker, locked by means of a chain and padlock. Debbie locked two of the Kryptonites in the middle, augmenting the Swiss Bastards' chain system, then put two on each hinge, locking the gates to the gateposts. In the unlikely event that an emergency took place on the dump site, she stuck around with the keys so that she could open the gates for ambulances or fire trucks. We aren't careless fanatics and we don't like to look as though we are.

I was on the *Blowfish*, explaining this gig to the crew. Jim, the skipper, and hence their boss, was hanging around in the background.

Jim does this for a living. He lives on the boat and sails back and forth between Texas and Duluth; along the Gulf Coast, around Florida, up the Atlantic Coast, down the St. Lawrence Seaway into the Great Lakes, and west from there. Then back. Wherever he goes, hell breaks loose. When GEE wants an especially large amount of hell to break loose, they'll bring in professional irritants, like me.

Jim and his crew of a dozen or so specialize in loud, sloppy publicity seeking. They anchor in prominent places and hang banners from the masts. They dump fluorescent green dye into industrial outfalls so that news choppers can hover overhead and get spectacular footage of how pollution spreads. They blockade nuclear submarines. They do a lot of that antinuclear stuff. Their goal is to be loud and visible.

Myself, I like the stiletto-in-the-night approach. That's partly because I'm younger, a post-Sixties type, and partly because my thing is toxics, not nukes or mammals. There's no direct action you can take to stop nuclear proliferation, and direct action to save mammals is just too fucking nasty. I don't want to get beat up over a baby seal. But there are all kinds of direct, simple ways to go after toxic criminals. You just plug the pipes. Doing that requires coordinated actions, what the media like to describe as "military precision."

This crew doesn't like anything military. In the Sixties, they would have been stuffing flowers into gun barrels while I was designing bombs in a basement somewhere. None of them has any technical background, not because they're dumb but because they hate rigid, discipline thinking. On the other hand, they had sailed this crate tens of thousands of miles in all kinds of weather. They'd survived a dismasting off Tierra del Fuego, blocked explosive harpoons with their Zodiacs, lived for months at a time in Antarctica, established a beachhead on the Siberian coast. They could do *anything*, and they would if I told them to; but I'd rather they enjoyed the gig.

"These people here are environmental virgins," I said. We were sitting around on deck, eating tofu-and-nopales omelets. It was a warm, calm, Jersey summer night and the sky was starting to lose its darkness and take on a navy-blue glow. "They think toxic waste happens in other places. They're shocked about Bhopal and Times Beach, but it's just beginning to dawn on them that they might have a problem here. The Swiss Bastards are sitting fat and happy on that ignorance. We're going to come in and splatter them all over the map."

Crew members exchanged somber glances and shook their heads. These people were seriously into their nonviolence and refused to take pleasure in my use of the word "splatter."

"Okay, I'm sorry. That's going a little far. The point is that this is a company town. Everybody works at that chemical factory. They like having jobs. It's not like Buffalo where everyone hates the chemical companies to begin with. We have to establish credibility here."

"Well, I forgot to bring my three-piece suit, man," said one of the antisplatter faction.

"That's okay. I brought mine." I do, in fact, have a nice three-piece suit that I always wear in combination with a dead-fish tie and a pair of green sneakers splattered with toxic wastes. It's always a big hit, especially at GEE fundraisers and in those explosively tense corporate boardrooms. "They're expecting, basically, people who look like you." I pointed to the hairiest of the *Blowfish* crew. "And they're expecting us to act like flakes and whine a lot. So we have to act before we whine. We can't give them an excuse to pass us off as duck squeezers."

There was a certain amount of passive-aggressive glaring directed my way; I was asking these people to reverse their normal approach. But I was directing this gig and they'd do what I asked.

"As usual, if you don't like the plan, you can just hang out, or go into town or whatever. But I'll need as many enthusiasts as I can get for this one."

"I'm into it," said a voice from the galley. It was Arty, short for Artemis, author of the omelets, the best Zodiac jockey in the organization. Naturally she was into it; it was a Zodiac-heavy operation, it was exciting, it was commando-like. Artemis was even younger than me, and military precision didn't come with all the emotional baggage for her that it did for the middle-aged *Blowfish* crew.

At 4:00 A.M., Artemis powered up her favorite Zode and prominently roared off, heading for some dim lights about half a mile away. The lights belonged to a twenty-foot coast guard boat that was assigned to keep an eye on us. It happens that boats of that size don't have cooking facilities, so Artemis had whipped up a couple of extra omelets, put them in a cooler to keep them warm and was headed out to give these guys breakfast. She took off flashing, glowing and smoking like a UFO, and within a couple of minutes we could hear her greeting the coast guards with an enthusiasm that was obscene at that time of the morning. They greeted her right back. They knew one another from previous *Blowfish* missions, and she liked to flirt with them over the radio. To them she was a legend, like a mermaid.

That was when Tom and I took off in one of the other

Zodes. This one had a small, well-muffled engine, and we'd stripped off all the orange tape and anything else that was easy to see in the dark.

The *Blowfish* was three miles off the coast and maybe five miles south of the toxic site that had just been locked up by Debbie and Tanya. Jim waited fifteen minutes, so the coast guards could eat and we could slip away, then cranked up the *Blowfish*'s huge Danish one-cylinder diesel: whoom whoom whoom whoom. We could easily hear it from the Zode and if anyone ashore was listening, they could probably hear it too. Normally, for environmental reasons, Jim used the sails, but this was right before dawn and there wasn't any wind. Besides, we were aiming for military precision here.

Around 6:00 we heard them break radio silence with a lot of fake traffic between Blowfish and GEE-1 and GEE-2 and Tainted Meat, which was my current code name, and loose talk about banners and smoke bombs. We knew that the rent-a-dicks were monitoring that frequency. Meanwhile, Tanya was in Blue Kills, trailing a parade of Lincoln Town Cars, rousting the media crews from their motel rooms, handing out xeroxed maps and press releases.

The import of the press releases was that we were mightily pissed off about the toxic marsh north of town. You know, the one that two Zodiacs were converging on at this very moment. I was imagining it: Artemis undoubtedly in the lead, spiky hair slicing the wind, thrashing the morning surf at about forty miles an hour, as some lesser Zode pilot desperately tried to keep up with her. She'd been through a special GEE course in Europe where she'd learned how to harass two-hundred-foot, waste-dumping vessels, dipping in and out of their bow wave without getting sucked under. She knew how to massage a big roller with her Mercury, how to slide up and down the troughs without going airborne.

We were listening too, but we already knew what was going on. The whole flotilla was headed for the estuary. There was nothing the coast guard could do except watch, because there's nothing illegal about riding a boat up a river. By now, the Swiss Bastards would have dispatched all available rent-a-cops and rent-a-dicks to the scene, ordering them to drive into that toxic waste dump and stand shoulder-to-shoulder along the shoreline to prevent the GEE invasion forces from establishing a beachhead.

When they arrived, pushing through the horde of media, they would find the gate impregnably locked. They would find, as they always did, that no boltcutter in the world had jaws that opened wide enough to cut through a Kryptonite lock. They would then find that their hacksaws were dulled useless by the tempered steel. If they were exceedingly bright, they would get a blowtorch and heat the metal enough to destroy its temper; then they could hacksaw it, and, after a few hours, get inside their own dump. Meanwhile, the cameras would be rolling, as would the GEE demonstration, unmolested, on the other side of the transparent fences. Unless, in full view of the NYC minicams, they wanted to send rent-a-cops clambering over their own fences, or chop them up with boltcutters.

Tanya and Debbie had parked the Omni right in front and were propagandizing with a bullhorn. Listening to the radio, I could occasionally make out a word or two of what they were saying. Basically they were encouraging everyone to stay cool—always a major part of our gigs, especially when state troopers were present.

Riding in one of the Zodiacs was a man dressed up in a moonsuit, one of those dioxinproof numbers with the goggles and the facemasks. Nothing looks scarier on camera. This Zodiac was about three inches from the shore—no trespassing had yet been committed. He had some primitive sampling equipment mounted on long poles, so that he could reach into the dump and poke around pseudoscientifically.

In the other Zodiac was a guy in scuba gear, who, as soon as they arrived, jumped into the water and disappeared. Every few minutes he would resurface and hand a bottle full of ugly brown water to Artemis. She would take it, wearing gloves of course, and hand him an empty. Then he would disappear again.

They hated it when we did this. It just drove them wild. From previous run-ins with me, they knew the organization now had some chemical expertise, that we knew what we were talking about. Neither the guy in the moon suit nor the diver ever showed his face, so they didn't know which one was Sangamon Taylor. This sampling wasn't just for show, or so they thought. All of this shit was going to be analyzed, and embarrassing facts were going to be, shall we say, splattered across the newspapers.

That had started the day before, with an article in the sports section by well-respected journalist/sportsman, Red Grooten, who detailed, with surprising sophistication, the effects of this swamp's toxins on sports fishing. Next to it had been a shocking picture of a dead flounder. GEE authorities were quoted as speculating that this entire estuary might have to be closed to fishing.

In half an hour, the *Blowfish* would pull into view, and earnest GEE employees would begin examining the riverbanks downstream for signs of toxicity. If they were lucky they'd find a two-headed duck. Even if they found nothing, the fact that they went looking would be reported.

Tom and I were converging, slowly and quietly, on the real objective.

7

MUCH OF NEW JERSEY'S COAST is protected from the ocean by a long skinny barrier beach that runs a mile or two offshore. In some places it joins to the mainland, in some it's wide and solid, and in other places (off Blue Kills, for example) it peters out into islands or sandbars.

"Kill" is Dutch for "creek." What we have here is short, fat river that spreads out into a network of distributaries and marshes when it reaches the sea. The kills are braided together along an estuary that's supposed to be a wildlife refuge.

The estuary was north of us. The town of Blue Kills and the little principality of Blue Kills Beach were built on higher and dryer ground on its south side. The whole area was semiprotected from the Atlantic by a dribble of isles and sandbars. We were out on the toxic lagoon enclosed behind them.

I'd been studying my LANDSAT infrared photos so I knew where to find a shrub- and tree-covered island pretty close to our target, about a mile off Blue Kills Beach. We beached the Zodiac among the usual clutter left behind by teen beer-chugging expeditions. Tom checked his gear and climbed into the Darth Vader Suit.

Normally divers wear wet suits, which are thick and porous. Water gets through them, the body warms the water up, they insulate you. But you wouldn't be caught dead wearing something like that when you are screwing around with toxic waste. So the Darth Vader Suit was built around a drysuit, which is waterproof. I'd added a facemask made from diving goggles, old inner tubes, a patching kit, and something called Tennis Shoe Repair Goo. When you wrestled it down over your face, the scuba mouthpiece fit into the proper orifice and there was kind of a one-way valve over your nose so you could breathe out. When it was put on correctly, it would protect you from what you were swimming through, at least for a little while.

Tom didn't like drysuits but he wasn't arguing. Before he put it on, we protected the parts of his skin that would be uncomfortably close to leaks or seams in the Darth Vader Suit. There's a silicone sealant that's made for this kind of thing—Liquid Skin. Smear it on and you're semiprotected. The suit goes on over that. We equipped him with a measuring tape, a scuba notepad, and an underwater 8-mm video camera.

"Just one thing. What's coming out of this sucker?"

"Amazing things. They're making dyes and pigments back in there. So you have your solvents. You have your metals. And lots of weird, weird phthalates and hydrazines."

"Meaning what?"

"Don't drink it. And when you're done, take a nice swim out here, where the water's cleaner."

"This kind of shit always bugs me."

"Look at it this way. A lot of toxins are absorbed through the lungs. But you've got a clean air supply in those tanks. A lot more get in through your skin. But there's not enough solvents in that diffuser, I think, to melt the suit."

"That's what they told us about Agent Orange."

"Shit." There was no reason for me to be astonished. I just hadn't thought of it before. "You got sprayed with that stuff?"

"Swam through the shit."

"You were a SEAL?"

"Demolition. But the Viet Cong didn't have much of a

navy so it was mostly blue-collar maintenance. You know, cleaning dead buffaloes out of intake pipes."

"Well, this stuff isn't like Agent Orange. No dioxin involved here."

"Okay. You've got your paranoia and I've got mine."

We *were* being paranoid. I'd already admitted it. After our midnight ride through Brighton he had a pretty good idea of how my mind worked.

"I don't care if they see me checking out their pipe on the surface, Tom. I don't even care if they recognize me. But if they see a diver, that's a giveaway. Then they know they're in trouble. So just bear with me."

So he climbed into the water and I towed him, submerged, to a place where the water turned black. Then I cut the motor. He thumped on the bottom of the Zode.

I gave him a minute to get clear, then restarted the motor and just idled back and forth for a few minutes. I already had pretty good maps, but this was a chance to embellish them, note down clumps of trees, docking facilities, hidden sandbars, and media-support areas. About half a mile south was a public pier belonging to a state park; then, moving north, there was a chainlink fence running down to the water, separating park land from the Swiss Bastards' right-of-way. A few hundred feet past that was another fence and then some private property, some old retired-fishermen's homes.

The Swiss Bastards' right-of-way was deceptively wooded. When the wind came up a little, the trees sighed and almost covered the rush-hour roar of the parkway. Just out of curiosity, I took the Zode closer to shore and scanned the trees with binoculars. One of the rent-a-cops loitering back there was giving himself away by his cigarette smoke. Or, knowing the habits of rent-a-cops, maybe it was oregano somebody had sold him as reefer.

I knew what direction the pipe ran, so I could follow it inland using my compass, trace its path under some swampy woods and crackerbox developments, out to the parkway, a couple of miles inland. Then a forest of pipes rose up behind the real forest. Whenever the wind blew the right way, I got a whiff of organic solvents and gaseous byproducts. The plant was just coming alive with the morning shift, the center of the traffic noise. Tomorrow I'd make a phone call and shut it all down.

The big lie of American capitalism is that corporations work in their own best interests. In fact they're constantly doing things that will eventually bring them to their knees. Most of these blunders involve toxic chemicals that any competent chemist should know to be dangerous. They pump these things into the environment and don't even try to protect themselves. The evidence is right there in public, almost as if they'd printed up signed confessions and sprinkled them out of airplanes. Sooner or later, someone shows up in a Zodiac and points to that evidence, and the result is devastation far worse than what a terrorist, a Boone, could manage with bombs and guns. All the old men within twenty miles who have come down with tumors become implacable enemies. All the women married to them, all the mothers of damaged children, and even those of undamaged ones. The politicians and the news media trample each other in their haste to pour hellfire down on that corporation. The transformation can happen overnight and it's easy to bring about. You just have to show up and point your finger.

No chemical crime is perfect. Chemical reactions have inputs and outputs and there's no way to make those outputs disappear. You can try to eliminate them with another chemical reaction, but that's going to have outputs also. You can try to hide them, but they have this way of escaping. The only rational choice is not to be a chemical crook in the first place. Become a chemical crook and you're betting your future on the hope that there aren't any chemical detectives gunning for you. That assumption isn't true anymore.

I don't mean the EPA, the chemical Keystone Kops. Offices full of mediocre chemists, led by the lowest bottom-feeders of them all: political appointees. Expecting them to do anything controversial is like expecting a hay fever sufferer to harvest a field of ragweed. For God's sake, they wouldn't even admit that chlordane was dangerous. And if they don't have the balls to take preventive measures, punitive action doesn't even enter their minds. The laws are broken so universally that they don't know what to do. They don't even look for violators.

I *do* look. Last year I went on an afternoon's canoe trip in central Jersey, taking some sample tubes with me. I went home, ran the stuff through my chromatograph, and the result was over a million dollars in fines levied against several offenders. The supply-side economists made it this way: created a system of laissez-faire justice, with plenty of niches for aggressive young entrepreneurs, like me.

A rubber-coated hand broke the water ahead of me and I cut the motor. Tom's head emerged next to the Zodiac and he peeled back the Darth Vader mask to talk. His mouth was wide open and grimacing; he was surprised. "That is one big motherfucker."

"How long?"

"It's so long I can't swim to the end of it. I'll need a lift."

"And there's black shit coming out of it?"

"Right." Tom placed the little video camera on the floor of the Zode. I picked it up, rewound the tape, put the camera to my face and started to replay the tape through the little screen in the viewfinder. "Some shots of the diffusers," Tom explained. "Each one is three and a quarter inches in diameter. The crossbar is three-eighths inch."

"Nice job."

"Wasn't doing much when I showed up, then it started really barfing that stuff out."

"Morning shift. You missed the rush hour when you were down there. Let's see."

Through the viewfinder I was looking at the smooth, unnatural curve of a large pipe on the seafloor. It was covered with rust, and the rust with hairy green crap. The camera zoomed in on a black hole in the side of the pipe; understandably, nothing was growing near that. Cutting across the center of the hole was a crossbar.

"This remind you of anything?"

"What do you mean?" he said.

"Looks like the Greek letter theta. You know? The ecology symbol." I held up a press release bearing GEE's logo and he laughed.

"I guess this means to hell with the secrecy fetish," I said. "Hang on and I'll take you out farther."

We worked our way offshore about a hundred yards at a

time, then, and when we got bored and started thinking about lunch, a quarter mile at a time. The slope of the bottom was gentle and the water never got deeper than about fifty feet. I'd motor him out, following the pipe with my compass, and he'd drop off and swim down to see if it was still there. When Tom finally found the end of it, we were pretty close to our starting place on the little shrub-covered island. The fucking thing was a mile long.

I hadn't worked with him before, but Tom was good. When you dive for a living I guess it pays to be precise. I knew some other GEE divers who would have said. "Whoa, man, it's a big fucking pipe, it's, like, about this wide." Tom was a fanatic, though, and came up with pages of measurements and diagrams.

We hung out on the island for an hour, savored a couple of beers, and talked it over.

"The holes are all the same size," he said. "Spaced a little over fifty feet apart. That tape measure is just an eighteen-footer, so I had to be kind of crude."

"All on the same side of the pipe?"

"Alternating sides."

"So if the thing is about a mile long . . . that works out to something like a hundred three-inch holes we have to plug up."

"It's a big job, man. Why did they build it that way, anyhow? Why not have your basic huge pipe, just barfing the stuff out?"

"They used to think this was the answer. Diffusion. There's a strong current up the shore here."

"I noticed."

"The same current that created this island we're on, and all the barrier beaches. They figured if they could spread their pollution out across a mile of that current, it would more or less disappear. Besides, a big barfing pipe is mediapathic."

"And you're sure it's illegal?"

"In about six different ways. That's why I want to close it down."

"Think you can bluff them?"

"What do you mean?"

"Call them up, say, 'This is GEE, we're going to shut off your diffuser, better close down the plant.' "

"Anywhere else I could, but they wouldn't go for it here. They know how hard this thing would be to plug up. Besides, I want more than a bluff. I want to stop pollution."

He grinned. So did I. It was a catch phrase we repeated when frustrated by a hopeless task: "I want to stop pollution, man!"

"So what do we do? Postpone it?"

"Naah." I started to rewind the tape for the third time. "Necessity is the mother."

HE DUMPED HIS GEAR into the Zode and we headed up the shore to rendezvous with the *Blowfish*. It was easy to find, as it turned out, since they'd set off some huge military surplus smoke bombs near the dump. Gluttons for attention, I guess.

I had Tom drop me off. It was time to do some ruminating, and that wouldn't be possible in the groovy chaos of the *Blowfish*. They'd all be exhilarated by the gig, they'd want to talk too much, and I wanted to think. So we brought the Zodiac right up on the public beach. I waded to shore in my underwear, the only bather present who was smoking a cigar, and put my clothes on once I reached the beach. Normally guys in their underwear attract a lot of attention, but none of the kids and oldsters who were here noticed. They were all gathered in a clump a hundred feet down the beach, staring at something on the ground. I figured someone had stroked out while swimming. It was ghoulish, but I walked down there anyway to have a look.

But it wasn't a dead person they were looking at. It was a dead dolphin.

"Hey, S.T., come to help this poor guy out?"

A geezer had snuck up on me. No one I knew. He'd probably seen me at the civic association meeting I'd attended the month before. A lot of these retirees keep an eye on the tube, read the papers every day, go to the meetings.

It seemed an odd thing for him to say, so I moved forward to the front row and took a closer look. The dolphin wasn't dead, just close to it. Its tail was oscillating weakly against the sand.

"I wish I knew the first thing about it," I mumbled.

A couple of young muscleheads decided they did know about it. One of them grabbed the dolphin's tail, hoping to drag it back to the water. Instead, its skin peeled back like the wrapper on a tray of meat. I turned around and walked as fast as I could in the other direction. People were screaming and vomiting behind me.

"Looks like another victim of you-know-what," the old guy was saying. I looked over to see him matching me stride for stride. There wasn't much to say, so I checked him out. We were talking appendectomy from long ago and a fairly recent laparotomy. Exploratory surgery, maybe. His tubes seemed okay; probably a nonsmoker. I gave him fifteen years; if he'd worked at the plant, five years.

"Didn't know I had a name around here," I said.

He grinned, shook his head, and converged on me, chortling silently. He was laughing, but swallowing it. A born conspirator. "Oh, those guys hate you. They hate your guts up there!" He allowed himself an audible laugh. "Where you guys have your headquarters?"

Exactly the kind of information I hate to give out. "Somewhere out there," I said, "on a boat."

"Uh huh. What do you do when someone wants to get ahold of you?"

"Got a cellular phone in our car."

"Oh yeah. For the media. That's smart. You give 'em all your number then."

"Yeah, you know, on the press releases."

"Hey! You got one of those? I'm kind of a news junkie, you know, get the *Times* and the *Post* every morning; got a satellite dish behind the house and I'm always following it, got a shortwave. . . ."

I had a few press releases folded up in my pocket, always

carried them with me, so I handed one to the guy and also gave him a GEE button that he thought was hilarious.

"Where's a good hardware store?" I said. A trivial question for him to answer, but priceless for me.

"What kind of stuff you looking for?" he asked, highly interested. He had to establish that I deserved to have this information. Blue Kills probably had a dozen mediocre ones, but every town has one really good hardware store. Usually it takes about six years to find it.

"Not piddley-shit stuff. I need some really out-of-the-way stuff. . . . "

He cut me off; I'd showed that I had some taste in hardware, that I had some self-respect. He gave me directions.

Then, what the hell, he gave me a ride to the damn place. Dropped me off in the parking lot. Drove me in his Cadillac Seville with the Masonic calipers welded to the trunk lid. This guy was a goddamn former executive. With an obvious grudge.

"You know Red?" I said on the way over.

Dave Hagenauer (according to the junk mail on his dashboard) laughed and thwacked his maroon naugahyde steering wheel. "Red Grooten? I sure as hell do. How the hell do you know Red?"

"Old fishing buddies?" I asked, ignoring the question.

"Oh, hunting, fishing, you name it. We been going out for a long time. Course the most we do now is a little fishing, you know, plunking off a boat."

"Not in the North Branch I hope."

He whistled silently and glinted his eyes at me, Aqua-Velva blue. "Oh, no. I've known about that place for a long time. Shit no."

By that time we were at the store. "Stay out of trouble!" he said, and he was still laughing when I slammed the door.

Most of my colleagues go on backpacking trips when they have to do some thinking. I go to a good hardware store and head for the oiliest, dustiest corners. I strike up conversations with the oldest people who work there, we talk about machine vs. carriage bolts and whether to use a compression or a flare fitting. If they're really good, they don't hassle me. They let me wander around and think. Young hardware clerks have a lot of hubris. They think they can help you find anything and they ask a lot of stupid questions in the process. Old hardware clerks have learned the hard way that nothing in a hardware store ever gets bought for its nominal purpose. You buy something that was designed to do one thing, and you use it for another.

So in the first couple of minutes I had to blow off two zesty young clerks. It's easy for me now, I just mumble about something very technical, using terms they don't understand. Pretending to know what I mean, they direct me off toward another part of the store. Young clerks like to use a zone coverage, whereas the oldtimers prefer a loose man-to-man, so you can wander and think, pick up an armload of items, frown, turn around, put them all back and start over again.

I did a lot of that. After half an hour, an old clerk orbited by, just to be courteous, to establish that I wasn't a shoplifter. "Anything I can help with?" he asked understandingly.

"It's a long, long story," I said, and that put him at ease. He went back to coffee and inventory and I took another swing down the plumbing aisle, visions of theta-holes dancing in my head.

What we had here was your basic hard-soft dilemma. I needed something soft that would form itself to the gentle curve of the pipe and make a toxic-waste-tight seal. But it had to have enough backbone that the pressure wouldn't destroy it. Two laps around the Best Hardware Store in Blue Kills had demonstrated that no single object would do the trick. Now I was trying to break it down, one problem at a time.

First, the soft part. And there it was: ring-shaped, four inches across, rubber. Attractively blister-packed and hanging there like fruit on a tree.

"How many of these toilet gaskets you have in stock?" I shouted. The young clerks froze in dismay and the old clerk took it right in stride.

"How many toilets you got?" he called.

"A hundred and ten."

"Wow!" piped a younger clerk, "Must be some house!"

"I'm a plumber missionary," I explained, wandering toward the front of the store. "Going down to . . ." almost said Nic-

aragua, but caught myself " . . . Guatemala next week. Figure
the only way to stop the spread of disease down there is put
in modern plumbing facilities. So I need a whole shitload of
those things."

Of course they didn't believe me, but they didn't need to.

"Joe, go see how many," said the boss. Giggling nervously,
Joe headed for the basement. I turned around before they
could bother me with questions and moved on to Phase II:
something hard and round that could hold the pressure, hold
those toilet gaskets against the side of the big pipe. Some
kind of disk. God help us if we had to cut a hundred disks
out of plywood. I could see us up all night on the deck of the
Blowfish, running out of saber-saw blades. Somewhere in this
great store there had to be a lot of hard round cheap things.

To summarize: they were having a sale on salad bowl sets
in the housewares department. Cheap plastic. A big bowl,
serving implements, and half a dozen small bowls nested inside. I borrowed a small bowl from the display set and carried
it over to plumbing, where I could hold it up against the toilet gaskets: a perfect match.

Now I just needed something that would hold the salad
bowls with their rims pressed against the gaskets pressed
against the pipe. All along I'd known that the crossbar running across each hole could serve as an anchor. In the back
they had yards and yards of threaded steel rod, which would
do just fine. Cut it into five-inch chunks, use a vise to bend
a hook into one end, hook it over the crossbar, run it
through a hole in the center of the bowl and use a wingnut
to hold the bowl down. It'd take some work, but that's what
nitrous oxide was for.

I bought a hundred and ten toilet gaskets, nineteen salad
bowl sets, fifteen three-foot-long threaded quarter-inch rods,
a hundred and fifty wingnuts (we were sure to drop some), an
extra vise, a chunk of lead pipe (for leverage when bending
hooks into the rods), four hacksaws, some files, some pipe cement, and a couple of spare 5/16-inch drills for drilling
through the bottoms of the bowls. Paid in cash and persuaded them to deliver it to the public dock at Blue Kills
Beach at the close of the business day. Then I walked out

into the bright Jersey sunlight, a free man. It was well past noon and time for a burger.

This place was a little out of the way, as good stores usually are, so I found a phone booth and dialed the number of the phone in our Omni.

All I could hear was Joan Jett, very loud, singing a song about driving around in New Jersey with the radio on. This was hastily turned down, then I heard the phone shuffling around in someone's hand, the roar of the road coming through the tinfoil walls of that little crackerbox and the coyote howl of the engine, doing at least five thousand RPM and approaching the redline.

"Shift!" I screamed, "Shift!"

"Shit!" Debbie answered. The phone dropped from her shoulder and bounced off something, probably the handbrake, then got crushed against the seat as she rammed the tranny into a higher gear. The engine calmed down. "Where the fuck is the horn," Debbie said dimly, then found it and described someone as a "rich bastard." Then, cut off in traffic, she had to downshift. I rummaged in my pocket for more change; this might take a while.

"Such a fucking right-handed car!" Debbie said. "The shift lever, the stereo, now the phone. What's the problem with the horn?"

"The whole middle part of the steering wheel is the horn button," I said.

"Oh, S.T. Stress. I love it. I adore stress."

"How'd it go?"

"Real fine. They gave up on the Kryptonites. Tried to send some boats up the channel to get us from that direction, but Jim blocked the deep part of the river with the *Blowfish* and they skragged one of their propellers on an old oil drum. One of theirs, probably."

"Wonderful. Very mediapathic."

"Didn't find any deformed birds but we got some trout with scuzz on their bodies. What did you find?"

"Toxic Disneyland. Want to come pick me up?"

I stayed on the phone and guided her on a hunt-and-miss expedition through the metropolitan area; did not hang up until the bumper of the Omni was in contact with my knees.

The grille was a crust of former insects, and waves of heat issued from the louver on the hood. As I checked the oil, she emerged to hover and squint, skeptically, at the engine.

"Master's degree in biology from Sweetvale, and you're driving around with a dry dipstick."

She couldn't believe what a jerk I was being, but that's okay, I even surprise myself sometimes. "What kind of macho crap is this?"

"You can call it macho, but if you redline it with no oil, it's going to go Chernobyl in the middle of the Garden State Parkway and we'll have to take the Green Tortoise home again."

She laughed. "Oh, fuck." We remembered half a dozen granola Green Berets, staggering onto a hippie bus at three in the morning wearing scuba gear and carrying a blown-up motorcycle.

I opened up the back and took out a couple of cans of oil. "You ever read *The Tragedy of the Commons?*"

"Environmental piece, I know that."

"Any property that's open to common use gets destroyed. Because everyone has incentive to use it to the max, but no one has incentive to maintain it. Like the water and the air. These guys have incentive to pollute the ocean, but no reason to clean it up. It's the same deal with this."

"Okay, okay, I can make the connection."

"Putting oil into the Omni is another form of environmentalism."

I shoved the oil sprout into the can, immediately making a sexual connection in my own mind. Then I poked the spout into the proper hole on the Omni, and looked at her, smearing the oil around on my fingers. She was looking at me.

The TraveLodge maid barged in and found us dorking each other's brains out on the rug, right in front of the door. Above us, Debbie was being interviewed on the telly. For some reason we had turned on all the hot water taps in the bathroom and the place was boiling with steam; Debbie's interview, and her other sound effects from below, were half drowned out by the buzz of the Magic Fingers. She slammed the door on her way out. What the hell did they expect, giving us the honeymoon suite?

"If you're planning to stay more than one day, it's traditional to inform the hotel," I said when we were finished. Debbie didn't answer because she was laughing too hard.

9

I⊤ WAS THREE O'CLOCK. Debbie called the front desk and told them we'd stay another day. Big surprise. We took a shower, then went down and hauled our CB out of the Omni and checked in with the mother ship. I told them that I had an idea for tomorrow that I'd like to bring up with them, and made arrangements to be picked up at the public dock at five.

Debbie and I had first run into each other when I was doing a full media splatter number on that toxic pond on the Sweetvale campus. It stirred up lot of interest among the student body, the idea that the green ivy of New England academe was just like algae growing on a rusty drum of industrial waste. They asked me to show up on campus and I went, foolishly expecting to be treated like a hero.

In fact, most of them were incredibly pissed off. They had pulled some blame-reversal thing where they felt the existence of toxic metals in their soil and swimming hole was somehow my fault. That if I'd kept my mouth shut, it would have been safe. This shouldn't have surprised me, because the ability to think rationally is pretty rare, even in prestigious universities. We're in the TV age now and people think by linking images in their brains. That's not always bad, but it led to some pretty ludicrous shit there at Sweetvale, and when some student leaders really started getting on my case in the media, I regrettably had to strip them naked, figuratively, before the toxic glare of the TV cameras. At some point during all that ugliness, Debbie found something decent either in me or GEE International and got involved with one or both of us, I'm not sure. We'd never been in the sack until now, but we'd both been considering it.

One of the New York City remote crews drifted by in their van, reminding me: we've got a media apocalypse to run tomorrow, and these guys don't even know it yet.

For that matter, neither did the victims. They'd been waiting for us to arrive for a month. Today we'd created a big noise and made them look like jerks. Now they were sitting back, holding meetings with their PR flacks, getting started on the damage control. That was awful, they were thinking, but now it's over, and we can stop the bleeding and pour some more death into the oceans.

Hardey-har-har. Tomorrow they'd need both hands just to hold their intestines in place. But we had to prep the media.

"Sangamon Taylor? Quite a show. Were you involved?"

This was one of the local media types, a classic horse's-ass TV reporter with a pneumatic haircut. He was winking at me, assuming that I was the man in the moon suit.

"Wait until tomorrow," I said. "Then we'll have some great visuals for you."

"You're doing something else tomorrow?"

"Yeah. Not one of these media events, you understand. I mean, what we did today, I'm sure you can see that it was intended just to look kind of flashy on TV. No real news value."

Shock flashed over his face like a blue beam from a cop car, then he managed a grin. "I gathered that," he said, a few tones higher than his baseline anchortone. "You did a good job of it."

"Thanks, but I'm sure a journalist like you can understand

there's more to GEE than just a bunch of clowns waving at the camera. We do serious work, too. Stuff that'll make for a real story—not just a piece of fluff."

What could I lose? His piece of fluff was already cued up in a videotape machine at the station.

"Tomorrow?"

"Yeah. We'll start real early in the morning, but this is going to be a long operation. All day long."

"Where?"

I told him how to get to Blue Kills Beach and gave him a xeroxed handout we prepared for the Fourth Estate—tips on how to protect and use your camera on a rocking Zodiac and that sort of thing. I also tossed him a videotape, stock footage of GEE frogmen working off of Zodiacs, plugging pipes.

"Thanks," he said, "I'll copy this and get it back to you."

"Keep it. We've got others."

"Oh, thanks!" He hefted the videotape and did a doubletake on it. "Jesus! This is three-quarter inch!" Then he gave me a sly wink and promised to see me tomorrow.

In the Omni, Debbie was on the phone to a reporter who'd been sent here from one of the New York papers. He'd be more portable than a minicam crew, shrewder, harder to manipulate and a lot more fun to hang out with.

We and the reporter—a round grizzled type named Fisk— and the *Blowfish* and the truck from the hardware store and a Lincoln with two rent-a-dicks all converged on Blue Kills Beach. I considered trying to hide our purchases from the dicks, but even if they saw what we had, they'd never anticipate our plan.

The driver from the hardware store was severely rattled. He was just a sixteen-year-old, probably doing his part-time on his way to being an artillery loader at Fort Dix. His dad probably worked at the plant. He'd never seen men with hair before.

"You know anything about outboards?" I asked him by way of male bonding. We got into a long rap about whether I needed to check the carburetor on one of our Mercs. Artemis got involved and soon the kid relaxed completely. He allowed as how he'd never seen such big motors on such small boats and she took him for a ride while we unloaded the truck. When he came back, half drenched with salt water, phthalates and hydrazines, he thought we were pretty cool. And that's fine, because we were pretty cool—Artemis is, anyway—and it wouldn't be fair for him to go away with the wrong impression. We take people for rides while the chemical companies lay off their cancerous dads, and sooner or later they decide on their own who the good guys are.

Several of the *Blowfish* crew wanted to do laundry and bathe in real tubs, so Debbie and I handed over the keys to the Omni and the honeymoon suite, after I talked to them briefly about dipsticks and redlines. Then we headed out to sea on the *Blowfish.*

I sat down on the foredeck with Fisk, who accepted one of my illegal cigars. We smoked and drank beer and traded environmental stories for a bit, then I showed him the pictures of the theta-holes, sketched the diffuser, laid out the whole gig.

He was interested, but not overly. "I figured you had something big planned," he said, "but my main reason for coming was this."

"What?"

"*This,*" he said, and swept his arms out wide. Then I noticed that we were sprawling on the deck of one very fine handmade wooden ketch, on the open ocean, under a golden afternoon sky, cooled by the breeze and warmed by the sun, sailing along strongly and quietly, smoking fine Cuban cigars.

"Oh, yeah," I said. "Fringe benefit."

Over dinner it came out that this was Captain Jim's birthday. Tanya had brought out some kind of politically incorrect cake, buried an inch deep in frosting, with a crude picture of a ketch on top. Debbie took the opportunity to give him something she'd been meaning to give him anyway.

She'd put in a lot of time on banner duty. More time than anyone should. She had a knack for visual thinking, Debbie did, and we knew it. These days she just sketched them out and canvassers—our student gnomes—did the sewing. One of her better efforts was a big square banner that we shackled to the top of a Fotex water tower one fragrant spring evening. It was simple: a skull and crossbones with the international circle/slash drawn over it in red.

Given the same assignment, I would have written a twenty-five word manifesto with a little picture down in the corner. Debbie said the same thing with a picture. I was impressed. When drunk, I referred to it as the Toxic Jolly Roger. The next time I went down to my Zodiac, someone had been there and attached a little fiberglass pole to the transom, a segment of a fishing rod. A little hand-sewn nylon flag was flying from it: black, with the skull and crossbones in white and the circle/slash in red. That was when I knew this woman liked me.

Then she came up with the idea of making a big one for the *Blowfish*. For some reason, I had to help, so we went to fabric stores and I loitered among the heavy, manly fabrics in the canvas section and scared off business while she charged up yards of ripstop nylon on a credit card that turned out to be mine. Then we laid it all out on the floor of her living room and drew the patterns. She had to educate me in basic cloth facts: if you draw the pattern on a chunk of cloth that is stretched out of shape, the pattern will be messed up. Then we had to seal the edges against fraying by running them through a candle flame, filling the apartment with every toxic fume known to man; I could feel the dissolved brain cells dribbling out my ears. Debbie insisted that no operation connected with sewing could really be toxic. And finally we ran it through her fucking Singer. I just went to the other room and watched the static from the sewing machine tear across the screen of her television. I don't like sewing machines. I don't understand how a needle with a thread going through the tip of it can interlock the thread by jamming itself into a little goddamn spool. It's contrary to nature and it irritates me.

So when we presented it to Jim, everyone applauded Debbie, and I just sat there like a turd on a platter. Then it was time for boy stuff. I cranked on the ship's generator and started ripping open boxes.

We drilled holes in bowls until 11 P.M., when I went to sleep. Debbie and I crammed ourselves into a berth meant for one. That was okay, since today was our first time. But in a week or so we'd need a kingsize waterbed. Fisk hung out on the deck in a sleeping bag, drinking brandy and making Artemis laugh. Jim just curled up next to the tiller, looking at the stars and thinking about whatever a forty-five-year-old sea drifter thinks about. The Atlantic rocked us to sleep, even as it was killing some more dolphins. The Toxic Jolly Roger grinned down over one and all.

And I woke up in the middle of the night sweating and panting like a pesticide victim, Dolmacher's slack skull-face staring at me. *It's the Holy Grail, as far as you're concerned.*

"What are you thinking about?" Debbie asked.

I hate that fucking question. Didn't answer.

Up there, a couple hundred miles north of us, Dolmacher was up—I knew he was still awake, still at the lab at two in the morning—tinkering around with genes. Looking for the Holy Grail.

I'd never play with genes. Wouldn't touch them. Any molecule more complicated than ethanol is too scary for me; bigger than that and you never know what they'll do. But Dolmacher *was* fucking with them. And the thing of it was: I always got higher scores on exams than him. I'm smarter than Dolmacher.

10

THAT WAS THE LAST SLEEP I got for about twenty-four hours. At four in the morning, I got up, destroyed the rest of the cake and chased it down with two cans of Jolt. Got a scuba outfit all ready, tromped around on top of the boat to get people awake and moving, then got into the best Zode with Artemis and we took off. At the last minute Fisk woke up and joined us.

The rent-a-dicks were lurking nearby in an open boat. There was no need for stealth, so we just warmed up the Mercury and let them eat our wake. We were quickly out of sight, and it's hard to track by sound when your own motor is blatting away ten feet behind you. Headed north, just to give them the wrong idea, then doubled back and homed in on the end of the diffuser.

I can dive if I have to, but it's not my thing. This time we needed lots of divers, though, and in any case the principle had to be tested. Arty saved me from certain embarrassment and possible demise by pointing out that I'd hooked up my tubes wrong. As we got them fixed, Fisk winked at me. "From here on out," he said, "I'm an objective journalist, sort of."

"Funny you should say that, since I'm about to commit a criminal act. Sort of." And I fell off the Zodiac.

After a certain amount of aimless swimming around, I located the diffuser. It wasn't putting much out right now, so I couldn't follow the black cloud. And Tom was right, the current was powerful, and a greenhorn like me would end up in Newark if he didn't keep swimming south.

But I had some big old magnets, things that would grip with a force of a hundred pounds, and I'd brought one along. Once I found the diffuser, I slapped the magnet on and tied myself to that with some rock-climbing webbing. This way I could plant my flippers and lean back against the tug of the rope while I worked.

From here on in it was just a problem of industrial engineering. How many holes could we plug per diver per hour, and how could we make it go faster? The key was to assemble the bowl/gasket/bolt/wingnut contraptions in the Zodiacs and hand them to the divers as they were needed.

The plug fit better than I deserved. There would be some leakage owing to the curvature of the pipe, but the diffuser's ability to emit toxic substances would be cut down to a thousandth of the norm. It was easy to hook the curved end of the bolt under the crossbar and twirl the wingnut down to tighten it. I took my time and estimated how far we could pretighten the wingnuts in the Zodiacs so that the divers wouldn't have to spend cumulative hours twisting them down.

Then I smeared some pipe cement over the threads. Hopefully it would harden up and prevent the wingnuts from being removed.

Not bad. I pretightened the wingnut on another assembly, checked my watch, swam to the next hole, and plugged it. That took five minutes. Five minutes per hole meant five hundred diver-minutes. They'd spend half their time farting around with air tanks and other friction, so we needed a thousand diver-minutes, or something like sixteen diver-hours. If we wanted to do it in four hours, we'd need four divers.

When I broke the water, our objective journalist was in a truly passionate clinch with Artemis. His fault. I'd made a point of waving my light around to warn them. When making love to granola commandos, leave your eyes open. They broke apart and I pretended to be looking the other way.

"I'm in luck," I said. "We only need four divers. And we happen to have four, besides me—so I can stay on top. Where I belong."

Artemis dunked me for that. Then we went back to the *Blowfish*, which blazed with light and cast a heavenly garlic smell across the water. Jim was up cooking—it had to be Jim, whose passion for garlic was fine by me.

"I'm not trying to sound, like, militaristic," I announced to the tofu-eating multitude, "but we have a go, Houston."

Everyone said "all right" and some raised an herbal toast. Now that these people were used to me, they were getting into the project. The prospect of destroying a mile-long toxic waste diffuser—hell, destroying *anything* a mile long—was a fiendish temptation.

"You want to call the plant, then?" Jim asked.

"I figure, as soon as we're done eating, we go over there and start. We've got two divers here and two at the TraveLodge and they'll be meeting us in half an hour. So once we get it working smoothly, get all those initial bugs worked out—"

"The part of the operation where we look like assholes," Debbie said, translating.

"—correct, we shut down the plant. That'll take about thirty seconds on the phone. Then we start the carnival." With Fisk present, I wasn't going to get any more explicit than that.

It all went pretty well, except that Fisk suddenly admitted, when the *Blowfish* was halfway there, that he had a gram of coke in his photographer's vest. He decided to fess up when he noticed that we all went through one another's clothing, looking for anything that could be construed as a drug or weapon; for obvious reasons we always did this when we were likely to get busted. And once Fisk owned up, I felt guilty and admitted to a square of blotter acid in my wallet which, since it was on a Boston Public Library card I didn't think would ever be noticed. But guilt is guilt.

LSD is a violation of Sangamon's Principle. It's a complicated molecule and hence makes me nervous. But sometimes you get in situations so awful, or so physically taxing, that nothing else will penetrate.

So the library card was burned, its ashes scattered, and Fisk's coke went up certain noses. We attacked our task with renewed vigor.

The TraveLodge people showed up a little late and we hustled them off to work. I hung out on shore, watching the media and authorities gather. They took pictures of me inflating a child's large wading pool. Hard to look like a commando when you're doing that; we'd have to get us a pump.

I have to get the toxics off the bottom of the sea and onto the cathode-ray tubes of the public in order for this kind of gig to work and, because the diffuser was completely hidden, this wouldn't be easy. All we had to show was a bunch of scuba divers jumping into the water with salad bowls and toilet parts and coming back up without them. So about the time all our media were in place, I took a Zode out and borrowed Tom from the salad-bowl operation. We went out to the *Blowfish*, picked up a portable pump and motored back in toward shore. Tom swam down to the diffuser and put the pump's intake hose into a diffuser hole, and I hauled the Zode up onto the beach and dragged the pump's output hose into the wading pool. Minicams clustered like flies on a muffin. I'd chosen a pool with a nice bright yellow bottom, so the Swiss Bastards' black sludge hit it with a nice mediapathic splash.

We ran the pump until the pool was nearly full. Along with Zodiacs and moonsuits, wading pools are among my favorite tools. We were lucky here, because the waste *looked* really bad. Sometimes you get stuff that's clear as water, and it's hard to convince people that it's really just as dangerous. After the pool, we also filled a couple of 55-gallon drums— these we'd chain to the doors of the New Jersey Statehouse in a couple of days—and then we were all done with the pump. I went over to the Omni and picked up the phone.

Every large corporation has its own telephone maze, its juicy numbers and dead ends, its nickel-plated bitch queens and sugary do-gooders. I'd already navigated this particular maze from Boston on my WATS line. So I dialed a particular extension three or four times, until I got the receptionist I wanted, and she punched me through to the plant manager.

"Yes?" he said, kind of groggy. I checked the Omni's clock. It was only 8:30.

"Yes, this is Sangamon Taylor from GEE International. How are you today?"

"What do you want?"

"I'm fine, thanks. Uh, we've discovered a big pipe sticking out into the ocean that's putting very large amounts of hazardous wastes right into the water. In fact, of the six pollutants that had EPA has licensed you to discharge into the water at this point, you're exceeding the legal limit on all six. And since they're very dangerous substances, what you're doing is illegally endangering the health and welfare of everyone who lives in this region, which is a lot of people. So, uh, we're shutting the diffuser off now, and I'd recommend that you stop putting wastes into it, for obvious reasons. If you'd like to get in touch with us, we're down at Blue Kills Beach. Would you like to take down our phone number here?"

"Listen, buddy, if you think that's just some little old pipe, you're wrong."

So I gave him a complete description of the pipe and what we were doing to plug it.

By this time the Omni's window had become kind of a TV screen for all the media to watch. I rolled the window down and turned the phone over to the "speaker" setting so that they could hear the whole conversation. On the whole, it was calm and professional, no fireworks. I go out of my way to be polite, and people entrusted with running huge chemical plants, unlike some of their bosses, tend to be in control of themselves. One techie to another. It's the flacks and executives who fly off the handle, because they have no understanding of chemistry. They don't imagine they might be wrong.

Half an hour later, our divers told me that nothing was coming out of the diffuser any more.

By that time I was the ringmaster of a full-scale media circus. Each crew had to be taken out on a Zodiac, given a thrilling ride through the surf, given a chance to videotape our divers and to walk around on the *Blowfish* and nuzzle the ship's cat. Meanwhile, Debbie hung out on the beach to placate those who were waiting their turn, giving them interviews, telling jokes and war stories—and later, confronting the small army dispatched here by the corporation. Fortunately she was well cut out for that; dinky, tough, quick-witted and exceedingly cute. Not the flummoxed rad/fem/les they were hoping for.

For a big outfit, the Swiss Bastards were pretty quick on their feet. They'd already xeroxed up their press releases, and they always had reams of prepackaged crap about eye-droppers in railway tank cars and the beneficent works of the chemical industry. You know: "These compounds are rapidly and safely dispersed into a concentrated solution of dihydrogen oxide and sodium chloride, containing some other inorganic salts. Sound dangerous? Not at all. In fact, you've probably gone swimming in it—this is just a chemist's way of describing salt water." This is precisely the sort of witticism that TV reporters love to steal and pass off as their own, granting their stories a cheery conclusion on which to cut back to the beaming anchordroids. It's much more upbeat than talking about liver tumors, and it's why we have to do this business with wading pools.

When I got back from taking a local TV reporter on his joyride, the suits were fully mobilized. They'd set up a folding table on the beach with their nicely forested property as a back-drop. Tactical error on my part! I should have strung a nice big banner out across that fence so they couldn't use it. We had a big roll of banner stuff in the Omni—green nylon cloth on a white backing—so I asked Debbie and Tanya if they could try to whip something up real quick.

They'd propped one end of their table up on some bundles of press releases, because the beach sloped toward the water, as beaches do. It was too much to hope that the incoming tide would undermine and topple it. I was tempted to speed that process up with the pump, but that would be openly juvenile and too close to actual assault. Their head flack was waddling around in the sand, which was pouring in over the tops of his hand-tooled dress shoes. They even had makeup people handy to spackle his trustworthy face.

To watch a big corporation throw its PR machine into action can be kind of imposing. I got scared the first couple of times, but fortunately I was with some GEE veterans who were old hands as trashing press conferences. You have to attack on two levels—challenging what the PR flacks are saying, and at the same time challenging the conference itself, shattering the TV spell.

I waved Artemis close in to shore. As soon as the Swiss flack started in with his prepared statement, I nodded at her and she cranked up her motor pretty loud, in neutral, forcing him to raise his voice. That's very important. They want to be media cool, like JFK, and if you make them shout they become media hot, like Nixon. I started thinking about five-o'clock shadows and how we could cast one on a flack's face. An idle inspiration that was probably too subtle for us.

The flack unleashed his poster about eyedroppers in tank cars. I ran to the Omni for my poster about banana peels on football fields. He talked about sodium chloride and dihydrogen oxide, and I countered that calling trinitrotoluene "dynamite" doesn't make it any safer. He showed a map of the plant, then of Blue Kills, showing where the big pipe ran underneath the city and out to this beach.

That was fine with me. If he wanted to show people how their toxic waste was passing under their homes, let him.

In fact, I couldn't figure out what the hell he was thinking. Why did he want to emphasize that? I started flipping through one of their press packets and found the same map, with their underground pipe highlighted. Exactly what they didn't want people to know.

Then the bastard drygulched me. He almost nailed me to the wall.

"By plugging up the diffuser at the end of this pipe, the GEE people are running the risk that the pipe will burst, somewhere back in here . . ." (pointing to a residential neighborhood) ". . . and release these compounds into the soil. This should lay to rest any misconceptions about their concern for the people of Blue Kills. What these people are, pure and simple, is t—"

"What he's saying," I shouted, stepping up behind him and holding a salad bowl in the air, "is that this pipeline . . ."

I pointed to the map ". . . that's carrying tons of toxic waste under people's homes, is so fragile, so shoddily made and poorly maintained, that it's *weaker* than a contraption made from a salad bowl and a toilet part that we just whipped up on the spur of the moment."

I could see the guy deflate. He refused to turn around. "And if these compounds are as safe as he says, why is he worried about them getting into the soil? Why does he equate that threat with terrorism? That should tell you how safe it really is."

And, finally, I got to deliver my traditional *coup de grâce*, namely, handing the flack a glass tumbler full of the awful black stuff and inviting him to drink it.

Sometimes I feel sorry for flacks. They don't have a clue about chemistry or ecology or any of the technical issues. They just have an official line they're told to repeat. My job is to get them fired. The first few times I did this, I felt great, like an avenging angel. Now I try to coopt them. I go easy. I don't blow their brains out on-camera unless they get sleazy, attacking me or GEE. I've been responsible for a lot of people getting fired—security guards, PR flacks, engineers—and that's the most troublesome part of my job.

THE COPS SHOWED UP. All kinds of cops. Blue Kills cops, state police, coast guardsmen. It didn't much matter because we'd already plugged ninety-five of the holes.

All the cops stood in knots on the beach and argued about jurisdiction. What they came up with was this: several state troopers and Blue Kills policemen took a coast guard boat out to the *Blowfish*—which a trooper boarded, just to show the flag—and then their boat escorted us way around to the north and into a dock that was part of Blue Kills proper, not Blue Kills Beach.

It was a fun trip. The wind had come up and the Blue Kills cops, on that dinky CG boat, spent most of it doubled over the side, chucking their donuts. On the *Blowfish*, I chatted with Dick, the state trooper, a pretty affable guy of about forty. He asked me a lot of questions about the plant and why it was dangerous and I tried to explain.

"Cancer happens when cells go crazy and don't stop multiplying. That happens, basically, because their genetic code has gotten screwed up."

"Like nicotine or asbestos or something."

I glanced up and saw Tom Akers sidling over in our direction, listening to the conversation.

"Yeah. Nicotine and asbestos have some way of altering your genes. Genes are just long stringy molecules. Like any other molecule, they can have chemical reactions with other molecules. If the other molecule happens to be, say, nicotine, the reaction will break or damage the gene. Most of the time it won't matter. But if you're unlucky, the gene will be changed in just the wrong way. . . ."

"And you get the Big C."

"Right." I couldn't help thinking of Dolmacher—the world's biggest carcinogen—cracking genes up there in Boston. "The thing is, Dick, that for a chemist it's pretty obvious, just looking at any molecule, whether it's going to cause cancer or not. There are certain elements, like chlorine, that are very good at breaking apart your genes. So if you're dumping something into the environment that has a lot of available chlorine on it, you have to be a jerk not to realize it's cancer-causing."

"But you can never prove it," Tom said, sounding kind of sullen.

"You can never prove it the way you can prove a case in court. That's why the chemical corporations can get away with so much. Someone gets a tumor, it's impossible to trace it back to a particular chlorine atom that came from a molecule that was discharged by such-and-such a plant. It's all circumstantial, statistical evidence."

Dick said, "So this stuff coming out of this pipe down here—"

"Some of it has chlorine on it. Also there are some heavy metals coming out, like cadmium, mercury, and so on. Everyone knows they're toxic."

"So why does the EPA allow these guys to do it?"

"To dump that stuff? They don't."

"What do you mean?"

"The EPA doesn't allow it. It's against the law."

"Wait a minute," Dick said. I could see the methodical cop mind at work; I could see him writing up an arrest report. "Let's take this from the top. What these guys are doing is against the law."

"Exactly."

"So how come we're arresting you?"

"Because that's the way of the world, Dick."

"Well, you know, a lot of people around here . . ." he leaned forward, though nobody was even close to us ". . . are on your side. They really like what you're doing. Everyone's known that these guys were dumping poison. And people are sick of it." He leaned even closer. "Like my daughter for example. My seventeen-year-old daughter. Hey! That reminds me! You got any stuff on this boat?"

"What do you mean?" I thought he was talking about drugs.

"Oh, you know, bumper stickers, posters. I'm supposed to get some for my daughter, Sheri."

I took him down below and we redecorated Sheri's room with big posters of adorable mammals.

"How about stuffed animals? You got any stuffed animals?" Then his eyes went wide and he glanced away. "Sorry. I didn't mean that as a joke."

For a second I didn't catch the reference. Then I figured that he was talking about an incident a couple of weeks before when a van of ours, completely jammed with stuffed penguins, had caught fire on the Garden State Parkway. Our people got out, but the van burned like a flare for three hours. Plastic is essentially frozen gasoline.

"Yeah, we're a little short."

I got some coffee for Dick and we hung out in the cockpit watching Blue Kills approach, watching the cops on the CG boat do the technicolor yawn. "How long you staying in Jersey?" he asked.

"Couple days."

"You know, Sheri just thinks you guys are great. She'd love to meet you. Maybe you could come by for dinner." We fenced over that issue for a while—God help me, getting involved with an underage Jersey state trooper's daughter—and then Dick and his friends busted us and took us to jail.

We were each allowed one phone call. I used mine to order a pizza. We'd already notified the national office of GEE, down in Washington, and they had dispatched Abigail, the attack lawyer. She was on her way now, probably in a helicopter gunship.

By the time our mug shots and fingerprints were taken and we'd exchanged business cards with our new cellmates, it was eight in the evening and I just wanted to sleep. But Abbey showed up and sprang us.

"It's a totally awful, bogus bust," she explained, dragging on a cig and massaging her aluminum briefcase. "Jurisdiction is totally coast guard, because it all happened offshore. You were working out of the town of Blue Kills Beach. But the cops who busted you were from Blue Kills. So it's just a total fuck-up. And the charges will probably be dropped anyway."

"The charges are—"

"Sabotaging a hazardous-waste pipeline."

I looked at her.

"Honest to God. That's actually a crime in New Jersey. I do not make this up," she said.

"Why do you think they'll drop the charges?"

"Because that will force the company to go into court and testify that this pipeline is carrying hazardous waste. Otherwise, it's not a hazardous-waste pipeline, is it?"

When I got out to the Omni I sat there for a while with the seat leaned back, dozing, waiting for them to let Debbie out of girl jail. The phone rang.

"GEE?" said an old voice.

"Yeah."

"I want to talk to S.T."

"Speaking."

And that was all it took. The guy just started to ramble. He talked for fifteen minutes, didn't even pause to see if I was still connected. He didn't tell the story very coherently, but I understood pretty clearly. He'd worked at the plant, or ones like it, for thirty-two years. Saved up money so he and his wife could buy an Airstream and drive around the country when they retired. He went on and on about that Airstream. I learned about the color scheme, what kind of material the kitchen counters were made of, and how many pumps it took to flush the toilet. I could have rewired that trailer in the dark by the time he was done describing it.

Now he had a form of liver cancer.

"Hepatic angiocarcinoma," I said.

"How'd you know?" he said. I let him figure it out.

His doctor said it was a very rare disease, thought it seemed to be pretty common around Blue Kills. This guy knew three other people who had died of it. All of them had the same job he did.

"So I just thought you might like to know," he said, when he'd finally come around to this point, when he was ready to drive the knife home, "that those bastards have been dumping waste solvents into a ditch behind the main plant for thirty year. They're still doing it every day. The supervisors do it now so the workers don't know about it. And I just know they're scared shitless that someone like you is going to find out."

A guy in a suit had materialized right outside the Omni. When I suddenly noticed him it was like waking up from a dream. For a second I thought he was a hit man, thought I was going to die. Then he pressed a business card up against the glass. He wasn't a hit man or a rent-a-dick or a PR flack. He was an assistant attorney general from a particular state or commonwealth somewhere between Maine and the Carolinas. His last name wasn't necessarily Cohen, but Cohen is what I'll call him.

I reached around and unlocked the passenger-side door. Then I tried to think of a way to end this phone conversation. What do you say to a guy in those circumstances? He was halfway between this world and the next, and I was a twenty-nine-year-old guy who likes to watch cartoons and play ski-ball. He wanted Justice and I wanted a beer.

This assistant A.G. was polite, anyway. He stood outside the passenger door as long as I kept talking. The old guy gave me exhaustive directions on how to find this ditch. It would involve sneaking onto the plant grounds in the middle of the night, avoiding security cops here and here and here, going one hundred yards in such-and-such direction, and drilling. We would have to backpack a soil corer all the way in.

All of this was slightly more illegal than what I was used

to. Besides, that trench wasn't a secret. Others had already spilled the toxic information to the media. The neighborhood plague of birth defects and weird cancers had already been noticed; red thumbtacks had already gone up on the map, splattering away from the trench like blood from a bullet. In a couple of months the first suit would be filed. That trench was going to be an issue for the next ten years. There was a pretty good chance it would drive the corporation into bankruptcy.

"I just hope you can use this because I want those son of a bitches to dry up and fall into the ocean." And on and on, more and more profane, until I hung up on him.

Talking to cancer victims never makes me feel righteous, never vindicated. It makes me slightly ill and for some reason, guilty. If people like me would just keep our mouths shut, people like him would never suspect why they got cancer. They'd chalk it up to God or probability. They wouldn't die with hearts full of venom.

It is a strange world that Industry has made. Kind of a seething toxic harbor, opening out on a blue unspoiled ocean. Most people are swimming in it, and I get to float around on the surface, on my Zodiac, announcing that they're in trouble. What I really want to do is make a difference. But I'm not sure if I have, yet.

Cohen rapped on the window glass. I motioned him in, but I didn't move my seat to the upright position. I just lay there while he got in, and tried to remember all the crimes I had committed in Cohen's particular state/commonwealth. None in the last six months.

"Phoning home to Mom?"

"Not exactly. Hey, look, Cohen, our lawyer's inside, okay? I have nothing to say to you."

"I'm not here to prosecute you."

When I looked him in the face, he nodded in the direction of a Cadillac that was aswarm with suits from the company. "I want to prosecute *them*."

"Shit. Four different kinds of cops, now five, all arresting different people. I need a scorecard."

"Could you prove in court that someone like that was violating the law?"

"I can run a chemical analysis that proves it. But any chemist can do that. You don't need me."

"Why are you laughing?"

"Because this is unbelievable. I just get sprung from jail and now. . . ."

"You have a pretty low opinion of law enforcement in my state, don't you?"

A delicate question. "A lot of laws get broken there, let's put it that way." But that was a dodge. Of course I had a low opinion. I'd seen this before. GEE draws attention to a problem and suddenly the cops—particularly the category of cops who have to be reelected—are on the ball.

"It might interest you to know that our state is tired of being used as a chemical toilet so that people in Utah can have plastic lawn furniture."

"I can't believe an assistant attorney general came right out and said that."

"Well, I wouldn't say it in public. But we don't need this image problem."

"Sounds like strategy and tactics, man, like some important up-for-reelection type sat down with a chart, in the Statehouse maybe, and said: 'Item number two, this toilet-of-the-United-States business. Cohen, get out there and bust some corporate ass.' "

Cohen was nice enough to give me a bitchy little smile. "If that's how you want to view it, fine. But real life is more complicated."

I just sneered out the windshield. After I've gotten the date and done the work for them, ecocrats love to give me some pointers on real life. If it makes them feel better, I don't care.

"We want to prosecute these people," Cohen continued, "but getting evidence is hard."

"What's so hard about it?"

"Come on, Mr. Taylor, look at it from a cop's point of view. We aren't chemists. We don't know which chemicals to look for, we don't know where or how to look. Infiltration, sampling, analysis, all those activities require specialists—not state troopers. You're very scornful, Mr. Taylor, because for you—with your particular skills—for you all those things are easy. You can do them with your eyes closed."

"Holy shit, is this going where I think it is?"

It was. Cohen wanted me to break into a fucking chemical plant in the middle of the night, with cops and a warrant, in his home state, and get samples. Me, I was far too tired to hear this bizarre stuff. I desperately needed cold beer and loud rock and roll. So Cohen went on and on, about how I should think this over, and then I found myself sitting alone in the Omni, leaned back in the reclining seat with Debbie's Joan Jett tape blasting on the stero—*I'm in love with the modern world / I'm in touch, I'm a modern girl*—drawing stares from the company suits, wondering if I'd just dreamed the whole thing.

12

BACK IN BOSTON, we worked out a settlement with Fotex. They had just lost their most vicious negotiator, my oldest and wiliest enemy in this business, who had toppled off a rusty catwalk into an intake pond, been sucked into a pig pipe, shredded into easily digestible bits by rotating knives and processed into toxic sludge. I guessed it was suicide. This Fotex deal was a big hassle since Wes, who runs the Boston office, was using the Omni for a business trip through northern New England. I had to ride my bike to and from their goddamn plant, way up north in the high-chemical-crime district and reachable only by riding on the shoulder of some major freeways. I could feel the years ticking off my life expectancy as the mile markers struggled by.

Someone had donated an old computer system, a five-terminal CP/M system about ten years old. Boston already had a Computer Museum, but we were neck-and-neck with them as a showcase of obsolete machinery. Old used computers are economically worthless and we pick them up for little or nothing. Usually they're good enough for what we want to do: telecommunications, printing up mailing lists, slowly crunching a few numbers.

Debbie and I took a vacation up to Quebec City and then over to Nova Scotia for a couple of days. I had a terrible time.

"If we get up now—" I said one night at about 3:00 A.M., looking at my digital nerd-watch.

"—and roll up the tent real fast," she continued, and by this time I was already embarrassed, but she kept going, "and jump into the car and drive all night, we could reach the ferry that runs down to the states, and be in Boston, wallowing in sludge, within twenty-four hours."

"Yeah."

"Instead of being out here on the beach, listening to the waves, relaxing and screwing," she continued.

"We aren't screwing," I pointed out, but suddenly we were. Debbie insisted on following the rhythm of the waves. Typical duck-squeezer sex: slow, frustrating, in tune with nature. Fortunately there was a trawler out there somewhere, maybe a mile out, and when its wake attacked the beach, the waves started piling in on top of each other, blending into one fast pounding whoosh-whoosh-whoosh. I burst the zipper out of my sleeping bag, Debbie kicked a pot of cold hot chocolate out into the sand, and for a while we just lay there, half tumbled out onto the beach, feeling the cold and the warmth on opposite sides, and I said to hell with the damn ferry. Every so often I got some hint that this woman really wanted me, and it was scary. When she wanted other things she was so crafty and effective.

Eventually we found our way back and then didn't see each other for a while. It was a nice summer and I spent more time at the beach, or playing ski-ball, than working. Bart had a friend in Tacoma who mailed us a shitload of powerful fireworks he'd bought on an Indian reservation. We got arrested shooting them off in a park and I had to sell off some shares of my old Mass Anal stock to pay the fine. The guy who arrested us was good—some kind of ex-military man. He waited until we lit off a whistle, so we couldn't hear his engine, then he closed on us at some huge speed, with his lights off, stopped right in front of us, pinning us against a retaining wall, and hit us with all of his cop lights at once.

Brilliant tactics. I congratulated him heartily; it was useful to remember that smart cops did exist.

The *Blowfish* showed up. It was about to turn the corner around Maine and head into the Buffalo area. But first we took a trip out to Spectacle Island, a couple of miles off of South Boston. It really ought to be called Gallagher Tow Island, because it was kind of a patrimony for that family. The guy who'd founded Gallagher Tow—I don't know his first name—had held down the city garbage-towing concession for fifty years. He'd clung to that concession like something out of an *Alien* movie; he couldn't be removed without killing the patient. He'd used everything—graft, blackmail, bullshit, violence, Irishness, defamation of character, arranged marriages, the Catholic church, and simple groveling. He'd hung on to that garbage contract, built up his fleet of tugs from one to fifteen, created an entire goddamn island out in the middle of the Harbor, and, like a true magnate, died of a massive stroke. Now his grandson, Joe, ran Gallagher Tow, and he'd moved on to other forms of envirocide. They had a brand new behemoth named *Extra Stout*, a 21,000-horse tugboat that could probably haul Beacon Hill out to sea if they could figure out where to attach the hawser. Instead they used it to haul oil rigs through twenty-foot swells in the North Atlantic.

So the Gallagher garbage-dumping days are over, but the evidence is still there. You can go walk around on it. Someday, I'm sure, a set of yuppie condos will spring up on Spectacle Island. The heating bills would be low, because all that trash is still decaying; if you stick a probe into its bowels in the middle of the winter, you will find that the entire island is blood-warm. It just sits there decomposing, throwing off heat and gases. As far as I'm concerned it kind of sums up Boston Harbor.

You can dig a hole and sample the blood of Spectacle Island, a reddish-brown fluid that permeates the entire dump, a cocktail of whatever's been piled up there, mingled together and dissolved in rainwater. But once you analyze it, you know there's more to the island than used diapers, rotting sofas and Sox scorecards. There are solvents and metals, too. Industry has been out dumping its trash.

Sometimes I got the impression that companies were still coming out here and unloading difficult pieces of garbage. That was hard to prove, unless I camped out on the island and waited for them to show up, and I didn't want to live on a mound of garbage. Roscommon's house was close enough.

Our *Blowfish* expedition was an experiment. I'd been reading about a place in Seattle where they'd constructed houses close to an old covered-over dump site. The houses started to explode spontaneously and it was found that methane gas, created by the decay, was seeping into their basements. So the city sank pipes into the ground to let the gas escape, and if you lit them they'd make nice flares.

We loaded a number of long pipes onto the *Blowfish*, rented a drilling rig, and cruised out there on a sunny Saturday morning. When we got there, the obligatory crew of under-age shitheels, half a dozen of them, were throwing a party on the fetid beach. They were all standing around a bonfire because there's no place on Spectacle Island where you'd want to sit down. They were drinking Narragansett, which had put them into kind of a traditional Russian mood; whenever they finished a bottle, they'd fling it down and shatter it. They were drinking in a hurry, because it was windy and cool, the place stank and they probably knew the whole trip was a mistake. The tinkling explosions were almost nonstop. Gulls circled, hoping some edible garbage would show up, swooping down to intercept the flying glass.

We anchored a little ways offshore and used a Zode to ferry the equipment onto the island. The Narry drinkers had come out here in someone's dad's boat, an open, four-seat fishing cruiser, and had pulled it up onto the best landing spot. It hurt just to see that, because the bottom of that nice fiberglass hull had probably picked up some long, deep scars. We settled for a less-convenient spot about a hundred yards away, and started piling up our equipment.

I was happy to avoid them. They wore the uniform of the teen nonconformist: long hair, unsuccessful mustache, black leather. If Bartholomew were here, he could identify their favorite band just by looking at their colors. I stayed on shore with the equipment while Wes ran stuff back and forth. He'd dumped off some pipes and was on his way back to the *Blow-*

fish when he noticed that the partyers had found a stack of junk tires. They were swarming like ants on candy, shouting, laughing, calling each other "dude," and throwing them on the bonfire.

My attitude was, who the fuck cares? That's why I'll never be in charge of a regional office. Wes was a different type.

To me it was just some black smoke into the air. Kind of unsightly, a little toxic, but unimportant in the big scheme of things. To Wes it was a symbolic act, a desecration of the environment. It didn't matter that, in this case, "the environment" was an immense garbage dump to begin with. So before I could tell him not to worry about it, he was drowning out my voice with his outboard, buzzing over there to intervene.

Once they got over being stunned, they reacted exactly as you'd expect: went into a blind testosterone rage. "*Fuck* you! *Fuck* you!" "Now listen . . ." "*Fuck* you!" One of them dragged a strip of burning Goodyear out of the fire, whirled it up into a flaming spiral, and let it fly toward Wes, who had to knock it aside with an oar before he had time to get scared. He shot away, bottles splashing in his wake, and then, of course, they noticed me.

Standing there with a five-gallon can of gasoline, recalling the *Road Warrior*, I could think of a thousand interesting ways to scare these twits off. Unfortunately, these were the sort who'd be apt to carry guns. If there wasn't a Saturday Night Special in one of their belts, you could bet they had one in the boat. So a frontal assault wasn't a wise idea.

Wes believed anyone could be converted to an environmentalist by negotiation. It hadn't worked, but at least he had the presence of mind to see that they were headed my way. Wes was no expert with the Zodiac, but the water was calm and he could make it faster than the goons could run. Unfortunately the goons had a head start. I ran away from them along the shore, and as Wes caught up with me I waded out so he wouldn't have to pull his motor up, or, worse, forget and skrag the prop.

When I was up to midthigh, he reached me and I took one last step forward, half-falling into the boat. My foot came down on a sharp piece of metal and I felt it slash through the sole of my tennis shoe and gouge me. Then I was lying crosswise on the Zodiac, random pieces of Gallagher's trash pile were splashing into the water around us, and we were headed back to the *Blowfish*.

We changed course halfway there when Wes noticed that the goons were trashing the equipment we'd left on shore. They were especially interested in the drilling rig, which they started wrecking with the primitive weapons at hand. It was like watching Homo Erectus discover how to make tools out of flint.

Wes brought us to within about a bottle's throw from the shore and shouted at them. I don't think they even looked up.

They did seem to notice when they heard the sound of a second Zodiac motor cranking out some high RPMs. We all looked down the shoreline. Artemis had taken her Zodiac in to shore, tied its stern rope to the back of their fishing boat and tugged it off the beach. Now she was hauling it ass-backwards out to sea.

Later there were loud and long and dull debates about whether this was consistent with GEE principles. It wasn't exactly violence, but it did imply a certain willingness to let these guys starve to death on a pile of garbage, within sight of home. Like most of these debates, this one never got resolved.

It modified their attitudes, though. They stopped pounding on the drill motor and ran back to inform Artemis that she was a "fucking cunt." When this didn't work, they quieted down, watching their boat go out to sea.

In about five minutes, the jerks had dumped all the Narries out of their cooler and were using it to haul water up from the surf and dump it on the bonfire. It never really went out—tire fires never do—but it stopped billowing smoke.

I asked Wes to take me out to Artemis, then clambered on board their boat, hopped around leaving bloody waffle prints on the deck and checked in the glove compartment.

The gun wasn't the little .22 revolver I'd expected, but a big, chrome-plated cannon, stuck in a stiff new shoulder holster. When I pulled it out, it took me a minute to untangle the straps.

"All six chambers are loaded," Artemis observed. "Not a great idea unless you want to shoot yourself in the armpit." When I shot her an odd look, she shrugged. "My dad was into guns, what can I say."

It looked like someone else had a real jackass for a dad too. I chucked the weapon into the sea. Then, just for the hell of it, I kept rummaging. We had all day, we were already into some serious criminality, and we'd never be prosecuted. But if these pricks gave us any more trouble, I wanted to know where they lived.

Couldn't find a damn thing. Other than the gun, this boat was eerily clean. No papers, no registration, no old beer cans. The life vests were brand new and unmarked. When I climbed back onto the Zode, I had no information at all, nothing but a chemical trace. There was an odor about that boat, and it followed me, unwelcome, onto the Zode. It was on my hand. The smell of some goddamned men's cologne. I'd picked it up from the revolver.

Artemis mocked me with no mercy. "Shit, I'd rather have PCBs on me," I said. "PCBs you can wash off; other people's perfume sticks with you like a bladder infection." I trailed my hand in the water.

We reunited these little fucks with their transportation and they left, quietly. The injured dignity on their faces was something to behold. You'd think we'd just busted up a monastery.

They didn't say a word until they were a hundred yards out, almost out of earshot. Then, I think, they looked in the glove compartment. They just exploded with more lusty fucks, cunts, and pricks. I could hardly make it out, and I didn't want to.

Wes turned to me with just a grin on his face. "Did you hear that?"

"What?"

"Satan will get you."

"That's what they said?"

"I think so."

"Shit. Then I'll tell Tricia to expect a call from the Prince of Darkness."

"She'll probably hang up on him."

We didn't have the stuff we needed to repair the drilling rig. That was okay, since I didn't really think it would work anyway. It was made to bore down through reasonably soft dirt, not a pile of trash that included lots of iron fragments. We had something more reliable: a couple of sledgehammers. I picked out a promising place on the north end, visible from both South Boston and downtown, and we started pounding pipe segments down into the bowels of Spectacle Island.

Ridiculously slow work. We spent about four hours on it, taking turns on the sledgehammers and keeping an eye out for the goons on the boat.

My foot had a one-inch gash in it, ranging from not very deep to pretty fucking deep. Back on the *Blowfish*, I scrubbed it out with soap and water, taking scientific care to probe the deepest parts of the cut, squeezing it to make it bleed, the whole bit; disinfected it with something incredibly painful and wrapped a sterile bandage around the foot. Walking around was painful, so when I wanted to do a little investigating I had to go by water, on a Zodiac.

What I wanted to see was near the northeast corner of the island. It was a huge, rusty, old barge, a piece of shit, but apparently seaworthy. There was no cargo on it. It looked like it had simply run aground.

Right now the tide was almost out and about three-quarters of the barge was high and dry. It was way, way up there; when it had rammed this island, the tide must have been especially high, or it must have been going very fast, or both.

Or maybe it had been deliberately abandoned. Maybe Joe Gallagher had come here and put the nose of the *Extra Stout* against the ass end of the barge and just tossed it up onto the rest of the garbage. The interesting thing was that it was new—it wasn't here three months ago, the last time I was out—and it must have carved some pretty deep gashes into the island.

Geologists love earthquakes and other natural upheavals because they tear things open, providing views into the

earth's secrets. I had a similar attitude about this barge.
There was no way to drag it off the island and then jump
down into the cavity it had dug, but I could skulk around the
edges with my sampling jars and see what was coming out.

But I probably wouldn't bother. If I were doing a Ph.D.
dissertation on Spectacle Island, I'd go wild over it. But I
know what Spectacle Island is: a big heap of garbage. As long
as there were bigger issues in the Harbor, no point in getting
obsessed with the details.

But just for the hell of it, because it was new and interesting, I circumnavigated the barge, partly on the water and
partly by foot. Nothing much to see besides hundreds of feet
of vertical, rust-covered wall. Graffiti was sprinkled near the
waterline and on the part that stuck out into the Harbor.
The walls were a natural for graffiti, but Spectacle Island
wasn't accessible to your average jerk with a spraycan. The
SMEGMA man had made it out here—some guy who'd been
wandering around Boston for a couple of years painting the
word SMEGMA everywhere. Super Bad Larry had made it,
probably swam one-handed all the way from Roxbury. Someone in the Class of '87, and VERN + SALLY = LOVE apparently
had had access to a boat. Three-quarters of the graffiti was in
red, though, done by a single group. Besides being red, it had
a distinctive look to it. Most graffitists just scribble something down and run away, having made their point, but the
people with the red spray-paint were performing black magic,
exercising ritual care. This was most obvious with the penta-
cles, which were inscribed in a circle. It's hard to stand on a
rolling boat in the middle of the night and draw a perfect
five-foot circle with a spray can, but the Satan worshippers
had done it repeatedly, all around the barge. Then they drew
upside-down stars in the circles, forming your basic pentagram, and an inverted cross underneath that. Arched over
the top of the circle were the words PÖYZEN BÖYZEN—a
heavy-metal band with a thing about nuns and pit bulls.

They weren't finished with the umlauts, though. They put
another in the center of the pentagram. If you stood back
and looked at it the right way, the inverted star then became
a face. The umlaut made two beady red eyes, the bottom

prong of the star made a sharp muzzle, the top prongs a pair of horns, and the two side prongs a pair of goatlike ears.

The name of the brand was written a few other places, billboard-sized, along with a bunch of incantations I didn't recognize. Old magic symbols cribbed from a book on the occult, I guess: circles and lines and dots connected in rigid but meaningless patterns. A nonchemist might mistake them for molecular diagrams.

The Satan worshippers had left a few other symptoms of their presence scattered around the island. For example, a wrecked toilet with a cross painted on it, surrounded by the remains of five bonfires. A mock shrine, I guess. I knocked it apart by throwing football-sized rocks at it, not because I'm some kind of heavy Christian, but only because it got on my nerves. Besides, there's no incentive to keep a garbage pile neat, which was the problem with Boston Harbor to begin with. I kicked at one of the old bonfires and noticed that they had been burning old wood that had been pressure treated with some kind of preservative. That was fine with me. When you burn that kind of wood, the smoke contains an amazingly high concentration of dioxin. Let's hope Pöyzen Böyzen fans like to roast marshmallows.

A curl of that toxic smoke rose up out of the ashes. This fire was brand new, left over from last night.

I hadn't seen any boats beached near here, so they must have all gone home. Hell, maybe it was the same group we'd been arguing with. I went down to the pseudobeach next to the barge and looked for signs of activity and, sure enough, a few footprints. This obviously was their landing zone, and the graffiti was dense. WELCOME TO HELL, it said, and a few yards after along, written higher than I could reach, a small pentacle and the word SATAN with an arrow pointed upward.

THE ANTICHRIST IS

That's why the unrusted area caught my eye. It was way up at the top of the barge, above the SATAN sign. A pair of little spots, a silver umlaut, where the rust had been worn away. They were a little more than a foot apart. At first I thought they were paint spots, but then caught them glinting in the sun.

I went over and stood beneath them. This patch of ground looked smoother, harder-packed. There were some weak indentations, a little more than a foot apart. The Pöyzen Böyzen people had been using a ladder to climb up into the barge.

It didn't look like a rusted-out hulk to me anymore. It looked like an iron-walled fortress, something out of Tolkien. God knows what was going on inside of it.

I had a pretty good idea: high-school kids came out here to drink Narries and fornicate. Maybe they traded in cocaine, or cheaper highs, but at any rate the lunatic fringe to this group owned a lot of red spray paint and had been to some bookstore in Cambridge with an "occult" section in the back.

There was no reason in the world I would want to discover their purpose, so I limped back to the Zode and went back to our pipe-pounding operation.

Frank, the biggest guy on the *Blowfish* crew, had broken through for us. Something was definitely escaping from the pipe. If you held your hand over it, the warm, moist draft made your skin crawl. I had everyone stand back, lit a 4th of July sparkler, and threw it toward the pipe from about ten feet away. I didn't see the rest, because I turned away instinctively, but I heard a large but quiet *thwup* as a big ball of gas went up. Then there was a mild roaring sound, like distant traffic. The crew of the *Blowfish* applauded and I turned around. We had a nice flare going, a big raggedy yellow flame.

We lengthened the pipe so that its outlet was about ten feet off the ground and then we left it there, burning. In my fantasies, I wanted to encircle Spectacle Island with a blazing corona of yellow flares, a beacon to ships at sea, a landmark for airline pilots, permanent fireworks for the yuppies in the new waterfront condos. It wouldn't really accomplish that much, other than to remind people: Hey. There's a harbor out here. It's dirty.

13

WHEN I GOT HOME I washed my foot again, applied vodka
(a particular brand that I keep around strictly as an organic
solvent) and rebandaged. My dreams were hallucinatory
nightmares about fleeing from oversized, heavily perfumed
PR flacks with chrome revolvers. I got up three times during
the night to vomit, and when my alarm went off I couldn't
move my arm to hit the snooze button because all my joints
had gone stiff. My vision was blurry and I had a 104° fever.
My muscles and joints were all welded into a burning, smoking mass. I lay there and moaned "two hundred pounds of
tainted meat" until Bart came in and brought me a Hefty.
When I took enough nitrous to get to the bathroom and fin-
ish up with the vomiting and diarrhea, I looked in the mirror
and found that my tongue was carpeted with whitish-brown
fuzz.

Bart drove me to the big hospital downtown to see Dr. J.,
my old college roommate. He'd gotten his M.D. on the six-
year shake-and-bake program, done an Ivy League residency,
and now he worked ERs. Not very prestigious, but the pay is
steady. A fine way to subsidize other life projects.

When I explained how I'd cut my foot, he looked at

me as though I had just taken both barrels from a twelve-gauge.

"There's some very serious stuff out there in the Harbor, man. I'm not kidding. All those decay organisms? They work on your body too, S.T.," he said, shooting me up with some kind of stupendous antibiotic cocktail. He gave me more of the same in pill form, but in the end I was to take only about half the bottle. Whatever those antibiotics were, they just blew the shit out of whatever was in my system. That included the natural bacteria in my colon, the E. coli, so I had continuing diarrhea. Life is too short to spend on a toilet, wondering if there's more, so I stopped taking the pills and let my own defenses handle the mop-up work. And yes, I got a tetanus shot.

"I ran into some people you'd like," I told Bart as he drove me home. "Pöyzen Böyzen fans."

He sniffed the air and frowned slightly. Bartholomew was a sommelier of heavy metal. "Yeah. Not bad for a two-umlaut band. First album was so-so. Then they ran out of material—they write maybe two songs a year. Got into a black magic thing for their videos. Already passé."

"Isn't that the whole point of heavy metal?"

"Yeah. I'm the one who told you that," he reminded me. "Heavy metal will never leave you behind."

"Where are they from?"

"Long Island somewhere. Not the Brooklyn end." He looked at me. "Who were these dudes? How'd you know they were fans?"

"Instinct." I told him about the barge.

"Shitty bargainers," he said.

"What do you mean?"

"These people sold their souls to the Devil and all they got was a rusty old barge? I would've held out for something with a wet bar. Close to the T."

When we got home, he went to his racks of albums and tried to remember whether Pöyzen Böyzen was filed under P or B. The answering machine was blinding, so I rewound it, listening to the message fast and backwards. And when you run it backwards, it's supposed to be gibberish. But this wasn't. It was a melody, a song with a strong beat that was compressed into a tinny tik-tik-tik by the machine. And above that rhythm, a little high-pitched voice was babbling: "Satan is coming. Satan is coming."

When it rewound all the way, I played it forward. It was heavy-metal thrash. Bart came running in, amazed. "What the fuck?" he was saying. "That's on the machine?"

"Yeah."

"That's Pöyzen Böyzen, man. Second album. It's called 'Hymn.'"

"Nice song."

They'd left the entire song for us. When it was over, there was about ten seconds of a woman screaming. And that was it.

It didn't sound like Debbie, really, but then I'd never heard Debbie scream. She wasn't the type. So I dialed her number and she answered the phone, sounding fine.

"I'd like to talk to you," she said, and I knew I was in trouble.

"You want to get together?" I said.

"If that's okay with you." Okay, so I was in trouble.

We had dinner at the Pearl. She let me twist for a long time before she got down to business.

"Are you still interested in seeing me?" she asked.

"Shit, of course I am. Jesus!"

She just fixed me with a big-eyed stare, penetratingly cute, yet one of keen intelligence.

"I'm sorry that I haven't been calling you enough," I said. "I realize that I don't call enough."

"How about if I just stopped calling you? Would that give you any more incentive?"

"Isn't that what you did?"

"Not like that, I didn't."

"You lost me, Debbie. Explain."

"I like you, S.T., and I've tried, a few times, to reach out and get in touch with you. And now you're addicted to it."

"Howzat?" She was a speck on the horizon.

"We're getting into this shit now where you expect me to follow you around. To keep track of where you are, pick up the phone and call you, do the social organizing, set up our dates. And then, when we're together, you give me this gruff shit."

"I do?"

"Yeah. You make me come on to you, and then you pretend you don't want it. I had to put up with that once or twice on the Canada trip and I'm never going to do it again. No way. You want something from me, call me up—you've got my fucking number—and ask for it."

After that, my eyes didn't blink for about half an hour. It reminded me a whole lot of being popped by that smart cop when Bart and I were having our boys' night out. You go around thinking you're cool, a veritable shadow in the night, and then you find out that someone's got your number.

Like the Pöyzen Böyzen fans. A band of assholes I probably wouldn't even recognize in civilian dress.

"That reminds me of something," I said. "I'm being kind of threatened, kind of, by a bunch of Satan worshippers. I want you to look out."

"How the *fuck* . . ." she said, then got up and walked out of the restaurant.

I finished her five-spices chicken and doodled around with my nerd watch. After a major social fuck-up, it's good to have machinery to screw around with. I programmed the alarm to go off in ten days. When it did, I'd give her a call.

Between now and then I could drink a lot, meditate on my own unfitness to live, and get nice and shit-eatingly lonesome. And worry about the Pöyzen Böyzen thing. When I got done wandering home slowly, I played the tape backwards again, listened to the backwards message, then erased it.

For cavemen, they were quick on their feet. Was I that easy to track down?

The thing of it was: nobody had my number. Six months ago I'd gotten another damn call at 3:00 A.M. from some GEE hanger-on who'd just landed at Logan and wanted to be picked up and given a free place to crash. That was enough of that, so I changed to an unlisted number and didn't tell anybody. Not even my employer. If GEE wanted to reach me, they had to get clever.

Which brought up another sore point. Usually they called

Debbie and got her to call me, and she had said a few things about not being a receptionist. Another relationship felony. Just another reason to get to drinking.

But I still didn't know how the crew from the island had tracked me down. Maybe one of them worked at the phone company or something. Maybe one of them knew someone who knew someone who knew Bart.

When my watch alarm went off, I called Debbie, and found out she was vacationing in Arizona for three weeks. So I set my alarm watch for three weeks later.

It went off around Labor Day, in the middle of the night. I was deep in a chemical factory in another state, nestled up against a fifty-five-gallon drum on a loading dock, doing a bag job for Cohen. Had to press the damn watch against my thigh to muffle the sound, unstrap the wristband, pry the back off with a screwdriver, and scramble the innards. That's the last digital watch I'll ever own.

Despite that, the job was a cakewalk. It was just like being a criminal, except it was all pretend. If they caught you, you could just stand up and show them your warrant. They didn't.

I SENT ESMERELDA a box of Turtles and she went through the *Boston Globe* Index and checked out all the entries under Spectacle Island for the last three months. I was interested in something along the lines of "Spectacle Island—Abandoned barges running into."

She found it, and I should have figured it out myself. It was Hurricane Alison, or the last remnants thereof, which had hit us when we were having an abnormally high tide. Whenever a big, systemic disaster hit, a blizzard or heat wave, the *Globe* ran enormous articles "compiled from reports by" followed by lists of twenty names. They had to list every single bad thing that had happened to Massachusets or else people would call in, claim they'd been neglected and cancel their subscriptions.

Buried in one of those was a paragraph about an old barge, due to be scuttled anyway, that had broken loose from Winthrop during the storm and had been batted around the Harbor all night. It wasn't much of a problem because no boats were out in that weather. By the time they even noticed it was missing, the barge had dug itself into Spectacle Island, which was a fine place for it anyway.

I was throwing a lot of work into Project Lobster. I wanted to get the damn thing finished, and Debbie was deliberately unavailable, and I was out of nitrous, and by that point in the summer I didn't have enough money for anything but newspapers and ski-ball.

All those tainted lobsters had to be run through a pretty complicated chemical analysis. It required equipment GEE didn't have, so I'd worked out an arrangement with a lab at a university. Tanya, the Blue Kills Marauder, who'd been working for GEE since her high school days in California, was one of their grad students. She helped with various projects, and in return for "educating" her we got access to nifty analytical equipment.

This particular university had a glut of it anyway, having been so successful in attracting the devotion of big Route 128 corporations that you had to think they'd made their own pact with Satan, negotiated by their toughest lawyers. The high-tech companies coughed up gobs of expensive equipment and the university had to hold hysterical fund-raising drives just to build buildings big enough to keep it out of the rain. You could wander through the basements and find analytical devices costing half a million dollars, so powerful, so advanced that no one was even using them. Once I had gotten access, I had to go down, study their owner's manuals, take off the plastic, and calibrate the gizmos.

Then we were in business. Tanya or I, usually Tanya, broke the lobsters open and located their livers. Whether you're a human or a lobster, your liver filters the toxins out of your system, so that's where you find the bad stuff. We checked them for obvious signs, like tumors or necrosis, and then we ran them through the big machines from Route 128. We got their levels of various metals and organic bad things and put it all into our database.

And we stood around a lot, edgy as hell, because Tanya was Debbie's roommate, and though she was willing to work with me, forgiveness had apparently not yet been earned.

In the weeks surrounding Labor Day we were working at this for twelve or fourteen hours a day, I out on the Zodiac nagging my pals for fresh samples, and Tanya down in the basement cutting bugs. The university wasn't far from the

Charles, so once or twice a day I'd bring the Zode around—as I said, the fastest Boston transportation—and she'd come down to the water and we'd make a handoff.

I was a little perturbed when she missed one, but not surprised. Probably in the middle of something. I hung out on the Zode for maybe half an hour. Why not? Even if the water below me was dirty, I was in the middle of a park. But I got sick of waiting, fast—I was tired of this project and wanted to get on with it. I tied the boat to a tree, took out the fuel line, and hiked inland, schlepping the beer cooler. Trotted up out of the water-side park and into the campus.

Our lab was down in a corridor that still smelled like fresh paint and linoleum glue. One room after another filled with microchips. But the odor got sharper as I approached our lab. Smells trigger memories, and this one made me think of building model airplanes when I was a kid.

It was the smell of spray paint. And on the brand-new laboratory door was some graffiti, still wet, done up in cherry red. A rough pentagram, the inverted cross below, the staring umlaut in the middle. Above it: SATAN SEZ: STAY THE FUCK OUT. The laboratory was dark.

Didn't touch a thing. I ran upstairs to the lobby and phoned Tanya and Debbie's place.

Debbie answered, sounding kind of tense, even though she didn't know it was me yet. "Yeah?"

"Don't hang up, this is business. Tanya there?"

"She can't come to the phone right now. What the hell have you guys been doing? What's with her?"

"I was going to ask you."

"Why is she acting so bent?"

"What's she doing?"

"She came home crying, ran into the bathroom. I heard her throw up a couple of times and now she's been in the shower for about half an hour."

"Sounds like—"

"No. She wasn't raped."

"You got your door locked anyway?"

"Damn right."

I hung up and ran back downstairs. Call me strange, but I tend to carry latex surgical gloves around in my pocket, because it's my business to touch so many nasty things. I put them on before I did any touching.

Good. She hadn't been too freaked out to lock the door when she left.

No signs of struggle. The gas chromatograph was still turned on. I could smell organic solvents in here, the same ones we didn't like big corporations to use, and something else too: an oily, foul odor, mixed in with the marine stench of the lobsters. I recognized it. Some of the lobsters I'd gotten off Gallagher's boat had smelled that way. In fact that was the reason they'd given them to me. Big enough to sell, but they stank too bad. They had come from the entrance to the Inner Harbor.

Just for the hell of it, I locked the door. And that made me think, wait a minute. Tanya had gotten home half an hour ago? And it would have taken her at least half an hour to get home. So whatever was bothering her had taken place an hour ago. But the spray paint on the door was a lot fresher than that.

I opened the door again and checked out the graffiti. It was shitty work. The stuff on the barge had been carefully done. This was done in a hurry, and done badly, with lots of drips and runs.

Spray paint is messy. It throws a fog of paint into the air. Standing in the doorway, I could see a penumbra of paint mist fading out across the white floor. And right in front of the door the red was interrupted by a pair of white ovals where no paint had fallen—shadows cast by the graffitist's feet. The shadows were pointy-toed, but bigger than a woman's feet.

When he'd walked away, he'd gotten paint mist on the soles of his shoes, and tracked it down the hallway some distance. They were faint tracks, but they'd been made by dress shoes.

That was charming. The Pöyzen Böyzen now had yuppies working for them. So that's how they afforded those Back Bay condos.

Just as important, Tanya hadn't left any tracks. She'd cleared out of there before the graffitist had.

So I went back into the lab. What had freaked her out so bad? Something she'd seen during the analysis?

I approached the workbench. Slowly. This reminded me of when you hear a rat trap go off in the middle of the night, and when you go down in the morning you know you're going to find something really unpleasant. You just don't know when or where it's going to hit you.

Whatever had set Tanya off wasn't obvious. Not two-headed monsters, no parasites squirming loose on the bench. Hell, that wouldn't have bothered her anyway. She was a biochemist, a scientist, and she had listened to a full recitation of my relationship crimes. Nothing could gross her out.

She was about halfway through dissecting one of Gallagher's big stinky lobsters. She'd removed the legs and tail and pried back the shell around the body to expose the liver. The bug was sprawled out on its back under a hot light, and the odor was billowing out of it like smoke from a fire.

Had she gotten the liver out? Hard to tell. Something was definitely wrong down in there.

No, she hadn't. There was hardly any liver left. It had necrosed—a fancy word for died. Rotted away, inside the body, leaving just a puddle of black stuff. Surrounded by blobs of yellowy material, vesicles or sacs of something that I'd never seen inside a lobster before. Some kind of toxin that the liver had desperately tried to remove from the lobster's system, killing itself in the process. I found a ballpoint pen and poked one of the sacs; something greasy poured out and a wave of the oily scent rose up into the light.

There used to be a plant in Japan that made oil out of rice. The oil had to pass through a heat exchanger to cool it down. In other words, it flowed over a bunch of pipes that had a colder fluid running through them. The cold fluid was a polychlorinated biphenyl. A PCB.

If you're an engineer, and you're not very bright, it's easy to love polychlorinated biphenyls. They are cheap, stable, easy to make and they take heat very well. That's why they end up in heat exchangers and electrical transformers. It's how they got into that machine in Japan and, when the pipes started to leak, it's how they got into a lot of rice oil.

Unfortunately, rice oil is for human consumption, and as

soon as human beings enter the equation, PCBs no longer look very good. If we were robots, living in a robot world with robot engineers, we could get away with using them, but the problem with humans is that they have a lot of fat in their bodies and PCBs have this vicious affinity for fat. They dissolve themselves in human fat cells and they never leave. They are studded with loose chlorine atoms that know how to break up chromosomes. So when that heat exchanger started leaking, the city of Kusho, Japan started to look like the site of a Biblical plague. Newborn babies came out undersized and dark brown. People started to waste away. They developed a fairly disgusting skin rash called chloracne—the same one Tom had gotten in Vietnam—and they felt very sick.

Now the plague had come to Boston Harbor.

15

A PERSON MIGHT WONDER why I, Sangamon Taylor, didn't
run out and go home and scrub myself raw like Tanya did. It
had nothing to do with male/female issues, or personal brav-
ery or any of that crap. It had to do with how we viewed ourselves. Tanya was pure as the Antarctic snow. She wore a gas
mask when she rode her bicycle. She was born vegetarian,
the child of hippies. She didn't smoke and she didn't drink;
her worst vice was mushrooms—organically grown mushrooms. When she'd looked down into that puddle of PCBs,
she'd gotten the first whiff of her own mortality, and she
didn't like it.

We all owe a toxic debt to our bodies, and sooner or later
it comes due. Cigarettes or a chemical-factory job boost that
debt to the sky. And though Tanya had hardly any debt at
all, when she figured out she was staring at PCBs, smearing
them on her skin, breathing them into her lungs, she probably felt like all her carefulness had been erased. All that
tofu was for nought. Suddenly she was up there with the I.V.-
drug abusers.

I have no illusions about my own purity. I avoid the really
bad stuff, I use common sense. I refuse to work with the nas-

tier solvents and I don't inhale my cigars. But I could look at those PCBs and say, okay, I'm poisoned, maybe if I give up cigars and ride my bike a little more I can pay off this debt.

You don't get PCB poisoning from the air anyway. You get it by eating the stuff.

When I thought of that, I thought of Gallagher and his crew. Those bastards lived on lobsters. I had to get in touch with them right away. Easy enough.

The tough part was this. Where were the PCBs coming from? I was used to finding trace amounts just about everywhere. Basco had put lots of them into the Harbor. But I'd never actually *seen* the stuff before; just detected it with exquisitely sensitive instruments. To actually stand there and watch it running through a lobster's viscera like melted butter—that was a fucking nightmare. Unheard of. Somebody had to be dumping it into the Harbor by the barrel load.

First things first, so I got myself decently protected and wrapped the lobsters up in many layers of PCB-proof plastic, marked it as hazardous waste, and left it there for the time being. I wasn't normally in the business of disposing of hazardous waste and wasn't sure how to begin. Scrubbed the counter down and locked the place up, then went to a different lab and hosed myself off. Finally got Tanya on the phone; she was jittery as hell, but laughing a little now. I tried to tell her she was okay as long as she hadn't been licking her fingers, but with her background she knew more about it than I did. I asked her to put Debbie on.

"Yeah?"

"We have a big thing coming up. A huge thing. Would you like to work on it?"

"Sure."

"And sometime, if I can find some time, I would like very much, more than I can really say here at this pay phone, to, like, take you to dinner or something of that nature."

"Well, you have my number," she said.

And you've got mine, I refrained from saying. And then what? How could I explain the Pöyzen Böyzen thing?

"Gotten any weird messages on your phone lately?"

"Have you been doing that?"

"What?"

"Putting that awful music on our phone machine?"

"No. That's being done by some—some assholes. Heavy-metal fans."

"What do they want?"

Actually, that was a damn good question. What did these guys want? If they wanted to scare me, it was working. But what did they want to scare me into? Thugs can be so non-specific.

"They're pissed about something. Something to do with Spectacle Island. And the lab."

"Drugs?"

"There you go." Spectacle Island—specifically, that old barge—would be a great place to process drugs. A nice, abandoned, lawless zone, only minutes from downtown.

Bart had said that PCP was very hip among the Pöyzen Böyzen drones. PCP was easy to make—even a metalhead could manufacture it by the fifty-five-gallon drum. And I could detect it, by the wastes and smell it generated. No wonder they didn't want me taking samples out there.

"You want to know exactly what happened?" I said. "Those poor idiots overheard me saying I was hunting for PCBs, and they thought I said PCP!"

"Great. So you've got a band of dustheads after you?"

"No. We have a band dustheads after us."

"That's great. I'll never take another shower."

I refrained from offering showering privileges at my place. Without being her official boyfriend, there wasn't much I could do.

Reassuring was my best bet, but I wasn't. I wanted Debbie and Tanya as scared as I was, because that way they'd be careful. "Watch your ass. I have stuff to do."

"Going to call the cops?" she asked.

"About what—the PCBs?"

"No, the PCP."

"Uh, no. Look, the angel dust is weird and exciting; the PCBs are ten times as important. So right now I'm thinking about the PCBs. Sorry."

Went to a bank machine and took out a hundred dollars.

I'm not sure why. Called Bartholomew and told him where I was going, just in case. And had an idea.

"How'd you like to become a Pöyzen Böyzen fan?"

"I have to anyway. Amy is."

"Oh. Is that your woman?" Amy was his new girlfriend. Hadn't met her face to face, but I'd heard her in the next room, late at night; the second loudest copulater I'd ever heard.

"Yeah. Have you guys met?"

"Indirectly. Well, go hang out with the hard core if you can, okay? The young ones—teenagers. Shit, I'll even subsidize it."

"But teen Böyzen heads are like two-legged cockroaches or something."

"So bring some Raid. Come on, you're the social critic, right? This is it, man."

"We'll see."

Then I headed for Fenway Park, only a few blocks away. Everything in Boston's only a few blocks away. It was approaching dusk and the wind was coming up, with something cold and wet behind it. The baseball game probably wouldn't make it to the seventh inning. Tonight it was going to rain like hell—the first Nor'easter of the fall.

When I was almost there, I walked by another phone booth, saw its white pages fluttering in the wind and remembered Dolmacher. Formerly of Basco and presently of Biotronics, a subsidiary of Basco, he was now my prime suspect. "I'm in the book—look me up," he'd said. So I did. I knew for damn sure he wasn't about to tell me anything, but if I hit him with a frontal assault, and he was his emotionally retarded self, I'd know he was totally ignorant. If he went into adrenaline overdrive and called me a terrorist, I'd know Basco was involved. So I dropped a dime on Dolmacher and let the phone ring twelve times.

"Hello?"

"Dolmacher, this is S.T."

"Hi!" He sounded terribly cheerful, and a cheerful Dolmacher was almost unbearable. It meant that his work was going wonderfully. "I just got in the door from work, S.T."

"Dolmacher, just tell me one thing. Why is the floor of the Harbor, right off Castle Island Park, a lake of solid PCBs this evening?"

He laughed. "You're taking too many of those hallucinogenic alkaloids, Sangamon. Better get a real job."

I hung up—he didn't know shit—then I bought a bleacher ticket and ran around to the dark side of Fenway Park.

A toxic crime had been committed. I had witnesses and an address. The witnesses were bleacher creatures, and the address was underwater. First I had to see those witnesses, and it was easy to track them down. Like dolphins, Townies communicate with high-pitched sonar: "Heyyy, Maaahk! I'll meet ya at the Aaahk afta da geem!"

"Mr. Gallagher," I said.

"Heyyy, S.T.! Heyyy, guys, look who's here! It's the invironmintle!"

"Heyyy, S.T., how ya doin?"

"Barrett grounded out, Horn flew out, now it's 0 and 2 on Dewey. He's swinging for the bleachers, that stupid bastard."

"Look. Those oily-smelling lobsters. You haven't been eating any, have you?"

"Shit no. Tried it once but they taste awful. When you gonna do something about that, S.T.? That whole area there, it's for shit now."

S.T., when are you going to stop pollution? "Which area?"

Gallagher looked around at his buddies and they all threw out rough descriptions: "Right out there, you know." "South of the airport." "North of Spectacle Island." "Right off Southie."

"Since when?"

"Month or two."

"Look, Rory. I gotta tell you something. I know sometimes you guys give me shit, you think I'm kind of flaky, but I'm telling you that shit is dangerous. I'm not talking about maybe getting cancer in twenty years, I'm talking about croaking next week. Don't eat those lobsters. I want to go find all the other lobstermen and tell them not to use that area."

Gallagher took me seriously until I got to the last part,

then his face turned even redder and he laughed. "Hell, S.T., no one uses it anyway. They all found the same thing we did. But shit, it's a big area, I got no business telling people not to use it."

Fenway Park turned on its lights. I knew Gallagher was right. He couldn't personally embargo half the harbor. Maybe I could get through to the state authorities. But the last time I'd done that, I had to dress up in a Santa Claus suit. What was the drill this time, Bozo the Clown?

I had my back to the field, standing with one foot propped up on the bleacher. I felt a big guy beside me, trying to get past, so I moved aside and he scrunched through. It was a hot prestorm afternoon and he wasn't wearing a shirt. This was kind of unfortunate, since he had a skin condition.

Now, a lot of people have skin conditions. Especially fair-complexioned people who work under the hot sun, around salt water, for a living. This guy who sat down next to Rory was blanketed by a rash of little blackheads, so small and close together that they looked like a five o'clock shadow. I was trying not to stare, but that's no good when the person you're staring at is a little touchy.

"You got a problem?" he asked.

"Nope. Sorry."

What was I going to do, demand a close examination right there under the lights? The guy was gripping a large, fresh brew in his left hand and I saw a wedding band.

"Just remember, Rory," I said, real loud, loud enough for even this guy to understand. "The oily lobsters. Those things are poison. Especially for kids and pregnant women. Throw 'em away and go eat a Big Mac or something. Eat too many of those things, you get a skin rash and it's downhill from there."

I turned around and left. "What was he talking about?" said the guy with chloracne.

It was time to mobilize GEE's PR machine, phone all my media connections and make a lot of noise about oily lobsters. Had to contact some kind of healthy authority too. Maybe Dr. J. could spread the word. So I phoned the ER.

"What's the word?" he said.

"Chlorachne."

"Whoa!"

"Look out for it. Tell your colleagues. Fishermen, Southeast Asians, anyone who eats fish from the Harbor."

"What's the source?"

"I don't know. But I'm going to find them, and then I'm going to blow them away."

"Nonviolently."

"Of course. Gotta run."

"Thanks for the tip, S.T."

Back at the Zodiac I replaced the vital parts and buzzed over to the MIT docks, where I tied up and jogged over to the office.

No one was around. Probably at the Sox game, in better seats. I got the Darth Vader Suit and an air tank, a supply of sample containers—peanut butter jars—and some binoculars with big wide light-gathering lenses. Until the rain came, the light diffusing off the city should be enough to navigate by. Took a huge nautical-rescue strobe that we keep around just because it's powerful and irritating, and on the way back to the Zode I picked up a couple of gyros and a six-pack.

When I got to the water between Spectacle Island and South Boston—the address of the crime—the sky was blue in the east and black in the west. I had no interest in wasting time. I was tired as hell, all alone, the wind was coming up, the temperature dropping, and below me was a sea of poison. I struggled into the scuba gear, double-checked when I remembered that I'd done it wrong once off Blue Kills, peeled on the Darth Vader mask, turned on the big strobe, and dove.

This kind of work is a pain in the ass, and taking actual samples off the bottom is a last resort. That was the whole purpose of Project Lobster. The lobsters, I'd hoped, would tell me where to concentrate my efforts. This afternoon it had paid off in a big way and now I had to follow through.

It was hard to figure: how had that lobster found so much PCB on the Harbor floor, *here*? If he'd been hanging out along the shore of some Basco property, or under one of their pipes, I could understand. But down here, there was nothing.

When I got to the scene of the crime, though, and flashed my spotlight, I was reminded that "nothing" is a relative term. Humans have been flinging garbage into Boston Harbor for three and a half centuries. I was standing in the foothills of Spectacle Island itself, staring around at everything from Coke cans to wrecked trawlers. Maybe, if I spent hours cruising the bottom, I'd find a cluster of fifty-five-gallon drums, thrown overboard by some corporation with too many PCBs on its hands. If I could do that, and trace them back to the owner, I could go ahead and paint their logo on the prow of my Zodiac. I already had two logos there and was eager to become an ace.

But there were no drums sitting around within ten feet of me, and this wasn't the time for a full-scale search, so I scooped up some muck into a peanut butter jar. While I was screwing the lid down I shone my light into the sample and saw a condom spiraling through it. Reservoir tip, ribbed and used.

A chunk of latex could definitely queer my sample, so I had to abandon that one and take another. I swam around for just a minute or so, hoping I'd get lucky, then headed slowly for the surface. Upstairs the weather was turning to shit. I'd been out on the water since 7:00 A.M. and it was time for normal recreation.

One of my uncles grew up in New York and he used to tell me about diving for condoms in the Hudson. There was one stretch where you could dive down, holding your breath like a Polynesian pearl diver, and pick them off the river bottom. They'd dry them out, put them on broomsticks, dust them with talcum powder, roll them up, and sell them for a nickel. This was during the war and there were plenty of sailors in the market.

When I was a kid I'd wondered how those condoms had ended up in the river. Did the sailors peel off their used condoms, take the bus out to the West Side and fling them into the water, all in the same place? No. When I went to my current job I figured it out. The sailors flushed them down the toilets and into the sewers. In most of your old cities, you have combined sewers—one system carrying human waste, rainwater, and industrial crap.

But a sewer is just a collection of tubes that run downhill.

It's an artificial river, with tributaries and out outfall. A tube, like a river, can only carry so much stuff. Then it overflows.

There's no reason for a sanitary or an industrial sewer to overflow, because it gets steady, predictable inputs. Storm sewers are totally different. Take tonight, for example.

When I broke the surface, it was raining. The Zode was flashing and rocking like mad about fifty feet away. By the time I climbed in, which is pretty difficult when there's no one on board to hold it steady, the rain was coming down hard. I stripped naked, turned of the strobe, and just lay there in the rain until I started to shiver.

Sure, I'm a good environmentalist and I know that this rain was acidic because of coal-burning plants in Ohio, that it was carrying oxides of nitrogen because of automotive emissions from the Boston area. Maybe even a trace of nitrous oxide. But it was easily pure enough to drink. It was purer tha.1 I was, and there was no comparison with the sewage I'd just come out of. I could let it fall into my open mouth and not think for a minute about bioaccumulative toxins.

It was falling all over the Boston Basin, running into the sewers and heading for this Harbor. If enough of it fell, the sewers would overflow.

Sometimes, geysers of shit arise from downtown-Boston manholes after heavy rains. That's an example of combined sewer overflow. Normally it's kept under control. The engineers know that overflows will occur, so they have CSOs— Combined Sewer Overflows—all along the waterfront. If the sewers get too much runoff, they overflow directly into the Harbor and the Charles. What comes out of those CSOs isn't just rainwater, though. Industrial waste and sewage are running down the same tubes. It all comes out together. If it's really bad, and even the CSOs can't discharge enough sewage to empty those tubes, that's when manholes start to pop.

There was a CSO near Castle Island Park. It explains why I'd found a condom out in the middle of the Harbor. There was probably a CSO in the Hudson River, in New York, upstream of my uncle's old condom-diving beds. Of course, he didn't have scuba gear. He just swam through the raw sewage with his eyes open. He must have had the immune system of a junkyard dog.

I cut slowly through the rain back toward the yacht club, chopping through big rollers the whole way.

The visibility was next to nothing. So I was rather surprised when I came face to face with something big, shiny and blue, floating about a hundred yards from where I'd been diving. It was a boat, a good-sized powerboat, sitting there dark and quiet. And about the time I saw it, it saw me, and suddenly there was a tremendous whh*ooosh* echoed by a second one as its engines were started; the storm was drowned out by the sound of about a thousand horsepower digging a hole in the water. Its nose angled up like the prow of a starship, and it vanished into the night. No running lights. The only evidence it had ever been there was a clashing, foaming wake that knocked me around for a few seconds, and a high roar that dwindled to nothing in a hurry.

I realized kind of slowly, on my way back, that it was a thirty-one foot Cigarette. The same one I'd seen before, up in that channel, sitting idle on the water. And the son of a bitch *was* watching me. As the man says: just because I'm paranoid doesn't mean everyone isn't really out to get me.

For a second, I wanted to chase it down, try to see some identifying marks. Then I figured out why they were going to the trouble to use a hot-rod speedboat, a Miami penismobile, up here in this land of bankers' sloops and wallowing trawlers. Why they'd put nine hundred horses on its back, when it was only rated for six. They were using a Cigarette because it was the only boat in the harbor that my Zodiac couldn't catch.

Or to look at it another way, the only boat I couldn't get away from. That one didn't occur to me until a few hours later, when I was trying to sleep.

I took a long shower in the yacht club and then sat out under an awning, waiting for Bart to pick me up, watching yuppies destroy their umbrellas in the wind. I was wasted. But I was alert. If some Satan-worshipping heavy-metal dustheads decided to hurt you, or kill you, how would they go about it? The old multiple shotgun blasts probably wouldn't suffice. They'd want to cart me off somewhere, make a ritual of it. For the nth time in my career I considered owning a gun. But guns were tricky and hard to aim. I should think in terms of chemical warfare—something really obnoxious I could use to slow down whoever came after me.

I had an idea already: 1,4-diamino butane; a.k.a., putrescine—the distinctive chemical scent given off by decaying corpses. I could whip up a batch and carry some on me. That would give anyone second thoughts.

When Bart pulled in, he cranked up a Pöyzen Böyzen tape and I half-breathed all the way home—half a breath of air, half a breath of nitrous. Phoned Debbie and Tanya to make sure they were all right. Tanya's boyfriend was holed up there, answering the phone, and armed. He was into some kind of martial art that involved samurai swords, so I felt better. I took another shower and then started drinking. Bart and I sat in the living room watching the Stooges on Deep Cable until about two in the morning, and I think Amy came over, though I never heard a single moan, shriek or wail. Roscommon drove through sometime during the night and sideswiped Bart's van, streaking it with white paint.

I took the T into the university, ran into the lab, locked the door behind me, and ran a test on my sample. It was full of PCBs. The concentration was roughly a hundred times higher than the worst ever recorded in Boston Harbor. The lobsters and Gallagher and Tanya and I had discovered a toxic catastrophe.

16

I THOUGHT, SHIT. The Mafia. I'm fucking around with the Mafia. It would be just like them to take this blatant approach, just haul a few barrels of PCBs out into the Harbor and throw them overboard.

For two reasons I didn't want to fuck with the Mafia. The first reason is obvious. The second reason is that I can't do anything about them. I pressure large corporations by hurting their image. By making them look like criminals. There wasn't much point in trying that approach on the Mafia. Besides, we already have cops to fight them. Not just EPA officials. Cops with guns. Recently they'd been doing a pretty good job of it and they didn't need my help.

If it was the Mafia, they were being awfully subtle. The goons in the Cigarette first had hidden from me, then had run away. I should have found a horse's head in my bed by now, at the very least. Why so coy?

You had to figure they'd warn me off before killing me. That's what I'd have to bet on. As soon as I got a warning, I'd forget about it. Maybe issue some dire warnings about lobsters from the Harbor, but not cause any real trouble.

If I didn't hear from them, this was going to get interesting fast.

In the early days, GEE didn't play anything close to the vest, they took what they had and ran with it. But I've got this chemistry background and it's given me some habits I can't break. I won't go to the media until I've got lots and lots of information. One shit-filled Jiffy jar didn't qualify.

What I needed was a lot more samples and a rough plot of the spill's distribution on the Harbor floor. Then a lot of poisoned lobsters to freeze for later display. In the meantime I could make a few discreet media contacts. When the story broke, there was going to be a lot of background to explain, so I contacted Rebecca at *The Weekly*, the *Globe's* environmental reporter and a local freelancer who had been eating macaroni and cheese for three weeks.

"I'm kind of busy with your friend, Pleshy," Rebecca told me.

"The big one? Alvin?" I never could keep them straight. For Brahmins they multiplied quickly.

"Alvin. You know, he's kicking off his campaign. . . ."

"Don't tell me. Faneuil Hall. Shit! I wish I knew about it—"

"Forget it. Look, S.T., to you he's just a local hack, but he's important nationally. He's got Secret Service three deep. You don't want to get near him."

"Oh, I don't know. Maybe we could borrow a rocket launcher from Boone—oh, I almost forgot. This line's tapped."

When they first started bugging my phone, I went out of my way not to use keywords like "ammo" and "detonator." But after a couple of years I figured, fuck it. The poor bastard who sat there listening to me talking to Esmerelda about her grandchildren, talking to my roommates about which movie we should go see, explaining to reporters the difference between dioxin and dioxane—he must have been bored out of his mind. So from time to time I'd toss in a reference to an RPG-7 or a shipment of Soviet plastique, just to spice things up a little.

They say that the people who listen to bugs for a living are all thirty-five-year-old men who still live with their mothers. That was the image I kept in my own mind. Some kind of balding, spare-tired paleface in wirerims, sitting at a desk, monitoring my life and worrying about the carburetor on his Chevette. I didn't care what he heard, because if he didn't know by now that I wasn't a terrorist, he'd never figure it out.

"Anyway, S.T., I have a proposal," Rebecca said. "He's supposed to be the Democrats' Great White Hope, right? But you seem to think his environmental record is less than clean."

"Got that impression, huh?"

"So I want to borrow you as an expert consultant. Sangamon Taylor on Alvin Pleshy. Front page of the Politics section. Basically a dossier piece. You'd look at his career at Basco, then his political career, critique his work on the environment."

"Very tempting. But I'm skeptical. Because you know what'll happen?"

"What?"

"His Basco career will stink. The Vietnam part, you know, when he was undersecretary of state for napalm, that'll reek. But that's all back in the Fifties and Sixties. Then when we get into the political part, it's going to be straight Democratic party line. Doesn't matter what he's been doing behind the scenes with Basco. So I'll have to say, 'Uh, well, he voted for the Clean Water Act, that's good. And a wilderness area in Alaska, that's good.' Very boring."

"If there's that much of a contrast, we can play it up. Say, 'Well, he votes nice and pretty, but look at what he did to Vietnam.' What do you think?"

"I'll give it a shot. But I don't have time to research every move he made back three decades ago."

"You're not supposed to, S.T. I've got an intern working on that. Down at the library, night and day."

"Oh. Tell him to talk to—"

"Esmerelda. I already did. And it's a she, not a he."

"Excuse my sexist ass. Rebecca, I must be off."

"Bye. And thanks."

I went into the lab and synthesized a few liters of 1,4-diamino butane. That's too much—you could render Boston uninhabitable with that much putrescine. But I was imagining possible future uses for it. I took my time hooking up a reactor that was closed-cycle, or else my host at the university would have to dynamite the building after I was finished. Decanted the substance into jars and packed them into a cheap, sheet-metal safe that I kept in my desk. I was praying that the FBI would break in and go through my stuff again. But for immediate use, I put a tube of the stuff in my pocket. Would have been more effective to load it into Bart's enormous battery-powered squirt gun that looked exactly like an Uzi, but that could be dangerous.

One of the divers from Boston was on vacation, plying his trade in the Caribbean, so I called down to the national office and they persuaded Tom Akers to come out again. He was always happy to visit Boston and was coming east anyway, to work with the *Blowfish* in Buffalo.

I met him at Logan. In the airport lounge I relaxed for the first time since the Pöyzen Böyzen thing started. No heavy-metal dustheads here.

Then I remembered those footprints in the hallway: dress shoes. The whole operation couldn't be run by burnouts. It took capital to build a PCP lab, some chemical expertise. Maybe I had an Evil Twin. Somewhere there was a higher, suit-wearing echelon. So I couldn't make assumptions as to what these guys looked like. High-tech yuppies, maybe. People who knew chemistry. Or Mafia.

We didn't get abducted and mutilated on the way home, though. I took Tom to our house and we sat down with a six-pack. "There's two ways you can help," I said. "First, by diving. Helping us get samples off the floor."

"I thought you already did that, man."

"I got one sample and a bunch of oily lobsters. But if I'm going to make the kind of noise I want to make, I need more. At least a dozen samples, preferably forty or fifty, distributed around the area, so I can show a pattern."

"One time around is enough for me. I don't need no more chloracne."

"That brings me to the second thing. You can be a witness for us. A victim of the same poisoning."

Tom frowned and shook his head. Then he finished his

beer. As soon as I brought up the subject, his beer consumption jumped to the chug-a-lug level. "Not the same. Remember? Agent Orange, man. That's what I have. This is PCBs."

To Tom and most everyone else, Agent Orange *was* a different thing from PCBs. But the underlying problem was the same, and I'd have to explain how in a press release. Just another goddamn thing to get working on. This was turning into a paper-shoveling operation, more time spent at my desk than on my Zodiac.

If this was the kind of house that had napkins, I'd have sketched it out for Tom. But Tess, Laurie, and Ike were all recycling maniacs and I usually had to wipe up spills with my shirt sleeves. Cloth towels were very nice if you had someone doing your laundry for you, but they sucked when all you had was a washing machine with a burned-out engine, and a landlord who filled the basement with water whenever he laid hands on a pipe wrench.

"I want you to explain all this shit to me anyway," Tom confessed.

"Okay, first of all, the bad thing about Agent Orange wasn't the Agent Orange. It was an impurity that got into it during the manufacturing process: dioxin. That's what you had, dioxin poisoning. But dioxin is just a shortened version of the full name. The full name is 2,3,7,8-tetrachlorodibenzo-*p*-dioxin. Also known as TCDD."

"This doesn't mean shit to me, man."

"Just hang on. TCDD belongs to a class of similar compounds that are known as polychlorinated dibenzodioxins."

"And that's related to polychlorinated biphenyls?"

"More or less. In both cases you've got a bunch of chlorine atoms, which is why it's called polychlorinated, and an organic structure that they're carried around on. In one case it's a biphenyl, in the other case a dibenzodioxin. You know what a benzene ring is? Ever take any chemistry?"

"No."

I looked around for six similar objects I could arrange in a ring. Of course, they were right in front of me. "A benzene ring is a six-pack of carbon atoms. The six-pack is held together with this little plastic holder. That's like a benzene ring. It's stable. It's strong. The six-pack stays together. It takes some effort to pull one of the cans away. There's a couple different kinds: benzenes and phenyls. Both six-pack holders, but the phenyl has one less hydrogen atom."

"Okay."

I went and pulled another six-pack out of the fridge. "If you put two six-packs together, you have a twelve-pack. If the six-packs are phenyls, then it's called a biphenyl. If the six-packs are benzenes, it's a dibenzodioxin—because the connection between six-packs is made by using a couple of oxygen atoms. But it's basically similar to a biphenyl. So polychlorinated *biphenyl* and polychlorinated *dibenzodioxin* are structurally similar compounds."

"So these six-pack things, they're the toxic part?"

"No. The toxic part is the chlorine. That's what gets you."

"Well, shit, you should get chloracne from being in a swimming pool then, right? That's full of chlorine. Hell, drinking water's full of chlorine."

"Yeah. That's why half of the people in GEE drink spring water. Because they've heard about chlorine and don't know shit about chemistry."

Tom noticed the salt shaker on our table, laughed, and dumped a little salt out onto the table. "Shit, man! Sodium chloride, right? Isn't that in seawater? Hey, maybe that's why I got sick. It wasn't Agent Orange at all, man, it was the sodium chloride in that seawater."

"Okay, you're asking me: why is chlorine so incredibly toxic in dioxin and not in table salt?"

"I guess that's what I'm asking."

"Two reasons. First, what it's attached to. That biphenyl or dibenzodioxin structure—the twelve-pack—dissolves easily in fat. Once it gets into your body fat, it never leaves."

"That's what they said about the Agent Orange, that it sits in your body forever."

"Right. That's the first bad thing. The second bad thing is, the chlorine there is in covalent form, it's got the normal number of electrons, whereas the chlorine in salt is in ionic form. It's got an extra electron. The difference is that covalent chlorine is more reactive, it has these big electron clouds that can fuck up your chromosomes. And it slips right through your cell membranes. Ionic chlorine doesn't—the cell membranes are made to stop it."

"So the six-packs are like the vehicle, the gunboat, and the chlorines are like the soldiers with the machine guns who ride on it."

"Yeah, and the electrons are their ammunition. They ride up and down the river—your bloodstream—and slip into your cells and shoot up your chromosomes. The difference between that and table salt is that table salt is *inorganic*, ionic chlorine—soldiers without a boat, with no ammunition—and this other stuff is *organic*, covalent chlorine—bad stuff."

Tom sat back, raised his eyebrows. "Well then, if you think I'm going to go down there, forget it."

"Look, that's fine, and I don't blame you, but let me just say that I'm as paranoid as anyone and I went down there. I'm pretty sure we can do this without getting contaminated."

"I'll do other diving but I won't go to the bottom. I got enough of this shit in my body already."

"Fair enough."

I phoned Esmerelda. After this was over we'd have to give her an honorary membership in the group. If GEE was like the Starship Enterprise, then I was Scotty and she was Spock.

We had an extremely pleasant chat about her granddaughter's brand new pink dress, which had involved roughly a hundred manhours of shopping, and about the weather and the Sox. Standing in the library, she spoke quietly, and I always found my own voice dwindling to a whisper during these conversations. It was like talking to an important Japanese warlord. You had to hem and haw and nibble around the edges for a few hours, just to be polite, before you got to the point.

"There's some kind of intern working there, a woman, working with *The Weekly?*"

"Yes. She had a little trouble threading the microfilm machines but now she's doing just fine."

"If someone ever invents a self-threading microfilm machine, half you guys are going to be out of a job. No offense to you."

"How can I help you, S.T.?"

"If that woman comes up with anything really interesting, could you shoot me a copy?"

"About Mr. Pleshy?"

"You know it."

"Anything in particular?"

"Oh, I don't know. Something with photos in it. That always makes them nervous. Would you mind?"

"Certainly not. Is there anything else?"

"No. Just wanted to see how you were doing."

"Have fun, S.T." That's how she always said goodbye to me. She must have some queer ideas about my job.

The next day we organized, and the day after that we did it. With another diver from the Boston office I swam around scooping muck into sample jars. We'd hand them off to Tom, who'd relay them up to the Zodiac, where Debbie was waiting. That way we wouldn't have to decompress every time we had a full load of samples. Debbie was our navigator, using landmarks on shore to judge our position and mark down roughly where each sample came from. We could plot the results later on. If the PCB concentration increased sharply in one direction, that would give us a clue as to where the source was. If we were really lucky, we'd be able to track it down, probably to a few barrels on the bottom.

The ultimate success would be to find some barrels with PCB still in them, and to get some photos. We couldn't salvage them ourselves, but the EPA probably could and, more important, they probably would. We could save the Harbor a lot of grief and we might find evidence that would lead us to the criminals.

I didn't want Debbie sitting out there alone on a Zodiac. We knew the Pöyzen Böyzen people had a boat, and they seemed to know a hell of a lot about who we were and where we hung out. So we looked through our donor list and found a couple of yacht owners, then convinced them that it really would be fun to spend a day bobbing around in the Harbor, showing the flag. We hoisted another Toxic Jolly Roger, persuaded Tanya's black-belt squeeze to join up, and ferried a few media people out from Castle Island Park. Rebecca came, as did the starving freelancer and the reporter from the *Globe*. So far it was background.

We started roughly where I'd taken my first sample and worked our way outwards, covering about half a square mile of the Harbor floor. We ended up with thirty-six peanut butter jars full of raw sewage, and some very sore muscles.

There's one advantage of hanging out with groovsters: they give good massage. A couple of hours of massage, beer, nitrous oxide, and Stooges after a day of diving—nothing could beat it.

The next day we began to run the samples and got semidisastrous results. Disastrous for me—we weren't reading any PCBs at all. This was unbelievable—there had to be contamination inside the machine—and the whole operation went on hold for two days while I took the gas chromatograph apart, piece by piece, cleaned each one, and put it back together. Pure joy.

Then I started to test the samples again. No one had stuck around for the two days of cleaning, so by this time I was working alone. No matter, I got exactly the same goddamn results. The level of PCBs in these samples was no different from those taken anywhere else in the Harbor.

As we headed south, in the direction of Spectacle Island, the concentration dropped rapidly—not what I'd expected—and to the north of Spectacle we couldn't get any PCB readings at all. It was totally virgin.

The Granola James Bond, the Toxic Spiderman, had fucked up. I'd overreacted to some oily lobsters, seen a guy with excema and called it chloracne. Then I'd gotten a bad sample, or run it wrong, and rushed the gig.

It was hard to believe, but I had no choice. The only other possibility was that the culprits had somehow hoovered up the PCBs while I was shuffling papers. But that kind of a Cecil B. De Mille operation would have cost billions.

It happens. Seen from the laboratory, the universe looks a lot more complicated than it does in your neat mental blueprints. But this time it really burned my ass. Debbie could have helped, but I didn't give her a chance. To be lonely and pissed feels better. So after I'd gone through the burning embarrassment, the denial and the anger, I got down into some serious depression.

It was raining, cool for the season, and I wandered drunkenly until I hit an obstacle: a huge, overdressed throng in the marketplace. On a sunny weekend this wouldn't have been unusual, but today it was a little out of place. Then I saw the banners, the buttons, all the cheap, shimmering detritus of a political campaign, and heard The Groveler's voice ringing dingily out of some big speakers.

These were just the groundlings out here. Bostonians practice idolatry in their politics—Curley, Kennedy, O'Neill, now Pleshy. Inside were the bigshots, the power structure of so-called liberal Massachusetts politics. All the people who bleated about cleaning up the Harbor until they discovered that people like Pleshy were responsible for making it dirty.

This was too disgusting to witness, so I turned on my heel and headed across into Government Center. A couple of Secret Service types were watching me; one had stopped to buy a soft pretzel on the curb, and when I went past him we nodded at each other.

At a phone booth I called the Boss collect, and told him I had to get the fuck out of town, that I needed a vacation.

"You deserve it," he said.

"GEE deserves it," I said. "I'm so into my job that I'm fucking up."

Thank God Project Lobster was over with and I could say goodbye to skeptical lobstermen. They'd never let me forget this one. Busting into the middle of a ball game in Fenway to give them dire, unbelievable warnings, then showing up a week later and taking it all back; exactly the image I'd been fighting all along.

I remembered Hoa's busboy giving me that sneer, that duck-squeezer look, and decided to eat Chinese for a while.

"Where are you going on vacation?" the Boss asked.

"Shit, I don't know, just hang around town."

"How about Buffalo?"

"*Buffalo?*"

"Why not?" he said, sounding terribly innocent.

"Let me tell you a story about Buffalo. Last time I drove

through there was in the middle of a windstorm. Huge, record-setting windstorm. Sixty-miles-an-hour winds in broad daylight. It was clear, but there was so much dust in the air that the light turned all brown, you know? And you couldn't even stand outside because the wind was picking up god-damn rocks, little pebbles, and flinging them through the air like hailstones. And I got to this place on the way to the bridge, in between a couple of embankments with big petro-chemical tanks on either side of the road. Your basic indus-trial Mordor. The embankments acted like a wind tunnel and they were picking up coal dust off a huge pile beside the highway and so I was driving downhill through this thick, black, sulfurous cloud, sticks and stones hailing down against my windshield, caught between a couple of semis carrying gasoline, and I said to myself, shit, I accidentally took the off-ramp to Hell."

"The *Blowfish* got there ahead of schedule," the Boss said, "and we've got an extra project that needs doing."

"Forget it."

"It involves plugging a dioxin pipeline."

A good boss always knows how to dangle the right thing in front of your nose.

"And we'll pay your way. Debbie's going."

That meant I could go on the train, in a sleeper coach, with Debbie in there too.

I cruised home to pack, only to discover a little display was waiting for me. Someone had grabbed a stray neighbor-hood cat who hung around our home sometimes—Scrounger—and had beaten his skull in, then wrapped an unbent coat hanger around its neck and strung it up in front of the door.

I cut Scrounger down, carried him around to the side and threw him into the garbage, burying the carcass under some other trash so my housemates would be spared the sight. Out back, I noticed some spots of blood on the ground, and fol-lowed them straight to the murder weapon: a fist-size hunk of concrete, smeared with blood.

The house had been broken into through the back, and trashed. Not a thorough trashing, but a decent effort never-theless. The TV was kicked in, as was my computer screen.

They'd even yanked up the bottom half of the computer, a separate box, and stomped on it a few times. A lot of food was strewn around the kitchen in the messiest way possible, and they'd poked a screwdriver into the tubes in the freezer and let all the freon evaporate.

And there was a black handprint on the door to my room, at about eye level.

Fake Mafia or real Mafia, I had no way of knowing. But I was damn tired and depressed; I just wanted out of town. My big scandal had turned into a bad joke. And now someone was getting violent. Game over, case closed.

17

IONIC CHLORINE'S EASY TO GET. It's in seawater, as Tom Akers pointed out. But if you want to manufacture a whole stinking catalog of industrial chemicals, you have to convert ionic chlorine into the covalent variety. You do that by subtracting an electron.

And it's just about that simple. You take a tank of seawater and you put a couple of bare wires into it. You hook a source of electrical power up between the wires, and current—a stream of electrons—flows through the water. The molecules get rearranged. The ionic chlorine turns into the covalent kind, which is what you want. The sodium joins up with fractured water molecules to form sodium hydroxide. Or lye or alkali, depending on how educated you are. This process is called Chloralkali.

Simple enough. But to make industrial quantities of DDT, or PCBs, or solvents, or whatever it is you're shooting for, you need industrial quantities of chlorine. That takes a lot of electrical power. And if you want to manufacture a Niagara of chemicals, guess what? You need a Niagara-sized power source.

Hence Buffalo. Its blessing, the beautiful Falls, was also its curse. And even though the Falls were getting all broken down and full of rocks, all those chlorine compounds remained. We call it toxic waste. Without Chloralkali, toxic waste would hardly exist. The only hazardous waste that doesn't flow from that fountain is the heavy-metal variety, and heavy metals are a pretty small trickle in the toxic stream. Chloralkali, also known as Niachlor (Niagara + chlorine) is virtually synonymous with toxic waste.

Despite all my moaning and bitching, it's getting tougher to be a toxic polluter in this country. In the last three decades, especially since about 1974, the Chloralkali business has taken a nosedive, down by about forty percent. I'm shooting for a hundred.

Going after the chemical industry in Buffalo meant going after Boner Chemicals—which was like shooting ducks in a barrel while half a million people stood around cheering you on—and this time it was going to be even easier. We didn't have to use shotguns on those toxic ducks anymore, because a friend of ours in Albany was providing us with flame-throwers.

The EPA is so anemic, and this country so dirty, that they have to contract out a lot of their work. After the toxic catastrophe in Buffalo, they farmed some work out to a group of chemical consultants in Albany, similar to Mass Anal. In effect, that gave these consultants subpoena power over Boner, the sole cause of the catastrophe. They got to raid Boner's files and cart off the relevant maps and documents. They learned toxic secrets that would turn your blood to dioxin.

One of the consultants resigned because he wanted to build a geodesic-dome house and start his own computer software company. I think you know the kind of guy I'm talking about. He got involved with GEE. He no longer had any secret documents, but he knew how to operate a Xerox machine. When my train pulled into Albany on its way to Buffalo, he joined Debbie and me in our sleeper coach; we poured him a Screwdriver and talked about things to come. His name was Alan Reading.

Debbie and I had kept the bunks fastidiously folded away. We'd talked all the way from Boston to Springfield, paused so

I could read the last couple of days' *Wall Street Journal*, and were just getting into the terrible subject of Commitment when we pulled into Albany. We weren't exactly in a good mood.

We sat in the coach and studied a bunch of documents that Alan had illegally xeroxed. One was quite interesting: a map of the main Boner plant, showing in detail the boundary between Boner property and the public streets. There was an indentation in the boundary: a street that ran for half a block into Boner territory and then dead-ended. It was still public property, though it was surrounded on three sides by the plant. The only reason it existed was as a place to put a manhole. There was a sewer line running from the middle of boner Chemical out to Buffalo's general sewer system. This line ran along underneath the deadend street; at the end of that street, right up against the gate to Bonerland, was a manhole. Alan happened to know that at this very spot, Boner Chemical was dumping dioxins into the sewers.

"This is great stuff," I told him. "I have something you might want to read too." And I showed him the *Journals*. Seems as though another big corporate merger was in the offing. Basco was buying out Boner.

"Why on earth would anyone want to own it?" Alan mumbled. "It's a black hole."

"If it makes money on paper, for the first year, it must be a good investment."

Debbie had other things to concentrate on. Up at the Falls, she and the *Blowfish* people had some big splashy affair planned for the media, involving Canadians and Indians. It appeared that the Indians in upstate New York, the Seven Nations, continued to approve of us.

This wasn't always the way it worked. GEE scouts were always pursuing the Indians, asking to sleep in their teepees and groove on their most sacred ceremonies. You couldn't be cool in some GEE circles unless you'd seen the inside of a Lakota sweat lodge; it was like a fetish. Usually the Indians were tolerant, but not always. The night before, I'd been on the computer, poking around in GEE's international message system, and learned that one of our boys was in the hospital in Rapid City. He had been smoking the peace pipe with some Sioux and had taken it upon himself to put in some marijuana. So they broke his arm. Little misunderstandings like this were common, and I was always amazed when the Northeastern tribes showed any interest at all in working with us. They had as much to lose from being slowly poisoned by large corporations as anyone, I guess. Maybe more, since they tended to be fishermen or factory workers.

A donated car was waiting for us in Buffalo, a half-devastated Subaru with loose speakers dangling out of the door panels and ecostickers all over the windows. I dropped Alan and Debbie off at the marina where the *Blowfish* was parked. They were having a party for local supporters and I couldn't bear the thought of it. Sometimes, actually, I do feel like having fun, pretending to be charming, putting on my suit with the toxic tennis shoes, regaling local environmentalists with war stories, describing the variety of crap they have in their tap water. But other times, like now, I just wanted to drive around in the dark and look for trouble.

We were going to be plugging a few pipes here, I knew that much. Pipe-plugging technology is pretty well established by now. For pipes less than about four feet across, you just stack bags of cement in them. The cement swells up and gets hard.

If the pipe gets any larger, you have to plug it with a disk of some kind. But that's hard to do if any significant amount of crap is pouring out of the pipe, because it obviously tends to force the disk out. So you have to use a butterfly plug, which was invented by one of our people in Boston who has since gone into the computer biz. You cut the disk in half down the middle and fold the halves together, pointing them upstream, like the wings of a butterfly. You install it in that position and then release the sides of the disk. The pressure hits them and they slam open, sealing against the walls of the pipe. Then you can add extra devices to complicate removal if you really want to be an asshole. For example, you can clamp the plug on with C-clamps, then saw off the screws.

The sewer coming out of the Boner plant was much larger than four feet across, but we couldn't construct a plate to go across. Why? Because it would have to go in via the manhole. So we'd have to use lots and lots of cement. Cement is more permanent anyway, and permanence was the key to this job. Those butterfly plugs are just media events. You put one in, with a big GEE logo painted across it, and the minicam crews hang around and film the seasick plant workers struggling to remove it. But this was underground and so there was no point in showing off. And the Boner waste was much too serious. Dioxin, man. Unacceptable stuff. Dump dioxin, you're playing for keeps, you die.

First I drove up to the Falls and looked for a hotel room. It's funny. Everywhere I go, I like to rent the honeymoon suite. What the hell, GEE's picking up the tab. And the honeymoon suite is the best place to unwind after a rough day of humping cement bags and being hauled around in manacles. You can sit around in the heart-shaped tub, you can romp on the waterbed. And now, here I was on the road to Niagara Falls, where every room was a honeymoon suite. All I had to do was pick the best one.

Took a while, but I found it: lava lamps, eight-foot waterbed with fur, mirrored ceiling, view of the freeway. The manager hated my looks but liked the idea that I was going to stay for a while. I charged up a few days on the GEE gold card, told her I'd be back later and headed back toward Buffalo.

Now the only thing on my mind was the pair of suits who'd been tailing me every since I'd left the train station. They were driving a Chevy Celebrity, conspicuous by its very dullness. My Subaru was smaller, more maneuverable, and probably just as fast, if the tranny didn't fall out. Once we got back into Buffalo, I got to engage in my favorite sport.

I topped off the tank first, checked the tire pressure, emptied my bladder, bought a six-pack of Jolt. Then I headed for the on-ramp and gave them a chance to line up behind me. They wouldn't follow me directly onto the ramp because this was a covert tail. So I cruised up the ramp, cranking it as hard as it would go, then shut off my lights and braked onto the shoulder, using my handbrake so the taillights wouldn't give me away.

A few seconds later they shot past me, their brake lights blazing in embarrassment, and I took off and followed them.

And followed them and followed them. For four hours I followed those stupid fucks. My car had a shorter range, but I'd just filled it up.

Nothing's more fun than following someone whose orders are to follow you. I could do it forever: cruising flamboyantly behind them, playing classic rock on the jury-rigged stereo and flicking cigar ashes out the window.

They didn't even figure it out for twenty minutes or so. They decided to play it cool and stay ahead of me for a while before gradually dropping back. But I wouldn't let them. Finally they came to a full stop on the shoulder and waited. I stopped behind them and waited. They started up and pulled an illegal U-turn across the median strip. Obviously they weren't cops, because cops are trained how to do that maneuver, and these guys had never done it before. I followed them through that exercise, after pausing on the shoulder to give them a little time.

Then they went into the next phase: wondering what to do now. They got off at the next ramp and I followed them around downtown Buffalo, listening to three Zevon songs about hapless mercenaries, back-to-back, no commercial interruptions. I doubt they had classic rock and roll playing on their stereo. They had a regular discussion in progress, with lots of hand-waving and glancing back over their headrests at me.

Finally they pulled off at an IHOP. I watched them through the windows until they had ordered coffee, then opened my door, peed on the asphalt, and reclined the seat so I was below window level. They came out in a few minutes and took off. I gave them a minute to think they'd finally made it, then pulled in behind them again.

Then they knew they were fucked. They thought: this isn't just a joke. This guy's going to follow us until we have to report in, and then he'll know who we are.

Some bad driving ensued as they tried and failed to shake me. It's hard to shake a tail in a totally deserted downtown. These guys had learned how to drive by watching "Hawaii Five-O" reruns: if our tires are squealing, we must be going fast.

So they definitely weren't cops. Cops or G-men would just

stop the car and come up to me and say, "Okay, okay, very funny, asshole, now go home." And they weren't Mafia, or else I'd be bleeding in the dark. Some kind of cheap private dicks, or amateurs.

If they were locals, they probably worked for Boner. If they'd followed me out from Boston, maybe they were connected to the PCP thing. Maybe we were talking about a drug lab, financed by yuppies, run by dustheads, and now that we'd gotten into this cloak-and-dagger stuff, the upper echelons didn't know quite how to handle it.

They realized too late that most of the gas stations in downtown Buffalo are closed at three in the morning. They ran out of gas right in the middle of a lane. I came up behind them, bumper to bumper, and shoved them into a parking space. But at the last minute, thinking of Scrounger, I downshifted, gunned it and shoved them right through the space and into the back of a parked car. The Celebrity's power brakes didn't work when the engine was dead.

They were really ticked. They jumped out of the doors and came after me. I backed down the street a couple of blocks, letting them chase me, getting a good look at their adrenalin-flushed all-American faces, then blew them off and found a phone booth and dialed 911. There had been a fender bender downtown, I said, and the culprits had abandoned their car and run away from it, and I suspected that maybe the car was stolen. Yes, I'd be happy to give my name. Yes, I'd be there to give the police a statement.

The cops were on the scene within two minutes. We had a huge, fortyish black cop with a pissed-off demeanor, and his younger, female partner. The two suits were loitering grimly nearby, huddled together in the dark like aborigines. When they coughed up their driver's licenses, I got a peek over the woman cop's shoulder. Massachusetts licenses. The pissed-off cop got on the radio and was kind enough to speak their names for me: David Kleinhoffer and Gary Dietrich. A couple of good Americo-Aryan rent-a-thugs.

That was all I was going to learn out here. I went to a pay phone and called the car rental company. I used my flack voice.

"Yes, this is Mr. Taylor. We've rented a vehicle from your

office," and I gave her the description and license plate number, "we've misplaced the rental agreement, and there seems to be some confusion as to which account it's being charged to. I'm working in the accounting department and I need to know. Would you mind reading to me the impression from the charge slip?"

She did. Turns out Kleinhoffer and Dietrich were working for a company named Biotronics.

Now that I knew, it made sense. I should have guessed it. First Pöyzen Böyzen, then the Mafia, leaving me threats. And the Mafia thing didn't start until right after I began worrying about it.

Some assholes in fancy shoes had been trying to scare me. And for the most part they had done a damn fine job. But this bit with Scrounger was too fucking much.

The tip was the computer. A Mafia goon would kick in the screen and say, that's it, that sucker's busted. Actually, monitor screens are cheap. The expensive part is the box underneath. Whoever trashed our place had known that much. He'd known about it, and cared. The thing with the freon, too. That was a pretty suburban way to trash a kitchen— letting the freon out of your fridge.

Now that I'd seen the faces of the people who were trying to scare me, I was a lot less scared, and a lot more interested. Maybe they were really making PCP, or maybe they had some other nasty secret. When I got back from Buffalo I'd have to find out, and do these people some damage. In the meantime, I'd have to content myself with charging up tens of thousands of dollars' worth of lingerie on their credit card number.

18

Still, the disappearing PCBs were keeping me awake at night. I'd gone over the whole thing a dozen times in my head, trying to find my error. I wasn't even sure which time I'd screwed up—on that first lone sample or on the whole batch we collected later.

That's the difference between being a toxic detective and some other kind. You're a regular detective and you find a dead person on the floor, you know murder's been committed; your eyes tell you. But if you're a toxic detective, your eyes are a gas chromatograph, not always as reliable. If that mechanical eye tells you there are PCBs in this sample, you have to ask: how was the sample taken? Is the machine okay? Who else has been dicking around with it?

For a second, I had an inspiration. Maybe someone had gotten to our samples overnight, while I was in getting massaged and drunk. They'd been sitting out in the back of the Omni, and high-tech goons could be just clever enough to get in there, dump out the samples, and replace them with fakes.

But there were too many problems with that. First of all, it was just too implausible. Second, I remembered seeing a flash of red in one of my samples—a fragment of a Coke can—which I also saw again later, the next day. And most conclusive, when we plotted the results on the map, the samples showed an even, steady pattern of decreasing PCB levels as we headed toward Spectacle Island. That couldn't be duplicated with fakes.

My next inspiration: maybe the PCB spill was extremely localized. And maybe, just by dumb luck, I had come down into a hot spot on my first trip and gotten a really dirty sample by chance. This was just barely conceivable. Maybe there was some really big, old shark that had been hanging out in the Harbor for decades, eating bottom fish, building up incredibly high levels of bioconcentrated PCBs. Then it had croaked, settled to the bottom and decayed away to nothing, leaving a puddle of PCBs behind.

Stranger things had happened. When you're being rational and scientific, you have to take into account that bizarre events can throw off your results. That's why good scientists take a lot of samples and check their numbers before they go public. I could at least feel good about that.

I snagged a few Z's on the *Blowfish* and then went out and rented a U-Haul box truck. Debbie went out on the boat to plan the Niagara gig, while Alan and I, along with Frank, the largest member of the *Blowfish* crew, took the U-Haul outside of town to a big home-and-garden store. We filled the truck to its limit with hundred-pound sacks of dry cement and gravel and we also got ourselves some really vicious epoxy resin glue. Canvas gunny sacks we already had.

We parked the truck near the marina for the time being and then I drove out to a nearby Indian reservation and met a guy named Jim Grandfather, whom I'd worked with before. He was shaped like me, in his forties, lived with his wife and dogs in a doublewide back in the trees, and drove a big old Dodge pickup with an Indianhead hood ornament that he'd lifted out of a junkyard somewhere. He had a couple of years of college and was the tribe's historian, archivist, and preserver of weird knowledge. Whenever environmental issues came up, he was the point man for the tribe. I don't know if he had an official position in the tribal government, or if he was appointed by consensus, or by himself, but that was definitely his role. When I showed up, he was out on the front yard throwing sticks and frisbees for his dogs. There were two dogs and only one frisbee and consequently I had to sit there and wait while a tug of war was waged across the middle of the road. Finally Jim shouted something in a language I'd never know, and they both dropped it simultaneously. He stalked up to the car with a big grin.

"How's the Granola James Bond?"

"A little more toxic than last time, but good enough. How are you, dude?"

"Check this out." He opened his wallet and took out a folded piece of paper. It was a computer printout. A blood test.

"What, they testing you for drugs or something?"

"No, no, this is for cholesterol." He pointed to one line with one of his stubby fingers. "Low normal." He stepped back and held his hands off to his sides. "So? Does this look like a body with low cholesterol?"

"Congratulations, Jim."

"Well, I thank you for it." The last time I'd seen Jim was about a year ago, and I'd hassled him about the amount of greasy food he ate. He belonged to some kind of a pig raising and butchering co-op, so he hit the bacon and sausage very hard. His wife, Anna, started getting on his case too. He had gone in for a checkup and found out that his cholesterol level was pretty high. So this was quite a turnaround.

"You been eating a lot of fish?"

"You see any oceans around here?"

"Tofu?"

He snorted. He already knew my opinion of that. "Venison, baby. Lean and tough. Like me. Take some sausage to work every day."

"Why'd you do it?"

"Shut my wife up." Which might give you the wrong impression, because they loved each other.

I parked my car half in the ditch and let his dogs smell me. At least I thought they were dogs.

"How can you tell these things from wolves?" I said.

"These have collars," he explained. "Don't worry, they're checking you for dioxin."

They didn't find any, so we wandered up toward his house. "Who's this asshole in South Dakota?" he said.

I almost asked how the hell he'd heard about that, but then caught myself. If we had a computer bulletin board, why couldn't they? I'd seen this before, though. Go out to Alaska, California, talk to tribe officials, and it's like they've been poring over my dossier. They kept in touch.

"I don't know him myself. You can probably expect the national office will fall all over itself trying to apologize."

"It's no longer necessary. They made their point."

We sat down in his kitchen and he got me some coffee. "Anna's in town shopping," he said. "Soon as she gets back, we can take off."

"No hurry. I don't have to be back until midnight."

He laughed. "Typical. Most people have appointments at noon. You have them at midnight."

"That's when all the midnight dumping takes place."

"What's up with you these days? What's shaking in Boston?"

"Who the fuck ever knows?" I explained the PCB/PCP story to him, and included my speculations from last night. He seemed to favor the grand conspiracy theory.

"You don't want to fuck around with the Mafia, do you?"

"Not at all. They can do whatever they want. You think it's the Mafia, Jim?"

"Yeah. Something about the whole style of the operation."

"I disagree. Too wimpy."

He meditated on his coffee for a minute. "Well, look. If they get after you—if you get in trouble—get your ass to the Adirondacks."

"I don't ski."

"Doesn't even have to be there. Just any reservation. You go there and ask them for help and I'll make sure you get taken care of."

"Yeah. I guess Sicilians stand out pretty bad on the res."

He let my flip comment sail right out the window. "If they're suspicious, give them my name, have them call me or whatever. But don't hang around and let yourself get greased."

I was surprised by his offer, and honored. It's not as though I'd helped him out all that much. But a reservation would be a great place to disappear.

We talked about the week's operations, which were going to be split between grungy mechanic's work and full-splatter media events. For the time being I was worried about the grungy part, in Buffalo, while Jim was going to be hanging around up at the Falls, looking noble for the cameras. Later, after the cement had hardened, I'd join him up there.

While we were waiting for Anna, we wandered around his property a little. He had a shooting range out back, for both archery and guns, and we farted around there for an hour or so. "This is what you should be packing," he recommended, hauling down a huge rifle with lots of scrollwork on it. "Lever-action. You seem like a lever-action kind of guy. Look at the size of that magazine."

"What magazine?"

"Jesus, S.T., the tube on the bottom is the magazine. Forget it." He put the rifle back. "This is more your speed. We'll set you up with a fucking bow and arrow."

He had a lot of those. He made them in the Nez Percé style, the Lakota style, the Iroquois style, you name it. He figured the only way to keep the knowledge from being lost was by using it. He could go into the woods armed with just a knife and make himself a birchbark canoe from scratch. "Only did it once, though," he had explained, "took me two weeks. Anna had to keep coming out with coolers full of baloney sandwiches. I ended up with viral pneumonia." Which sounded very humble, but he'd finished the canoe, and he still had it in his garage. The bows he made in his workshop, and he had no compunction about shaping them with a belt sander. "The idea," he said, "is to keep the information in my hand, not to live like a caveman."

I couldn't really use his bows, even if I'd wanted too. I could draw them but I couldn't hold them steady long enough to sight in on the target. Also, I was nervous. The bowstrings were made of twisted horsehair. I was convinced that one of them would snap, and its ends whip into my eyeball at supersonic speed. Jim killed a few bales of hay for me, and that was about the time Anna came home.

19

THE REST OF THE DAY was brute labor. We lined the back of
the U-Haul with plastic and dumped the cement and the
gravel in a big mound and stirred it together. Then I went
out and found a bar. Around 11:30 I tore myself away from
a ski-ball game and allowed myself to be picked up by Alan
and Frank in the U-Haul. We drove down to the Boner
plant, found the cul-de-sac, and backed the truck up to the
manhole. The rest was simple, stupid and obvious. We lifted
the lid. We didn't have a manhole cracker, but a big strong
guy like Frank can do it with a prybar and a chisel. We
formed an assembly line, shoveling the cement and gravel
mixture into the gunny sacks and stacking them in the sewer
line until it was filled, top to bottom, side to side. Then we
did it again so we had a double-thickness wall. We even
pounded a few segments of rebar into it to make it all the
stronger. By that time the sewer had backed up about halfway
and dioxin-laden juices were oozing out between the sacks.

I got sick because I'd had three dozen red-hot chicken
wings in the course of my ski-ball, and I had to toss them
right down the manhole. Probably not the first half-digested
load of hot wings to visit those sewers.

Then we took sandpaper and files and removed all the rust from the rim of the manhole lid and its iron seat in the pavement. We squeezed the epoxy glue onto both and glued the lid back in place, then poured a layer of wet cement over the whole thing and just paved it over. We threw a sheet of plywood over the wet cement, then parked the truck's rear wheels on it. We deflated the tires, unscrewed their valve stems, and removed the distributor cap from the engine, and, for our finale, secured the gate into the Boner plant with some Kryptonites. The cement would take three days to set properly and we intended to do a proper job, so we set Alan up as the night watchman, rolled out sleeping bags in the back, and went to sleep, breathing mildly carcinogenic cement dust.

For a night gig, this one turned out to be not bad from the media-circus point of view. No one knew why we were parked here—we figured we'd let them puzzle it out for themselves—but Buffalo loves to see scruffy environmentalists irritate Boner Chemical. A crew came around with donuts at 7:00 A.M. and interviewed us for a local morning show. A whole series of panjan-drums from Boner came around and told us to get off Boner property or we'd be arrested, and we told each one that we were on a public street, not Boner property. Then they sent some lawyers around to tell us the same thing, as though the messenger would make a difference. The cops came around once or twice and we showed them the official city maps. We also pointed out that there were no NO PARKING signs in this vicinity. That satisfied them. California cops would have beat us up and searched our rectums for crack, but these guys thought we were nice, spunky kids.

Then the citizenry started coming around and bringing us food. Two layer cakes. A cherry pie. Seventeen bags of chips. Five assorted six-packs. Six more bags of chips. A total of forty-six donuts. Chips. Frank was horrified. "This is all junk food," he said, in the privacy of the U-Haul. But when another lady showed up with a blazing red, cherry-flavored cake, he thanked her profusely.

Boner stationed security people around us on all three sides. They hadn't figured out the thing with the sewer yet.

They thought we were using this as a base camp for some kind of illegal assault. Stupid as this would have been, this is how the Boners saw the world.

Once it was dark, they wheeled out big spotlights and aimed them at us. It was very bright. For the people sleeping in back, this was no problem, but for the person on watch it was irritating. What the hell, we wore sunglasses. I had Debbie come around with our big nautical strobe and we set that going on top of the cab. You could see that thing through a brick wall. The flash was so intense it knocked the wind out of you. For the person in the cab, it wasn't bad, but for those security people, staying up all night, staring at us, it must have been lethal. By sunrise, the words U-HAUL were permanently chiseled into their optic nerves.

On day two, the Boner people got a little smarter and called the fire department. This we hadn't counted on. A car pulled up, one of those station wagons with the red light on top, and a guy who was obviously the fire marshal got out. Some of the Boner lawyers scurried up again and flanked him as he approached, as though they were on his side. He identified himself and I told him I was in charge.

"You seem to be blocking a public street," he pointed out.

"Nobody's using it," I countered, "It's a dead-end; this gate is locked, and Boner lost the keys."

"Normally I wouldn't care, but every once in a while this factory catches on fire."

"Goddamn. That must be hell to fight."

"Eh?"

"All those chemicals. You practically need a reference book for each one."

"Yeah. Let me tell you, when we get a call for this plant, we're not all that damn happy."

"Time to roll out the Purple K, huh?"

His face crinkled up. "Yeah, exactly."

Purple K is a foaming compound they keep at airports to put out exploding 747s. Sometimes useful for chemical fires.

He continued, "But anyway, if there were a fire here, we'd have to get in through this gate."

"No problem. We're here twenty-four hours a day. If there's a fire, we'll move."

"What about the gate? I'm told that you've locked the gate."

"The key's nearby. If there's trouble, we can have the gate open within five minutes."

"Too slow."

"Thirty seconds."

"Okay, that's fine then," the fire marshal said, then got in his station wagon and drove away. True story. The Boner attorneys just stood with their briefcases twisting in the breeze.

Not much happened on day three. Boner had decided to view the whole thing with amused tolerance. They still didn't have a clue about the sacks of concrete. Back in the plant, toxic waste was backing up in a holding pool somewhere, but they hadn't noticed. Tonight we'd drive away and, if they were very sharp, they'd notice that a manhole had vanished.

In the afternoon Debbie and I decamped to the honeymoon suite where we talked and almost had sex. I refused to leave the bed, just sat there watching the Home Shopping Network, charging up microwave ovens on the Biotronics card, sending them to random addresses in Roxbury, and drinking beer. The three days on the U-Haul had taken a lot of out of me. Jim Grandfather showed up and I put the beer away, because the smell bothered him, and he and I sat there quietly, watching football with the sound turned off, listening to Debbie sing in the shower.

In the morning I bathed, borrowed a blow dryer and blew on my hair until I looked like the tail end of a cross-country motorcycle trip. Then I slipped into a fairly modest three-piece suit, put on tube socks, pulled plastic bags on over those and got out my bright-green high-top sneakers, stained and splattered with various toxic wastes. I kept them locked up in a small beer cooler until they were ready to be deployed. Wore a tie that simulated a dead trout hanging from my neck. Jim drove me downtown in his pickup truck and dropped me off. He went out to look for a belt for a washing machine and I walked into the front doors of a large office building.

The security guys were waiting for me and they took me right up to somewhere near the top floor. We did your basic whisk number, whisking through the secretarial maze, and then they showed me into a nifty boardroom where the top-management echelon of Boner Chemical was waiting for me.

It was all choreographed. There were a dozen rich white guys and one of me. Actually, I'm a white guy too, but somehow I keep forgetting. So the white guys were seated in a crescent, like a parabolic reflector, with a single empty chair at the focal point so that they could all point inwards and concentrate their weirdness energy on me. Instead, I wandered over and sat down on an empty chair way off to the side, over underneath the window. Shoe leather creaked and invisible clouds of cologne and martini breath wafted around the room as everyone had to turn around and rearrange. The chairs were massive; a lot of physical effort was involved. They had no coherent plan, so things got pretty raggedy, with some execs sitting way off to the sides and others peering over pinstriped shoulders. All of them were squinting into the sun—a fortuitous accident. I leaned my chair back against the windowsill so that my green sneakers rose into the air. I leaned back there and regarded this nervous phalanx of upper-crusters and got to thinking about what a twisted job this was. I spend days living and working with people who would probably be street puppeteers if GEE didn't exist to hire them. People who keep quartz crystals under their pillows to prevent cancer, who feel the day is lost if they don't get a chance to sing a new 2-4-6-8 chant in front of a minicam. Then I threaten the boards of directors of major corporations. On off days I go scuba diving through raw sewage. My aunt keeps asking me if I've gotten a job yet.

They all introduced themselves but I lost track of the names and ranks pretty quickly. Top execs don't wear "Hello! My name is . . ." tags on their charcoal-grey worsted. Most were Bonerites, but there were some Basco people there too.

"Sorry about your dioxin outfall," I lied, "but don't worry. It's nothing that a few hundred pounds of dynamite won't fix."

"If you think you can just plug up a Buffalo sewer line, you're wrong, mister," said the executive with eyeglasses the size of portholes.

". . . and get away with it?"

"Yes."

"Just did. Now, moving on to Item Two," I said, "we're steamed about your hidden outfall at the base of Niagara Falls. Tomorrow we're going to reveal its existence to the media."

"I don't know what you're referring to," said an executive I had mentally christened Mr. Dithers. "We'll have to take it up with Engineering."

"Item Three: you guys are getting bought out by Basco?"

"The details of that transaction are secret," said a half-embalmed guy with pale eyes.

"Not totally," I said.

An executive with a hard-on shifted uncomfortably in his seat. "What exactly are you getting at?"

I whistled. "Insider trading, baby. SEC's number-one no-no."

Actually, I just made that up on the spur of the moment. But I knew insider trading was going on. There always was. And it would really scare the shit out of these people if they suspected we had some way of bringing the SEC down on them.

"Mr. Taylor, I wonder if I could work an item into the agenda," said a Class-IV yuppie who'd been spending too much time on the Nautilus. He grinned at me, which was kind of an unusual move in these surroundings, and there was a little stir of, not exactly laughter, but a relaxation, a few moments of unlabored breathing around the room. The air in here was desperately stale and hot.

I threw up my hands and said, "At your service, Mr.—"

"Laughlin. It's kind of hard to remember all these names, I know."

All this groovy informality was calculated, but up here I'd take informality where I could get it. I dropped the front legs of my chair to the carpet and crossed my legs in the all-American figure-four position, letting the shoe dangle way out to the side. I sipped some of Boner's toxic decaf and stifled a fart. "Okay. What's your beef, Laughlin?"

He looked almost injured. "No beef. Why does it always have to be a beef? I'm just interested in talking to you in less . . ." he waved his hands around the room ". . . claustro-phobic surroundings."

" 'Bout what?"

"Well, for one thing, whether Sam Horn's going to be as lucky in a tight spot as Dave Henderson."

"The world is full of Red Sox fans, Mr. Laughlin, and I only sleep with one of them."

"*Touché*. Another thing, then. We've got some work going on at Biotronics that would interest you."

"The Holy Grail?"

He was a little nonplussed. "I don't know about any Holy Grail."

"Dolmacher's phrase."

"Ah, yes! He mentioned that the two of you had had a lit-tle chat."

"Verbal combat is more like it. You work for Biotronics, Laughlin?"

The executives crinkled up and chortled.

"I'm the president," Laughlin said, kindly enough.

Oh yeah. I'd seen his picture in the paper, a couple of months ago.

Thirty floors below, Jim was waiting for me in his rusty pickup, reading the warranty on his washing machine belt. "This must be reality," I said, climbing in.

"Take it or leave it."

"Let's go to the Falls," I said, "and raise some hell."

"What happened?"

"Zip. Made an appointment with a young rising star in the cancer industry."

"To do what?"

"To shop for Grails."

We went to the Falls. Jim stood up near the top, wearing 501s and some Indian gear, squinting a lot, looking sad and noble for the camera crews and telling dirty jokes to the print reporters. A bunch of GEE people had come down from the Toronto office to give us a hand, so things were well under way by the time we got there. I kept asking where

Debbie was and people kept saying "over there," and eventually I got pointed over to a heavy railing overlooking the Falls. Three climbing ropes were tied to it, leading down the cliff, and Debbie was hanging from one of them down near the bottom, dressed in a stunning Gore-Tex coverall. She and her Toronto pals had located Boner's hidden outfall, right where Alan said it would be, and then started driving pitons into the rock. Toronto had prepared a banner, a forty-foot strip of white ripstop nylon with a big red arrow blazoned on it. They nailed that banner to the cliff, pointing right to the outfall. They took their time, used a lot of pitons and strung eighth-inch aileron cable around the edge of the banner so that the wind wouldn't stretch it away from the cliff. Finally, Debbie took a can of fluorescent-orange spray paint and did what she could to highlight the outfall, make it visible to the cameras. It wasn't a total success, since everything was cold and wet, not ideal conditions for spray paint, but some of it stuck. And if it didn't, well, that's what the arrow was for.

20

WHEN I GOT BACK HOME there was the usual post-trip crap
to take care of. Mail and messages. Had to get a birthday
present for Auntie. Had to sign a bunch of papers to continue Tanya's "studies" at GEE. They shut off our phone service so we all had to sit down and thrash out about three
months' worth of unpaid long-distance bills. In the middle of
a spirited discussion of who had made seven consecutive calls
to Santa Cruz at three in the morning, Ike got up and announced that he was moving out. He was tired of the plumbing problems, he said, and the weird messages on the
answering machine, and Roscommon had come in while he
was at work and torn down the Mel King campaign poster on
our front balcony. That was okay. Ike was a shitty gardener
anyway and he complained when I ran my model trains after
bedtime. Tess and Laurie, the lesbian carpenters, announced
that they liked the kitchen better after we'd untrashed it and
cleaned it up, so why not try to keep it that way? I pointed
out that I had bought three new badminton birdies before I
left for Buffalo and now they were all gone. Should we call
this place a "co-op" or a "commune"? How about calling it a
"house"? Who had scrubbed the Teflon off the big frying pan?

Since Tess had weeded the garden, how many tomatoes did she get? Whose hair predominated in the shower drain—the women's, since they had more, or the men's, since they were losing more? Was it okay to pour bacon grease down the drains if you ran hot water at the same time? Could bottles with metal rings on the necks be put in the recycling box? Should we buy a cord of firewood? Maple or pine? Did we agree that the people next door were abusing their children? Physically or just psychologically? Was boric acid roach powder a bioaccumulative toxin? Where was the bicycle-tire pump, and was it okay to take it on an overnight trip? Whose turn was it to scrub the green crap out from between the tiles in the bathroom?

They had gone to extreme inconvenience to save a message for me on the phone answering machine. I had to listen to it three times because I couldn't believe it. It was Dolmacher. He sounded friendly. He wanted me to go up to New Hampshire with him and participate in the survival game—pretending to be a commando in the woods. He was trying to get more people to come up from Boston, he explained, and—get this—the people he worked with were "all terrible nerds."

I did have to give him one thing: he had the intestinal fortitude to go up there every weekend and do combat with those shaggy inbreds from New Hampshire. They didn't use real bullets, but the dirt and cold were real.

He sounded so damn happy, that's what bothered me. The Grail project must be doing well. And later on the tape, he reminded me of my appointment with Laughlin. What the hell did they want from me?

Shit, maybe they really were on to something. Maybe they'd come up with a way to clean up toxic waste. If so, wonderful. But for some reason the thought bugged the hell out of me.

Maybe I was the only one who was supposed to be a hero. Maybe that was my real problem. If Dolmacher and his grinning, musclebound boss found a perfect way to clean up toxics while I was still sitting hairy and grubby in a Zodiac, riding my bicycle to work, where would it leave me? Left behind and worthless. Meanwhile, Biotronics was pulling some

kind of bad cop/good cop drama on me. Scare me and my
friends shitless, then, when I figure it out, smile a lot and in-
vite me over for a meeting.

There had also been a series of messages from Rebecca,
which they hadn't saved, but they were all the same: I'm trying to get in touch with you, asshole, why don't you call
back? So the next time I was in the office I gave her a call.

"How's the wounded warrior?"

Rebecca always had to call me by epithets: the Granola
James Bond, the wounded Warrior.

"What do you mean?"

"Pride, S.T. I'm talking about your pride. Last time I
talked to you . . ."

"Oh yeah. The Case of the Disappearing PCBs. Yeah, that
one still smarts a little. But I had a good time in Buffalo." I
briefed her on it.

"Been following the Pleshy campaign?"

"That reminds me. They're buying Boner. Big merger, you
know. Rumors of insider trading."

"Let's talk about it. And about the article—remember?"

So we made an appointment. I wasn't sure about the article yet. It might be some fun, in the fish-in-a-barrel department. But then, every once in a while I took a shot at
political credibility. A couple of surprisingly well-known local pols have come to me to write policy statements on hazardous waste issues. If I got in the habit of banishing The
Groveler in the alternative press, they might shy away from
me.

While I was gone, someone had put some clippings on my
desk about that jackass Smirnoff. The Terrorist Boy Scouts
had held their first meeting and invited all the local press,
one or two of whom had shown up. Smirnoff had issued a
statement, a rambling statement, just what I'd expect, alter-
nately heaping shit on GEE's head for being too conservative
and praising our direct-action techniques. One of the clippings had a photograph, and I could see the back of a member's head, staring up adoringly at Smirnoff, and I was just
positive it was Wyman, the guy who had shifted into reverse
on the freeway. So I tried to get ahold of him for a while, but

he had moved out of his old place and no one knew where he was.

"He's very secretive," his old roommate explained, "because the FBI is after him."

"Big fucking deal," I said, miffing the hell out of his unindicted coconspirator.

I spent the rest of the afternoon writing letters and press releases denouncing the likes of Smirnoff and his idol, Boone, and explaining, in very short sentences, the differences between us and them. Then I trashed them, had the computer wipe them out. They'd never see print, because we don't talk about people like Smirnoff, we just ignore them.

I did have some fun during that first week back. No big actions on the way, no court appearances, no wrecked cars. I mixed up a shitload of papier-mâché and added a new mountain to my train set. I hocked a few more shares of my old Mass Anal stock and bought an antique locomotive. Bartholomew and Debbie and Tess and Laurie and I played a few hundred badminton games after work.

But the most fun of all was when Esmerelda sent me a copy of a photo from the July 13, 1956, *Boston Globe*, second page of the Business section. It was a picture of Alvin Pleshy, back in his squirrelly, young-engineer days, in Basco's main facility on Alkali Lane. I recognized the building just by its size: it was their big Chloralkali plant. Same process that had ruined Niagara. They made a lot of chemicals, so they needed a lot of power. They needed equipment that could handle the power fast. That meant big equipment and lost of it—huge transformers. Many transformers, each the size of a two-car garage.

"NEW EQUIPMENT FOR BASCO. Alvin Pleshy, Senior Engineer, supervises as modern equipment is installed in Basco's Everett facility. The equipment will be used in the production of industrial and agricultural chemicals."

Which will be sprayed over most of Vietnam, I mentally added. But the caption didn't matter, I was looking at the photo. Anyone could see that we weren't dealing with just any "equipment" here. We were talking whopping transformers. They were being lowered through holes in the roof.

The fact that Basco bought a bunch of new transformers

in 1956 was not interesting to me. What was interesting was that they had had to get rid of some old transformers to make room for the new ones. And all of them had probably been full of PCBs, hundreds of thousands of gallons of the bad stuff. Basco had been having PCB problems for years, but nothing of that magnitude.

Pleshy had stashed away a lakeful of toxic waste somewhere, and he'd been keeping it under his belt for thirty years. I wonder if he thought about it at night. I wonder what the stockholders would say when I informed them of it, sent them copies of this photograph.

Suppose they'd taken those transformers and just dumped them on the floor of the Harbor somewhere. Or taken them to one of their lots and covered them with dirt. Sooner or later they'd bust open and then all hell would break loose. It might take a long time—say, thirty years. But it would happen.

And they'd know about it. They'd be sitting there, waiting, worrying. Maybe worrying enough to cover the site with some goons in a Cigarette.

Pure speculation. But it might explain the lobster. Unfortunately, it didn't explain the disappearing PCBs.

I looked at the photo again. Pleshy was smiling that big bright smile that hasn't been seen anywhere since the Fifties. Twelve years later, when he read about the rice oil in Kusho, I'll bet the smile wasn't there.

But there were plenty of smiles at Biotronics, at least for the first ten minutes or so. Laughlin actually sent a car around to pick me up. He said he'd feel terrible if I got run over riding my bike to their offices. Either he was indiscreet as hell, or he wanted to let me know that he knew a lot about me.

So it was high time for me to learn a lot about Laughlin, and I had a few ways of doing that. Most of them would have to wait until after the meeting, though, so I rode, relatively ignorant, in a big fat company car out to a high-tech office building along the river, not far from Harvard. Not even that far from where I lived. Took the elevator up to the top floor and found Biotronics easily, by following its smell. They were using solvents in there, mostly for cleaning and sterilizing stuff. Ethanol and methanol. Some kind of disinfectant with an aromatic perfume added to make it smell more impressive. Whiffs of hydrochloric acid, probably used for heavy-duty cleaning. Sweet acetone. None of this was unusual, just the basic lab odors. No wonder they were on the top floor; they'd use hoods to contain the toxic stuff, and then exhaust it all out vents in the roof.

Laughlin met me at the door, swooped his right hand around like a Stuka dive bomber and nailed me with a gym teacher's handshake and a game-show host's smile. And on top of all those other odors, a wave of familiar cologne rolled up my nostrils.

But he wasn't wearing a shoulder holster at the moment. And you could buy that perfume at any sufficiently pretentious store. Or, if you had access to a gas chromatograph, you could manufacture it yourself at a hundredth the price. So I had to take it easy here and not jump to any paranoid conclusions. Big guys and big revolvers didn't necessarily go together. I wiped my hand on my jeans, discreetly, then followed him past all the smiling secretaries, the cheery bottle-washer pushing a cartload of glassware, the unresponsive Xerox repairman, the hale-and-hearty fellow executives, blah blah blah. Being in an office just makes my skin crawl. All that good cheer. All that fine wool, the processed air, the mediocre coffee, fluorescent tubes, lipstick, new-carpet smell, the same fucking xeroxed cartoons tacked on the walls. I wanted to shout: one Far Side on the door does not an interesting person make. But somewhere back in here they had a lab, which made it a little better.

Not much of a lab, as it turned out. They had a gas chromatograph, sort of a cheapie, and some other analytical machines, and they had one very odd piece of work, up against a wall, called a Dolmacher. He held a printout in his hand and was moving his lips.

"S.T.!" he shouted, somewhat too loud, blinking spasmodically as his contact lenses tried to catch up. "Sorry we didn't see you on Saturday."

"I was in Buffalo. Did you kill anyone?"

"Yeah! Nailed an R.O.T.C. cadet right behind the ear. From thirty yards. God, was he embarrassed."

"Yeah. So this is where you work?"

"Part of the time."

"Where's the DNA sequencer? Where are the big bug-growing tanks? Where's the tobacco that glows in the dark?"

"We're in Cambridge," Laughlin said, managing to crank out a surprisingly throaty laugh.

"Oh, yeah. And people like me have ruined it for people like you."

"God, S.T.," Dolmacher said, not quite whining, "you guys really made it tough on us in this town. We can hardly even have offices here."

"Wasn't me," I said. "Genes aren't my bailiwick." Years before, another bunch of duck-squeezers had rammed through some laws making life hard for genetic engineers in Cambridge.

"That might be true now, S.T.,'" Laughlin said, "but it's about to change."

"Yeah, I've been getting all kinds of dark hints to that effect."

Laughlin jerked his head toward the exit, letting his politeness drop for a second. I guessed that meant we were leaving now. Dolmacher followed automatically.

"Where's the rest of it?" I said, killing time as we wandered down the hallway.

"Unfortunately we don't have a consolidated facility at this point in time," Laughlin said. "Depending on various environmental regs, we have different parts of Biotronics scattered around the area. This is the headquarters. And as you saw, we have a small analytical lab."

"Small molecules only?"

"Small molecules only," Laughlin said, then turned and fixed me with a glare over his shoulder. "Sangamon's Principle."

I couldn't believe this fucker. He'd been twisting my dick this entire time and I hadn't even figured it out until now. He was just begging me to punch him in the nose so that he could throw all those big uncoordinated Nautilus muscles into action. And then call his lawyers.

He ushered me into a conference room. I sat down with my back to the window. Laughlin closed the door and Dolmacher hovered.

"You know, Laughlin, you're the nicest guy who's ever hated my guts," I said.

He laughed freely, the laugh of a man with a clear conscience. "I doubt it."

Dolmacher just swiveled back and forth like a spectator at a tennis match. Me, I was trying to avoid going into a fight-or-flight reaction. I drank some of their ice water—natural spring water, of course—and breathed slow, trying to keep my vocal cords nice and loose. I was wondering if Laughlin had done it—killed Scrounger—or those two pricks, Kleinhoffer and Dietrich. Or all three.

"Well! Shall we get started with the presentation," Dolmacher hollered.

"Got any kids, Laughlin?" I asked.

"I think you're going to find this interesting," Laughlin said.

"Should we tell him about the secrecy thing?" Dolmacher asked.

"This research is not generally known," Laughlin explained, "for competitive reasons."

"Competing with the police?"

"With all the other players in this industry. Of course, you can say anything you want about this meeting, after you've left, but we'll just deny it. And all it will do is give a slight edge to our competitors."

"Okay," I said. "Let's get this shit over with. We're all busy people. You guys have been working on some kind of genetically engineered bug that deals with the organic chlorine problem."

"Actually, yes," said Dolmacher.

"I'd guess you got yourselves some time on a Cray supercomputer, or something, and did some kind of heavy quantum mechanics, worked out a rough numerical-solution Hamiltonian for chlorine, devised some kind of transition state between covalent and ionic, figured out a way to introduce an electron into those chlorines to make them ionic again. Some reaction that could be carried out by a string of genetic material—what do you call it?"

"A plasmid," Laughlin said.

"A plasmid that could be introduced into a bacterium and therefore reproduced in unlimited quantities. And now you want to get approval to use this thing to clean up toxic waste spills. Turn all that covalent chlorine back into salt."

"Sheesh," Dolmacher said, and not for the first time.

"You want a job, S.T.?" Laughlin said.

"I could use one. Need to replace my computer."

"That's a shame."

"Yeah. The Mafia sent a hardware engineer around to bust it."

For once, Laughlin had nothing to say. He was just a little rattled, or pissed. Probably thinking that he'd been kind of stupid, here and there, along the way.

"You should buy one of the new ones," Dolmacher said. "With the 80386 processor. Hottest thing going."

"You bastards. You already did it, didn't you?"

Laughlin checked his Rolex. "Let me see. Two weeks, three days, and about four hours. It took you that long to figure it out?"

"Took your magic bug and dumped it into the Harbor. Ate those PCBs right up. Turned them into salt."

Laughlin shrugged. He had his eyebrows way up on his forehead now, up there in the zone of total innocence. "Is there some problem with that?"

"Tell me. How long since Dolmacher put this bug together for you? A month or two? When I talked to him at the yacht club, he wasn't finished with it yet. He said he was working on the Holy Grail, not finished with it."

"Something like that."

"Jeez, S.T., chill out."

"How much testing did you do on that bug before you put it into the environment?"

Laughlin shrugged. "Wasn't necessary."

"I think the EPA would disagree."

"Don't insult my intelligence by talking about them."

I snorted. "Alas, we agree, Laughlin. But didn't you even think about the dangers?"

He grinned. He had me. "What dangers? The bug eats covalent chlorine compounds. S.T. That's its food. When it's eaten them all—when the Harbor is perfectly toxin-free—it starves to death. End of bug."

"Yeah, I get the secret message loud and clear. If I go out there and try to get evidence—to find some of these bugs and blow your company away—I won't find zip. They're all dead."

"Which is fine, isn't it? Because we don't want genetically engineered bugs in the environment."

"And we don't want PCBs either," Dolmacher reminded us.

Laughlin smirked at Dolmacher behind his back.

"You guys went out and stopped pollution, huh?" I said, beating him to it.

"We stopped pollution. No PCBs left in the Harbor. No bugs either. No evidence to harm our company. The only person who's screwed is you, S.T."

Suddenly Dolmacher turned nasty. "Yeah, S.T., you're screwed."

"Everywhere except in bed," Laughlin added.

"Laughlin, my man," I said, "I didn't realize it was going to be that kind of fight."

He dropped into a boxing stance, waved his guard around, snapped a big meaty right hook into thin air. "Fight's over," he said. "First-round knockout. Ever do any boxing, S.T.?"

"Nope. I prefer to kill helpless animals."

Dolmacher cleared his throat with a sound like pebbles rattling in a can. "What we're hoping is that we can get you on our side."

"That's not what we were going to say, Dolmacher," Laughlin said. "We were going to say, 'What we're trying to demonstrate is that we're already on the same side.'"

"You and us," Dolmacher continued, right in stride.

"Lumpy, you ever get your boss up there for the Survival Game?" I asked. "I could slip you some dum-dums."

"It's a stupid game," Laughlin said. Dolmacher looked a little wounded.

"All your boss's ammo is on the bottom of the Harbor," I said. "In his chrome-plated revolver."

"I got a new one," Laughlin said, "even bigger. To protect myself from terrorists."

"How's your son?" I asked. "The Pöyzen Böyzen fan. He been spending a lot of time on the Nautilus lately?"

"Christopher lacks the maturity for a concerted power-building program," Laughlin said, showing a little tension.

"I'll say. He and I had a chat, out there on that big mound of garbage in the Harbor, where he hangs out with the rest of the Junior Achievement League. How old is he—fourteen, fifteen?"

"Seventeen."

"Oh. Well, I was impressed with him. He throws a mean beer bottle."

"Thank you."

"What's his ambition, then? Arsonist?"

Laughlin started for me, quick little boxer's steps. I just sat there. Harder to punch a guy's face when it's down around your waist.

"Think about lawyers, Laughlin," I said. He did, and he stopped.

"Let's get to the end of this," I said, "because we're both about to kill each other. You want me, noted eco-asshole Sangamon Taylor, to come out and say that your PCB-eating bug is a good thing. That it should be rushed into general use right away."

"All of which is the God's truth," Dolmacher said.

"Before you ever used that bug, you knew I might fuck it up for you. You heard from Christopher that I was hanging out on Spectacle Island, and you were afraid that I'd discover the old Basco transformers leaking PCBs there."

"Continue."

"The ones buried under the north shore of the island. The ones that accidentally got ruptured by that old barge during Hurricane Alison, and spilled a whole lake of PCBs down into the Harbor. You were afraid I'd figured that all out. Which, actually, I hadn't. As you noticed, I can be pretty slow sometimes. But you tried to scare me off, to slow my investigation down, so that you could use the bug to wipe out the evidence before I went public."

"And it worked."

"It worked fine. The question is: did the bug really eat all those PCBs? What about deep underneath that old barge? Maybe there's an unruptured transformer down there. Or maybe there's a pocket of bugs down there, still working on some PCBs, bugs that I could sample and show before the public. You're still worried about that. You want me off your trail, you want me on your side."

"Why shouldn't you be on our side?" Dolmacher said. He really meant it. "S.T., there are no covalent chlorine compounds left in Boston Harbor. Isn't that what you wanted?"

"Sangamon's Principle," I said. "This plasmid, it's a huge molecule you're messing around with. You don't know what it's going to do. The answer is no."

Laughlin didn't bother to show me out. Dolmacher followed me, going on about the Survival Game, until I body-checked him into a wall. He gave me a vacant yet somehow piercing look, and as I rode the elevator down, I got to thinking that Dolmacher was nothing but a big complicated molecule himself, and you never knew what he'd do either.

21

REBECCA CAME AROUND for our appointment about half an hour after I got back. I'd forgotten about it. Damn it, I was still just stewing in my emotions, trying to wash Laughlin's perfume off my hand. I hadn't had time to consider anything. I wanted to tell all, but first I had to come up with a plan. I shoved my clippings under some other crap when I heard her voice approaching; she walked in and said she had some interesting stuff for me.

She did, but nothing better than what I'd already seen. There was another copy of that same picture. The intern had also discovered a vague little article from the late Sixties saying that Basco had put some "junk machinery" on the floor of the Harbor, giving the usual feeble excuse.

"They claim that this junk was going to become a habitat for marine life. You don't buy that?"

Bless her, she did know how to blow my lid. "Rebecca, goddammit, since the beginning of time, every corporation that has ever thrown any of its shit into the ocean has claimed that it was going to become a habitat for marine life. It's the goddamn ocean, Rebecca. That's where all the ma-

rine life is. Of course it's going to become a habitat for marine life."

"You think those things pose an environmental hazard today?"

"Nothing compared to those transformers. I've got Basco
in my crosshairs, Rebecca."

"I don't think I can print that in the paper, S.T."

"I just don't have any ammunition in my magazine."

"Look. Do you want to do the article? S.T. on Pleshy?"

"Can't. Not yet. Have to figure out what's going on." I
leaned forward and looked ponderous. "If I seem a little
stressed out, well . . . the FBI is after me."

"You're kidding, S.T.!"

"Recess. I'll get back to you when Basco's in the grave."

When I'd gotten back from that lovely chat with Laughlin
and Dolmacher, there'd been a message waiting for me, a
worried message from Gallagher's wife. It was still early
enough in the day to catch him on his boat, and I needed an
excuse to get out on the water. I persuaded Rebecca to drive
me downtown, got on the Zodiac, and buzzed around to
Gallagher's berth in Southie. He was still out on the water
somewhere. So I persuaded one of the neighboring boats to
hail him on the CB, and in about twenty minutes I was
screaming flat-out across calm water to intercept the *Scoundrel*, which was just returning from the Bay.

They recognized me at a distance, since I'm the only one
who travels in that way, and cut their engines so I could
come up alongside.

"Jeez! You guys run into an oil slick?" I said when I got
close enough to talk. Maybe it was the late-afternoon light,
but they were all dark, greyish looking. They mumbled some
kind of defiant, bullshit response. They sounded tired. I
tossed one of them my bow line and then they helped me
scramble on board.

They all stood around and stared at me, quieter than
they'd ever been, sunk, depressed. The reason their skin was
dark was that they were covered with chloracne.

"You guys have been into some bad chowder," I said in a
weak murmur, but Gallagher, skipper of the plague ship
Scoundrel, held up his hands and cut me off.

"Listen. Listen, S.T., we stopped setting our traps there. I swear to God we haven't touched any of them oily lobsters."

When was this damn thing going to start making any sense? Why did I feel like such an asshole? "You absolutely didn't eat any of those oily ones?"

"Only Billy. The guy you saw at Fenway."

"How's he doing?"

"Fine. He felt real sick and took a couple days off, stopped eating lobster."

Billy came up from belowdecks. He was pristine. A little residual scabbing from his old case of chloracne.

"But you guys have been eating lobster and you got sick."

"Yeah. Real bad, just in the last couple of days. So we switched to Big Macs."

"Good."

"But it's getting worse anyway. When I left this morning, S.T., I was okay, I really was. But now I feel like shit."

"The lobsters that you ate since the last time I talked to you—"

"Goddamn it, S.T., I'm telling you the God's truth. We looked at them all real careful and they didn't smell oily, they didn't taste oily."

"Where'd you get 'em?"

"All over the Harbor. Mostly Dorchester Bay."

That didn't help me at all. Dorchester Bay was a pocket of water below South Boston, ringed with sewer overflows—CSOs—but not much industry. It was three or four miles east-southeast of the area I'd been concentrating on.

"Have you pulled up any traps that were oily?"

"Yeah. We put one down near Spectacle, just as a test, you know. See, S.T., we're starting to become invironmintles. Pulled it up this morning. Check this out, S.T."

I knew it had to be bad because they had just chucked the whole thing into a Hefty bag and left it out on the fantail. I pulled it open and looked. There was no lobster in there, but the trap was still glistening with oil. It had all dripped off the trap and run down into one corner of the bag where I could grab it and squish it around and feel it through the plastic. Oily, but transparent. This trap had been dipped in PCBs.

This was orders of magnitude worse than the lobster Tanya had found—the lobster had just had a few drops of the stuff, built up slowly over time.

There was more to this business, but I had no idea what. Each new piece of evidence directly contradicted the last.

Billy ate oily lobsters and got poisoned. When he stopped eating them he got better. Fine. But the rest of the crew never did. They got poisoned anyway. They stopped eating them but it didn't help. Where were they getting PCBs?

"The only thing I can think is that you're absorbing them from traps like this one," I said. "You didn't try burning anything, did you? Any old traps or ropes?"

"Why would we do that?"

"Beats me. But let me just warn you that PCBs don't burn. They just turn into dioxin and escape into the air." Maybe someone was running a clandestine toxic waste incinerator in Southie. I just don't know.

"Activated charcoal," I said. "Go home and buy some aquarium charcoal. Grind it up fine, heat it up, and eat it. Give yourself an enema."

It took me a while to make them believe that. "Or you could grind up some briquets very fine. Don't use the self-lighting kind."

"Yeah, we're not dumb micks, S.T."

"Sorry. Ever hear of an activated charcoal filter? The carbon grabs onto organic molecules, anything that's reactive, and holds it long enough for your body to get rid of it."

Gallagher laughed. "Okay. I'll tell my wife we're getting an aquarium. Just what I need, more frickin' fish."

By the time I got the Zode back downtown, filled the gas tanks, made it back to the office, loaded myself down with diving equipment, got it all back to the yacht club and hit the water again it was dark and a little bit foggy. Which was fine by me. I was a little dark and foggy myself; I didn't even know what I was going to look for, or where.

The oily trap—now, that was evidence. No gas chromatograph was needed, just my trusty schnozz. It contradicted the evidence from the gas chromatograph at the university but, by now, contradictions seemed par for the course. I was willing to believe the most recent piece of evidence to drift past me.

I'd gotten Gallagher to show me, on a chart, exactly where he'd pulled that trap. A quarter-mile north of Spectacle Island, in sort of a depression in the sea floor. I could go down into it and look for puddles of oil. For fifty-five-gallon drums or old Basco transformers. We'd already sampled the area, though, and found nothing at all.

What would that prove anyway? It wouldn't help with the real mysteries—why my analysis was all fucked up; why Gallagher was sick.

Maybe it wasn't PCBs at all. Maybe some other form of organic chlorine, that didn't taste oily, didn't show up in our analysis. That was the only plausible way for those guys to get poisoned. I could be dealing with two separate problems here: a busted transformer dumped thirty years ago by Basco, causing oily traps, and some other kind of subtle, nasty waste-dumping, something really new and vicious. New technologies were being invented all the time out on Route 128, and new forms of toxic waste along with them. Maybe someone was using the CSO system to get rid of their corporate shit—flushing it down the toilet during heavy rains, knowing it would immediately overflow into the Harbor and never be noticed down at the sewage treatment plants. It was coming from one of Dorchester Bay CSOs and contaminating lobsters in that area.

That was the thing to look for, then. Take a sample from Dorchester Bay and analyze it. Analyze it every which way, look for every damn thing under the sun: bromine and fluorine and the other compounds that could mimic chlorine. If nothing else, it would help me rule out this new hypothesis. And if I found something, I could trace it to a particular CSO, and then I had the criminals by the balls. Each CSO drains a specific set of toilets in a specific part of town. By lifting the right manhole covers, paying a lot of attention to my sewer maps, I could trace the trail right back to the perpetrator.

This strategy had another advantage as well: I wouldn't have to dive as deep. Diving just isn't my thing. Under normal conditions it's scary enough, but diving at night, in murky water, with no backup—that was fucking stupid. I was only doing it because I knew I wouldn't be able to relax until I did something. So I anchored my Zodiac a hundred feet off the shore and worked from there.

First I just found the bottom and nosed around some. In front of me was a CSO that had littered the bottom with condoms, toilet paper and other sewage for at least half a mile out. Behind me, I suspected, was a huge PCB spill. In between was total confusion: lobsters saturated with poison, bottom sludge that was utterly clean, clean-looking lobsters that gave massive doses of chloracne to the people who ate them.

There was a lobster crawling on an old oil drum right in front of me. I gave the drum a poke with my knife and it crumbled; there couldn't be anything in there. Then the lobster and I did hand-to-hand combat. I pretended it was Laughlin. Couldn't smell it or taste it, but I had enough time to chop it open and find its liver.

It had no liver, just sacs of oil, like the one Tanya had found. I scooped its viscera into a jar and took it with me. Maybe it was PCBs, maybe something completely different. So I swam into the shallow water and mucked around a little, breaking the water every so often to get my bearings, until I'd located the CSO pipe. Thank God it wasn't raining.

Having taken a good jarful of sludge from right under the pipe, I surfaced, trod water and studied the shoreline. I needed to know which CSO I was dealing with here, triangulating off the positions of U. Mass, South Boston High, Summer Street, and other landmarks. When I was convinced I could pin this place down on a map, I decided to call it a day.

While I was heading for the Zodiac I heard a propeller, or maybe more than one, and that bothered me because when I broke the water earlier, I hadn't been able to see any running lights. Somebody was nearby, using the fog to hide, and I had to guess he was hiding from me.

So I started one very slow orbit, and that's how I found the Cigarette. Sitting there with its motor idling, just far enough away that I couldn't see it from the Zode. It could see me because it was running dark. But the lights on my boat would splash against the surrounding fog and make it impossible for me to see them.

What now? I could try to get a close look at them. But they might have a negative attitude about that. Somehow I didn't relish my chances if they decided to chase me down. Besides, I was running out of air, and I couldn't stay underwater that much longer.

I could abandon the Zode and swim to shore on the surface, but why abandon ten thousand bucks worth of GEE equipment? These guys were just watching me. And they'd been watching me for a long time. I'd even provoked them once before, and all they did was run away. I didn't burn down my house when the FBI bugged it, did I?

So the only sensible idea was to go back to the Zode and proceed normally. But that's exactly what they were expecting me to do. It irritates the hell out of me to be in a situation where I'm forced to do exactly what's expected. But when you run out of air, you run out of air.

The best tactic was stealth. I swam back under the surface, broke the water on the far side of the Zode, in case they were using infrared, and started to take my stuff off while remaining in the water. My one concession to paranoia was dropping some gear: I just let the empty tank sink to the bottom because hauling it up into the Zode would be noisy and time consuming. Same with the clanky weight belt. It was just some chunks of lead and a nylon strap.

The problem was that I had to haul myself up into the boat. I weighed more than all that other crap together. Getting over the side of the Zode wasn't like hopping over a fence. It was more like sumo wrestling in a pool filled with Crisco.

So I tried to be quiet about it until I accidently made a godawful amount of noise, and then I just tried to be quick about it. And at about the same time, I heard the Cigarette's engines rev up, heard it being thrown into gear. That scared the shit out of me and I waddled to the back of the Zode and began hauling on the ripcord, trying to start up the outboard. I hauled on it like a maniac about three times, felt something pop in my back, and then the Cigarette materialized like a ghost, shiny and blue and slippery, and I finally got to look

at the owners. They were wearing ski masks. One of them
was driving and the other was staring at me through unnat-
urally large binoculars. These were high-tech, Route 128
thugs: they had me on infrared. The driver's eyes glinted pale
blue; Kleinhoffer or Dietrich. The other one set his binocs
down and aimed a gun at me.

I remembered having tried to pistol-shoot at Jim Grandfather's, noticing how hard it actually was, after having
watched TV and movies my whole life, to actually hit something with a handgun. These guys were on a small boat and
so was I. I didn't figure they were going to nail me with one
shot. Which didn't prevent me from being scared shitless;
when I saw the gun, I fell back on my ass, tipping the whole
Zode up. The Cigarette overshot me and had to turn around
for another pass.

That gave me time to notice a little surprise they'd left behind: a pair of small darts stuck into the side of my Zodiac,
and they were sputtering at me, throwing off a transparent
bluish light. I'd heard about this from Dolmacher. It was a
Tazer. If I hadn't fallen back, those darts would be stuck in
my skin and that electrical charge would be running through
my nervous system. And I'd be unconscious, or wishing I was,
long enough for them to rev up and run over me in their
Cigarette at about eighty miles an hour. Sorry, officer, it was
foggy.

The wake of the Cigarette was throwing the Zode around
like a teeter-totter. Something heavy smashed into my foot.
It was our big nautical strobe light. So when the Cigarette
cruised by me for the second attempt, I turned the strobe on,
held it over my head like a basketball, and made a three-
point jump shot right into their cockpit.

"Nice second effort, boys!" I hollered. The light had half-
blinded me, too, but I didn't need perfect vision to start the
motor. They needed it to take a shot at me.

Time for another try at the motor. This time I did it right:
set the throttle on START and choked it. Three more hauls on
the ripcord and it started.

Then it died. I put the choke back in and hauled once
more, getting a good start. I had to lean way over to shift it
into forward gear and that's how I got tossed out of the boat.

Kleinhoffer and Dietrich weren't total losers. While they were clearing the purple spots out of their vision they could buzz me and throw me around with their thousand-horsepower wake. It had succeeded beyond their wildest dreams. I had gotten the Zode into forward gear, but I got tangled up with the throttle handle when I was tumbling out, so now the motor was cocked all the way over to one side. It was puttering around in tight little circles, a little faster than I could swim. The Cigarette came around once more and I had to assume that Old Deadeye was using his infrared specs. If it had been calm they would have seen me instantly, but tonight, thank God, it was a little choppy.

The immediate problem was that my throat and nose were full of water and I hated to draw attention to myself by coughing and sneezing it out. So I tucked my head under the surface, blew some of it out and swallowed the rest. Yummy. Then I didn't have any air in my lungs so I had to come up and breathe.

My turn for a break. The Zodiac was spiraling in my direction. I just tried to present a small target, to look like a wave, and to dogpaddle toward it. The Cigarette was tearing back and forth, trying to locate my head with its propellers.

This went on maybe ten minutes. Between trying to breathe, trying to hide, coping with the tsunami wakes of the Cigarette and trying to get closer to the Zodiac, it was hard to keep track of time.

The Zodiac's bow rope brushed over my leg and I grabbed it. That was a nice reminder: if I let it trail behind me, it would get caught in the propeller. What other useful tips had Artemis given me? One thing for damn sure: take it reasonably easy; don't give it full throttle right off the bat or it would just do a backflip and toss me into the Harbor again.

Finally I got the prow of the Zodiac right up in my face, waited for the Cigarette to overshoot me, then threw myself up over the nose and into the boat. That was the theory, anyway. In reality it took a little longer than that so, as I was crawling on my hands and knees back toward the outboard, I looked up and saw the Cigarette cruising by me, slow and methodical, and I saw that Tazer gun pointed in my direction.

The gun didn't make any sound. I didn't even know I was hit until I felt a hot buzzing sensation in the arm of my wetsuit. But that was all I felt.

"You assholes," I shouted, "it's a rubber suit!"

Artemis would have been proud: I throttled it up slowly, establishing a stable attitude in the water. Then I ripped it open and blew right past the bow of the Cigarette. It was choppy, but not that bad, and I was aiming for Zodiac nirvana here: the boat airborne, just the screw in the water. At that speed, the water might as well be asphalt. The Cigarette slices through it, the Zodiac just skitters—like being dragged down a cobblestone street by forty rabid mustangs.

If I could just make it out of Dorchester Bay and out toward Castle Island Park, I could take dead aim at the heart of downtown. Then I'd cross a small channel, cut past navy territory, and then I'd be passing the ends of the south Boston piers, all in a nice line. The worst part was the first, where I had nothing to protect me, but I'd covered half of it by the time the Cigarette caught up. They came after me dark, running a zigzag search pattern through the fog and, when I was almost to Castle Island Park, they found me.

Then it was raw power versus maneuverability. They tried to cut across my bow and swamp me, but I spun away from them, did a two-hundred-seventy-degree turn, went airborne off their wake, half fell out of the boat and cut in behind them, the water clawing at my right leg. They recovered faster than they wanted to and ended up ahead of me— shades of Buffalo—so I fell back into the Zode, aimed for their asshole, and throttled it up. They headed into a turn—a very fast turn, but slower than me. We turned and turned, me spiraling round right behind them, sticking to the calm spot in the center of their wake. They twisted it the other way, trying to shake me, and I followed them in the other direction until I saw the lights of downtown swinging past. Time to turn the corner. I broke out of the curve and drilled the throttle.

They tried to spin, got slapped around by their own wake for a little, then cranked it up to about twice my speed and came for me like a Sidewinder missile. They were trying the same attack, but this time I knew it. Jived left, spun right, cut directly in front of them, just missed being sliced in two by that samurai sword of a hull, and pulled the same trick: whipped around and cut behind them. They were trying to reverse direction so I blew them off and aimed for the sky-scrapers.

The assholes should have realized I'd be wearing rubber. It was an excellent plan, though. Like something I would think up, if I was Laughlin.

Environmentalist Dies in Bizarre Hit-and-Run Boating Accident
Self-Styled Maverick Was Cavalier About Safety Procedures

I faked them out by sprinting in the direction of the air-port, half a mile away, and when they bit, I flipped a hairpin turn and shot past them in the opposite direction, close enough to see the whites of their eyes. That gave me enough room to make it across the navy channel, and they almost lost me again in the fog.

I'd made it to the piers of South Boston, goddamn it, and it was low tide. The low tide was going to save my life. The piers stood up on piles and I could squeeze between them.

Time for some serious Zodiac abuse. I was hanging onto the Zode in about six different ways because the piles kept trying to punch it out from under me. I was flying every which way, like riding a bronco, so the barnacles on those piles left a nice series of parallel gashes in my hands and arms. Long years of video-game experience were coming into play. I just kept worrying about the next set of piles, cutting and jiving through the gaps, ducking under the occasional strut. Cigarettes aren't made for that particular kind of abuse, so all they could do was parallel me and then try to cut me off when the piers came to an end and I had to emerge into the Harbor again.

But that was like a defensive lineman trying to stand in the way of a running back. A fake here, a fake there, and there's just no way to do it. I screamed past with them no more than ten feet away, because it's harder to draw a bead on something that's going by close and fast—ask any Indian circling a wagon train—and then I swung around, heading inland again. I was all done with Southie; downtown was a hundred yards away.

Paranoia is my way of life, and for a couple of weeks, some creeps had been shadowing me in a big powerful speedboat. I'd lost sleep, irritated Debbie and wasted a lot of gasoline because of these creeps. Instead of sleeping I had sprawled on my bed trying to think of what I would do if they ever came after me. In other words, I wasn't unprepared for this. I'd given it some thought.

So I knew exactly how to send these bastards to their graves: lead them into the Fort Point Channel at high velocity.

Boston used to be just a round island at the end of a sandbar. The airport, Back Bay, and much of Southie's waterfront are all artificial land. The bay between Southie and downtown Boston had been narrowed until it was just a slit—a canal, really—called Fort Point Channel. It was only a couple hundred yards wide, and it was no place to race speedboats. It was spanned with several bridges and completely fouled with old, half-rotten pilings. In its one-mile length it had more snags and shallows and lurking dangers than any hundred miles of the Mississippi. Like a riverboat pilot, I knew where all that shit was. I could navigate this channel at full speed with my eyes closed. Or so I'd bragged. This was my chance to find out.

First I got them excited, acted like I wanted to head home toward the yacht club, made a desperate break for the airport, got cut off both ways. Got them going very fast in the wrong direction, then broke the opposite way and just headed for the Channel at a flat sprint. Finally broke the motor in—hit full throttle—never thought I'd be that scared of anything. So I had a quarter of a mile lead before they even got turned around. I knew that Deadeye was looking right through the fog with his infrared specs, zeroing in on the heat signature of my motor, which must be blazing like a nova. He found me, probably fading fast, and his partner did exactly the right thing: leaned on the throttle, asked for all thousand horsepower, and got it. They hauled ass into the Channel, passed under the Northern Avenue Bridge, and I led them right through the safe part so they wouldn't even know they were in mortal danger. They were driving right up my ass when I led them toward a picket fence of foot-thick pilings next to the Boston Tea Party ship. I pulled into a violent turn and the Zode went between them, on its side. Then I got out of the way.

They plowed into the pilings doing upwards of sixty miles an hour. Their sexy fiberglass hull shattered like a potato chip in a meat grinder. Those big oversize motors took a lot of gasoline and all of it exploded at once. I remember one of the big outboards tumbling through space like a comet, trailing pale blue flames, its screw cutting on air. The Cigarette was a big boat going fast, and it took a long time for all that crap to stop moving.

Myself, I crossed the Channel and got onto dry land at the Summer Street Bridge. I squatted on the shore for a while, watching the flames coming up off the water. Then I wandered up into civilization, stood in the road and flagged down a BMW. It overshot me a little bit so I got to see the SAVE THE WHALES sticker on the rear bumper. A young guy in a suit climbed out. "What's burning?" he said. "Are you okay?"

"I am. You got a tire patch kit in that thing?"

"You bet." The guy even knew my full name. We carried his kit down to the water and fixed the Tazer holes in my Zodiac. Then he got back in his BMW and drove away. I told him he didn't even have to think about donating more money to GEE this year.

22

EVEN THESE PUSSWADS couldn't afford to own more than one Cigarette, so I figured I was okay as long as I stayed on the water. The yacht club was definitely not an option, but I could come ashore just about anywhere else.

So I took the Zode up and out of Fort Point Channel and up to the Aquarium docks, where I found a pay phone.

"What's up?" Bartholomew asked.

Where to begin? "Well, I just killed some guys."

For once he didn't say anything, just sat there uncomfortably silent, and I realized that this was a stupid way to commence a conversation. "Look, how many people are at the house this evening?"

"Just me. Roscommon's banging on something downstairs. Shut off our water."

"Could you track the others down?"

"I think maybe. Why?"

"Because everyone should stay away from the house for a while. Somebody's trying to kill me."

"Again?"

"Yeah. But for real this time."

"You call the cops?"

Of course. When people try to kill you, you're supposed to call the cops. Why hadn't I done that? "Don't let anyone in. I'll get back to you in a minute."

Then I called the cops. They sent a detective around to the Aquarium and we sat there beside the Seal Pool for a while. I gave them a statement. A harbor seal sat behind us the whole time, looking up at us and shouting, "Thunderbird, Thunderbird!" The bums who hung out around the Seal Pool were skilled instructors. "Spare change? Spare change?" But the detective had the courtesy to concentrate on me. Didn't see much point in trying to explain all the stuff with the PCBs, since all I had was conflicting evidence. I just told them I was taking some samples and these guys tried to kill me.

Then I called Bart again. He was still sitting there watching the same Stooges flick and I could still hear Roscommon's thuds resounding from the basement.

"I feel like a sap. Why don't I own a gun?" I asked rhetorically.

"Beats me. I don't have one either."

Actually, I knew the answer. I didn't own a gun because then I'd look like a terrorist. And because, hell, I didn't need one. "You got any plans for tonight?" I asked.

"No more than usual," Bart said. "Amy's in New York."

"There's a chance that, if I get crazy enough, I'll ask you to drive me around all night sewer-diving and possibly being chased by amateur hit men."

"Whatever."

I buzzed off into the darkness again, going a little slower now, trying to keep my head on straight. Paused at MIT and ran to the office to get the manhole lifter, a bandolier of test tubes and a bucket on a rope. Went across the river and re-emerged at the university. Went straight to the lab and ran a test on the sample I'd just taken from the Dorchester Bay CSO.

It was stuffed with organic chlorine compounds. Not just PCBs, but a whole stew of venality. To go back to the gunboat metaphor, what we had here was soldiers with machine guns, riding not just on patrol boats, but on surfboards, Zodiacs, water skis and inner tubes. All the compounds were polycyclic aromatics—carbon atoms in six-packs, twelve-packs, and cases. Some kind of crap was definitely getting dumped out of the CSO.

Tomorrow it was going to rain—a big storm coming in from the Atlantic—and the sewers were going to overflow. If there was any evidence in them, it was bound to be washed out to sea. So now was the time for executive-hunting. I called my roommate and asked him to meet me under the birdshit, then I hung up.

It was a fifteen-minute walk from our house on the Brighton side of the river to the mall on the other side. Along the way we had to walk below an overpass, a highway bridge made of metal girders. For some reason, pigeons happened to like those girders very much, and the sidewalk underneath was thick with birdshit. This was a reference only Bart would understand.

For me, it was just a pleasant nighttime cruise on the river. The fog had cleared off as the wind had risen, and now the air was cold and smelled cleaner than it was. It was a chance to relax, get my head clear.

The Charles wasn't as bad as it used to be. From here it seemed like the Main Street of civilization. Beacon Hill behind me, Harvard ahead, MIT on one side and Fenway Park on the other. After playing fatal video games on the Harbor, it was comforting to go for a slow putt-putt out here, watch the traffic on the riverside boulevards—comfortable, normal people in nice cars, listening to the radio—and stare into the lights of the university libraries, and listen to the Sox hounds celebrating a run-scoring double.

Within a few minutes, Harvard came up on the right, dark and ancient, with a neon corona rising up from Harvard Square behind it. Then around a bend, and suddenly the Charles was narrow, just a minor river surrounded by trees. Past the big cemeteries, then the IHOP reared up on the left and I tied my Zodiac to a tree. A short hike took me to the birdshit, and, voilá, there was the van, sitting there dark, ZZ Top rumbling from within. Bart opened the door, which was nice, because that way I didn't have to wonder who really was inside.

"Anyone follow you?"

"If they did," he said, "they did a good job of it. You have any more trouble?"

"No."

"Hey. Check this out." He unzipped his leather jacket and pulled it open to reveal a .38 Special stuck in his belt.

"Where the fuck did you get that?"

"Roscommon."

"*Roscommon?*"

"Once, when he got really pissed, he started threatening me. Told me that he had an equalizer in his car. So after you called, I just went out and busted the window and took it."

"There's beauty in that, Bart."

Call me a fool, but I felt a lot tougher now. We pulled the van onto the grass along the river beside Soldiers Fields Road, and hauled up the Zodiac's gas tanks and the outboard motor. We put them in the van and then put the Zodiac on top and tied it down. We went to the IHOP and got big fat coffees to go. Then we turned up the stereo and went out sewer-diving.

This I had done before. Put me in the sewers and I'm in my element. The tendency of Boston's sewers to gush directly into the Harbor whenever more than three drops of rain fell made them an ideal place for companies to dump their hazardous waste without the embarrassment of a mediapathic pipe. Sometimes I'd discover a bad thing coming out of a CSO and then I'd have to go on one of these expeditions. Bart knew the drill.

The principle is simple. If there's poison coming out of a sewer, you should be able to trace it to its source. It helps to have a map of all the sewer lines and where they feed into one another. I find the CSO on my sewer map and, just like that, I know which neighborhood it's coming from. Once I get to that neighborhood, my map tells me where the key manholes are and, by running tests under those manholes, I can narrow it down even further.

Besides a manhole tool, the only requirement is some kind of quick, simple test for the presence of the toxin you're tracing. Preferably it's a test you can perform right in your vehicle. I had something like that for organic chlorine compounds, a test built into small plastic test tubes. They were about the size of shotgun shells, so when this whole mess had started I'd made up several dozen and stashed them in an army-surplus bandolier. With that slung over my shoulder and my manhole cracker in my hands, I was a toxic Rambo, prepared to rain media death upon the bad guys. We were all set.

It wasn't that romantic, though. I sat down in the back with my coffee and a penlight while Bart drove around aimlessly on the Mass Pike, trying to determine if we were being tailed. I studied my sewer map. Dorchester Bay had many CSOs and I had to figure out which one of them I'd been looking at. My technique was kind of like Boy Scout orienteering. I was about four blocks over from Summer Street, I knew how a couple of landmarks happened to line up, and that allowed me to figure my position on the map.

My toxic CSO wasn't just any CSO, certainly not of the neighborhood variety. It wasn't even a Boston CSO. It was the outlet of a long tunnel that ran all the way from Framingham, out in the extreme southwestern suburbs. Framingham had no place to dump its overflow—they didn't even have a river—and they'd had to construct an underground river that ran for some twenty miles east-northeast to Dorchester Bay. Overflow from Framingham and the neighboring town of Natick ran down that pipe. Somewhere along those twenty miles, someone was throwing huge amounts of organic chlorine compounds into the flow.

I was tempted to go straight to Natick and start sampling there. Although it's a little outside Route 128, it is prime territory for Route 128 corporations. But there was also a chance that someone had tapped into the line between Natick and the outlet. If we got out that far, ran a test and found nothing, we'd have wasted an hour driving out and back. So I traced the tunnel eastwards and picked out a promising manhole in a Boston street. We would start there.

"Roxbury, James," I said.

"Oh, good. Right near the museum, right?"

"Wishful thinking. It's a mile south of here."

"Oh. You mean for real Roxbury."

"Sorry, that's where the tunnel is."

Let me explain something about Bart: he wasn't as dumb

as he sounded. He had a sense of irony that ruled his life, made it impossible for him to use his considerable brains in any kind of serious job. Kind of like me.

We didn't know how to get there and had to find it by reputation—"don't go down that street any farther—it'll take you right into Roxbury." We had to follow a bunch of that kind of streets.

But eventually we found our manhole. It was in the right land of a four-lane street. I had Bart pull just past it, then I threw open the back doors of the van, reached out and snared the lid with my tool and hauled. It took some doing but I got it off. I climbed down in there with my bucket-on-a-rope and had Bart back up to conceal the hole. He closed up those back doors and switched on the emergency flashers.

The main thing was not to act like a pair of scared, lost, white guys. Bart was pretty good at it. In his black leather and his black van, with his longish hair and loud music, he clearly was not a lawyer with a flat tire.

Plus, I had my part of it down to a science. I went down the ladder, braced myself so my hands were free, lowered the bucket on the rope and took my sample. Took a leak, too. Twenty seconds' work. Then back up the ladder. But I could hear the roar of a radiator fan, I could see headlights in the van's undercarriage. Someone was pulling up behind us. And until the van moved, I was trapped in the manhole.

Door slam. Footsteps. Knock, knock. Music turned down, window descended.

"Can I help you officer?"

I didn't know how to take that. Cops.

"You have a problem here?" Old white Townie voice. I could draw you a sketch of this cop without having seen him: fifty, stubby iron-colored hair, a big, solid spare tire.

"Stalled the engine and my battery's too low to turn it over now. And I know this is a bad neighborhood, officer, so I just rolled up the windows and locked the doors and waited for one of you guys to show up."

"Good move, son, you did the right thing. Hey, Freddy! Bring her around here."

Freddy moved the cop car up and they performed the jump-start. I relaxed. Right above my head was more evidence of Bart's concealed intelligence: he'd gotten one of those magnetic key holders, and hid some spare keys in the undercarriage of the van. "Okay, now get out of here, kid!"

"Okay! I'm just gonna sit here idling for a few minutes and let the battery recharge, okay?"

"Son, if you don't mind, I'd prefer to escort you right out of this neighborhood." Wonderful idea from my point of view.

"Hey, I appreciate that, officer, but it's okay. I got an equalizer in here."

"Okay. Well, don't press your luck. This ain't your part of town."

"Thanks again!" And then, deliverance. Bart pulled the van forward; I got out and replaced the lid; and we were the fuck out of there. Not a single gang even looked our way. Bart had to be physically restrained from stopping at a Louisiana catfish restaurant for a 1:00 A.M. dinner.

I pointed him west, toward Brookline, and ran my test in the back. Positive for organic chlorine poisoning. The crooks were west of us. My prejudices were well-founded.

To be fully scientific I should have stopped at every manhole between Roxbury and Natick, following the trail, but sometimes you have to take your science with a grain of salt. First there was Brookline. Not the scummy northern part of Brookline with its two-hundred-thousand-dollar condos. The nice part, with its fifty-room slate-roofed mansions. Then there was Newton, where Roscommon lived, where every front door was flanked by Greek columns. The folks in Brookline and Newton weren't dumping organic chlorine compounds into the sewers; they were making their money from doing it.

We drove straight to southern Newton for another check. Getting samples was tricky out here because there were even more cops, and just owning a black van was reason enough for a life sentence. I'd had success before, though, just on pure balls. "Yes, officer, I'm Sangamon Taylor with GEE International, we're working on a sanctioned investigation here [whatever that meant] tracking down illegal dumping in the [insert name of town] sewer system. You live in this town, officer? You have children? Noticed any behavioral changes lately, any strange rashes on the abdomen? Good. I'm glad to hear it. Well, it looks like my assistant is just about finished, thanks for your help."

We had to check three manholes before we made a bingo. Newton had its very own sewer system with its own manholes, which made things confusing. I was forced to deploy the above-mentioned speech while Bart was checking number two. Usually it was hard to convince them that you worked for a real environmental group, but the Zodiac on top of the van, with GEE in orange letters, made it all look plausible. I'd have to remember that trick. Word got out on the radio, and at manhole number three, a cop actually stood there and directed traffic around us while we worked.

Which doesn't necessarily mean we fooled them, but they could see we weren't out to cause trouble, and things went a lot more smoothly when they stood there with their flashing lights. And that's mainly what a cop wants: things to go smoothly.

More organic chlorine. We headed west. Once we got out into Wellesley we were sampling more often. That got us into the city limits of Natick, and this was where things got really tricky. Until now, we'd been following a single line, but here the possibilities were branching out in every direction and it was necessary to check manholes at every branch.

My maps didn't run this far out, so things got primitive: drive around slow, look for manholes in the street, scratch your head. We got lost immediately, just past Lake Waban, did a lot of U-turns and sketching of diagrams on the old McDonald's napkins in the back. We sort of thought that there was a major branch here—a lot of Natick sewer lines feeding into the big tunnel.

"This is going to take fucking forever," Bart pointed out. By now it was three in the morning and we had about eight manholes to check.

"Hang on for a sec," I said. There was a 7-Eleven half a block away and I trotted over and scoped out their phone book.

All they had was a white pages, so it was kind of a random search. I was trying to think of all the prefixes that high-tech companies give themselves. "Electro," "Tec," "Dyna,"

"Mega," "Micro." In ten minutes or so, I had found half a dozen of those, and the last one had an interesting address: "100 TechDale."

TechDale had to be some kind of high-tech industrial park. I looked it up by name: TECHDALE DEVELOPMENTS, followed by an office address in downtown Wellesley and one for their development in Natick.

And then, gods of Science forgive me, I couldn't help it. It was biased thinking, but I couldn't help it. I looked up Biotronics Incorporated. They had a facility in Natick, alright: 204 TechDale.

Inside the 7-Eleven they sold maps of the area. TechDale was so new it hadn't shown up on the maps yet, but the clerk showed me where it was: a couple of miles away on Cochituate Avenue, out in the direction of the lake by the same name. I spread the map out on the counter and simply traced Cochituate Avenue backwards toward us. It crossed our path a quarter of a mile away. We'd already driven up and down it a couple of times, and found a manhole in it.

I got back into the van. "We want the manhole on Cochituate Avenue," I said. "Over there."

"Why do you say that?"

"Prejudice. Sheer blind prejudice."

"You think black people did it? Is that why we were in Roxbury?"

We checked the manhole. It was the right one. The chlorine was still there.

Or so I told myself, because I was tired and we were running out of time. What I had was a substance in a test tube that would turn red in the presence of organic chlorine compounds. When I used it on the Dorchester Bay sample, or the Roxbury sample, it came out looking like burgundy wine. This last sample looked a little more like rosé. The concentration was getting weaker as we approached the source. And that didn't make a damn bit of sense. Obviously it should've been the other way around. I could think of a few bizarre hypotheses to explain it, but they sounded like the work of a pathological liar.

This, friends and neighbors, was depressing as hell. As we moved west on Cochituate Avenue, the concentration kept decreasing. The toxin was still there, definitely at illegal levels, but it was doing the wrong thing.

We tested it on one side of a residential subdivision and it was high enough to be illegal. We tested it on the other side and it wasn't there at all. We'd lost the trail.

"So they don't want to dump right from the company property. They put it into tank trucks. They drive a couple of miles to the subdivision with the curvy streets. The trucks drive down the streets dumping the shit into the gutters."

We drove down every street in that fucking division and didn't see anything. We tested its sewer system and didn't even find a trace.

"Explain that to me, goddammit," I shouted at Bart. "Upstream of the houses, no chlorine. Downstream, there's chlorine. We check the place where the houses dump their shit into the stream, and there's no chlorine there either. So where the fuck does it come from?"

Bart just looked out the windshield and tapped his steering wheel to the beat of the radio. He was tired.

"Let's see what else is on Cochituate Avenue," I said. He shifted into gear without a word. We drove one more mile and arrived at TechDale.

I'd seen these things before. They looked just like suburban housing developments, with the same irritating maze of curved streets, but instead of houses, they had big boxy industrial buildings, and instead of lawns, parking lots. We coasted to a stop and read the logos on the buildings, and about half of them all said the same thing: Biotronics.

"Well, I'll be dipped in shit," Bart said.

"I've already tried that," I mumbled, watching the horizon think about letting the sun come up.

Instead of cruising around this well-scrubbed development at four in the morning in our battered black van with an environmetal group's Zodiac strapped to its roof, we pulled in at a gas station-café on Route 9, just a couple of blocks away. We topped off the van and filled up the Zodiac's tanks with 50:1 mix, all on the GEE gold card. We went in for more coffee. What the fuck, we scarfed down tremendous breakfasts and punched some tunes on the jukebox. We struck up a warm relationship with our waitress, Marlene. We asked her about the industrial park and she started rattling off the names of the occupants.

". . . and then there's Biotronics. But we don't see much of them."

"Why? What's different about Biotronics?"

"Safety regs. They have to take a shower when they go in every morning, scrub with disinfectant, and again when they go out. So it's kind of a hassle for them to come over here for lunch."

"You want to go in there, before it gets light?" Bart said when Marlene had disappeared. My respect for the man continued to grow; he was ready for just about anything.

"You'd make a great terrorist," I said, "or criminal."

"Look who's talking."

"No. If we got caught, we wouldn't have any toxic evidence to back us up. Shit! I can't believe this. I was all ready to phone up all my media contacts. It's the same thing as with the PCBs in the lobsters. I have hard evidence, I start tracking it down and it slips through my fingers. Like picking up a handful of sludge: squeeze too hard and you loose it."

"That must be nice. Phone up all the newspapers and start a crusade."

"Credibility, my man. Carefully and slowly accumulated through years of being almost right. If I say anything now, I'll have none at all."

I considered hanging out here and waiting for Dolmacher to drive by, but it was too much wait for too little gratification. I wanted to see the look on his face when he saw our van sitting outside his Grail factory like the Grim Reaper's chariot. But I had nothing to back up the threat. It was time to get up and beat the rush hour and coast home.

23

WHICH IS WHAT WE DID. There was a nice blue heap of shattered safety glass out in front, where Bart had busted into Roscommon's car. Tess's car wasn't there, which was good. She was steering clear from trouble, our house.

I had a little trepidation about finding a bomb or something in there, but it was paranoia. We'd beefed up all the doors and windows, making the place hard to break into. Anyone could have broken in, of course, but they'd have to cause some obvious damage in the doing and there wasn't any of that. So we went in and filled a couple Heftys. The answering machine was blinking. We stood around it with our Heftys, breathing and listening, doing lip-synch impressions of the voices on the tape.

"S.T., this is Tess. What the fuck is going on? Please call me at Sal's. The number's in the back of the phone book."

Beeep.

"Uh . . . this is Roscommon. I hate these machines. Don't go into the basement. It's, uh, dangerous now—got some exposed electrical cables and there's water on the floor. So I nailed the door shut. Don't try busting in there, you hear me? Or else you're out of there. You're fucking out on your ass."

Beeep.

"This is Domino's. Is Bart there? He ordered some pizza and we're calling to double-check the order."

Beeep.

"It's Debbie. It's about 1:00 A.M. Look, I borrowed the Omni and took it to a party, and then I drove it home and someone ripped it off. I can't believe this is happening. I heard something outside, looked out the window, there was a big guy out there—in a suit—and there was a big black car waiting next to him, and this guy just got into the car with keys and started it up and drove away. They already had keys made."

Beeep.

"Your house has a huge fucking bomb in the basement. Get out, now."

Beeep.

"Hi, this is Dolmacher . . ." but I missed the rest because Bart was throwing a chair through a window.

About ten seconds later my train set got scattered all over Brighton and points downward. We were lying down in Boston's largest backyard, behind a heap of Roscommon's concrete trash. A few pieces of his stupid vinyl siding fluttered down on our backs, but that was it.

I got an A in chemistry and I could tell it wasn't a gas explosion. It was high explosives. Planted there the night before. Which meant it had been done with Roscommon's help. But why would he help? Because they were big. Big enough to make him an offer he couldn't refuse—a Bascosized organization—and because he wanted to get rid of this house anyway.

BRIGHTON BOMB FACTORY EXPLODES, KILLING 2
FBI SAYS TAYLOR WAS ACTUALLY A TERRORIST
"DIRECT-ACTION" CAMPAIGNS A COVER FOR
VIOLENCE?

Bart rolled over on his back. "Intense," he said.

I yanked the revolver out of his belt, grabbed it by the barrel, and laid open his right eyebrow. I grabbed his keys and ran for the van.

"I Thought S.T. Was Man of Peace,"
Says Shocked Roommate.
GEE TERRORIST'S DESPERATE ESCAPE FROM BOMB SITE
INSIDE: *Sangaman Taylor: Jekyll & Hyde Personality?*

While I was headed crosstown, it started to rain. Downtown there was a waterfront park and that's where I assembled the Zodiac. Out on the water, a coast guard cutter was towing an eighty-foot pleasure palace out away from a yacht club, into the open water.

GEE Car Found Near Yacht Club
ABANDONED IN MINING ATTEMPT?

I recognized the yacht; Alvin Pleshy liked to go fishing in it. It was being shadowed by a couple of fireboats and cops were swarming around on the decks.

PLESHY'S TERROR CRUISE
S.T.'S BOMBS ON EX-V.P.'S YACHT
"He hated Pleshy from the beginning"

I just took it out of there nice and easy, didn't crank up the throttle until I was out past the airport, and then ran full tilt until all I could see was waves, and rain, and rain—a Nor' easter bearing down from Greenland. A big blue nasty-looking son of a bitch. We had an exposure suit in there, so I pulled it on, then crammed myself back into my Levi's so I wouldn't be so fucking orange. I pointed her north, into the stormclouds, into the waves. Nothing could find me in that. Not Cigarettes, not CG cutters, neither helicopters nor satellites.

Or so I thought until the helicopter gunship came up on my stern.

This was just what I was afraid of. Once they pinned the terrorist label on me, they didn't have to screw around with cops and warrants anymore. Life during wartime.

It was one of the new ones with the incredibly skinny bodies, the occupants sitting virtually on top of each other. A guy on top to fly it, a guy on the bottom to manage all those guns, missiles, bombs and rockets.

They couldn't possibly fly through this shit. The rain was

just starting to come down heavy, we had a forty- or fifty-knot headwind. But I was remembering a rescue operation in the spring when they plucked some Soviets off a freighter in weather this bad.

Of course, the freighter had been stationary. I sure as hell wasn't. I'd long since stopped cutting through the waves and started riding up and down them. The water doesn't actually move; the surface of it just goes up and down. So if you're in a Zodiac, and you head into a thirty-foot roller—like that one, right in front of me—you are going up, skipper. Fast. And then you're going down, virtually in free fall. As soon as you bottom out, the acceleration squashes you into the floorboards again and you're on your way up, leaving your stomach somewhere down between your testes. If your boat is strong enough to handle the G-forces, you're fine. Otherwise it just gets thrust beneath the surface and breaks apart. That wasn't about to happen to the Zodiac.

First I thought a bolt of red lightning had struck, but actually it was a river of Gatling gun fire digging a hole in the wave right in front of me, or was it above me? When there is no horizon, you can never tell. This was called firing across the bow. A warning.

But it was too kind to call it a river of fire. It was a series of tentative spurts, all in different places, kind of like my first orgasm. One of those spurts landed about thirty feet behind/below me, and I got to thinking maybe it wasn't a warning at all. Maybe it was just poor workmanship.

Just for the hell of it, I tried sighting down my index finger, tried to see if I could keep it aimed at that helicopter. And it was impossible, I couldn't even keep my eyes aimed at it. Those poor bastards couldn't shoot straight. They didn't have a hope.

I figured this out as the water was tossing me full into the air, into free fall off a liquid cliff. A big gust of wind hit me at the top and almost flipped the boat over. I saw a wall of black rain from that vantage point, and then all I could see was the next wave; it was bigger. The chopper was a few yards away, I could look the bastards right in the goggles. Then it was far above me, twisting in a gust, and I almost lost sight. Which meant they could lose me. So I tried to head diagonally away from them.

Anyway, it didn't matter, because they couldn't hit me with any of that firepower. Not in this. So I flipped them the bird—maybe they'd pick it up on infrared—and headed for Maine. I had full tanks to run on, and they'd take me fifty miles. All the raindrops in the sky suddenly merged. I didn't see the chopper again.

I ran out of gas half a mile off the coast sometime before noon. It was time to start hitting the LSD. I'd been up for more than twenty-four hours, I hurt real bad, I'd thrown my back out hauling on that ripcord and now I had to paddle this son of a bitch through a rainstorm. Fortunately the swell had gone down to about five feet. I was carrying the acid on a sheet of paper in my wallet, a sheet of blotter paper with a bogus map drawn on it, stuck behind Debbie's graduation picture. When I took it out, I sat and looked at that photo for a while and started crying. A poor, utterly fucked, duck-squeezer castaway, bobbing in the Atlantic, soaking in the rain, sobbing over his girlfriend.

That went on for about ten minutes and then I put a little corner of the paper into my mouth and sat down to wait. In about twenty minutes I was able to paddle the boat without groaning in pain. In thirty minutes I didn't feel anything. In forty I was enjoying it more than I'd enjoyed anything since my last time in the sack with this girl, so I took another half. In an hour, I was ready to take on a Cigarette. My teeth hurt because I was paddling through the cold rain with them bared in a huge shit-eating grin. Once every hour or so I actually remembered to check the compass to see if I was headed for land.

It was stupid for a fugitive terrorist to go to a gas station, but in order to be a fugitive you have to fuge, and it's hard to fuge without gas. So I got a refill. The guy running the gas station was a dead ringer for Spiro Agnew and I couldn't stop laughing. He got pissed off and told me to hit the road. I did, gladly; if I saw Nixon, I'd shit my pants.

I guess in order for me to have gone to the gas station I must've made it to the land, right? Because that's where gas stations are. So I'd paddled all the way to Maine. To the

Maineland. Now it was time to fuge inland, to ply my fugitive trade on freshwater. Like the Vikings, whose shallow-drafted ships enabled them to sail up previously unnavigable European rivers and pillage villages—that rhymed—previously considered invulnerable to marine forces. The Zodiac was the modern equivalent of the Viking ship. Someday I'd mount a dragon on the prow. By God, there was the dragon now! Or was it a seagull?

There was something involving a lake. This led me to a river, and from there to another, smaller lake. Ran out of gas, deflated the Zodiac, and sank it, using its own motor as a weight. Threw the gun in there too; it hadn't worked. Then I was in the White Mountains. Wandered there for forty days and forty nights. Before the Indians found me.

24

My punishment: dreams of a silver Indian who stood off in the distance with a tomahawk face and refused to look at me. Then I woke up in someone's Winnebago, sick as a dog and weak as a Pleshy handshake. When I stopped trying to sit up and just lay down again, I could look straight out a gap between the drapes and see Jim Grandfather's pickup parked outside the window with that Indianhead hood ornament.

They wouldn't let me look at newspapers for a week. The only newspapers they had were *USA Today*, which had dropped the story by that time, and a local rag that didn't pay much attention to Boston. I spent a lot of time staring at my exposure suit, which was hanging on the wall, torn to shreds and covered with muck. Jim didn't have to tell me it had saved my life.

I was being nurtured by the Singletary family, and indirectly by the whole tribe to which they belonged. Either they didn't understand how nasty the U.S. government could get when it thought it was fighting terrorism, or they didn't care.

Probably the latter. What could the government do to them? Take their land? Give them smallpox? Herd them onto a reservation?

The first couple days I used all my energy on dry heaves. We worked our way up to water after that, then Sprite, then duck soup, then fish. Every so often I'd wake up and Jim would be sitting there, hunched over a shoebox, making arrowheads. Tick, tick, tick. Little crescents of volcanic glass ricocheting around as he squeezed them off. "This one's in the Zuñi style. See the detailing around the base?"

"You should get back to Anna," I finally told him, one afternoon. "Don't fuck with me, man, I'm poison. I'm toxic waste at this point."

"Welcome to the tribe."

"Have they come looking?"

"They think maybe you went to Canada."

"I thought I did."

"No. You're still in love-it-or-leave-it land. Nominally. Actually you're in the—" he rattled off a twenty-syllable Indian name.

"That's fine, Jim. Can I buy some fireworks?"

When I succeeded in keeping a Big Mac down for a whole morning, they pronounced me one healthy white-eye. Jim administered his own exam, which involved a cigar. When I passed, he let me see the clippings from the national press.

They'd had all kinds of time for psychoanalysis. I learned many interesting things about myself. I got to see my high school graduation photo, in which I truly did look like a budding psychopath. It seemed that I, Sangamon Taylor, was a man with deep-seated psychological problems. There was some debate as to whether they were purely mental problems, or neurological too, caused by the risks I took with toxic wastes. But they were rooted in my unhappy childhood—my many moves during the early years, being dragged around by my father, a troubleshooter for a chemical engineering firm, and then my unstable home situation as a teenager. My folks had split up and bounced me around from one relative to another.

This, and my academic struggles, the newspapers said, had given me a deep-seated resentment of authority. When I'd scored around 1500 on the SATs, proving that I had near-genius intellect, that resentment was magnified. These fucking teachers had just been holding me back. Never again would I respect anyone in a tie. My career at B.U. had been one scrape after another with the autocratic administration. My only outlet: hacking up the academic computing system, which I did "with a kind of savage brilliance." I sort of liked that phrase.

GEE was the perfect way for me to lash out against the chemical industry, which I saw as responsible for the destruction of my parents' marriage and for my mother's fatal case of hepatic angiocarcinoma. But even this had proved too confining. I chafed under the restrictions of GEE's nonviolent policy. I was a maverick, a hellraiser. I wanted to take truly direct action, they speculated.

All of these factors became focused in my irrational, all-consuming hatred of one man: excabinet official, now presidential hopeful, Alvin Pleshy. As a privileged person, an authority figure from my childhood and a leader of the chemical industry, he was everything I despised. I did everything I could to implicate him in chemical scandals, but I just couldn't pin him down. I was geared up for a media blitz against him just a couple of weeks before "the explosion," but had to call it off, sheepishly, when the evidence didn't pan out. Slowly the plan took form in my mind: employing the commando techniques of the eco-terrorist Boone (whom I had secretly come to admire), I would mine Pleshy's private yacht and blow him sky-high, like Mountbatten. Using my chemical expertise, I constructed a highly sophisticated explosives laboratory in the basement of a house I was renting from Brian Roscommon, a hard-working Irish immigrant and upstanding Newton resident. By purchasing my raw materials, bit by bit, from different companies, I was able to evade the ATF's monitoring system, which had been designed to foil plots such as mine. In an ironic twist, I bought the materials from Basco subsidiaries; they had records to prove it, which they had readily agreed to turn over to the FBI. I was able to build an extremely powerful mine in my basement and take it out into the Harbor on my GEE Zodiac. While I was planting the mine on the bottom of Pleshy's yacht, I was noticed by a couple of private security guards patrolling the area in their high-powered Cigarette boat. Using my commando skills, I slipped into their vessel in my scuba gear, killed them both and then burned their vessel in the Fort Point Channel to hide the evidence. I was so cold and calculating, the more lurid newspapers suggested, that I actually called the police and gave them an account of the incident.

Unfortunately, the whole plot unraveled when the highly unstable chemicals I'd (allegedly) stuffed into my basement deteriorated and touched themselves off. Bartholomew, my roommate, who had been growing ever more suspicious of my strange behavior, tried to place me under citizen's arrest, but I knocked him down and stole his van. Then I escaped, probably to Canada and, with the help of an underground network of environmental extremists left over from the days of the baby seal campaigns, eventually to Northern Europe, where I can live undercover, supported by Boone's clandestine operation.

"What do you think," I asked Jim. "Is it just plain old savage brilliance, or have I taken in too many organophosphates?"

"What's that?"

"Nerve gas. Bug spray. They're all the same thing."

The clippings taught me one thing for sure: Bart was playing it cool. I should have guessed it from the way he handled those cops in Roxbury. He was so full of shit he must be ready to burst. He was giving out one interview after another, sounding pained and shocked and kind of sad, and the media were lapping it up, portraying him as kind of a latter-day flower child in black leather. This man could survive anything.

"It's time for me to get out of here," I said.

"Why?"

"Because sooner or later they'll track me down. I mean, correct me if I'm wrong, but I'm an official terrorist now, right?"

"Certified by the U.S. government."

"Right. And they have all these Darth Vader things they can do in the name of national security, right? They can bring spooks, Green Berets, rescind the constitution. Federal marshals, Secret Service, all the Special Forces cops. Sooner or later they're going to find my Zode in that lake. Then they'll just seal off these mountains and I'll never escape."

"Seal off the mountains? Don't insult me."

"I tell you, they'll find the Zode."

"Let's check it out," Jim said.

First things first. I shaved off my beard. I'd lost twenty pounds, which would also help. Jim scraped up some new clothes for me. The sun was shining, so I had an excuse to wear sunglasses. We borrowed a boat on a trailer and drove down to a small, clear lake. To the southeast it ran into a much bigger lake. From the northwest it was fed by streams falling clean out of the White Mountains. I could have taken the Zodiac a little farther up one of those streams, but they were shallow, and without a hole deep enough for a righteous sinking. So I'd left it in the lake, next to a bent-over scrub pine. Jim found us a boat ramp and we put in and headed for that pine. But there wasn't a damn thing. Not that I could see.

It was only twenty feet deep, and we could almost see the bottom from the boat. Jim went down in a mask and snorkel, looking.

"I wasn't that stoned," I said. "I put it here for a reason. That tree there, that was my landmark. I'd never forget that tree—there can't be two like it."

"I'm telling you there's not a damn thing there," Jim said.

I ended up going down myself. Jim didn't want me to, but by now I was feeling good enough for a short dive. I was nauseous most of the time, but sheer terror has a way of overcoming most anything. And Jim was right. The Zode was gone. I'd just about convinced myself that we were in the wrong place when I noticed a black splotch on the bottom. I went all the way down and checked it out: Roscommon's revolver.

"If the Feds had found it, they'd have brought an armored division to pick it off the bottom, right? We'd see cigarette wrappers and footprints on the shore over there."

There was nothing onshore either. "Except over here, where you tried to hide your footprints," Jim said.

"Okay, give me a fucking break."

Finally Jim convinced me that there just wasn't anything to be seen. "Maybe some of the Winnepesaukees found it. It's pretty valuable. Shit, if I found it, I wouldn't care if the Feds did want it. I'd take the damn thing and use it myself."

"It's some kind of weird mind game. Now I don't even know if we can go back. They're back there waiting for us."

"No way, S.T. They're not that subtle. This is more like something you'd do."

He was right. But I hadn't done it, so that didn't help me much. There couldn't be that many environmental direct-action-campaign coordinators running around this neck of the woods.

He persuaded me that I was totally unrecognizable, that it was okay to go into town and get a cup of coffee. Actually I didn't want coffee because my stomach was so jumpy. I had some milk. We sat and watched the traffic coast by. And once, Jim tugged on my sleeve and pointed to the TV set up in the corner.

My Zodiac was on it. Upside down. Washed up on a beach in Nova Scotia. No footprints.

Then they cut to a map entitled "Intended Escape Route." It ran from Boston up the coast, about halfway up Maine, then straight east to Nova Scotia. But three-quarters of the way there, it was cut, severed by a question mark and a storm cloud. And then they had the obligatory footage of coast guard choppers searching the seas, CG boats cruising along the beach looking for bodies, picking discarded fuel tanks off the rocks, examining washed-up flotation cushions.

"There was a big storm the day after we found you," Jim said. "Maybe the Zodiac flipped over in that, and you drowned."

"Look me in the eyes, Jim, and with a straight face, tell me you don't know anything about this."

He complied. We got back in the truck and headed for the reservation.

"I can only think of one thing," he said when we were almost there. "And it doesn't really lead us anywhere. It's just an anomaly. After we found you, a couple of the guys made a little side hike down to the river to refill our water bottles. They ran into some guys, some backpackers, who were crouching on the riverbank, running their stove, drinking some coffee. Hairy-looking guys, bearded, real granola types.

Maybe with accents. And these people said they wanted to get across the river. They asked where they might be able to find a rubber raft—you know, had we seen any around here recently."

"Kind of funny. Why didn't they find themselves a bridge?"

"Exactly. Kind of funny, since you were in the area, on a raft. But our guys didn't tell them anything."

"Special Forces, man. They can wear their hair any way they like. Shit." I didn't say "shit" because I was worried about them, though I was. I said it because I was getting hit with some stomach cramps.

When we got back to the Singletarys' trailer, I had to sit in the truck a while until they subsided. Then we went inside.

There was a white man sitting at the kitchen table, warming his hands by wrapping them around a hot cup of tea. He had kind of an oblong face, curly red hair piled on top, a close-cropped but dense red beard, shocking blue eyes that always looked wide open. His face was ruddy with the outdoors, and the way he was sitting there with that tea, he looked so calm, so centered, almost like he was in meditation. When I came in, he looked at me and smiled just a trace, without showing his teeth, and I nodded back.

"Who . . . you know this guy?" Jim said.

"Yeah. His name is Hank Boone."

"Nice to finally meet you," Boone said.

"My pleasure. How'd you find my Zodiac?"

"We got a sighting of you, we knew the watersheds and we found it by the oil slick on the water."

"By following my trail of hazardous waste. Nice."

"Oh," Jim said, figuring it out. "*That* Boone."

Boone gave out kind of a brittle laugh. "Yeah."

25

"WE HAD TO TWEAK IT a little to get the right effect," Boone was explaining. We were sitting around the fire, Boone and Jim and Tom Singletary and I. They were drinking hot chocolate and I was drinking Pepto Bismol. "The tanks he had on there didn't have the range to make Nova Scotia. So we scattered a few extra tanks down the coast, let them wash up at random, as though he'd been using them up and tossing them out." Boone's face suddenly crinkled and he laughed for the first time. "You made a great escape," he said.

He was a peculiar guy. I'd never met him, just seen his picture and heard tell of him from the veterans of GEE's early days. They all agreed he was a hothead, out of his mind. Once, when the Mounties came after him on an ice floe, he knocked six of them into the water before they took him down. And I'd seen him on film, doing things that made my blood run cold: sitting right underneath a five-ton container of radioactive waste, getting thrown into the sea when it was dropped on his Zodiac then getting sucked under the vessel, turning up a couple of minutes later in its wake. And he was like that even when he wasn't working—a drunk, a bar fighter. But the guy I was looking at was totally different.

Shit, he was drinking herb tea. He talked in a slow, lilting baritone murmur, he paused in the middle of sentences to make sure the grammar was right, to pick just the right word. But it wasn't a wimpy Boone I was looking at. I had to remember the action he'd just pulled off, on short notice, on my behalf.

"How long you intend to stay," Singletary asked.

"I have a camp," Boone said, "out in the forest."

"No, I don't mean tonight. I mean in the area."

"If you'd like me to leave, I will."

"Not at all."

Boone turned and looked at me with his invisible smile again. "I'm here to talk to S.T. I'd like to see what he wants. That's my only business."

That line turned out to be an instant conversation killer. Jim and Tom took off and left me and Boone sitting there by the fire. We moved to different chairs, so we were facing each other, and the grey autumn twilight glowed in Boone's face, seeming to lift his luminous blue eyes up out of their sockets. We just looked at each other for a minute.

"What's your plan?" he said.

"You have to give me time to think about that. Until a couple of days ago, I had what I thought was a stable life in Boston. Now I'm a dead man, living on nuts and berries."

"You could easily pass for Northern European," he said. "We can set you up there, if you'd like."

"It's just about the last place I want to live."

He shrugged. "Sometimes we can't help our circumstances."

"Silas Bissel, Abbie Hoffman, they both set themselves up with new identities."

"Minor flakes. They didn't try to assassinate a future president."

"Neither did I."

"Exactly. They were guilty. You aren't. That's going to hurt."

"How should you know?" I asked. "You're the real thing."

"The real what?"

"A terrorist."

He closed his eyes for a second and then opened them and looked hard at me. "What makes you think that?"

I groped around for a minute, started to say something, then stopped; remembered things, then questioned my memory. I thought I knew all about Boone. Maybe I was just another dupe.

"The first one," he said, quieter than ever, but filling the room with his voice, "the first one was real. Off South Africa. Pirate ship. We'd seen them wing a baby whale with a nonexplosive harpoon, tow him around so he'd squeal and make noise. The other whales came to help. First the mother. They blew her away before she'd gotten to see her child. Then the others. A whole pod, a huge pod of them, and they just kept firing, kept slaughtering them, more than they could ever use. We sent out some Zodiacs and they fired on us. They killed one of our people."

"With a—"

"Nothing that mediapathic. Not a harpoon. Just a rifle shot. Drilled her through the ribcage. When that happened we all pulled out.

"We were totally insane. It was pure blood lust. We were going to board them and take revenge with our bare hands. Berserk, literally.

"We had this Spanish guy on the boat. Remember, this wasn't GEE, it was a European outfit, much less principled, and they didn't really check out their people. This guy suddenly reveals that he's actually Basque. He was also into whales, but his main thing was the Basque insurgency and he was on this trip as a cover. We'd stopped in for a while in Mozambique and he'd picked up a suitcase full of plastique. He was bringing it back to Spain to blow up God knows what. But he had a thing for Uli, this woman we'd lost that day, and so . . ."

"Boom."

"Boom. We gave them plenty of warning. Half of them got off on life rafts and the other half stayed aboard and died. It wasn't an environmental action at all. It was a bar fight."

"And then you turned it into a career."

He laughed and shook his head. "Let's say you own a whaling ship that needs a total overhaul. It's insured for three times its value. You've been thinking about getting out of the business. The bank has turned you down for a loan and your five-year-old granddaughter has a whale poster on her bedroom wall. What do you do?"

"Put a limpet mine on it and send it to the bottom of the harbor. Then say you'd been getting threats," I offered.

"From the well-known terrorist. And after it's happened several times, this Boone gets quite a reputation, it gets even easier to pull off that kind of a scam. So you see, S.T., I've sunk one boat with my hands and a dozen with my reputation. The new Boone is just a media event."

"Exactly how much have you really done?"

"I just told you the whole thing. Now I've got an organization with a grand total of five people in it, all people like you and me. Antiplumbers. We do a nonviolent action maybe once a year. Usually something technically sweet, like your salad bowl thing—we read about that. Laughed our heads off. The rest of the time we're looking for what to do next. Picking only the best projects."

"No media contacts?"

"Hell no. Media pressure doesn't work that well in Europe anyway. It's kind of sick. They *expect* criminal behavior."

"And I could be the sixth member of this group."

"It's not a bad life, S.T. I've done some good work. Some unbelievably satisfying work." He grinned. "I saw the kills painted on your Zodiac. I've got four on mine."

What it came down to was: I was tired, I felt bad and I had to sleep on it. He could relate, so he got up and vanished into the trees and I fell into bed.

I didn't feel much better when I woke up, but I felt itchy and got to thinking about how long it had been since I'd bathed, and about that lake water dried onto my skin. So I kind of staggered into the bathroom, squinting against the light, and took a shower. Washed my new short hair, felt soap on my whisker-free cheeks for the first time, started to wash my torso and noticed it felt kind of bumpy. Poison ivy, maybe, from my escape through the woods.

When I got out and looked at myself in the mirror, though, it wasn't that. It was a whole lot of little dark pimples, emerging together into a shadow. Chloracne.

I ate a breakfast of charcoal briquets and went through the Singletarys' deep freeze, checking the fish they'd been feeding me. All freshwater stuff, all caught locally. They ate more of it than I did and they weren't having any problems. I had brought the poison with me. Which was impossible, because I hadn't eaten any seafood since this thing had started. So how had it gotten into me?

The same way it had gotten into the Gallaghers? They hadn't eaten any tainted lobsters. I hadn't believed that, but now I had to.

During my dive to the CSO? Maybe it was a kind of toxin that was absorbed through the skin. But it seemed to have time-release properties, hitting me a week later.

I couldn't help remembering that sewer tunnel from Natick to Dorchester Bay. There was a similarity here. I'd thought the source of the chlorine was Biotronics, but it didn't show up right away. It showed up gradually, as it headed down the pipe. Time-release toxicity.

What had Biotronics wrought? Something new and strange. And at the very end, Dolmacher had been trying to get in touch with me.

I was a sick dude. My identity may have died, swept overboard into the Atlantic, but my body lived on, tied to Boston, to Biotronics and Dolmacher and Pleshy by a toxic chain.

Mrs. Singletary was up and about and I asked her if she had any enema stuff around the house. She went into her root cellar and came out with a hollow, long-necked gourd. I thanked her profusely and decided to forget about enemas for the time being.

Boone was sitting out in front of his tent, frying a trout. When he saw me, he gave me the biggest grin I'd seen from him yet, a genuine, unrestrained, shit-eating beamer. "I'd forgotten about this country, S.T. Ten minutes ago this fish was swimming through a stream that's clean enough to drink. And we're, what, a couple of hours away from Boston, is all?"

"Yeah. Welcome home. Let's work together."

"You're joining me, then?"

"No. You're joining me, unless I'm totally wrong."

I sat down and told him about everything. Was going to

show him the chloracne, but no, he'd seen it in Vietnam. He asked me all the right questions. He tried to explore all the blind alleys in the problem that I'd already explored. The only alley that wasn't blind led to Boston.

"Since the sinking," he said, "I haven't done an action in the U.S."

"Time to get on the stick."

"My people have all gone back to Europe."

"What am I, dog meat? Look, Boone, this could be the biggest action of all time. We know who the target is, don't we? Our probable next president. How are you going to feel if you go home and let this guy become the leader of the Free World?"

"Very risky. And my setup in Europe is too sweet to risk."

"Yeah, yeah. You see, Boone, that's exactly why I don't want to move to Europe. Because it's dirty everywhere. Because nobody has idealism, nobody gives a shit when you expose a toxic criminal. And because after six months there, I won't have any balls left. Geographic castration."

He tossed his trout on the ground and came after me with both hands. I'm no boxer, so I just get in close, too close to punch, and use my weight. A little of that and we were rolling around in the leaves together. Then I curled up with stomach cramps and he took pity on me. He just rolled over on his back and lay there, the first yellow leaves of the New Hampshire fall spinning down into his face. "I feel alive," he said.

"I feel like I'm dying," I said, "and we both have something to prove."

"The Groveler, man. His ass is grass."

26

As FOR JIM GRANDFATHER, I didn't want him along. I wanted him back with Anna. Everything I said just rolled off his back and he ended up driving the car.

Boone knew all about this identity-blurring stuff, to the point of knowing which brand of hair dye was the best. Before we left that reservation we were both brunettes. I was Tawny Oak and he was Midnight Ebony. Jim loitered outside the bathroom, loudly wondering if he should dye himself blond. "Greg Allman, man!"

We hit Boston around five in the evening. For the last half of the trip we were getting Boston radio stations and Boone went nuts. It was like he'd been on a desert island. The man was a Motown freak. He sat in the center of the seat with both hands on the radio, punching up and down the dial, hunting the beat.

Sometimes he had to settle for a news broadcast. They had pretty much stopped talking about me since my death. GEE was still in the news, repudiating my actions, covering its ass. That was fine, they had to do that. But Debbie, bless her, had come out in public, pointing out a few holes in the FBI's story, disputing my terrorism. Pleshy was on the prowl, visiting organizations in New Hampshire and, as always groveling. And then there was the usual crap: apartheid demonstrations downtown, murders, arson and some demented bandit who was stealing prescription drugs from pharmacies. His trademark was a Tazer gun. When the electrocuted druggists woke up, their shelves had been ransacked.

The first thing I wanted to do was get a message to Bart, so I wrote it down and gave it to Boone. We dropped him off near the Pearl and then pulled around to the alley in back to wait. He was going to give the note to Hoa and ask him to relay it to Bart the next time he came in, which, knowing Bart, would probably be within twelve hours. It was a pretty vague note. Hoa wouldn't understand it, but Bart would.

While we were waiting, watching the Vietnamese people come to the back door to buy cheap steamed rice, a motor scooter stopped next to us, by the dumpster. In the corner of my eye I saw the rider bending over on his seat and figured he was undoing the lock. Then the smell of vomit drifted past me. I glanced over; it was Hoa's busboy, doubled over, barfing in the alleyway.

Couldn't look any more than that because he might recognize me. I sank down in the seat and turned away. "Jim. That guy on the scooter, can you see if he's got a rash?"

"He's wearing clothes, S.T. Nothing on his face."

Boone, coming out the back door, noticed him. The guy was slowly getting off his scooter, looking pale and sick of the whole business. Boone started talking to him in Vietnamese, then switched to English. Then he got into the truck.

"He's got it," Boone said, and that was all we needed.

So we had another spill. This thing just kept getting more involved. The Dorchester Bay CSO couldn't possibly account for contamination under the public fishing pier.

What I wanted, real bad, was to have my maps of the sewer system. Then I could locate CSOs near the pier. Since I still had a few test tubes with me, I could trace them out and find the source of the spill.

But I'd done enough of those traces to have a rough idea. If there really was organic chlorine coming out near that pier, the source had to be up north.

We were driving past a pay phone when I remembered

Dolmacher for the nth time. "The Holy Grail . . . I'm in the book." I'd looked in the book once before and I knew where he lived: up north. Vague evidence, but visiting the poor fuck was high on my list anyway. We stopped at the booth long enough for me to get his exact address, and then we headed across the river.

To find his place we had to drive down some pretty dark and quiet streets, and the temptation was almost too much. I still had my bandolier, had worn it all the way to the Singletary residence and brought it back to Boston. I started looking around for manholes.

Then I remembered that the simple approach didn't work with this toxin. If it was the same thing we'd seen in Natick, the concentration would be zero up here in his neighborhood, and much higher downstream. Maybe we could check that out later.

Jim dropped me and Boone off in various places, then parked somewhere, and we all converged separately on the house. The lights were off in Dolmacher's place; this wasn't the kind of neighborhood where you needed to leave them on when you went out. Not that it was ritzy, just nice, out of the way and homey. The only criminals around here were us.

As evidenced by the fact that we broke right into his house through a basement window. I was wearing surgical gloves and the others kept their hands in their pockets. We didn't want to turn on all the lights, and it looks suspicious to beam flashlights around the inside of an empty house, so we just stumbled around in the medieval glimmer of my Bic.

The basement was true to form: a big war game was spread out on the ping-pong table. The U.S. was being invaded through Canada and Dolmacher was doing a great job fighting the red bastards off. And he had an active model-building studio down here.

We went upstairs to check out his collection of electronic toys and military-power books. Jim noticed a nightlight on in the bathroom and went to look at that. Boone and I checked out the living room, done up in classic Dolmacher Contemporary, now full of empty pizza boxes and used paper napkins.

"Holy fucking shit, I can't believe this," Jim said from the bathroom, and we convened. On my way, I tripped over something that fell over and scattered across the floor: a half-empty sack of aquarium charcoal. It goes without saying that Dolmacher didn't own any fish.

We went and gazed at the bathroom in the brown gloom of the nightlight. It stank. The first thing my eye picked out was the half-dozen used syringes scattered across the counter. Then the bottles, many bottles of pills. I started reading the labels. Antibiotics, each and every one. The place smelled like death and chlorine; there was a half-empty jug of laundry bleach on top of the toilet and an empty in the garbage. I bent over, bless my scientific heart, and sniffed Dolmacher's toilet. He had dumped a bunch of bleach into it. This was inorganic chlorine, the safe kind, not the bad covalent stuff we were looking for. He was using it to disinfect his crapper.

Dolmacher was real sick. He had a problem with some bacteria, a problem in his bowel. He knew it was a problem and he was desperately trying to deal with it.

Maybe I had a problem too. I went through Dolmacher's supply and scarfed some pills.

Boone and Jim were doing some mumbling, bending over the bathtub. ". . . or maybe buckshot," Boone was saying.

"No way, 9mm semi," Jim said.

"What are you guys . . ." I said, and then, for the first time, noticed the corpse in the bathtub. It was a guy in a suit.

"Your dude's a good housekeeper," Jim said. "Puts his bodies in the tub to drain."

"Should've recognized the smell," I said. "Putrescine."

"Say what?"

"Putrescine. The chemical given off by decaying bodies."

Dolmacher had already gone through the guy's wallet and tossed it on his chest. I picked it up, being the only one here with gloves, and checked it out. Basco Security.

"Nice grouping," Jim observed. The dead guy had six holes in his chest, all within six inches of one another.

Boone and I got beers from the fridge, Jim got water, and we sat around in the living room. I was thinking.

"You guys know anything about quantum mechanics? Of course not."

They didn't say anything, so I kept thinking out loud.

"Any reaction that can go in one direction can go in the other direction."

"So?"

"Okay. First of all, here's what we know: Basco, thirty years ago, dumped some whopping transformers on the north side of Spectacle Island. Covered them with dirt and forgot about them.

"In about '68, they started to worry, because they knew there was a lot of toxic stuff in those transformers. But there was nothing they could do about it until recently—the Age of Genetic Engineering. They bought out the best and brightest such company in the Boston area and told them to invent a PCB-eating bug.

"So they did. Put together some chlorine-processing plasmids and implanted them in a particular bug called *Escherichia coli*. It's a bacterium that lives in everyone's bowels, helps digest food. A good bug. A very well-understood, well-studied bug, ideal for these purposes. It's what all the genetic engineers use.

"It worked. But it just barely worked in time. An old barge came along and ripped the transformers open. So they had to release the bug quickly, before they'd had a chance to test it in the lab, to clean up that mess before yours truly noticed it. And that all worked just fine. The PCBs went away.

"That's what we know. Now, from here on out, it's just my theory. Like I said, any reaction that goes one way can be reversed. Now, somewhere along the line, when these guys were trying to design a plasmid to change covalent chlorine to ionic, they had to consider the possibility of making it go the other way. Ionic chlorine, like in seawater, to covalent, like in toxic waste."

"Oh shit," Boone said.

"Once they considered that, they'd never forget it. Because a whole industry—most of the chemical industry—is founded upon a single reaction: the Chloralkali process—turning salt water into covalent chlorine. Using a very old process that takes up a hell of a lot of electrical power. It's an industry that's been on the skids for decades. But if you could design a bug that would do the same process, with no electricity, think what a kick in the ass it would be for Basco and

Boner and all those other old, decomposing corporations. Suddenly, everything they wanted to make would be ten times cheaper. The environmental regs wouldn't matter, compared to that. It would be so fucking profitable. . . ."

"Okay, we understand why they'd want such a bug," Jim said. "You're saying they've got it?"

"They've got it. In two senses of the word. They own it, and they're infected by it. Someone screwed up. Someone at Biotronics picked his nose at the wrong time, or forgot to scrub beneath his fingernails, or something, and that wonder bug—the one that converts salt water to toxic chlorine—got into the wrong tank."

"But how did it get into that sewer line?" Boone said.

"You're Pleshy or Laughlin. You're a crafty guy. You've learned a few things since 1956 when you openly dumped your transformers on the island. This time you're going to be subtle. When it's time to eat up those PCB-eaters on the Harbor floor, you're not going to take the bacteria out in big drums and pour them into the water in broad daylight. You're not going to go out there at all. You're going to let the primeval Boston sewer system do it for you. It's full of *E. coli* already. You flush the bugs down the toilet at the place where they were made, out in Natick. You pick an evening when it's starting to rain heavily. That night the sewer overflow tunnel carries your bugs twenty miles under the city and dumps them into the Harbor through a CSO in Dorchester Bay, a CSO that happens to be right near Spectacle Island.

"In most places the bugs die for lack of PCBs to eat. But some of them find their way to your huge PCB spill.

"Your plan succeeds brilliantly. The PCBs disappear. The guy from GEE gives up on it.

"Then the covalent-chlorine level starts to rise. You're not dumping PCBs, but the levels are rising anyway. It's impossible, it doesn't make sense. But after some simple tests, one of your genetic engineers figures it out. Your tank of PCB-eaters got contaminated with a very small number of bugs that do the opposite thing. They got into the sewers along with the others. At first, they didn't do very much. The size of the colony was tiny compared with the size of the PCB-eating colony. But after a few weeks, they've multiplied. They can multiply as much as they want. They have an unlimited supply of food—all the salt in the seven seas."

I drank beer and let them ponder that one.

"And all of that salt could be converted into organic chlorine?" Boone said, sounding kind of breathy.

"Let's not worry about that right at the moment," I said. Boone and Jim laughed nervously.

"It's like not worrying about nuclear war," I suggested. "We'll get used to it."

"How does this lead to Bathtub Man?" Jim said.

"Well, you realize that you're in big trouble. The guy from GEE comes back and discovers rising PCB levels, tracing them back to your CSO. He doesn't understand the whole thing yet, but you're in serious trouble now and you can't take chances. You try to kill him.

"In the meantime, you're going on to Plan B. You knew all along that your crime might come to light one day. But you're ready for it. That's why you used the sewers in the first place. You pick out one of your employees, one who's known to be a zealous worker, a fanatic for the project, and you put some of the bugs in his food. They take up residence in his bowel. Whenever he takes a shit and flushes the toilet, he's sending more of them down to the Harbor. So if the bugs ever get traced to your company, you just say, 'Well, this employee of ours got too enthusiastic and violated the extremely rigid safety procedures we have set up. As a result he got infected, and every time he used the toilet, spread more of these bugs down toward the sea.'"

"And, in the meantime, the bugs are turning the salt in this guy's food. . . ."

"Into toxic waste. In his stomach. He gets chloracne and right away he figures out what's going on. He's being poisoned from within. So are all the people who've eaten lobsters or fish from the contaminated zones of the Harbor. Or who were dumb enough to swallow a mouthful of seawater near the CSO, like me. They're all getting chloracne, they're all getting organic-chlorine poisoning.

"Time out," Boone said. "I'm no chemist, but I know a little. It takes energy to convert salt to organic chlorine, right?"

"Yeah."

"So where do these bugs—the bad bugs—get their energy supply?"

"Just a hypothesis," I said. "All the stuff I was sampling was polycyclic. Carbon rings in various numbers and combinations. If our bugs knew how to make those rings, they could get a lot of energy that way. It takes energy to *break up* a six-pack of carbon, right? Which means that if you *make* a six-pack, you get some energy out of it. And if you use that energy to make some organic chlorine, and tack that chlorine onto the six-pack, you've just made some type of useful, but toxic, chemical. That's what I was seeing out by the CSO—all kinds of polycyclic-chlorine compounds.

"Anyway, say you're Laughlin, the guy running this sorry outfit. You didn't succeed in killing the environmentalist. He got away and he's been on the phone. The toxic information is spreading. There's no way to contain it. Your only choice is to destroy the credibility of that person. You have to put a stain on his character. And what's the worst stain a guy can have right now? Being linked to terrorism. So you blow up the guy's house and say it was a bomb factory. You put a mine on Pleshy's yacht, steal the guy's car, park it nearby and say he was trying to assassinate Big Daddy. Even if the guy survives, no one will ever believe him.

"Now let's say you're the infected employee, the zealot who has gotten infected with the PCB-eating bug. Dolmacher. You're smart, you know exactly what's happening, because you've been worrying about it. You tell your company that you've been infected and they say, 'Stay at home, Dolmacher, and we'll send you some antibiotics.' And they do. But they don't seem to work. And the company goes along day after day without announcing the extreme danger to the general public. You realize you've been set up. They've been sending you placebos. They're letting you die. And if they're willing to do that, maybe they're willing to assassinate you. You get intensely paranoid, you arm yourself. Some guy comes around from the company, God knows what for, and something goes wrong—he makes the mistake of threatening you and about a second later, he's wearing half a dozen slugs. So you hit the road. You get out of your house. You take one of your numerous guns, your electric Tazer, and start hitting drugstores and stealing mass quantities of antibiotics off the shelves."

"And then what do you do?" Jim asked, sounding as though he already knew.

"That, my friends, is the sixty-thousand-dollar question, and I'm not a good enough detective to predict the answer."

"This guy is a violence freak," Boone observed.

I agreed and told them about the survival game.

"Up in New Hampshire, huh?" Jim said. "Sneaking around shooting at people. Did it occur to you that Pleshy's stumping New Hampshire at the moment?"

We just sat there, stunned.

"Time to roll on down that lonesome highway," Boone said.

27

Dolmacher wasn't the type to own Tupperware, but he did have a big half-gallon vat of some kind of margarine substitute in his fridge. I scooped all this unknown substance out onto his counter, ran the container under hot water to wash out the remains, sloshed some of his bleach around in there, and rinsed it. Then I dropped my 501s, squatted over the thing and deposited a sample. I put the lid on.

Borrowed a razor blade from Dolmacher's medicine chest, sterilized it, and cut one of my toes. Just a little cut. We got on the highway and followed the first series of HOSPITAL signs we saw, straight to the emergency room. I had Jim and Boone carry me in. We waited half an hour and then they came to look at me.

"Early this morning we were playing soccer down in Cambridge by the Charles River and I waded in after the ball and cut my foot," I said. "Tried real hard to keep it clean, sterilized it and everything, but now, shit, I'm vomiting, got the shakes, my joints hurt like hell, diarrhea. . . ."

They shut me up by sticking a thermometer in my mouth. The nurse left me alone for a while so I put the thermometer on the electric baseboard heater until it was up into the lethal range, then shook it down to about a hundred and four.

Same as before: they shot me full of killer antibiotics, and gave me some more in pill form. We went out to the car and I ate some. I'd borrowed some of Dolmacher's essential supplies: aquarium charcoal and laxative. I took a lot of both and rode in the back of the truck. Enough said about that. We drove around to Kelvin's house in Belmont, a little suburb just west of Cambridge.

Kelvin is a difficult person to describe. We had gone to college together, sort of. He had this way of drifting in and out of classes. I'm not sure if he even registered or paid tuition. It didn't matter to him because he didn't care to have grades, or credits, or a diploma. He was just interested in this stuff. If one day's lecture was boring, he walked out, wandered up and down the halls and maybe ended up sitting in the back of an astrophysics or medieval French seminar.

Later I found out that he was on a special scholarship program that the administration had set up to lure in the kinds of students who normally went to Harvard or MIT. The university waived all tuition and fees, and set up a special dorm on Bay State Road. It wasn't really an expensive program because they didn't have to pay any money out. They just avoided taking any in from these particular students. That was no loss, because without the program those students wouldn't have showed up anyway.

Kelvin only showed up when he felt like it. He got in on the first year of the program, in the stage where they still had a few bugs to work out of the system. They decided that Kelvin was one of the bugs. So after the first year they started clamping down, insisting that he register for some classes and make decent grades. He registered for freshman gut courses, devoted an hour a week to them and aced them. The rest of the time he was hanging out in the astrophysics seminars.

The next year they insisted that he show steady progress toward a specific degree. That was his last year. Subsequently he went out and started his own company and did pretty well with it. He lived out in this house in Belmont with his wife, his sister and some kids, I could never tell exactly whose, wrote highly conceptual software, mostly for 32-bit personal computers and, every once in a while, helped me out with a problem.

It was past eleven when we got there and the house was mostly dark, but we could see him up on the third floor in his office, a kind of balcony surrounded by windows. He noticed us driving up; I stood there and waved since I didn't want to send the house into a frenzy by ringing the doorbell. He came down and opened the door.

"S.T.," he said, "what a pleasure." Completely genuine, as usual. His mutt came out and sniffed my knees. I was about to walk in when I realized that for once in my life I was in a house where children lived.

"I'm not sure if I should come in, Kelvin. I'm contaminated with a form of genetically engineered bacteria."

Kelvin was the only person in the world I could just say that to straightfaced, without giving him prior notice that we were venturing into the realm of the totally bizarre. He found it unremarkable.

"Dolmacher's?" he said.

Of course. Dolmacher would have done the same thing: thought of Kelvin.

"It's *E. coli*, with PCB-metabolizing plasmids, right?" he continued.

"If you say so."

"What do I smell?"

"I unloaded some of it in the back of the truck. Into a bucket."

"Just a sec." Kelvin went into his garage and came out with a can of gasoline. Taking the shit-filled bucket out of the back of the truck, he poured gasoline into it, walked about ten feet away and threw a match at it. We all stood around and watched it for a few minutes, not saying much. The Fire Department came around; the Alzheimer's victim across the street had called in a chimney fire. We told them it was a chemical experiment and they left.

"I'll let you in the back door. We can talk in the basement," Kelvin said, after it had burned down to ash.

We went into his basement, which was mostly full of electrical and electronic stuff. We sat around on stools and I put the sealed margarine tub up on his workbench. There was a naked light bulb hanging above it which filled the container with yellow light; the toxic turd cast a blunt shadow against the flower-patterned sides.

"Good. Dolmacher brought me a sample but he'd already weakened it pretty badly with antibiotics."

"How do you know this one isn't weak?" I asked.

"It's well-formed. If you were taking the kind of antibiotics that are effective against *E. coli*, you'd have diarrhea."

Boone and Jim exchanged grins. "Looks like we came to the right place," Boone said.

He was right. When it came to pure science, Boone and Jim had no idea what I was talking about. But Kelvin was as far ahead of me as I was of them.

"I'm sorry to come around at this time of night," I said, "but ... well, correct me if I'm wrong, but we are talking about the end of the world here, aren't we?"

"That's what I asked Dolmacher. He said he wasn't sure. It may be a little too simple-minded to make the extremest possible assumption—that it'll convert all the salt in the earth's oceans to polychlorinated biphenyls."

"Does Dolmacher know how to kill this bug?"

Kelvin smiled. "Probably. But he wasn't speaking in complete sentences. Had some undried blood on his pantlegs."

"Damn, Kelvin, you should have made him sit down and talk."

"He was armed," Kelvin said, "and he showed up during Tommy's birthday party."

"Oh."

"Anything can be killed. You could dump huge amounts of toxins into the Harbor and poison it. But there's a Catch-22 involved. If you aren't Basco, you don't have the resources necessary for such a big project. And if you are Basco, you don't want to use such obvious methods because ... because of people like you, S.T."

"Thanks. I feel a lot better."

"Of course, now that you're dead, maybe they'll loosen up a little."

"So what did Dolmacher come here for? Just to give you some warning?"

"Yes. And he phoned two days ago, between holding up

drugstores. He managed to find some trimethoprim and that seems to kill the bug pretty effectively."

"So why not dump a shitload of that into the Harbor?" Jim asked.

"We don't have a sufficient shitload," Kelvin said. "No, I don't think that antibiotics are the answer. They are large, complex molecules, you know. Totally against Sangamon's Principle."

"Kelvin, I am honored."

"It's hard to assemble big complicated molecules in Harbor-sized quantities. The only way to do that is through genetic engineering—turning bacteria into chemical factories. That is exactly what we're competing against, an army of little poison factories—but we don't have an army. There is no rival bug making trimethoprim. So we have to find the equivalent of a nuclear weapon. Something simple and devastating."

Here, Kelvin seemed to find something interesting in what he'd just said. "That's actually an idea," he said. "If the infection got totally out of hand, we might have to save the world by detonating some nukes in the Harbor. We'd lose Boston but it would be worth it."

At this point Jim and Boone had moved back into the shadows and were just watching Kelvin's performance open-mouthed. We heard the soles of someone's Dr. Dentons scraping against the linoleum upstairs, and then light spilled down the steps from the living room.

"Kelvin?" said a five-year-old kid, "can I have some cranraz?"

"Yes, honey. Use your She-Ra mug," Kelvin said.

"Cranraz?" Boone asked.

"Cranberry-raspberry juice," Kelvin explained. "I like this house, so let's not think in terms of nuclear weapons right off the bat. That was just supposed to be an analogy. We need to find some chemical susceptibility that these things have. And your sample here should make that a lot easier. I wish I had a better lab, though."

I told him how to get in touch with Tanya and Debbie. That should get him into the nice labs at the university. Kelvin's kid wandered down the steps holding the She-Ra mug, and Kelvin had him sit on his lap. The kid held the mug to his face like a gas mask and made rhythmic slurping noises, watching us.

"Do those people know you're alive?"

"Probably not. Hey, Kelvin. Did you know that I was? Were you surprised to see me?"

He frowned. "I was kind of wondering when your body was going to wash ashore. I didn't think you were that much of an asshole—to go out on the ocean without an exposure suit."

"Thanks."

"But are Tanya and Debbie to be told that you're alive?"

"Sure, as long as you don't do it over the phone, or in one of their cars, in their houses, in the lab. . . ."

"If you're worried about electronic surveillance, just say so."

"Fine. I am."

"Okay. I'll hand them a note."

"Kelvin, you are so—" I was going to say fucking, but the kid was looking at me "—eminently practical."

"Would you like to assist me in this project?"

"I wouldn't be able to go to the lab. Hell, we were sitting in an alley behind the Pearl and I almost got recognized."

"You're paranoid, S.T.," Jim said.

"I'm alive, too," I said.

Kelvin said, "You've got as much experience with these new species as anyone."

"You're saying there's more than one?"

"One that binds up oxygen in the water to create an anaerobic environment. Another that makes benzenes and phenyls, eats salt and poops toxic waste. The second one is a parasite on the first."

"Dolmacher's not such a dick-brain after all. He's the one we really need."

"Dolmacher is not available to us."

"We have this crazy idea. We think we can find him. If we can do that, maybe we can calm him down, get him to cooperate on killing the bug."

"I think he was headed northwards, when I saw him."

"How did you get that, Sherlock? Was he wearing muk-luks?"

"He borrowed my map of New Hampshire."

Great. Now Kelvin was going to be a coconspirator in an assassination attempt. I didn't mention that to him. He probably knew. Dolmacher had no guile.

"One more thing," Kelvin said, after he'd ushered us out to the driveway. "Did you blow up that speedboat last week?"

"Yeah, that was me."

He smiled. "I thought so."

"Why?"

"Because it was right next to the Tea Party Ship. The birthplace of the direct-action campaign."

"Good luck, Kelvin."

"Happy hunting." He and his kid stood there on their nice Belmont street, holding hands and waving to us, as we drove away.

28

THIS DOLMACHER GUY had no sense of personal responsibility. We needed him, damn it. Never thought I'd say that about Dolmacher, but we did. He'd invented the fucking bugs, nursed them, grew them, knew all about their life cycles, what they needed in the way of food and temperature and pH. If we made him settle down, if we grilled him, we could find out a simple way to massacre those bacteria. But no. He had to go up to the land of orange hats to seek revenge on Pleshy. And probably get killed in the process.

We headed north. It was 1:00 A.M. on a Friday night. Within a couple of hours we'd found Survival Game headquarters—a fairly new log cabin built up against some private forest. As we were pulling around into a parking space, our headlights swept through the cockpits of several parked cars, mostly beaters from the Seventies, and we caught brief silhouettes of men in baseball caps sitting up to look at us. Jim and I unrolled some sleeping bags on the ground, quietly, and went to sleep. Boone drove out to scavenge some newspapers and see if he could figure out Pleshy's schedule for the next couple of days.

I didn't sleep at all. Jim pretended for half an hour, then

went over to a payphone on the wall of the cabin and made a call to Anna.

"How's she doing?" I asked when he got back.

"I didn't think you were asleep," he said.

"Nah. Boone's sleeping bag smells like Ben-Gay and hydrogen sulfide. So I'm lying here trying to imagine what kind of action he went out on where he got real sore muscles and made contact with that type of gas. And I'm waiting for the next bulletin from my colon."

"She's fine," he said. "Went into Rochester today looking for wallpaper."

"Redoing your house?"

"Bit by bit, you know."

"That leads me to ask why you're here and not there."

"Beats me. This is a white man's screwup if ever there was one. But you helped me once and now I gotta help you."

"I release you from the obligation."

"You don't have anything to do with it. It's an internal thing, within me, you know. I have to stay with this a while longer or I won't have any self-respect. Besides, shit, it's kind of fun."

Boone got back a little before dawn, totally wired. He had hit every café in a twenty-mile radius, drunk a large coffee, and scooped up loose newspapers off the counter.

"He's at the Lumbermen's Festival," Boone said, "north of here, less than an hour."

"Staying there tonight?"

"Who the fuck knows, they don't put that kind of stuff in the newspaper."

"Going to be there all day?"

"Morning. Then to Nashua later. Looking at high-tech firms. With your pal Laughlin."

"How fitting." I was stirring through his damn newspapers with both arms. "You asshole, didn't you bring the comics?"

Boone was all hot to go straight to the Lumberman's Festival, but Jim persuaded him that we couldn't do much when it was still dark. I thought it was interesting that these Survival Game players went to the trouble to drive up here the night before and sleep in the parking lot—they must hit the trail at dawn.

Sure enough, a huge four-wheel-drive pickup pulled into the one RESERVED space at about 5:00 A.M. It was tall and black and equipped with everything you needed to drive through a blizzard or a nuclear war. A guy got out: not the stringy, hollow-eyed Vietnam vet I'd expected but a big solid older guy, more of the Korean generation. I heard people coming alive in the cars all around us.

Jim and I caught up with him while he was undoing the three deadbolts on the front door. "Morning," he said, ignoring me and taking a lot of interest in Jim. I knew he'd do that. That's why I'd persuaded Jim to get out of his warm sleeping bag and come up here with me.

"Morning," we said, and I added, "you guys get an early start up here."

He pressed his lips together and beamed. There are certain people who are just genetically made to get up at four in the morning and wake everyone else up. They usually become scoutmasters or camp counselors. "Interested in the Survival Game?"

"I've got this friend named Dolmacher who's told me all about it," I said.

"Dolmacher! Hoo-ee! That guy is a demon! Surprised I didn't see his car out there." He led us into the cabin, turned on the lights, and fired up a kerosene space heater. Then he hit the switch on his coffee maker. I caught Jim looking at me wryly. This was the kind of guy who put the coffee grounds and water in his Mr. Coffee the night before so all he had to do was switch it on in the morning. A natural leader.

"Is Dolmacher pretty good at this?" Jim said.

The guy laughed. "Listen, sir, if we gave out black belts at this game, he'd be, I don't know, fifth or sixth dan. He's got me completely bamboozled." The guy sized Jim up and nodded at him. "Course, you might have better luck."

"Yeah," Jim said, "my fifteen years as a washing machine repairman have really honed my instincts."

The guy laughed heartily, taking it as a friendly joke. "You ever done this kind of thing before?"

"Just bowhunting," Jim said. Which was news to me. I thought he'd killed all that venison with his big fancy rifle.

"Well, that's real similar, in a lot of ways. You have to get close, because you're using a short-range weapon. And that means you have to be smart. Like Dolmacher."

I suppressed a groan. In this company, Dolmacher was probably considered an Einstein.

"I thought you used guns," Jim said.

"Handguns. And they're all CO_2-powered. So the effective range is pretty short. Here."

He unlocked a gun cabinet full of largish pistols. He showed us where the CO_2 cartridge went in, and then showed us the ammunition: a squishy rubber ball, marble-sized, full of red paint.

"This thing hits you and ploosh! You're marked. See, totally nonviolent. It's a game of strategy. That's why Dolmacher's so good at it. He's a master strategist."

We told the guy that we'd get back to him. When we got back to the parking lot, Boone was standing in a semicircle of awed survivalists, explaining how to defeat a Doberman Pinscher in single combat without hurting it.

"Nice to see you're getting back to your old self," I told him, when we finally dragged him back into the truck.

"Those guys are troglodytes," he said. "Their solution to everything is a high-powered rifle."

"Maybe we should start an institute on nonviolent terrorism."

"Catchy. But if it's not violent, there's no terror involved."

"Boone, you sound like those guys. There's more to life than firepower. I think it's possible to create some terror just by confronting people with their own sins."

"What's your problem, you grow up Catholic or something? Nobody gives a shit about their sins anymore. You think those corporate execs worry about sin?"

"Well, they've poisoned people, they've broken the law, and when I show them up in the media, they get real bothered by it."

"That's just because it's bad for business. They don't really feel guilty."

By now Jim had us out on the highway. He pointed the silver Indian's face northwards and depressed the accelerator.

"How about Pleshy?" Boone said. "You think he feels guilty? You think he's scared? Shit no."

"They're still human beings, Boone. I'll bet he's scared shitless. He created a disaster."

"Yeah, he's showing all the symptoms of a man paralyzed with fear," Boone said, consulting one of his newspapers. "Let's see, ten o'clock, ax-throwing competition. Ten-thirty, grand marshal of log-rolling contest. He's running sacred all right."

"What do you expect him to do, run to Boston and hide? Look Boone, the guy is slick. He's got his gnomes working on the problem. Like Laughlin. Shit, I wonder what that bastard Laughlin's up to. Pleshy's job is to go around looking brave. But if someone confronted him, right in front of the TV cameras . . ."

Boone and I locked eyes for about a quarter of a mile, until Jim got nervous and started looking over at us. "You guys are nuts," he said, "you'll get popped. Or shot."

"But at the very least he'd break a sweat," I said.

"I'll buy that," Boone said.

"And we could publicize the whole thing." I was remembering my last action in New Hampshire—at the Seabrook nuclear site, years ago. We all got arrested, never made it onto the site. Some of us even got the crap beat out of us. But we got it on the news. And the reactor was still sitting there, uncompleted, a decade later.

"You'd have to get real close," Jim said. "Secret Service, you know."

"They'll be totally loose," Boone said. "What do they have to worry about? A dwarf like Pleshy—nobody even remembers the guy's name—early in the campaign, at an ax-throwing contest in New fuckin' Hampshire. Shit, if I was going to assassinate him, this is when I'd do it."

We found Dolmacher's car easily enough. The Lumbermen's Festival was staged in one of the many postage-stamp state parks scattered around New Hampshire, and there just weren't that many ways to get into it. We knew he wasn't going to park his car conspicuously, or illegally. He was going to park it like a proper Beantown leaf-peeper and then he was going to fade into the woods. And that was exactly what he'd done. We found it at a roadside camping/picnicking area, near the head of a nature-appreciation trail.

"Very clever," Jim said. "No one would expect him there."

I looked in the windows but didn't see much. One pharmaceuticals bottle, half-hidden under the seat. No ammo belts or open tubes of camouflage paint. Dolmacher was taking a remarkably buttoned-down approach to this totally insane mission.

Maybe the bugs could affect your brain. The media had been speculating all week that my contact with toxic wastes had fried my cerebral cortex, turned me into a drooling terrorist. I felt pretty calm, but Dolmacher had gotten a much worse dose, and was less stable to begin with. He hadn't turned into a raving maniac. He was acting more like the psychotics you read about in the newspapers: calm, methodical, invisible.

Jim was sitting in the truck, messing around with something, and Boone was watching intently. I went over, stood on the running board, and looked. Jim had pulled one of his homemade bows out from behind the seat.

"This is the Nez Percé model," he explained. "See, the limbs are strengthened with a membrane that comes from the inside of a ram's horn. They used bighorn sheep, but I get by using domesticateds."

"What the fuck are you going to do with that, Jim?"

"What the fuck are you going to do when you catch Dolmacher, S.T.? Remember? Your gun's on the bottom of that lake."

"Wasn't planning on shooting him anyway."

"You're a real prize, you know that? What do you think we're doing here? It's my understanding that we're going after a psycho with a gun."

"Only because we have to have his knowledge. We won't have that if we fill him full of arrows."

"You underestimate me, S.T." Jim pulled a bundle of arrows out from behind the seat. The shafts were straight and smooth, feathers at the back as usual, but without heads.

"Fishing arrows," Boone said.

Jim nodded and held one up for me. One short barb stuck backwards from the point, and a short perpendicular piece was lashed to the shaft about three inches behind that.

"This keeps it from going all the way through the fish, the barb keeps it from pulling out. Now, a game arrow, with the big head, that kills by severing a lot of blood vessels. The animal bleeds to death. But this will just stick into a big animal and annoy him."

I guess I still looked skeptical.

"Look, the guy said Dolmacher has a black belt in this game. If you think he's going to let us sneak up close enough to pluck the gun out of his hand, you're nuts."

"Okay. But if the Secret Service comes after us, you have to toss all that crap into the bushes."

"Obviously. Hell, this isn't for assassinations anyhow. It's the equivalent of a CO_2 gun with paint pellets."

29

BOONE INSISTED that he was the one. "Hell, you just tried to blow the guy up a week ago," he kept pointing out. "Your face is a 3-D wanted poster. They'll pop you. But everyone's forgotten about me. Unless Pleshy's secretly in the whaling business."

I couldn't argue with any of that. We agreed that Jim and I were going to hike up the trail and Boone was going to take the truck. He would swing around to the site of the Lumbermen's Festival and scope out the place. There wasn't any point in planning this out, because it was all random. If Pleshy happened to walk past him, he'd take the opportunity to stand up and state his case, get some media glare on Pleshy's reaction. If it was impossible to get near Pleshy, he'd forget about that, head for the back of the crowd and look for a tall, pale, psychotic nerd with his hand in his coat.

"Maybe we should call the cops and tell them Dolmacher's out there," Jim said at the last minute.

This was not an idea that had occurred to me. Frankly, if Pleshy ate a few bullets it was okay with me. I was worried about Dolmacher—probably the only guy in the world who knew how to stop this impending global catastrophe. He could easily get shot in the bargain. Even if he didn't, they'd truck him off to the loony bin where he wouldn't be of any use.

"Screw Pleshy. We have to coopt Dolmacher."

"If we warn them, they'll step up their security," Boone said. "We won't be able to get close to Pleshy."

"We have plenty of time to chase down Dolmacher," Jim explained. "And if we give the cops a complete description, they'll spend all their effort looking for him. That'll make it easier for anyone who doesn't look like Dolmacher to get close."

"Jim's right," Boone said. "If this all falls apart and we get popped, and Dolmacher gets found, they'll want to know why we didn't warn them. They'll say we're all working together. If we warn them, we're set up as good guys."

So we drove half a mile down the road to a gas station with a payphone, and I called the cops. We decided it should be me, because whatever I said would get recorded, and it would look good if we had this proof that I was terribly concerned about Pleshy's welfare.

"I can't give my identity because I'm being framed for a crime I didn't commit," I said, "and which only an asshole would think I really did—" Boone kicked me in the leg "—but this should help prove my innocence. I think an attempt is going to be made on Alvin Pleshy's life today at the Lumbermen's Festival." And I gave a complete description of Dolmacher, emphasizing all the ways he didn't look like Boone, and there were plenty of those.

"Uh . . . okay. Okay. Okay," the woman at the police station kept murmuring, all through the conversation. Definitely the shy type. Not equipped for presidential assassinations.

Finally, then, Boone dropped us off at the trail and headed around for the Festival.

Here I was totally incompetent, so I just followed Jim. He was wearing a kind of bulky, tattered overcoat that he kept in his truck for purposes like changing the oil. He had his bow underneath. It looked kind of stupid, but anything was better than brandishing a primitive weapon around the SS. He was half-running down the trail in kind of a crouch, keeping his head turned to one side. I was glad he knew bowhunting, that would help us. But I got to thinking about Dolmacher's black belt in survivalism, and I wondered just how clever and paranoid he was. There was only a mile, maybe a mile-and-a-half, of forest between us and the festival site: across some flats, up a ridge, down the other side. He had plenty of time. Wouldn't it make sense to go in a ways, then double back on the trail to see if we were being followed?

Naah. Who would follow him, why would he worry?

Because he'd been holding up drugstores. Maybe someone had gotten his license plate number. Maybe—I was just putting myself in his shoes, here—maybe his car had been noticed and they were sending in the cops.

How would cops do it? A frontal assault. Dozens of men, spaced a few feet apart, combing the whole area. He couldn't gun them all down.

Well, maybe he could, if he had a silenced weapon. And I wouldn't put it past Dolmacher to own a silencer, or even a submachine gun. He'd always had an obsession for Uzis and MAC-10s and such in college; this had clearly continued into his wiser years, and now, God help him, he had enough income to supply an arsenal.

Poor Dolmacher. All that priceless knowledge, that world-saving information about the bug, attached to a stunted personality. If we could stop him—not *if*, damn it, we *were* going to stop him—we'd have to deal with that personality for the next several days. A grim prospect either way.

Next question: what would he do if a couple of individuals came after him? First of all, they'd never find him without a dog. Jim knew a few things about tracking, but I doubted he was that good. If they did find him, they'd be in danger. Witness Bathtub Man.

Where the hell was Jim, anyway? I'd looked away and then he was gone. I went on for a few yards and stopped. Wouldn't be very smart to call out his name. There was kind of a gap in the foliage along the trail, so I stepped into it, wandered a few yards into the forest, and there he was, pissing on a tree.

"He probably came this way," Jim said.

"I don't get it. How can you tell?" I've never understood trackers.

He shrugged, continuing what was turning out to be an epic piss. "I can't tell. But the festival is off in this direction. There's an obvious opening in the trees here, it's just the easiest way to go. There are some tracks right there that look pretty fresh."

He nodded and I looked. The ground was wet and kind of muddy. Someone's size 13s had definitely passed through here. Not that Dolmacher was that tall. His wrists and ankles were like broomsticks. But his hands and feet belonged on a pro basketball player. Whoever it was, he'd been wearing those heavy-duty Vibram-soled running shoes that affluent people nowadays used instead of ten-ton waffle-stompers. Good traction combined with light weight.

And either he didn't care about being followed, or else he wanted us to find these tracks. I looked around at the forest and suddenly it all looked dangerous. The undergrowth wasn't that thick. If you squatted down and hid yourself, you could see of a hundred yards, but you'd be invisible to within ten. It was no fair.

"Change of plans," I said. "What if Dolmacher's waiting for us?"

"You know the guy, I don't."

"He's just the type who would do it. It wouldn't be complicated enough to just run through the woods and bore a few holes in Pleshy. He'd have to turn it into a war game."

"So? I thought you said you were smarter than this guy."

"Yowza, Jim! My eyes are watering."

Jim just shrugged.

I said, "Let's just go to the festival site. Let's take kind of an indirect route. We've still got an hour. We don't have to track the guy, we already know where he's going, so the only thing we can do by following his tracks is fall into a trap."

"We can swing way around and avoid the ridge," Jim said.

"Which would put us on the highway."

He sighed. "Or go over the ridge up there."

"Are you up to it?"

"We'll have to hurry."

"You have a watch, Jim?"

"Do you?"

"Shit no."

"Wonderful. We just have to go as fast as we can."

Time stretches out when you're in the woods and in a hurry. What seems like two hours is actually one. So if you have a deadline, you're always anxious about it. Usually you get there way ahead of time.

That's what I kept telling myself, anyway. It didn't make me feel any better. Actually I just felt like an asshole. We'd gone in all hot to track Dolmacher down and then realized we were in mortal danger. Meanwhile, Boone was out on his own. He was easily a match for two dozen SS men, but I at least wanted to see it.

When we got to the place where the ground went from flat to approximately vertical, we were already hurting. I was sick and starting to get cramps in the gut, and Jim had stepped in a hole and twisted his ankle.

I was opening my mouth to suggest that we run back and hitchhike to the festival when I heard a crinkling noise. Jim was unfolding a tinfoil packet that he'd taken from his pocket.

"Lunch already?" I said.

"Most people associate hallucinogenic mushrooms with the Southwest," he said, "but the Northwest tribes are familiar with fourteen varieties. I was there last summer."

"Studying their culture."

"That's for whiteys. I was taking my family to Expo in Vancouver. But I did stop in for a while, and look what I brought home." He popped something dry and brown into his mouth. "Legal for me, but not for you."

"What the hell, I can't get much more illegal than I already am."

The shrooms didn't help much on the first part of the climb but on the last part they did wonderful things. We still felt awful, but we were thinking about other things. Everything got very bright—of course, we were gaining altitude—and we believed that our senses were sharper. We lost track of time. But as I already said, this happens anyway when you're in the woods, in a hurry. Especially when you have to keep doubling back and going around obstacles. But eventually we made it to the top, and then we simply didn't give a flying fuck anymore. Without the drug, I would have been paralyzed by fear of Dolmacher. With it, we just started to run. When it got too steep, we put our feet down and skidded through old, wet leaves. There were a few short earthen cliffs and we slid down those on our asses.

Finally the ground leveled out, the woods got thick again and we realized that we were totally lost. Jim stayed cooler than I did and made us stand there for a while, getting our hearts and lungs under control. Eventually we were able to hear highway noises, in roughly one direction. Comparing that with a map and the location of the sun, we drew an approximate bead on the site of the ax-throwing competition. We spread out, about a hundred feet apart, and tried to move forward quietly.

Which is a joke when you're knee-deep in last year's leaves. The wind was blowing in the treetops, covering our noise a little, but I still felt kind of conspicuous, as though I was driving a tank through the woods. But down here the trees were skinny and widely spaced and I was pretty confident that Dolmacher wasn't lurking anywhere, ready to spin out from camouflage, both hands wrapped around his pistol, drawing down on me. I didn't want that to be the last thing I ever saw.

It got worse and worse. We saw brighter light up ahead and we knew there had to be a clearing. We heard a crowd, heard the cash register ringing at the concession stand. Dolmacher had to be between us and that. The undergrowth got a lot thicker and I came across a gully. Had to slide down one side and clamber up the other, helpless, white and stupid. I was thinking of those old World War II pictures of captives standing in the trenches, about to be gunned.

My first handhold ripped loose and I did a semi-controlled plunge back to the floor of the gully. Now I was ankle-deep in mud, covered with dirt and leaves, and wet. I moved downstream a few yards, toward where Jim was supposed to be. But I hadn't heard or seen him in ten minutes. Finally the walls of the gully opened out a little bit and I found an obvious way to get out of it.

And Dolmacher had preceded me. I stood there in stoned amazement and traced his tracks right up to the top. And at the top there was a wild-raspberry cane sticking out across his path; it was still vibrating.

Someone was moving around up there. I could hear him underneath the murmur of the crowd, the drone of the announcer. It was either Jim or Dolmacher or both. Then the sounds were all drowned out by the applause of the crowd.

I took that as a free ticket out of the gully. I clambered most of the way up, making plenty of noise, and flopped onto my stomach on the top. No reason to expose myself; if Dolmacher knew I was right behind him, he'd be waiting.

But he didn't know. I saw the bastard, walking slowly, carefully, toward the clearing, not more than fifty feet away from me. Through gaps in the trees I made out an awning over a raised log bandstand and a waving American flag, and when I climbed up to my feet I could see the parking lot. That's what I remember, because when you've been thrashing through mud and leaves for a while, nothing looks stranger than a bunch of cars glinting in the sunlight.

I couldn't see Jim anywhere. Had Dolmacher already taken him out? I turned around and checked the length of the gully, but no sign of Jim. He'd already made it across. He was somewhere out there, off to Dolmacher's right.

The Groveler was droning on about something through the P.A. system, but then there was a commotion. Dolmacher turned around and squatted behind a tree. Out at the edge of the clearing I could see a man in a trench coat appear from nowhere and run away from us.

Dolmacher saw it too, jumped to his feet, and headed for the clearing at a dead run. He knew he had his opening. He knew he could make noise, at least for a minute, covered by the shouting match that was now going on over the P.A. system.

"Let the man talk! Wait a minute, let's hear what the man has to say," Pleshy was shouting. "I have no qualms about my environmental record."

It was Boone. He'd done it. He was engaging Pleshy in mouth-to-mouth combat. And Pleshy was stupid enough to bite. Everyone remembered Reagan's performance in New Hampshire years ago: "I paid for this microphone!" It had won him the election. Anyone with Pleshy's instincts, and his reputation for being a wuss, would view Boone's challenge as an opportunity to pull a Reagan on national TV.

I got up and ran like hell. It looked like Dolmacher was making his move, but he slowed down when he was almost in the open, dropped back toward his crouch. If he turned around now I was screwed, because I'd dropped all caution and was just chugging along in the open, thirty feet behind him.

He turned around. I froze; he saw me.

He did it just like I'd expected him to: reached into his armpit, came up with the gun, clasped it in both hands, brought it down so all I could see was the barrel. I threw myself on the ground. But you can't throw yourself the way you'd throw a baseball. The best you can do is drop yourself—take your legs out from under and wait for gravity to pull you down at thirty-two feet per second squared. If you're falling off a bridge, that seems very fast. But if you trying to dodge a bullet, it's worthless.

Fortunately, at this point, Dolmacher got an arrow between his floating ribs; it went in three inches and stuck. He flinched, as though he'd been kicked, but he clearly didn't really know what it was. He just turned around, the arrow whacking against a couple of birch trunks, and strode calmly and purposefully into the open, taking his knowledge of the toxic bugs with him, stored up there in his big, unprotected melon.

The trench coat who'd left his position when Boone made his move was on his way back. Dolmacher nailed him with his Tazer, melted his nervous system, left him thrashing around quietly on the ground. Didn't even break his stride. A bunch of folding chairs were set up for spectators and he stood up on one of those, at the back.

"This is a hypothesis out of science fiction," Pleshy was saying. "To release genetically engineered bacteria into the environment—why, that's illegal!"

Jim Grandfather cut off my view by stepping in front of

me and drawing a bead on Dolmacher. The arrow got him in the left kidney just as he was pulling the trigger.

On TV it's amazing. Pleshy is standing there looking like a possum who has wandered onto an interstate. His eyes are wide open, his eyeglasses luminous in the TV lights, sweat breaking through the powder on his brow. He's looking every which way. Boone is standing six feet away, a rock, talking calmly and quietly like a nursery school teacher handling an obstreperous child. They're talking simultaneously about genetically engineered bacteria. But there's rising commotion in the background and suddenly the camera swings drunkenly away from them. It happens just as Pleshy's saying "Why, that's illegal!" Everything goes dim and grey for a second because we don't have the TV lights on our subject, but then the camera's electronics adjust to it and we have Dolmacher, pale and righteous, standing on a chair, calmly drawing down on Pleshy just the way he drew down on me.

If they stay on that camera you can actually see the arrow coming into the last frame. But if they cut to the other camera, the one that's still on the podium, you see Pleshy looking at something else—he never even saw Dolmacher—and you see Boone, confused for just an instant, then focusing in on the man with the gun. And for a second, he actually thinks. That's the amazing thing: you can see him thinking about it. Then he's moving forward, he puts up one arm and clotheslines Pleshy. Pleshy falls away like a tin duck in a shooting gallery and Boone raises his hands, almost in triumph. Just as he's turning to face Dolmacher, his face disappears, replaced by an eruption of red. It splatters everywhere—onto Pleshy's notes, onto the lens of the camera, onto Pleshy's stupid plaid mackinaw.

Back to the other camera and we see Dolmacher giving himself up, two arrows still dangling out of his torso; overwhelmed by trench coats so that there's nothing to see. Then back to the dais and we see Boone staggering around blind with his hands over his face, everyone up there standing with the expressions of developing shock you always see in assassination footage—eyebrows coming up and together, hands rising up from the sides, mouth forming into an O, but the body still stiff and unreactive. Boone is lost, out of control. Then he shakes his head, leans into the body of a local cop who has just run up to help him, and asks him for a hanky. He's just been hit in the face by a pellet of red paint and it's hurting his eyes.

30

JIM AND I TURNED TAIL AND RAN. First we ran in a state of terror, but then, when we figured out that we weren't being followed, drew closer together and started to skip and leap through the air, whooping, laughing like loons, like high school kids who've just egged the principal's house. I wasn't thinking, yet, about Dolmacher spending the rest of his life in the booby hatch, out of reach.

Finally, toward the end, we ran very slowly and made moaning and puking noises. And when we found our way back to the trailhead, Boone was waiting for us. In a helicopter.

It was a news chopper from one of the Boston stations. Boone had agreed to trade an exclusive interview for a lift back down to Boston.

"I'm finished," Jim Grandfather said. "I'm all done with this crap."

He went over to his pickup, leaned against it and breathed. I stood with my hands on my knees and did the same.

"You know, for ten seconds," I said, "I was sure you had saved my life."

"So was I."

"Let's just say you did."

"I don't care."

"I have a question for you," I said. "If you'd been carrying a real arrow—a big-game arrow—would you have used it?"

Jim stood up straight and shrugged. His big coat fell off his shoulders and his quiver tumbled out of it. All the fishing arrows had been used, but there were three in there with wide, razor-sharp heads. "No," he said. "Too dangerous."

I laughed because I thought he was joking, but he wasn't.

"You've drawn my bow. If I used one of these, it would go all the way through Dolmacher's body, out the other side and kill one or two other people."

"Well, I'm glad."

"Yeah. Considering that he was shooting blanks, I'd have felt like kind of a prick."

Jim and I hugged for a while, something I never do with another man, then Boone came out and they shook hands. Jim got in his truck and drove away. The copter's engine started to rev up, so Boone and I had a few private moments while we walked back through the rotor wash.

"What did you know," I asked, "and when did you know it?"

Boone gaped at me for a second, then laughed. "Shit. You don't think I'd step between Pleshy and a bullet, do you?"

We both laughed. I wasn't really sure. I wasn't convinced that he could recognize Dolmacher's gun that quickly.

"I always wanted to be a Secret Service agent," he confessed. "Because then you're the only person in the world who can knock down the president and get away with it."

We climbed into the chopper and Boone started giving a prolonged, monosyllabic, "aw shucks" interview about why he had put another man's life before his own. He was claiming to be a Boston environmentalist named Daniel Winchester. I seized upon a cat-nap; it wasn't that far back to Boston. I was hoping they'd swing over the yacht club, because I wanted to look down into our slip and see if Wes had gotten out the other Zodiac yet. If so, I'd probably be ripping it off sometime soon. I was in luck; they took us back to Logan itself.

That was fine, since the Blue Line took us right in to the Aquarium stop. I was still too recognizable around the yacht club, so I had Boone saunter by there while I loitered at a McDonalds. I had one of those milkshakes that's made from sweetened Wonder Bread dough extruded by a pneumatic machine. This, perhaps, would serve as a buffer against the toxic waste inside my system.

When Boone emerged from traffic he wore a grin. The Zodiac was there, all right, but with a wimpy ten-horse motor, and even that was missing a few strategic parts. So before we did anything else, we prepared ourselves. At a marine supply place out on one of the piers we bought ourselves a fuel line, spark plugs and other small important items that Wes might have removed to make the Zodiac unstealable. Boone flaunted his stack of credit cards.

We rode the Green Line to Kenmore Square and hopped a bus out to Watertown Square. Then it was a two-mile walk to Kelvin's. My pant legs had turned into stiff tubes from being saturated with mud and then drying out, and at one point I had to climb down an embankment into some dead shrubs and broken glass and take a quick squat on the ground. While I was there I looked through my wallet and realized that all my credit cards belonged to a dead man. My transformation into a derelict was almost complete. Jim had been supporting me through that bad week in New Hampshire, but now I was back in Boston, with nothing except a wicked case of diarrhea.

"You should bow out too," I said. "Shit, you've got your opportunity now. You're a national hero. You can rehabilitate yourself, tell your story."

"I've been thinking about doing that," Boone confessed.

"Well don't be shy. I can get along without you."

"I know. But this is more interesting."

"Whatever." This was a useful word I'd picked up from Bart.

"I'll stick with it a little longer and see what's happening."

"Whatever."

I'd been going through a lot of laxatives, trying to flush out my colon. It seemed to be working, because the nausea and cramps had subsided. Maybe I could ease off a little, get a Big Mac or something. Or if we could get to Hoa's, I could eat some steamed rice.

We got to Kelvin's just about twelve hours after our first, midnight visit. Since it was daylight, we came in the front door and got the full family welcome: dogs poking their muzzles into our balls, kids showing us their new toys, Kelvin's wife, Charlotte, fetching big tumblers of cranraz. All the kids were running around either naked or in diapers and pretty soon I joined them as Charlotte wouldn't let me out of the foyer without removing my pants. All I managed to hang on to was my colored jockey shorts and my t-shirt. Boone had to give up his socks and his shirt. All of it went into the laundry. We wandered half-naked down into the basement.

Charlotte's sister had decorated Kelvin's third-floor office just the way he wanted it—ergonomic furniture, a couple extra speakers wired into the main stereo, coffee maker, warm paneling. He went up there about an hour a week to write letters to his mother and balance the family checkbook. Then he spent about a hundred hours a week down here in this dank, dark, junk-filled basement. There was a workbench in the corner where he made stuff. There was a pool table in the middle where he relaxed. An old concrete laundry tub against one wall which he used as a urinal. He'd covered two entire walls with old blackboards he'd bought at flea markets. That was the only way he could think: on a blackboard, standing up. Sometimes it was long, gory strings of algebra, sometimes it was flowcharts from computer programs. Today there were a lot of hexagons and pentagons. Kelvin was doing organic chemistry, diagramming a lot of polycyclic stuff. Probably trying to figure out the energy balance of these bugs.

"Give up already?" he said, without turning around.

For once, I got to surprise him. "No. We found him."

"Really? How is he?"

"Leaking, but aware. I'm not sure what they're going to charge him with."

"That's for damn sure," Boone said. "They can't call it attempted murder."

Kelvin stood there watching us, then decided not to clutter his mind with an explanation. "I have some ideas on this," he said, sweeping his hand across the blackboards.

"Shoot."

"First of all, have you been following the news?"

"Look who's asking," I said. "You haven't heard about Pleshy?"

"Shit, we've been *creating* the news," Boone said.

"I mean the Boston news." Kelvin picked up a *Herald* that was sprawled on his pool table and flipped it over to expose the full-page headline.

HARBOR OF DEATH!

MIT PROF: TOXIC MENACE COULD "DESTROY ALL LIFE"

There was a picture of a heavy white man with his shirt off, showing a vicious case of chloracne.

"So they know about the bug," I said.

"Not exactly," Kelvin said. "A lot of people know of it, but it's not mentioned in there." He nodded at the *Herald*. "And in the *Globe*, as you might guess, it's just a farfetched speculation. Everyone thinks it's just a toxic waste spill."

"So why do they say that it could destroy all life?"

"To sell papers. If you read the article, you'll find that the quote was taken out of context. The MIT prof said it could destroy all life in Boston Harbor that happened to eat a large amount of it."

"Well, that's good," Boone said. "That's fine, from our point of view. We don't have to beg the media to cover it. The news is out."

Kelvin agreed. "It's really only a matter of time before the whole thing is exposed."

"Publicizing it isn't that important," I added. "The catastrophe's still going on. That's what we should worry about. Publicity doesn't kill the bug."

"Is that really you talking?" Boone said. "How do we kill the bug, Kelvin?"

"The chlorine-converting bug is an obligate anaerobe—" Kelvin said, then added for Boone's benefit, "—that means it has to live in an environment with no air in it."

"That's impossible," I said. "There's oxygen dissolved in the water. It wouldn't survive."

"Exactly. So they didn't make just the one bug. They

made two of them. The other is an aerobe—it has to have some air to survive. Its metabolism doesn't hurt anything—it just uses lots of oxygen and creates a locally oxygen-poor region where its salt-eating buddy can live. The killer bug is a parasite on the aerobe. Or symbiotic, or one of those terms—I hate biology."

"Look, I know I'm no expert here," Boone said, "but every environmentalist knows that a lot of water doesn't have any air dissolved in it. Right? Polluted water, anything that's got undecayed garbage or shit in it, doesn't have air."

"Right," Kelvin said, "because the organisms that break those things down use up all the air in the process. The more sewage there is in the water—that is, the higher the Biochemical Oxygen Demand—the less oxygen is present. When Dolmacher and company designed this bug, they had a simulated ocean environment for it to work in. They probably used something like an aquarium full of aerated seawater. The symbiosis worked just fine in that environment.

"It didn't occur to them that this pair of bugs might end up in an environment in which there wasn't any air. They probably weren't thinking of using it in a totally uncontrolled fashion, around raw sewage—or if they were, they didn't think about the BOD. Even if they were aware of that problem, it didn't matter because management got to the bug before they could test it in that situation. It was released into the Harbor."

"Into a part of the Harbor where there ain't no dissolved oxygen—because of all the raw sewage," I said.

"And Spectacle Island. That's got to be one big oxygen-sucker," Boone said.

Kelvin nodded. "Which means that in those bad parts of the Harbor, most of the aerobes are dead. Nothing to breathe. But the chlorine bugs, the ones we're worried about, did fine, because they didn't need the aerobes—in that particular situation. But if a lot of oxygen were injected into their environment, they'd all die."

"So if the contaminated parts of the Harbor can be oxygenated, the bugs die," Boone said.

"How do you propose we oxygenate whole, big patches of the Harbor floor? Get a shitload of aquarium bubblers?" I said. I was tired and I was wired. I was pissed and bouncing off the walls. Kelvin just stood there and took it calmly.

"Ozone. They use it at the sewage treatment plant. Put it on boats. Run tubes from the ozone supply down to the Harbor floor. Bubble the ozone through the sludge. GEE can't do it, it'll take a big governmental effort, but it can be done. The Harbor will stink like a privy for a few weeks, but when it's done, the bugs will be gone."

We enjoyed a moment of golden silence. Boone said, "Not much for us to do, then, is there?"

Kelvin shrugged. "There doesn't have to be. In this case, the governmental machinery might actually work."

Boone and I looked at each other and laughed.

"Kelvin," Boone said, "they can't even handle sewage treatment."

"Couple of days ago I called the Centers for Disease Control in Atlanta," Kelvin said. "This was after Dolmacher had told me everything. I got through to one of their investigators. He'd heard all about this epidemic of chloracne in Boston. The local hospitals had already noticed it, especially City Hospital. So I explained the whole thing to them, about the genetically engineered bug."

I'm an asshole, I do it for a living, so this shouldn't surprise anyone: in a way, I resented Kelvin for this. He knew everything before I did. And he'd made the right phone call. I never thought of calling the Centers for Disease Control. He'd probably saved a lot of people. The real reason was probably this: I wouldn't have the chance to make the Big Revelation, to call the press and inform them, to be the ecoprophet.

"Every doctor on the Bay knows about it now. They've been treating it with activated charcoal—in gastric lavage and enemas—and with trimethoprim. And they just put out an alert late last night, not to eat any fish from the Harbor. That's what inspired those headlines."

"Doctors can't put out that kind of alert."

"Right. You see, all the state authorities are aware of the problem now. They're dealing with it. I already called them and told them about this oxygenation idea. I have the impression they're working on it."

31

Boone and I sat down to wait for our laundry to run through the dryer. Charlotte went out to get some coffee and when she came back into the room, found us out cold. We woke up about four hours later. Boone felt spry as a puppy and I felt like someone had stuffed a rancid lemon into my mouth and flogged me with a hawser.

Kelvin gave us a ride down into Allston. When we walked into the Pearl, Hoa stared at me for a minute but he didn't say anything. I guess a Vietnamese refugee has seen it all. He recognized Boone, too, as the gentleman who'd brought in the message yesterday. Bard had received it, and he'd left a response: meet me at the Arsenal some day after work.

It was after work now. I borrowed Hoa's phone and called over there and asked for the long-haired guy covered with tire dust. The bartender knew exactly who I was talking about. "He just left," he said. "He was here with his girl and they took off. I think they're going to a concert. They were all decked out in leather." That didn't tell me much; they always looked that way.

We hadn't done any serious newspaper reading in a couple of days and, as Kelvin had pointed out, we were way behind on our current events. So I went down the street to a vending machine. I was feeling impatient so I made myself get up and jog, and about halfway there decided I wasn't sick, just stiff and tired. The trip to the emergency room hadn't been a waste of time.

When I went through my pockets looking for change, I found seventy or eighty bucks in cash. Kelvin and Charlotte had made a donation to the domestic terrorism fund. But there weren't any quarters, so I jogged another block to a convenience store and bought my paper there.

They had a TV going behind the counter, showing the seven o'clock news, and that was my first chance to see Boone's performance on TV. I couldn't hear the sound track, but when they flashed Boone's picture up over the anchorwoman's shoulder, they had him labeled as "Winchester." So nobody had recognized him. That was probably good, though I didn't really know if it mattered. They spent a while on Boone and Pleshy, then moved onward to Dolmacher, showing a police cordon around his house, and a closet shot of Bathtub Man being hauled out in a sack.

Then it was Dolmacher's picture, stolen from a frame of the videotape, above the anchorwoman's shoulder. Why don't anchorpeople ever turn around and look at this parade of mugs behind them? I insisted that the Babylonian behind the counter turn up the sound.

". . . found a large number of photographs and documents on Dolmacher's person which police and FBI agents are currently studying. While no official statement has been made, sources say that the information may be an attempt by Dolmacher to explain his reason for the bizarre assault."

The rest of the broadcast was about chloracne, and I didn't bother to watch. I brought a *Globe* and a *Herald* back to Boone, who had set us up with some beers. He took the *Herald*, I took the *Globe*, and while we were scanning the columns and pouring back those frosty brews, I told him about the newscast and what Dolmacher had been up to.

Boone was delighted. "You keep shitting on this guy, S.T., but he's smarter than you give him credit for."

"Shit, no. He got the whole idea from me. From you and me. I tell you, Boone, he's been following my career. If you want to get something covered in the media, do the loudest, most media-genic thing you can and then you've got your platform."

"Pretty strange way of doing it. Shooting an ex-V.P."

"Pretty strange, hell. That's *Dolmacher*'s way of doing it. He doesn't even own a Zodiac."

"So maybe the guy's not crazy."

"Let's put it this way. He's not irrational. I'll lay you odds he never spends a day in jail."

"Maybe all the vital information is in there. The secret of how to kill the bug."

"You really think so?" God, what a thought. "You think Dolmacher's that cool?"

"No."

"Neither do I."

"But Kelvin is."

"Kelvin is. Kelvin can handle the bug. We've got to handle Pleshy. We've got to handle his ass. People need to know about this crime."

"What's your plan?"

"Spectacle Island. Tonight. I'll lay you odds there are still some PCBs down under that barge. And plenty of bugs, too."

"All we have to do is hire a zeppelin to lift the barge off the evidence," Boone said.

"Just have to cut through the bottom of the barge. Or something. Have to go look at it first. Hell, it's not going anywhere. We can take our time. Shit, I wonder what Laughlin was doing there?"

"You never saw Laughlin on Spectacle Island, did you?"

"No, but he had this brand new boat. And he was carrying a gun around in it. And he knew about the Pöyzen Böyzen-barge-Spectacle Island connection. I'll bet you anything Laughlin's been going out there regularly."

"Why? He can't move the barge either."

"Basco put him in charge of Biotronics for one reason: to destroy the evidence under that barge. And he's nothing if not effective. Ever hear of hands-on leadership? I think Laughlin must have read some books on the subject. So maybe he has a way of getting through the bottom of the barge, getting access to the shit down there."

We went through several beers before we thought about ordering food. I'd eaten enough at the Pearl to earn this privilege, and Hoa seemed to enjoy playing bartender for a change. As much as he enjoyed anything, that is. He is always cheerful but I was never sure if he was happy. Of course, happy is a concept for fat Americans. Immigrants don't seem to care about happy very much. Healthy, wealthy and wise, yes, but happiness alone is something their children worry about, maybe. Now, the surly, toxic busboy, he was unhappy and wanted to do something about it. He didn't seem to be around tonight.

When we finally ordered some food, I asked Hoa about him. "Where's the busboy?"

He didn't understand. Since he was obsessed with my bicycle, I tried a different tack. "The one who rides the scooter?"

Hoa got serious for once, lost that fake pixie smile, and bent forward just a hair. "Very sick."

"Had a rash on his body and so on," Boone suggested, rubbing his hand around on his chest.

"We took him to the hospital and now they giving him medicine for it."

"Good, Hoa, they know exactly how to make it better." Which probably sounded kind of patronizing. But the Vietnamese got a little weird about their medicine sometimes, tried to cure themselves by putting containers of boiling hot water on their backs and so on. Which might work with evil spirits but not with the particular type of possession that busboy had.

"What, did he collapse at work, or something?" Boone said.

Hoa didn't understand.

"You said, you took him to the hospital."

"My wife took him. That boy is Tim. Our son."

At which point Boone and I both felt like assholes, apologized and said all the things one says, wishing Tim well and so on. Hoa was unruffled. "He going to get better soon, then I bring him back here and work him nice and hard."

We hung out there, leafing through papers and planning our reentry into impolite society. Things had to be done in the right order. We had to get drunk, I had to get in touch with Debbie, we had to tie up some loose ends on this whole PCB business and then we could make some noise.

Comics were entertainment and so what I had was the Entertainment section of the paper. They had a little advance-press article about a heavy-metal group that was playing a concert down at the Garden tonight: Pöyzen Böyzen. Unfortunately for Boone and me it was sold out. No Satanic rock for us tonight, but Bart and Amy were certainly in that number.

Boone was sitting there, going through the fine-print pages. "Hey," he said, "remember the *Basco Explorer?*"

"Never had the pleasure. But I know about it."

"Big old freighter of theirs," he said, wistfully. "They use it for ocean dumping, you know."

"Yeah, I know."

"Once we were harassing it out off the Grand Banks, and it dropped a big old drum full of black shit right into my Zode. A direct hit—snapped my keel. That was back before everything kind of turned sour."

"Back in your salad days. Boone, what is the reason for this misty-eyed crap about the *Basco Explorer?*"

He showed me the back page of the Business section, the one with the bankruptcy notices and exchange rates. They run a column back there listing what ships are in port now, what's coming in and going out. The *Basco Explorer* was going to be arriving in Everett tonight, coming in from the Basco plant in Jersey and probably going to their main Everett plant.

"That's pretty routine," I said. "It's almost like the Eastern Shuttle. It's always transferring crap back and forth."

"You don't think this might have anything to do with the bug?"

"Unless it's full of trimethoprim, no. I mean, what good would it do them to have the ship there? Use it for Pleshy's escape vessel?"

He shrugged. "I just thought it was an interesting coincidence."

Hoa brought our food, and we hovered, moaning with delight and breathing through our noses. Once Hoa saw the way we were chowing on this stuff, he turned away and didn't show up again until we were picking through the steamed rice.

"You talking about Basco?" he said.

"Yeah, Hoa, you familiar with them?"

"This is the company that poison Harbor?"

"We think so. Hell, we know so."

Hoa took the unheard-of liberty of pulling up a chair. He looked around the room kind of melodramatically. It would be melodramatic for an American, anyway. Hoa had spent six years in a reeducation camp in Vietnam and had led three escape attempts. This wasn't melodramatic for him.

"What you going to do?" he said.

"Go to the Harbor; get evidence against Laughlin. I mean Pleshy. Pleshy and the, uh, man who works for him."

"You think Basco—Pleshy—going to be punished? He should go to jail for long time, man!"

It was a little odd to hear this from Hoa. Hoa was a right-winger and I couldn't blame him. He had no respect at all for antiwar types. He thought the U.S. should have stayed in his country.

I was remembering an old black-and-white photo of Pleshy, in Vietnam, back when he was the world's leading exponent of chemical warfare, before the Sovs and the Iraqis took over the business. In my patronizing way, I hadn't imagined that Hoa was much into politics, or that he'd be aware of who the hell Alvin Pleshy was. That idea was dispelled by the way he pronounced Pleshy's name, the look in his eyes when he asked.

"What's your problem with Pleshy? He was on your side."

If it hadn't been his own restaurant, he would have spat on the floor. "Gutless," he said. "Didn't know how to fight. Thought he could win war with chemicals. All it did was make him rich. He make those chemicals in his own company, you know."

"Yeah. Well, we think it's pretty likely that Pleshy will get in a lot of trouble for this."

"You have to make him pay!" Hoa said.

It reminded me of Hoa's brother, a couple of months ago,

when he'd gotten upset about people who came into the Pearl and wasted food. Serene and cheery on the surface, but when they got pissed about something, they really got pissed. They let you know about it. They had long memories.

"We think we can trace this bad stuff through the sewers, back to a plant that's owned by Basco," I said, "and the guy who shot at Pleshy today also has evidence. I would say that Pleshy's in deep shit." But I didn't believe it for a minute. The man was a vampire. Only the light of a minicam could hurt him. Boone had winged him earlier today.

Tonight we had to drive a stake through his chest, or he'd recover. He'd appoint Laughlin his interior secretary, and use Laughlin's magic bug to bring more covalent chlorine into all of our bodies.

"I can help in any way, you will tell me," Hoa ordered. "This meal is for free. On the house."

"That's okay, Hoa, I've actually got cash tonight."

"No. Free." And he got up and went away, soundlessly as always, without displacing any air. For some reason it came into my head to wonder how many people Hoa had killed.

"Some of these immigrants were actually big honchos in South Vietnam, you know," Boone said. "I wonder if he knew Pleshy personally?"

"I don't think Pleshy's that hateful in person," I said. "To really dislike the man you have to be standing under an Agent Orange drop."

"That's right," Boone mused. "He's kind of a wimp in person."

"What did he say to you, anyway? I never got a chance to hear your conversation. I was too scared of Dolmacher."

"Well, he came right out and challenged me. He said, there's no bacteria like you describe. Go ahead and test the Harbor. Try me."

"So what do you conclude from that?"

"I conclude he was kept in the dark by his underlings. Like Reagan back during the contra thing. He didn't know what was going on."

"How charitable you are."

"Otherwise, why would he say something like that?"

I didn't figure Bart would be using his van while he was watching the concert, so we took a cab out to Boston Garden and cruised the local parking areas until we found it. I slid underneath and got his spare key. We got in and did some nitrous. Then we drove out to Debbie's place in Cambridge, a nice rent-controlled complex between Harvard and MIT. She wasn't there, so I left a note in her mailbox telling her we were going out on the water, and if she wanted to get together she should go out to Castle Island Park and build a fire or something and we'd circle back and pick her up.

We cut across Cambridge to the GEE office, where they hadn't bothered to change the locks. We loaded up on any kind of equipment that might come in handy—scuba gear, sampling jars, giant magnets, strobe lights, distress flares, radios—and threw it into the van and cruised back to the Garden. We got there just as the doors were opening up to spill a plume of black-clad Pöyzen Böyzen fans onto the streets of the North End. Dustheads galore.

Bart's old space had been taken so we just cruised around and made a nuisance of ourselves until he showed up.

"Hey, S.T., thanks for pistol-whipping me."

"I'm sorry about that, Bart, but—"

"You met my girlfriend, Amy?"

"Yeah, we've met."

"Hi, S.T.," Amy said, popping her gum explosively. Heavy metal, drugs and sexual passion had dissolved her brain to a certain point where she no longer distinguished between dead and living persons.

"Hop in," I said.

Boone introduced himself. They didn't take much notice of him. Amy wanted to know where we were all going.

"We're going to Spectacle Island," I said. By "we" I meant me and Boone and just possibly Bart, but Bart and Amy took it the other way.

"Alright!" he said. "That is going to be brutal tonight."

"That's what I was afraid of," I said. "A lot of Pöyzen Böyzen fans out there?"

"Tonight they are, man. It's going to be an all night party. I know someone who's got a boat."

"Christopher Laughlin?"

"Yeah, how'd you know?"

"It's okay. We have our own boat."

32

"ALRIGHT, MAN. A motley crew," Bart observed as we made our way across the piers to the GEE slip.

He had a point. There weren't deck shoes or yachting cap among us. We had walkie-talkies and Liquid Skin instead of Brie and baguettes. If there were any loose cops in the Boston area we'd be arrested on the spot. Fortunately they were all out in the streets training firehoses on Pöyzen Böyzen fans.

Amy found the trip down the ladder to the Zode extremely exciting. Bart had to help her down, using some holds he'd picked up as a high school wrestler in Oklahoma. Meanwhile, Boone and I were down there operating on the ten-horse. Wes had taken out the plugs. We didn't know what kind of plugs it took so we'd bought about twelve boxes of different types. Also we didn't know how to gap them. New plugs have to be gapped.

"It doesn't matter anyway because we don't have a gauge," Boone pointed out. But I was already one-upping him by whipping a set of leaf gauges out of my wallet.

"No wonder your fucking wallet's an inch thick," Boone

said. We guessed thirty-five thousandths on the plug gap and bent the electrodes accordingly.

The net result is that the motor started on the first pull. By this time Amy had mounted the prow like a sadomasochistic figurehead and Bart was thudding up and down the ladder loading the Zode with our war supplies. This included a nice stack of Big Macs and pseudo-shakes we'd picked up at the McDonald's. No telling how long we were going to be out. I shifted into forward and Boone cracked open a Guinness. Bart leaned back between Amy's thighs and trailed one of his hands in the black brine. For some reason I felt formidable.

With this worthless motor, the trip from downtown to Spectacle Island took almost an hour. I was expecting Amy to get bored and petulant, or at least seasick, but I underestimated her. She actually kind of liked it out here. She'd never seen Boston from the water, few people have, so we basically spent half the time telling her where shit was. The 747s were coming down fast and thick at Logan and that was a sight. Bart had a Walkman with stereo minispeakers that you could plug into it, so we listened to an old Led Zep tape and later to a Sox game, in California, on the radio. Boone told some kind of interminable story about hand-to-hand combat with a Canadian helicopter in Labrador. I kept an eye on Castle Island Park, hoping Debbie would show up and give me a sign, but she didn't.

Spectacle Island was easy to find in the dark, because half of it appeared to be on fire. If I shut off the motor, we could hear the stereos from a distance of three miles. We had the slowest boat in the harbor and everyone else had gotten there first. Small boats occasionally crossed our line of sight and made silhouettes against the light.

Somehow I doubted they had all brought firewood along. They were probably burning whatever was at hand. There must be some great toxins in the air tonight. Before long we smelled them, a profoundly nasty and foul odor drifting toward us on a southeasterly wind.

"I guess we picked the wrong night," I said.

Amy didn't understand. She thought that I wasn't sufficiently impressed by this party. Bart finally had to break the news to her: "They're not coming to party. They're coming to—" his silhouette turned to look at me "—just why the fuck are you coming?"

"Chris Laughlin ever tell you about his dad?"

"Yeah, he told me all about that fucking bastard."

"Remember my enemy at Fotex? Who fell into the pond?"

"Oh, yeah, the rotating knives?"

"Yeah. That's roughly what we're going to do to Chris Laughlin's dad."

"And what will that involve?"

"Beats me. Boone and I will just have to scope it out."

"Looks like you'll have plenty of light."

Amy was temporarily depressed that we were actually coming out to test a scientific theory, but she got over it. Meanwhile I was noticing something interesting, namely a big shadow that was blocking off about half of our view of Spectacle. We were getting to the point where we could make out some running lights, and eventually, Boone and I started aiming our humongous flashlights into that shadow, checking it out with binoculars. I already had an intuition about it. So did he, I guess, because we aimed our beams at the same place: high on the bow, where the name of the ship is written. It stood out nicely in rust-stained white: *Basco Explorer*.

"It's not going anywhere," he said. And when we got a little closer we could definitely see its anchor chains, coming out the hawsepipes up on the prow, descending straight into the water. The *Basco Explorer*, the toxic Death Star, was anchored about half a mile off Spectacle Island.

"Pöyzen fans," Bart said.

But Boone and I were just looking. He reached over and shut off the radio, and I dropped the motor to an idle.

"Spray paint," I said.

Boone rummaged through one of our bags and came up with a can of black Rustoleum we'd picked up with the spark plugs. Bart shook it up and blacked out the GEE lettering on the sides of the Zode.

Most of those boat silhouettes were heading to or from Spectacle Island. But when we noticed one that was going sideways, headed for the *Basco Explorer*, I cranked up the motor so that we didn't look suspiciously slow. We buzzed across the ship's bow, giving it a hundred yards of clearance, and checked out the other side, which was glowing an almost imperceptible red from the fires on the island. We had to look straight at it for a minute or two before our eyes adjusted. We asked Bart and Amy to look the other way, because anyone might feel nervous if four people on a Zodiac were staring them down.

A small boat, a Boston Whaler, was bobbing alongside. One of the *Basco Explorer*'s davits was active, lowering a drum of some godawful cargo toward the boat.

"Déjà vu," Boone said. "Just like the old days. Except the little boat's on their side."

That any of those Pöyzen Böyzen fans could tolerate Spectacle Island was amazing. The stench nauseated. Maybe the smoke was rising off the island so they didn't notice it, drifting downwind, hitting an inversion layer, and spreading out close to the water.

Bart was tugging on my sleeve, pointing in the opposite direction, toward the mainland. A small strobe light was flashing away on Castle Island Park.

I turned my back to the *Basco Explorer* and hunched over our walkie-talkie. This was just a guess, because I hadn't asked Debbie to bring a walkie-talkie along. But I thought she might. I switched to the channel we'd used in Blue Kills and punched the mike button.

"Tainted Meat to Modern Girl," I said. "Tainted Meat to Modern Girl. You there, toots?"

"This is Modern Girl," Debbie said, quoting the song: "I got my radio on."

"Nice to hear you, Modern Girl."

"Very nice to hear you, Tainted. Where are you? I can hear the little Merc."

"Right in front of you. Listen, you driving what I think you're driving?"

"What else?"

"How'd you get it started?"

"The guy who stole it put in a new coil wire."

I made a mental note of that; just another reason to kill Laughlin. No one should know that much about me.

"Checked the oil recently?"

"Just had it changed, asshole."

"Listen." This part was going to be tricky; if Basco was listening to the frequency, they'd get suspicious. "Seen much traffic in your area? Whalers, maybe?"

"I understand."

That was nice, but I didn't know how much she understood.

"We won't be able to swing by and get you for awhile. Until then, do you think you can entertain yourself? Go out for a drive and listen to some tapes, maybe?"

"Yeah. Maybe take some snapshots. Boston at night."

Fantastic. She had a camera. More importantly, she knew how to use it.

"Ten-four on that, Modern Girl. We'll catch you later. Drive safely."

"Always. Bye, Tainted Meat."

The idea of sending Debbie out by herself at night to follow and take pictures of Basco goons was a little troublesome. But she'd been on some wild gigs and had always handled herself well. She was good at this sport. As long as she kept her hot little right hand off the stereo, off the phone and on the shift lever, nothing was going to catch her. Besides, she adored stress.

We'd left the *Basco Explorer* behind. Boone started looking into the flames again. Amy was facing backwards and she let us know when the Whaler took off, headed for the shore. Spectacle Island was looking real big, the line of flames was breaking apart into individual bonfires, and the music was drowning out our motor.

The final approach was not smooth. Pieces of debris kept fouling our propeller. Fortunately it was soft, whatever it was, so the prop just chopped it up, coughed and kept going. Boone was leaning over the back of the motor to check it out when he almost got thrown out of the Zode by a boat's wake. Some jerk-offs had just shot by us in a small boat with a big motor, and now they were swinging around for another pass.

"Hey," Amy shouted, "alright, Chris!"

"Chris is too young for you, and he's actually a jerk," Bart said.

Two or three times a year, I got to hear one of Bart's relationships fall apart.

"Maybe you're too old," Amy suggested.

I was watching that fast boat. For a second I was afraid it was Laughlin himself. But asshole *père* must have had other items on his dancecard this night; Laughlin's awful son had tracked us down.

He'd brought his pals, maybe the same ones we'd seen before. The roar of their motor didn't drown out the sound of their laughter as they saw us wallow around in their wake. That was so much fun they came by for another pass, and another, and another. I could think of any number of ways to inflict injuries on them. For example, the Al Nipper approach: I took an empty Guinness bottle, of which we had several, wound up and drew a bead on Chris's head. But Boone caught my arm as I was about to throw.

"Why throw garbage at them," he pointed out, "when we can steal their motor?"

Within five minutes we were on the decomposing shore, doing exactly that. Laughlin had bought himself a real nice one, a Johnson fifty-horse, and also coughed up a couple of full gas tanks for us. With this rig we could really haul ass. We mounted it on the Zode and then we left our ten-horse sitting in the bottom of Laughlin's boat. They'd neglected to bring their oars. I would have been happy to maroon Dad on this mound of trash, but the son deserved some sympathy.

We did most of this without lights, not wanting to draw attention to ourselves. So when I was standing thigh-deep in the water, lifting our old ten-horse off the transom, I could tell that the bottom half of the motor was greasy and slippery, but I didn't know why. When we dumped it into the bottom of the other boat, Boone checked it over with his flashlight and whistled.

Our motor was splattered with a lot of gore that had been thrown up by the propeller. Wet, fishy-smelling gore. Chopped-up fish, as a matter of fact.

Once we got it running, we took the Zode around to a deserted stretch of beach and left it there. No point in allowing these people a glimpse of a free, fast ride. We went slow, and aimed our lights into the water, which was full of dead fish.

HARBOR OF DEATH. It made sense. The fish would get the PCB bug in their guts just like humans did, and they'd get sick and die in the same way.

Boone and I hiked back across the island toward the northern shore, toward the party. Bart and Amy were already there. It would be impossible to find them again, but that was okay. Bart was a survivor. Finding a way back to Boston would be as easy for him as getting out of bed in the morning.

We walked slow; on Spectacle Island you never knew what was going to poke up through the sole of your shoe. Eventually, though, we crested a junk-heap ridge with a smokey, fiery halo and looked down on the festival.

Three hundred people, give or take, twenty bonfires and a dozen kegs. There was also a garbage party—someone had brought a garbage can and people had dumped into it whatever alcoholic stuff they'd brought with them, creating a mystery punch. And a fire hazard.

And I finally got to see the Satan worshippers. A dozen of them. Their black leather was somewhat more bizarre and expensive than that of the average fan. They were up on the hillside, standing in a circle, working their way through some kind of ritual that involved torches and large knives.

The big knives weren't too dangerous compared to the cheap revolvers that half of the guys on the beach were probably carrying, and a few spells and incantations didn't worry me as much as the *Basco Explorer*. But we swung around them anyhow, since a few grams of PCP could make anyone feisty.

Sometimes, they said, drugs led to possession. Then you had to get yourself an exorcist. The exorcist would come and call out the name of the evil spirit, and that would scare it away. This was all it took—no surgical operations, no chemicals, not even much of a ritual. I figured I was in a similar business. I stood in front of the TV cameras and called out the names of corporations. I lacked the power to do much more than that, but it seemed to be pretty effective.

Dolmacher had called out Basco's name earlier today. If I

could find some kind of evidence under this barge, it would establish a link in my theoretical chain of events, and I, too, could call out their name. It wouldn't bring down Basco, maybe, but it would probably ruin Alvin Pleshy. And Laughlin would really be pissed.

33

Boone and i wandered straight through the party and over to the barge. Down by the shoreline, Boone kicked a couple of dead fish out of the way to establish his footing. Then I climbed up on his shoulders and got a handhold on the top of the barge. That got me over the top and then I helped him in.

There wasn't much here. The barge was made to carry some kind of dry, bulk cargo—coal or corn. It was divided up into garage-sized compartments that were open on top, and you could get around between them on catwalks that ran on top of the partitions. The Satanists had been here with their goddamn spray cans and labeled the whole thing with various kinds of nonsense; there was a HEAVEN sign with an arrow pointing toward the bow, and a HELL sign pointing to the stern. Right now we were in the middle, and it was labeled EARTH. Different compartments had been labeled with the names of different demons, or something, and little shrines had been put together in some of them, using household junk gathered from the island.

EARTH or HELL was the place to look. I didn't expect the transformers to be located in HEAVEN. When Basco had dumped them back in '56, they wouldn't have had any reason to drag them way up the slopes of the island. They'd have dropped them at the waterline, or below it, and covered them up. The impact of the barge might have dragged a few of them uphill, but not far.

We gave it a once-over to begin with, walked down all of those catwalks and aimed our flashlights into the compartments. If we were lucky we'd find something obvious. The Pöyzen Böyzen cult had made a mess of things, covered up a lot of shit, but this was a big barge and a small cult and they couldn't screw up the whole thing.

A whiff of cool wind came in from the north, bearing that nauseating smell. I hadn't smelled it since we'd landed. Apparently it wasn't coming from the island at all. Maybe it was coming from the reactions going on in the Harbor: rotting fish added to its usual delicacies. There was a strong overtone of putrescine, which I hadn't noticed before; maybe someone had found my cache of the stuff and poured it into the sea.

Actually, it came from the compartment below my feet, where three mutilated corpses were sprawled on the floor.

They'd been there for a few days. The blood was brownish-black, and they looked a mite puffy, about to burst the seams of their black leather pants.

"Boone!" I said. He was with me in a few seconds. We squatted, like archaeologists looking into a burial pit, and observed in totally rude fascination. But after a couple of seconds, he began shining his flashlight on the walls of the compartment.

"Fragged," he concluded. "Check out the walls."

A lot of shrapnel had gone into those walls. The impact points twinkled on the rust like stars in a shit-brown sky. "Fragmentation grenades," Boone continued, "or maybe Claymores."

We started beaming our lights at the trash strewn around on the floor. This wasn't random garbage; it was bright, colorful and interesting. The remains of a shrine. And a big, rust-free, stainless steel pipe, maybe six feet long, was toppled across one of the bodies.

"That pipe's weird," I said.

"There's all kinds of shit on this island," Boone said. "Check that out."

He was shining his light near the feet of a corpse. A wire was glinting in the light and at one end was a metal ring.

"Grenade."

After that he led the way. Boone knew more about booby traps than anyone. He searched the barge, one row of compartments at a time, and I tagged along behind to make sure he hadn't missed anything. When he said, "Shit!," I hit the catwalk. When he laughed, I got up.

We were a few yards past the shoreline, out in HELL. The compartment below had been dedicated to some demonic force named Ashtoreth. I'd already checked it out. There was a shrine here, basically a pile of junk—the obligatory toilet, some dolls' heads, wind chimes manufactured from old brake drums, rotating candelabras built on bicycle wheels. Boone had noticed something I'd missed. The shrine was built around an axis, a vertical pipe that rose from the floor of the compartment. The pipe was brand shiny new, not rusty, and it had a valve on the top. A padlocked valve.

"Laughlin's been prospecting," I said. "Digging down into the PCB deposits. The Pöyzen Böyzen devotees build shrines around the pipes. Or maybe he built them himself, as camouflage. And then he came around and booby trapped them."

"Because he was afraid of you."

"Maybe he knows I'm not dead?"

"No," Boone said, "you died a week ago. Those corpses were at least that old."

"I'll take your word for it. But I know why he was worried. This is great evidence, man."

"Yeah. Evidence that fights back."

Once we made damn sure there were no tripwires, we lowered ourselves down there. Then we squatted and investigated the heap of junk from a distance, saw the grenades, clustered around the pipe like coconuts on a tree, saw the wires.

Someone landed on my back. I turned my head a little so that when my face smashed into the floor, I was leading with my cheek and not my teeth. Whoever had jumped me was drunk and we ended up lying there, nestled like spoons for an instant, and then I just rolled over on top because it felt like he or she wasn't as heavy as I was.

I was right. But the second person, standing above me, astride my body, holding the ceremonial knife in his hands—he was heavy. He was obese, in fact. His floor-length leather cape spread way out, like Batman's.

There wasn't much I could do because I still didn't have my breath back. I gasped and moaned, getting my lungs push-started, but this didn't do anything about the guy with the knife.

Boone, over in the opposite corner, was giving a better account of himself. Someone had started by breaking a bottle over his head. She'd seen a lot of TV shows and thought that this would knock him out. Instead, Boone got pissed off and punched out her front teeth. Now she was shrieking like a bad set of air brakes, spinning and bouncing around the compartment like a top. A guy had gotten Boone in a bearhug from behind and lifted his feet off the floor, allowing him to kick with both feet—which isn't normally possible—and so he inflicted a bit of internal bleeding on a third attacker. I heard the ribs snap. But he didn't even notice. The person who was holding him off the ground spun him around and methodically rammed his face against a rusty wall about half a dozen times. The guy with the broken ribs was jumping up and down, shouting without using any words, stabbing at the air with his knife.

I happened to be looking at that person when he got about half his brains blown against the compartment wall. The obese guy standing above me stood up straight and I kicked him in the nads. Then I got showered with blood as he took a bullet in the middle of his back.

He staggered sideways into the shrine, rammed it like a tractor hitting a Christmas tree, and in the aftermath I heard a little tink-tink-tink that was probably the sound of a grenade pin bouncing around on the floor.

When I went over the top of the wall, I ran into Bart and took him with me; we landed hard on the floor of the next compartment. I was just starting to think about pain when the blast of the grenade came through like one beat of a heavy-metal tom-tom. The shrapnel hit the wall with an overwhelming pulse of static and then I could hardly hear anything.

Boone was above us, wiping blood out of his face and trying to get ungrogged. His head had already taken a lot of abuse. Bart was waving his revolver dangerously. "You better take this gun," he suggested. "I'm incredibly drunk."

"Lucky it wasn't a Claymore," Boone said, "or we wouldn't have had the time delay."

"That one seemed like about thirty seconds," I said.

"More like five."

The fragged compartment looked about the way I expected it to. The silver pipe had been severed halfway up. A golden fluid was welling calmly out the top, running down to the floor of the compartment. It wasn't necessary to run an analysis.

We weren't clear about what to do with the dead guys. If it came down to it, we could certainly defend ourselves in court. But you're supposed to bury corpses, or put sheets over them or something, not leave them sitting in a barge compartment that's slowly filling up with toxic waste.

"On the other hand, why not?" Bart said. "For them, this is like dying in church."

"That's good enough for me," Boone said, and jogged away down the catwalk. After about a nanosecond of careful thought, I followed him.

We came down on the opposite side of the barge, in case the Satanists had decided to bring in reinforcements. Once we hit the ground, I waded out into the water a little ways, sweeping my flashlight back and forth across my path. Just before Boone had discovered the shrine, I'd been starting to put a suspicion together in my mind.

The odor we'd noticed on our way over wasn't coming from Spectacle Island. It was coming from the water. But we hadn't noticed it in other parts of the Harbor. Only the part right north of Spectacle Island—where the *Basco Explorer* was anchored.

I scooped half a dozen dead fish out of the surf and tossed them up onto the land. We squatted around them and checked them over.

If the odor came from the dying of Boston Harbor—if

these fish had died from infection with the PCB bug—they would have died at different times. Some would be decomposed, some would be fresh. But if I may be excused another disgusting thought, these fish all looked good enough to eat. They had died within the last couple of hours.

"There's something new in the Harbor," I said. "Something that stinks real bad, and is incredibly toxic. And it stinks worst around the *Basco Explorer*."

"They must do something," Boone said.

"We didn't see any dumping."

"Sure. Years ago, when we started taking movies of them dropping barrels into the water, they got really shy and came up with a new system. They've got tanks in there that can be filled from the top and then drained out the bottom of the hull while the ship is in motion."

"What did Pleshy say to you this morning?"

"Make my day!" Bart said. "It was in the *Herald*."

"That's what he said," Boone said. "Go ahead. Test the Harbor for PCB-eating bugs. Test the sewers. Make my day. You won't find anything."

"Say they filled those hidden tanks with some kind of massively toxic, concentrated stuff, probably an organophosphate, and dumped it into the Harbor tonight. They'd want to anchor near Spectacle Island—the center of the infection. They'd dump it into the water. Everything in the water would die. No one would find it remarkable that fish were dying—remember, the *Herald* called it the Harbor of Death. But at the microscopic level, all those PCB bugs are dying too."

"Just like Kelvin said," Boone said. "If it gets real bad, we might have to nuke the Harbor."

"Jesus," Bart said, "Isn't that a little overkillish?"

"Not at all. Look. Twenty-four hours ago, these guys were dead. They had illegally put a genetically engineered bug into the environment and it was creating a toxic catastrophe. They'd rigged up a scapegoat—Dolmacher—but he'd gotten wise. A loose waste barrel on the deck.

"Now that's all different. Basco's dropping the bomb. Murdering the Harbor. Shit, the sewers too. The drums they were offloading into the Boston Whaler? Probably full of the same stuff. They're probably dumping it into the gutters right now. Exterminating the bug, covering up their traces."

"Kind of blatant," Bart said.

"Not at all," said Boone. "Shit, Basco's back on its home territory here. They're old hands at poisoning the water and getting away with it."

"It can't be traced to the ship, and it can't be traced through the gutters," I said.

"The bastards are getting off scot free," Boone said. He was just breathing the words, he was almost inaudible.

"Kind of looks that way," Bart said.

"We have to get onto that ship." Boone was in outer space now, in a kind of trance, staring at the incantations on the barge. "Before they get rid of the evidence. We have to board the ship and find the tanks they used."

"What would you do then," Bart asked. "Just getting on board wouldn't prove anything."

"We'd have to get the media on board," Boone said.

"No way to do that until they tie up somewhere," I said. "The ship is going to be moored on Basco property, and you can bet they'll have intense security. We can't even get within striking distance without trespassing on their property and getting popped."

"Maybe there's something real mediagenic we could do on board the ship, something the crews could film from a great distance."

"The toxin tanks are way down in the bowels of the thing. There's no way to make them visible from a distance without blowing the ship in two."

"We've handled this kind of thing before—remember the Soviet invasion? We could bring in our own cameras, do our own filming and distribute the tapes."

"That's one option," I said.

"One option. You have another?" Boone said.

"Yeah."

"What's that? Blow it up?"

"Shit no. This is a nonviolent action, I think."

"And what might it be?"

"Steal it. Steal the ship."

"Whoa!" Bart said.

Boone's blue eyes were giving off kind of a Tazer discharge and I felt the need to scoot away from him. We had found a plan.

"Steal the whole fucking ship?" he said. But he knew exactly what I meant.

"Steal the whole fucking ship, before they've had a chance to destroy the evidence—that means tonight—take it out into the Harbor, where the media will be waiting for us. Better yet, take it to Spectacle Island. Have the media in place out here. We can turn it into an all-night minicam slumber party."

"That is just fucking great, man," Boone said, levitating to his feet. "Let's do it, man. It's time to rock and roll."

34

Bart went around to the party side of the barge to find Amy, and Boone and I cut straight across the island to the Zodiac. We were trying to figure out a way to steal the *Basco Explorer*, but we were clueless. Our only real chance to get on board was right now, when it was on the open water. Once it was tied up at a pier, they'd have guards posted on it, toting machine guns and with every excuse to use them. But we didn't have a plan, so the only thing we could think of was to have Boone board it now and leave me on the outside to come up with the plan later. Boone was enthusiastic; he knew I'd think of something. Easy for him to say. We'd leave him a walkie-talkie and have maybe a fifty-fifty chance of being able to communicate with him.

We sat out on the Zodiac and got out two of my big old magnets. I used duct tape to coat them pretty thickly, so they wouldn't clang, and so they'd have good friction against the side of the ship. Then I rigged up little rope stirrups. Boone put on the Liquid Skin, put on a lot of it, then wrestled into a drysuit. It was black, the proper color for domestic terrorism during the evening hours, and would protect everything but his face.

I picked up the walkie-talkie once or twice and asked if Modern Girl was out there, but got no real answer. A walkie-talkie isn't like a telephone; you don't have a private line, just a thick chowder of noise that you try to pick something out of. I tried hard and only got a hint of Debbie's voice, like a whiff of perfume in a hurricane.

Bart came wandering along after about twenty minutes, alone. We went in and picked him up.

"Where's Amy," I asked him.

"Back there. We broke up."

He didn't seem too wrecked. "Sorry. We didn't mean to screw up a good thing."

"She's pissed off because I left her with this guy Quincy when I went and shot those dudes. But the reason I left her with Quincy was because I wanted to make sure she was protected."

"Who's Quincy?"

"The guy I stole this revolver from."

"So where's Amy now?"

"With Quincy."

Boone didn't say anything, just handed him a Guinness. Black beer for black thoughts.

We shoved off, taking it slow because we didn't know what we were doing. I tried the walkie-talkie again and suddenly Debbie's voice came through. Sometimes the radio works, sometimes it doesn't.

"Modern Girl here. I think we can pop the Big Suit for public urination."

The Big Suit had to be Laughlin. She'd never been introduced to him. But on my answering machine, right before the house blew up, she'd described the man as he was ripping off the car.

"He's doing it by the Amazing," she continued, "westbound."

Public urination had to mean that Laughlin was dumping something into the gutters. Just like we thought: the Harbor was dead, now he was killing the sewers too. The Amazing had to be the Amazing Chinese Restaurant out in west Brighton. He was heading down Route 9, heading for Lake

Cochituate, for Tech-Dale. Everything between Natick and the Harbor was going to be antiseptic tonight.

"Can you prove it, Modern Girl?"

"Yup. Losing you, Tainted Meat." And then our transmission got overwhelmed by a trucker, headed up the Fitzgerald Expressway, cruising the airwaves for a blow job.

Boone wrapped up a walkie-talkie in a Hefty bag along with a couple of Big Macs and a flotation cushion. The two magnets he slung from a belt around his waist. The cushion balanced out the weight of the magnets so that he could stay afloat and concentrate on swimming.

With three people and lots of gear, the Zode was near its weight limit, but fifty horses balanced that nicely. Traveling through the dark in an open vehicle made me think of biking through Brighton, so I clicked into my full paranoid mode. Instead of taking a direct route toward the *Basco Explorer*, I took us all the way around the south end of the island, swung a good mile or so out to the east, about halfway to the big lighthouse at the Harbor's entrance, and approached the ship from astern.

Boone said something that I couldn't hear, fell out of the Zode and vanished. The boat sped up by a few knots and we just kept going straight. By now we had nothing to hide, so we just swung right along the side of the *Basco Explorer*, checked it out like a couple of Pöyzen fans from Chicopee who'd never seen a freighter before.

It was pretty quiet. Blue light was flickering out of the windows on the bridge; someone was watching TV, probably the slow-motion replays of their boss getting chopped in the trachea by Boone. And they probably didn't realize that the same guy was crawling right up their asshole at this very moment. We could hear a couple of men talking above us, standing along the rail.

"Hey! Ahoooy, dude!" Bart shouted, "What's happening?"

I couldn't believe it. "Jesus, Bart! We don't want to talk to these pricks."

"Boone said we were supposed to create a diversion, didn't you hear him?" Bart cupped his hands and hollered, "Hey! Anybody up there?" I slapped my hands over my face and commenced deep breathing. I might get noticed, but my description didn't match the old S.T. anymore. No beard, different hair.

The deckhands murmured on for a few seconds, finishing their chat, and then one leaned over to check us out: a young guy, neither corporate exec nor ship's officer, just your basic merchant marine, standing on the rail having a smoke. With the cargo this ship carried, they probably weren't allowed to smoke belowdecks.

"Hey! How fast can this thing go?" Bart shouted.

"Ehh, twenty knots on a good day," the sailor said. Classic Jersey accent.

"What's a knot?"

"It's about a mile."

"So it can go, like, twenty miles in a day? Not very far, man."

My roommate had left me in his dust. I just leaned back and spectated. Technically he wasn't my roommate anymore, our home had been exploded by its owner. I guess that meant we were now friends; kind of terrifying.

"No, no, twenty miles an hour," the sailor explained. "A little more, actually. Hey. You dudes partyin'?"

Bart was getting ready to say, "Sure!," always his answer to that question. Then I imagined this sailor asking to go along, and me spending a couple of hours waiting for them to work their way to the bottom of that garbage can. So I said, "Naah, the cops came and started to bust it up, you know."

"Bummer. Hey, you guys know any good bars in this town?"

"Sure," Bart said.

"Are you Irish?" I asked.

"Bohunk," he said.

"No," I said.

"Hey, we got some Guinness down here. Can we come up there and check out your boat?"

"Ship," the sailor blurted reflexively. Then a diligent pause. "I don't think Skipper'd mind," he concluded. "We're under real tight security when we get into port. 'Cause of terrorists. But this ain't in port."

If Bart had proposed, back on Spectacle Island, that we board in this fashion, I'd have laughed in his face. But that

was Bart's magic. The sailor unrolled a rope ladder down the
side of the ship and we climbed up over the gunwhales.

"You know, in your own utterly twisted way, you've got
more balls than I do," I said to Bart as we were climbing up.
He just shrugged and looked mildly bewildered.

The sailor's name was Tom. We handed him a Guinness
and did a quick orbit of the deck, checking out such wonders
as the anchor chains and the lifeboats and the bit hatches
that led down into the toxic holds. The whole ship stank of
organic solvents.

"Fuckin' water sure stinks tonight," Bart observed. I
kicked him in the left gastrocnemius.

"Yeah, don't ask me about that," Tom said with a kind of
shit-eating chuckle.

After we'd checked out the butt end of the ship, exam-
ined the controls of the big crane, they headed up toward the
bow and I couldn't resist leaning out over the aft rail and trying to nail Boone with a loogie. He was there, all right,
though I wouldn't have seen him if I hadn't been looking.
He was totally black, there weren't any lights back here, and
when he saw someone above him he collapsed against the
hull and froze. I missed by a yard.

I took out a flashlight and shone it over my face for a second. Then I shone it down on his face. I'd never seen utter,
jaw-dropping amazement on Boone's face before and it was
kind of fulfilling. Then I just turned around and left. He was
doing pretty well; he was over halfway up.

Tom showed us the bridge and the lounge where the rest
of the crew was sitting around watching "Wheel of Fortune"
and drinking Rolling Rock. They all said quick hellos and
then went back to watching the tube. We were in your basic
cramped but comfy nautical cabin, with fake-wood paneling
glued up over the steel bulkheads, a semi-installed car stereo
strung out across the shelves, pictures of babes with big tits
on the walls. Up in one corner, a CB radio was roaring and
babbling away for background noise.

We watched the show a little, worked on our beers, exchanged routine male-bonding dialog about the wild scene
on Spectacle Island and the fact that women were present,
some good looking. I let Bart handle most of that; a cutaway

blueprint of the *Basco Explorer* was tacked up on the wall and I was trying to memorize its every detail.

The world's strange. You plan something like sneaking onto a ship and then you get completely paranoid about the chances of being noticed; you figure watchmen are spaced every twenty feet along the rail. But hanging out in that cabin, drinking bad beer and watching TV, surrounded by total darkness outside, I knew these guys never had a chance of noticing Boone. We might as well have dropped him on the deck with a helicopter. I just hoped he'd find a nontoxic hideaway.

They say that parents can pick out their babies' cries in the midst of total pandemonium. Maybe it's true. In Guadalajara, I've seen evidence to support the notion. Anyway, it seems some of those parental circuits were wired into my brain, since I caught Debbie's voice right in that cabin.

My heart was beating so hard it threw me off balance and I had to grab a bulkhead. I thought she was somewhere on board. I thought they'd taken her prisoner, then I traced the sound to the CB in the corner.

A powerful transmission was breaking through the clutter. I heard the sound of an outboard motor, the chuff of waves against a fiberglass hull and a man's voice, high-pitched and strained: "*Explorer . . . Explorer . . . come in.*" Debbie's voice was in the background, on the same transmission. I couldn't make it all out, but she was issuing some kind of death threat, and she was scared.

I took a swig of Guinness to relax, breathed deep and said, "Hey, I think someone's calling you."

That brought the skipper awake. He was a gleeful, potato-faced Irishman who'd been lying on a naugahyde bench, dozing through the tail end of a rough thirty-six hours, probably having been called out of a bar in Jersey to make an emergency run to Boston. He ambled over and picked up the mike. "*Explorer.*"

On the other end, a new voice had taken over. "It's Laughlin. We're coming in," he said, loud and tense and dominating.

"Dogfuckers!" Debbie called in the background.

Withering disgust passed over the skipper's face; he wasn't

in control of his own ship. The world's biggest asshole was running the show. "We're still out here," he said.

The crewmen turned away from the TV and laughed.

"We have some special cargo to bring on board and we need to do it quickly and quietly," Laughlin said, "we'll probably need a crane and a net."

I tried to think of nonviolent ways to torture Laughlin to death.

"I think you guys better go," Tom said.

"That's okay, I feel kind of sick anyway," I said.

Bart shrugged, clueless but cooperative. We cleared out. I remembered to turn around at the last minute and check the channel they were using on the CB: Eleven.

On the ladder, I was ready to jump into the water to get there faster. Then I thought about what was being pumped out underneath us. If they were unloading enough poison to kill every bug in the Harbor, it must be incredibly concentrated in the vicinity of the ship. So I took the slow way down; when you're in a hurry, it takes a hell of a long time to descend a rope ladder. But by the time Bart got to the bottom I'd started the motor; by the time Tom had leaned over the rail to wave good-bye to us, we were a hundred feet away, invisible, picking up speed.

Next challenge: picking out the boat where Debbie was being held. The obvious thing was to hang around the *Basco Explorer* and wait. Then I got to thinking: what if Laughlin changed his mind and decided to dump her in the Harbor? I picked up our walkie-talkie to listen, then realized it didn't even receive channel eleven.

They had to be coming from the mainland. We knew they'd been beaching their boats somewhere along Dorchester Bay. That still left us with a lot of water to cover, but with the fifty-horse motor, this Zodiac absolutely kicked ass. I cranked it up and headed for Southie in a broad zigzag. I told Bart what we were looking for: a Boston Whaler ferrying Debbie and a pack of goons.

The bastards weren't using their running lights; we almost ran right over them. Bart noticed it first and grabbed my arm and then I saw the side of the boat, white fiberglass with a harpoon logo, right in our path. Jerked the motor to one side, came very close to capsizing the Zode, and blew a twenty-foot rooster tail of toxic brine over their transom.

When I brought it around I was expecting them to be blasting out of there, trying to get away from us—make my day, Laughlin—but they were dead in the water, rooting around for flashlights. Bart speared a beam into the Whaler and blinded some goons, but we saw no signs of Debbie. She must have seen us, and jumped out, and now she couldn't call out for help because they'd hear her too. Either that, or her head wasn't above water.

I picked up a flotation cushion and frisbeed it back into her general location, then picked a different place and waved the flashlight. "She's over there!" I shouted, loud enough to be heard, cranked the Zode and headed out into the middle of nowhere. Within seconds I heard them behind me. I brought the Zode around to a stop and aimed the light into the water again as they headed toward us with all the horse-power they had.

When I knew they were going to overshoot, I twitched the throttle again and blew out of their path, spun the boat and returned to where I'd thrown out the cushion.

It was still there, bobbing up and down on the clashing wakes of the boats, and Debbie was clinging to it.

Laughlin didn't have a chance. Debbie only weighed a hundred pounds and we had two scared-shitless men to haul her into the boat. We hardly even had to slow down. Then we were plowing a trench in the murdered Harbor, heading for the lights.

35

BEHIND US WE HEARD the asshole emptying his fat chrome revolver in frustration—*kablam kablam kablam*.

Debbie was writhing around in Bart's arms. I wanted to take his place pretty badly, but if he took mine at the tiller we'd all be swimming within a couple of seconds. She managed to get her face aimed over the side of the boat and then vomited a couple of times. Probably swallowed some brine when she jumped overboard.

When she rolled over on her back, her wrists glinted, and I realized that Laughlin had handcuffed her. I could feel my balls contract up into my body and then everything went black. It's possible to go into a drunken rage without even being drunk; it's possible to black out on emotion. I just sat there, hunched over like The Thinker, not looking where I was taking us. And I didn't even pay attention to Debbie, which is what I really should have done. This wasn't for her benefit, unfortunately, it was for mine. Thank God the gun was empty, because I was ready to go back, before Laughlin had time to reload, and make the front page of the *Herald*: FOUR DIE IN HARBOR BLOODBATH.

Things got a little confusing. Debbie was leaning back between my thighs and I was kissing her. Bart was reaching out from time to time, grabbing my arm, steadying the course. I didn't even know where we were going; certainly not to U.Mass–Boston, which is where we were headed. We decided to aim for the skyscrapers, maybe to the Aquarium docks. The people at the Aquarium needed to be warned anyway, since a lot of their fish breathed water from the Harbor.

"They loaded those drums onto vans," Debbie was saying. It seemed like she wasn't pissed at all about being kidnapped, handcuffed and almost killed. She was totally calm. Of course she was totally calm; she'd made it, she'd survived. "I followed one of the vans out west, across Roxbury and Brookline and Newton. Every so often they'd stop along the gutter. I figured out they were dumping into the sewers. The vans had pipes or something that dumped the wastes out the bottom."

"Did you get . . ."

"Yeah, I got samples. Scraped them up out of the gutter. Real bad-smelling stuff. Of course they've got 'em now. The camera too."

"How did they catch you?"

"The car phone rang. Stopped by the curb for a few minutes to talk and they came from behind and got me with guns."

For a minute I thought that was the stupidest thing I'd ever heard. "Who the hell was it from? You should've told them to call you back."

"Couldn't. It was from Wyman."

"Wyman!? What did that silly fuck want?"

"He was tipping us off. He says Smirnoff is going to do something tonight."

"Oh, shit."

"Going to blow up a big ship in Everett. He's got some plastic explosive."

"A Basco ship?"

"Yeah."

Water was streaming down her face, though by now she should have been wind-dried. She was sweating and shivering at the same time. In the dim, grey light coming off the city, I could see a trail of saliva roll out the corner of her mouth and down toward her ear.

"He's got a navy demolition man," she chattered.

"Debbie," I said, "did you swallow any of that water?"

She didn't answer.

"I love you, Debbie," I said, because it might be the last thing she'd ever hear.

We weren't going especially fast. I cranked the throttle back up and asked Bart to put some fingers down her throat. It wasn't necessary, though, because she was vomiting on her own. By the time we were in the Charles River Locks, north of downtown, the odor of shit and urine had mixed with the vomit and the bile, and her wrists were bleeding because she was convulsing in her handcuffs.

The Zode got us to within a couple hundred feet of the best hospital in the world, and then I put her over my shoulders in a fireman's carry and ran with her. Bart ran out onto Storrow Drive and stopped traffic for me. The Emergency Room doors were approaching, a rectangle of cool bluish light, and finally they sensed my presence and slid open.

The waiting room was full. All the benches and most of the floor were infested with dustheads, half handcuffed, half in convulsions. Someone had been handing out bad chowder at the Pöyzen Böyzen concert.

This was no good. Debbie's nervous system was completely shorted out; she was thrashing so hard, like a woman possessed by Ashtoreth, that together Bart and I could hardly hold her.

"Organophosphate poisoning," I shouted. "Cholinesterase inhibitor."

"Drug related," said the nickel-plated nurse receptionist. "You'll have to wait your turn," she continued, as we blew past her and into the corridor.

We hauled Debbie from room to room, chased by a cortege of nurses and security guards, until I found the right one and kicked the door open.

Dr. J. turned around and was amazed. "Alright, S.T.! You have a new look! Thanks for coming around, man! I'm kind of busy now but . . ."

"Jerry! Atropine! Now!" I screamed. And being Dr. J., he

had a syringe of atropine going into her arm within, maybe, fifteen seconds. And Debbie just deflated. We laid her out on the linoleum because a two-hundred-fifty pound Pöyzen Böyzen fan was strapped to the table. Dr. J. began to check her signs. A lynch mob of ER nurses had gathered in the hallway.

"SLUD," Dr. J. said.

"What?"

"SLUD. Salivation, Lachrymation, Urination, and Defecation. The symptoms of a cholinesterase inhibitor. What, S.T., are you handling nerve gas now? Working for, like, the Iraqis or something?"

"These guys make the Iraqis look like fucking John Denver," I said.

"Well, that's a real drag. But your friend is going to be physically okay."

"Physically?"

"We have to check her brain functions," he said. "So I'm going to get a consult on this."

Pretty soon they brought a gurney and hauled her away to someplace I couldn't go. "We'll get word on this pretty soon," Dr. J. said, "so just chill out for a little."

He turned back to the Pöyzen Böyzen on the table. Despite his size and PCP overdose, he'd been pretty quiet. Mostly because he was strapped down with six-point leather restraints. Not that he didn't want to kill us.

"Hey, check it out!" Dr. J. was pulling some slips of paper out of the guy's studded vest. "Tickets to a private party, man! Or ticket stubs, I should say. Up in Saugus. There's three of them. Hey, I'm off in fifteen minutes, let's check it out."

The patient protested the only way he could, by arching his back and slamming his ass into the table over and over again.

"I'll bet his old lady's still up there. Hey, I'll bet she's cute!"

The guy figured out how to use his vocal cords at some preverbal level and Dr. J. had to shout to be heard.

"Jeez, can you believe I already gave this guy twenty-five mils of Haldol? PCP is amazing stuff, man!"

"Dr. J.!" a nurse was screaming. "We have other patients!"

"His keychain's right there, man," Dr. J. said, nodding to a big wad of chain hanging out of the guy's pocket. "Grab it and we can fuck around with his Harley."

This room was so loud that we fled into the hallway. "I hate these dusters," Dr. J. said.

A nurse was bearing down on me with a clipboard. I got to thinking about the bureaucratic problems that might arise. Which form do you fill out when a dead terrorist brings a handcuffed, SLUDding organophosphate victim in off the street? How many hours were we going to spend plowing through this question if I stuck around? So I didn't stick around. I told them Debbie had a Blue Cross card in her wallet, and then I split. Once we were a safe distance away, I called Tanya and told her to spread the word: Debbie was in the hospital and she could probably use some visitors. And some bodyguards.

Then I hung up. Bart and I were standing in the parking lot of the Charles River Shopping Center at three in the morning, in the Hub of the Universe, surrounded on all sides by toxic water. Boone was on a ship that was probably headed for Everett right now. When it got there, my favorite environmentalist, Smirnoff, was going to blow it up. Laughlin and the other bad guys would die. That was good. Our sailor friend, the skipper and Boone would probably die too, though. And the evidence we wanted so badly, the tank full of concentrated organophosphates down in the belly of the ship, would become shrapnel. The PCB bugs would be gone from the Harbor, with no way to trace them back to Basco. Pleshy would become president of the United States and eight-year-old schoolchildren would write him letters. My aunt would tell me what a great man he was and military bands would precede him everywhere. And, what really hurt: Hoa would say, well, maybe Canada needs some Vietnamese restaurants.

At least that's the way it seemed right then. I might have stretched a few things, but one thing was for damn sure: we had to stop Smirnoff.

"Is this what they call being a workaholic?" I muttered as we jogged through the North End, heading for Bart's van, chewing on some benzedrine capsules. "I mean, any decent human should be sitting by Debbie's bed, holding her hand when she wakes up."

"Hum," Bart said.

"I would give anything to kiss her right now. Instead, she's going to wake up and say, 'Where is that fucker who claims he loves me?' I'm out working, that's where I am. I've been working for, what, ninety-six hours straight?"

"Forty-eight, maybe."

"And can I take time out to hold the hand of a sick woman? No. This is workaholism."

"Pretty soon the speed'll kick in," Bart explained, "and you'll feel better."

We found the van where he'd left it, but someone had broken in and ripped off the stereo and the battery. He'd parked on a flat space by the waterfront so I got to push-start it. That was fun. The speed helped there. "I wish we had the stereo," he said.

We headed south along Commercial street, running along all the piers, and when we looked to the east we could see the *Basco Explorer* churning its way northward, blending the poison into the Harbor with its screws. A major crime was taking place right out there, in full view of every downtown building, and there wasn't a single witness. Toxic criminals have it easy.

Eventually we got ourselves to Rory Gallagher's house in Southie. He was back from the hospital now, healthy enough to threaten us with physical harm for coming around at this time of night. We got him calmed down and asked him how we could get in touch with the other Gallaghers, the Charlestown branch of the family.

Here's the part where I could cast racial aspersions on the Irish and say that they have a natural fondness for acts of terrorism. I won't go that far. It's fairer to say that a lot of people have fucked them over and they don't take it kindly. Gallagher, he loved Kennedy and he loved Tip, but he'd always suspected Pleshy, who was a Brahmin, who pissed on his leg whenever he spoke about the fishing industry. When I told Rory how Basco and Pleshy—to him they were a single unit—had poisoned his body and many others, he turned completely red and responded just the right way. He responded as though he'd been raped.

"But we've pushed them," I explained, "pushed and pushed them and made them desperate, forced them into bigger crimes to cover up the old ones. That's why we need your brother."

So we got Joe on the phone. I let Rory argue with him for a while, so he'd be fully awake when I started my pitch. Then I just confiscated the telephone. "Joseph."

"Mr. Taylor."

"Remember all that garbage your grandpa dumped into the Harbor?"

"I don't want to hear any shit about that at this time of the morning. . . ."

"Wake up, Joe. It's Yom Kippur, dude. The Day of Atonement is here."

I knew Rory's phone wasn't bugged, so we made all kinds of calls. We called an Aquarium person I knew and gave her the toxic Paul Revere. Called all the media people whose numbers I could remember, yanked them right out of bed. Called Dr. J. for an update on Debbie; she was doing okay. The Gallaghers made a couple of calls and inadvertently mobilized about half of the self-righteous anger in all of Southie and half of Charlestown. When we walked out Gallagher's front door to get back in Bart's van, we found, waiting in the front yard, a priest with chloracne, a fire engine, a minicam crew and five adolescents with baseball bats.

We borrowed a car battery from one of the adolescents and drove crosstown toward Cambridge, taking the two largest adolescents with us. Along the way, I gave Bart a brief lesson in how to run a Zodiac—one of the Townies kept saying "I know, I know"—and then dropped them all off on the Esplanade near Mass General.

Then I took the van to GEE headquarters. Gomez's Impala was there, and I met him in the stairway. "Thanks for the warning," I said. I'd had plenty of time to think about that voice on my answering machine—"your house has a huge fucking bomb in the basement. Get out, now."

"I'm sorry," he said.

"They probably came on to you real nice," I said. "Laughlin seemed so decent. All they wanted was information. They'd never hurt anyone."

"Fuck that, man, you cost me a job. I just didn't want to see you get killed."

"We should talk later, Gomez. Right now I have business, and I don't want you to know anything about it."

"I'm out of here."

He left, and I stood there in the dark until I heard his Impala start up and drive away.

Now was the time to use the most awesome weapon in my arsenal, a force so powerful I'd never dreamed of bringing it out. Locked up in a cheap, sheet-metal safe in my office, to which I alone had the combination, were a dozen bottles filled with 99% pure, 1,4-diamino butane. The stench of death itself, distilled and concentrated through the magic of chemistry.

During the drive here I'd started to wonder whether this was a good idea, whether this stuff was as bad as I'd built it up to be in my mind. All doubt was removed when I opened the safe door. None of the bottles had leaked, but when I'd filled them, a month ago, I'd unavoidably smeared a few droplets on the lids, and all those putrescine molecules had been bouncing around inside of the safe ever since, looking for some nostrils to climb up. When they climbed up mine, I knew that this was a good plan.

I put the bottles into a box. I took my time about it and packed crumpled newspapers around the glass. Plastic would have been safer but the stuff would have diffused through the walls.

Then I grabbed my scuba gear. This was going to involve underwater work and, once the putrescine escaped, I'd need bottled air anyway. I got the Darth Vader Suit. I stole someone's SoHo root beer from the fridge and chugged the whole bottle. It was made from all natural ingredients.

36

Just on a hunch, I took the long way around to Basco. Hopped Rte. 1 up into Chelsea and then peeled off on the Revere Beach Parkway, which runs west through the heart of Everett and just south of Basco's kingdom. When I saw the Everett River Bridge coming up, I slowed down a little and flicked on the high beams.

An abandoned van was sitting on the shoulder of the high-way—déjà vu—in exactly the same place where Gomez and I had stripped our old van after Wyman, the wacky terrorist, had left it there.

From here, you could get on the freeway, or you could slog across some toxic mudflats and boltcut your way onto Basco property, or you could go fifty feet up the shoulder, disappear under the bridge and mount an amphibian operation upstream into Basco's docking facilities. I could look straight across the flats from here and into the bridge of the *Basco Explorer*, now nestled into place in the shadow of the main plant. It was no more than a quarter of a mile away. Park a van on the shoulder here and you had a command outpost for any kind of attack on Basco.

What had Wyman been up to when he'd trashed our last

van here? Was it a dress rehearsal, or a failed operation? Or had it been a real accident, one that had planted the seed of this idea to begin with?

I sure as hell wasn't going to park here. Didn't even slow down. I drove the van across the bridge until I was out of sight of Basco, parked it on the shoulder and slogged down to the riverside under the bridge, carrying half my weight in various pieces of crap. Bart and his Townie friends were already there, smoking a reefer. They'd been joined by a couple of black derelicts who evidently lived here. Bart had fed them all of our Big Macs.

"Haven't you heard, man?" I said, "Just say no!" They were startled. Pot always made me more paranoid than I was to begin with; I couldn't understand how they'd want to smoke it here and now.

"Want a hit?" Bart croaked, waving the reefer around and trying to talk while holding his breath.

"See any action?" I asked.

"Big fuck-up over there," Bart said, waving in the direction of the flats. "Bunch of cop cars showed up and arrested some guys. Then one of them got stuck in the mud."

"It was great," one of the derelicts said. "They had to ask the prisoners to get out so they could push it out of the shit."

"So," Bart said, "I guess we don't have to worry about this Smirnoff dude any more."

"That was a diversion," I said. "Smirnoff's a jackass, but he's not stupid. He sent some people in through the obvious route, with boltcutters. Ten to one they're unarmed and they'll get popped for trespass. Meanwhile he's got a diver somewhere in this river with the real package. A navy veteran."

I wondered if the guy was an ex-SEAL. That would be great. What were my odds in man-to-man underwater combat in a dark sea of nerve gas with a SEAL? The only option was just to avoid the diver, find the mine and disconnect it. If Smirnoff had really rigged it up out of plastique, it had to be something pretty simple and obvious, probably timed with a Smurf wristwatch. Bart had brought the toolbox from his van and I grabbed wirecutters and a prybar.

"Did you get ahold of Boone?" I said, nodding at the walkie-talkie.

"Tried. Put out a call for Winchester, like you said, but no answer."

"That's okay. He'll figure it out. Too risky to talk on the radio anyway." I set down the box of putrescine and lifted the lid. "This is the bad stuff."

Two bottles went into my goody bag and the rest into the Zodiac. We all squatted together on the riverbank and went over it one last time, and then I made myself incommunicado by turning on the air valve and strapping my head into the Darth Vader mask. Everyone watched this carefully; one of the derelicts' lips moved and then I could feel them all laughing. I waded into the river.

First I swam across and checked out the opposite bank. Definite tracks in the muck here. Big, triangular, flipper-shaped tracks. I started swimming toward the *Basco Explorer*.

Technically I was swimming upstream here, but the speed of the current was zero. There had been a mild smell of the poison, not nearly as bad as earlier tonight. But I had to figure they were poisoning this river too, since it led straight to Basco Central and they wouldn't want any trail of PCB bugs leading in here from the Harbor.

Sometimes I couldn't believe the shit I did for this job. But if I could pull something off here, I'd have a good excuse for taking a couple of days off. Debbie and I could climb into a waterbed somewhere and recuperate together, not get out of bed for about a week. If she'd have me. Go out to Buffalo, maybe, get back into that honeymoon suite, buy a shitload of donuts and a Sunday *L.A. Times*. . . .

About ten seconds of those thoughts and I had got an erection and felt really drowsy and stupid. Hadn't taken enough speed. I checked the valve on the tank to make sure I was getting plenty of oxygen. Oxygen, oxygen, the ultimate addiction, better even than nitrous oxide. Tonight I needed lots. Had to keep alert, had to watch out for that SEAL. But it was such a boring trip, swimming through blackness and murk without a light. Easy to get scared, natural to fall into paranoia and despair. Every so often I broke the surface to check my direction and to see how close I was to the prow of the *Basco Explorer*. At first it was too far away, then, suddenly, it was much too close.

If I were a terrorist, where would I place my bomb? Probably right under the big diesels, amidships. Even if it didn't sink the ship, this would do the most damage.

The docking facilities here weren't huge. Basco owned the end of the Everett River. That's how rivers worked around Boston Harbor—ran inland for a mile and then just ceased to exist, fed underground by sewers and culverts. Basco surrounded the river in a U shape. On one side of it they had a pier, and the other side was just undeveloped, basically a siding for a railway spur that ran up into Everett. If they had guards, they'd be on the side with the pier. So I stayed on the right, the eastern half of the river, and started to slide on up the hull of the *Basco Explorer*.

For the first few yards, feeling my way over the sonar dome at the bottom of the prow, I had my head above water. Then I had to face the fact that if I stayed up here, the SEAL could come from below and gut me like a tuna. Either way, I was in his element. But if I tried to be half-assed about it, I was in double trouble.

So I dove. I swam straight down to the bottom, which was only about ten feet below the bottom of the *Basco Explorer*'s hull. I could almost stand on the bottom and touch the ship with one outstretched hand. They'd probably dredged this channel out to the *Explorer*'s dimensions.

Then I realized that we were dealing with small volumes of water. I was used to the open Harbor. This was a lot more claustrophobic. I was in a space about the size of a couple of mobile homes, and if the SEAL was still here, he was sharing my space.

The water transmitted a powerful metallic clang. Impossible to tell direction, but obviously something had struck the ship's hull. Possibly the magnets on Smirnoff's mine. If I hunkered down, pretended to be a chunk of toxic waste and waited, the driver would swim away and I could clip the wires. But I wondered: what was the time delay on the sucker? It had to be fairly long. The diver had to get away, the water-hammer effect could kill you from a distance. This was reassuring.

From using up the compressed air, I'd become slightly buoyant, a little lighter than the water, and it was hard to stay on the bottom. So I relaxed and let myself float upwards until I was spread-eagled against the bottom of the hull, facing down. I made sure I was a little east of the keel, so my bubbles skimmed off to the right, following the ship's curve, and came out on the unwatched side.

Another clang, very close, so close that I felt the vibrations through my tank and into my back. Then there was a light, coming toward me. You couldn't see a light more than a few feet in this shitty water. Then the light disappeared. Whoever owned it had shut it off.

Then another damn light, in front of and below me, almost on the bottom, cut into thick rays of shadow by the limbs of a diver.

Two divers. One swimming up where I was, his tank clanging against the hull. The second, the one with the light, heavier, using his weight to kick his way along the bottom. The one at my level had shut off his light so he couldn't be seen. The other was chasing him.

The prey almost got face-to-face with me and our masks looked at each other for just a second, amazed. He was wearing an underwater moonsuit, like mine, made for diving in a toxic environment.

Why? Smirnoff wouldn't know about the poison coming out of the *Basco Explorer*. He'd been planning this action for months. But this diver knew about it. Working for Basco?

He sank away from me because the other diver, below him, had grabbed him by the ankle and was pulling him down. He was kicking and thrashing but that's hard when you're underwater, and maybe a little tired of running. Steel glinted, and then the light was shining through a crimson thunderhead.

What was I going to do? All I could hope was that this killer with the knife hadn't seen me. I wasn't about to outswim him. If one of these guys was a SEAL, I had to figure it was the live one.

The light had gotten kicked by the victim, flailing around in his own blood, and the beam was slowly rotating as it sank. It spun by the killer's head and I saw a bare white face, long brown hair, blue eyes.

Tom Akers was working for Smirnoff.

Which meant the dead guy was Basco's. So maybe Tom wouldn't decide to cut me up. I pushed off against the hull and began sinking down into his level. He grabbed the light and nailed me with the beam, paralyzing me, getting a look at who I was. It was all up to him.

Through my eyelids I saw the light diminish as he pointed it somewhere else. When I could see again, I wished I couldn't. Tom was curled into a fetal position in the water, vomiting, groping around for his mouthpiece.

I was able to get over to him and shove the mouthpiece toward him again, but he just shot it out on a yellow jet of bile. SLUD. He was quivering in my arms and I saw him suck in a big bellyful of that awful black water and swallow it down. Then he looked up into my eyes—his pupils were dilated so there wasn't any iris left—and held up two fingers. Which could have meant two, or peace, or victory.

By the time I'd wrestled him up to the east side of the ship, he was dead. I left him bobbing there, face down, and swam back underneath to look for the mine.

And I found it—it was easy to look when I didn't have to worry about other divers—but it wasn't what I was looking for. This was a real mine, not a homemade one. An honest-to-god chunk of official U.S. Navy ordnance, stuck to the bottom of the hull, not exactly in the right place, a dozen yards forward of the engine room.

Maybe Tom had been trying to tell me there were two mines. That would make sense. Two divers, two mines. I swam back and found another one under the engine room, this one made from the bottom of a plastic garbage can and a couple of big old industrial magnets.

To pry it off and find the wires leading to the digital timer was easy enough. I clipped them off with the wirecutter and let this piece of junk sink to the bottom.

Now for the second. I swam back for a closer look and noticed a new fact: it was right in between a couple of vents in the bottom of the hull. Probably vents for toxic waste. This mine had been planted by a Basco diver, in protective gear because he knew the water was poisoned. They were sending their evidence to the bottom.

Laughlin was a goddamn evil genius. Poison the Harbor, kill the bugs, blow up the evidence, get rid of a rusty old tank, collect the insurance, blame it on wicked terrorists.

I tried to yank it off, but it wasn't going to come peacefully. Its magnets were bigger and more powerful than Smirnoff's. Bart's prybar got under it, but as Archimedes pointed out, the lever's no good without a place to stand. I had to invert myself and put my feet against the bottom of the hull. There were three divers down here tonight—The Three Stooges Stop Pollution—two of us were dead, and that left me to handle the slapstick comedy. That's probably what it looked like. But eventually the mine came loose and dropped to the bottom.

Next question: how much damage could it do from there? As my last major suicide attempt of the night, I swam down there and dragged it across the bottom until it was off to the side, maybe forty feet away from the ship. If it went off there, that was just too bad. The *Basco Explorer* would just have to take it like the sturdy old bucket she was.

When I paddled wearily away from that mine, I allowed myself to hear again, and what I heard was diesels. Immense diesels. Didn't need to break the water to know what it was. I swam under the ship, emerged under the Basco pier, climbed up a ways into the pilings, and lobbed one bottle of putrescine up there.

Bart's signal was the sound of projectile vomiting from the security guards on the pier. He came in fast and loud on the Zodiac, kept the *Basco Explorer* between him and the guards, and got his assistants to lob the rest of the putrescine up onto the ship. He was pretty good at this; maybe GEE should hire him as my replacement.

I'd always wanted to bomb a toxic waste ship, or a factory, with this stuff. If you really soaked it, the target would become worthless. You'd have to tow it out to sea and burn every last bit. That was going to be the *Basco Explorer's* fate, but not immediately.

All I could see was the side of the ship and the underside of the decking on the pier. I had to follow the action by noises. An awesome mixture of putrescine and vomit was dripping down through the cracks, raining down around me, and about the time Bart and company made their attack, I could hear some thudding and clomping as one of the guards staggered off the pier in the direction of an adjacent building.

There were guards on deck, too, and they didn't last long. The trick was going to be getting the putrescine below-decks. The crew was probably out carousing somewhere, but Laughlin might be downstairs arranging the evidence.

An alarm bell went off. The guards were asking for help. It was time to get the hell out of here. I'd already kicked off my flippers and now I worked my way over to a ladder and climbed up to where I could look out over the surface of the pier.

Three of the guards were doubled over on their sides, writhing around.

Did this count as violence? Assaulting the senses with something unendurably disgusting?

How about the strobe light on top of the U-Haul, back there in Buffalo? Same deal. A bunch of security guards had been assigned to look out for us and we had made life miserable for them.

I guess it all came under the heading of "obnoxious behavior, creative forms of." One of these days I'd have to work it all out. Someday, when I had a little free time.

It seemed like these guys weren't going to be shooting at me, but to make sure I picked up their submachine guns. They looked like Bart's UZI-replica water pistols but they were much heavier. I spun them off into the river. Then I ran for the gangplank, carrying my last bottle of putrescine like a grenade. "Gangplank" is a primitive word; it was an aluminum footbridge, complete with safety railings and a nonslip surface. And I was right in the middle of it when the hatch opened up, right in front of me, and Laughlin stepped out.

The jumbo chrome-plated revolver—the one he'd bought to protect himself from terrorists—looked a little tacky so close to his gold Rolex, but that's in the nature of a revolver. He was carrying a briefcase in his other hand, an executive to the fucking end. And when he saw me blocking the gangplank, he did a funny thing. He held it up between me and him, like a shield, and peeked at me over the top. I got a couple of steps closer. Then he dropped the briefcase.

Which didn't help me a bit. I wasn't here to subpoena the bastard. I kept moving, trying to decide when I was going to chicken out and jump off into the water.

Movement on a ship ain't easy. The stairs are narrowed and steep, the hatches weigh a lot and you have to step over a big ledge when you go through them. Laughlin was centered in the hatchway, but his right shoulder, the one attached to the revolver, was interfered with by the doorframe. When he tried to bring his arm up, he twitched against the trigger—already had the thing cocked, the guy was a born killer—and fired off a shot underneath the pier.

I wound up and tossed a kind of weak Bob Stanley palmball in the general direction of his face. The jar described a neat stinky parabola through space, bounced off the top of his head and exploded behind him. He fired again and drilled a hole in the Basco factory. I was scared enough to fall down on my face. Hard to run with an oxygen tank on your back, damn hard.

He had to be wading through a putrescine sea by now anyway, but he didn't notice. A good yuppie has no sense of smell. Laughlin's next shot hit a railing support right next to me and drilled a few metal splinters in my direction. Some of them stuck in my flesh and one shattered the face plate on my Darth Vader mask. Laughlin closed in for a closer shot, made the mistake of stepping through the hatchway and then Boone nailed him in the ear with the output of a CO_2 fire extinguisher.

I fucked up my hand trying to rip all those little triangles of glass out of my facemask. Managed to smear a nice gob of blood and putrescine directly on the bridge of my nose. I could still breathe bottled air, fortunately.

Several barfing blue-collar gnomes came up from below, stumbled over the writhing Laughlin and headed toward me, which is to say they tried to get the fuck out of there. Boone had grabbed Laughlin's revolver and that scared the shit out of them.

I grabbed the mask and pulled it away from my mouth.

"Take him!" I shouted, pointing at Laughlin. "Get that fucker out of here. Take him with you."

If we stole the ship with them on board, it'd be kidnapping: a serious charge. We had to get Laughlin off. But if we dragged him off, that might be kidnapping too.

They grabbed Laughlin and dragged him down the gangplank. The ship was empty. Boone had put on an oxygen mask, he'd stolen from a fire box somewhere.

He was pointing at Laughlin's briefcase. He gave it a kick so it slid a few feet away, then brought the revolver down and fired at it. The bullet dug a crater in the fine Moroccan leather, then stopped. Kevlar-lined. Anti-terrorist luggage for the paranoid executive.

For the first time, I got a chance to look down the river, toward the Mystic River and the open sea. The megatug, *Extra Stout*, was crawling toward us through the blue predawn light, looking like a power plant on a toboggan, plugging the entire river, kicking out a galaxy of black smoke. It was atonement time for Clan Gallagher. 21,000 horses of Irish diesel proceeded ass-backwards, shaking the earth and the water, rattling the windows of the factory. It almost drowned out the meaty splash made when we deposited the gangplank into the Everett River.

We had to get this damn ship disconnected from the pier. That was the whole objective. It was connected by a bow line, a stern line, and two spring lines: four lines. Something big and heavy slapped into my hand. Boone had gotten me a fire ax. He had one of his own.

"This is your only warning," said a voice over some loud-speakers. "Put your hands in the air now or we will be forced to shoot."

One warning. I was guessing we could each take out a rope during the one warning. We headed for the stern. There were two ropes attached to bitts back there.

Ever chop wood? Sometimes if you flail away in a panic, you don't get anywhere, but two or three solid chops will do the job. I used both techniques on the spring line, and I didn't chop it through, but I reduced it to a few shreds of yarn that could be relied on to break. Bone severed the stern line in about four strokes.

The guys with the guns had a basic problem here. The deck was a few feet higher than the pier. If we stayed on our bellies, they couldn't see us. So we spent the rest of the gig on our stomachs.

Boone had less stomach than I did, and he knew how to do this GI crawl, so he traveled about twice as fast as me. He ripped off the oxygen mask and splashed it.

By the time I made it to the other end, pushing Laughlin's briefcase in front of me, Boone was way out on the prow, feeding a rope down through one of the hawse-holes, the tunnels that the anchor chains passed through. Bart was down below us on the Zodiac, waiting. He was going to take it out to *Extra Stout*, now about fifty feet away; they'd attach it to a hawser, and we'd haul that up here and attach it to the *Basco Explorer*. I was several yards behind Boone, my Swiss Army knife deployed, sawing through the bow lines strand by strand.

I was lying on the deck with my head sideways, and I noticed that I could see a Basco water tower a thousand feet away. And I could see some guys climbing up there. Guys with guns. Three of them.

Something whizzed over our heads and we heard a distant crack-crack-crack.

"M-16s," Boone said, "or AR-15s, actually."

I slid the briefcase over to him. "I'm done with my part," he explained, and kicked it back to me.

Sawdust flew and a narrow trench appeared in the deck about four feet away from me. At this range, the rounds from the rifles had picked up a vicious tumbling action that would cause them to chew around inside your body like some kind of parasite from outer space.

My air tank exploded and I felt myself being stabbed in the back. There was continuing noise; I was hollering but that wasn't just me. It was the *Extra Stout*'s boathorn, giving us the signal to pull. Boone was going to need help so I got the briefcase in between my face and the water tower and crawled forward, toward the hawse-hole.

I found the rope and started pulling on it. Boone didn't seem to be helping any. There was a lot of slack and then it started pulling back.

Joe Gallagher had told me to look for the towing bitts—sturdy posts sticking out of the deck. If I looped the hawser onto anything else, the *Extra Stout* would just rip it loose. I found the bitts and rolled their way, trying to keep that briefcase with me, hauling on that rope. If I kept hauling, I'd find Gallagher's hawser. A Kevlar towing line. Kevlar—a wonder material, doubly useful tonight. A product of America's chemical industry. Helping to keep our nation strong. But it was heavy. I put a turn of the rope around the bitt so that it wouldn't slide back on me, and kept pulling on the fucker.

The briefcase jumped into the air as it soaked up a few high-velocity rounds and landed on the deck, out of my reach. I was judging the distance to it when everything was drowned out by sound and light. Maybe they'd thrown up some star flares and started artillery bombardment. This was deep-shit industrial noise, loud enough to cause kidney failure, and fulgurating light, brighter than the sun.

Time to surrender. I scooted away from the cleat, waving my hands. I writhed loose from the remains of the air tank, but it still felt like someone was standing on my back in hockey skates. That allowed me to roll over, belly up like every fish in the Harbor, and stare into the unpolluted heavens. But there was something in the way. Fifty feet above me, a symbolic eyeball looked down from a halogen tornado: a chopper from CBS News.

They wouldn't blow us away on national TV, would they? Highly mediapathic. If they were still shooting, they were missing. I started pulling on the rope again. Boone wasn't helping me because he'd been pretty badly shot.

It went on forever. CBS News would have to edit. The viewing public was sitting around and watching as I endlessly hauled on a fucking rope. On and on and on. CBS watched, the snipers and the guards watched, Gallagher's crew watched, Boone kind of watched through unblinking eyes. No one said anything.

And finally I was holding a big, fat eye splice in my hands, a loop at the end of the Kevlar line, thick as my wrist. The end of the rope. The one that's supposed to go over the bitt. Sailors call it the bitter end. So I tossed it over the bitt, crawled way up to the prow, pulled myself up to my knees, and gave the *Extra Stout* the thumbs up.

The navy mine exploded and sent up a waterspout and a shock wave that nearly swatted the chopper out of the air. Pretty soon the ship started to list—or was that me? I looked up to wave goodbye to the snipers, but the water tower wasn't there anymore. The Everett River Bridge was above me. The derelicts were down there raising a couple of Mc-Donald's pseudoshakes, toasting my health, cheering me on. Brothers in arms.

37

JOE GALLAGHER HAULED US DOWN the river into a sprawling media dawn. Everyone had come out. Tanya was the first on board; she and Bart climbed up on top of the bridge and hoisted the Toxic Jolly Roger. Tanya was perfect because she was a victim, she knew some things about chemistry, and she was pissed. The putrescine was a definite problem, but journalists who knew how to hold their noses could get down into the belly of the *Basco Explorer* and find incredible things.

It was all tremendously illegal, the evidence would have been useless in court—if we had been cops. We weren't. And if a noncop gets some evidence, even through a criminal act, you can use it to prosecute.

Of course, even when you have legally correct evidence, corporations rarely suffer in this country. Look at any big government contractor for the Pentagon or NASA. They can get away with murder.

In the media, it's a different story. Three hundred years ago, in Massachusetts, criminals were put in stocks in the public square and mocked. Today, we can't send those executives to jail, but we can kick them out of civilized society, put them through unendurable emotional stress, and that's just as effective. So Pleshy and Laughlin were being kicked out of civilized society while Boone and I were being taken to the trauma center on a chopped ambulance.

I was suffering from several pissant flesh wounds. Dr. J. gave me that disappointing news. Boone had a sucking chest wound, which I hadn't noticed because I couldn't hear it, and because I was distracted by other things. He'd been able to roll onto his back and press the forearm of his rubber suit against the wound, lubricating the seal with his own blood. That didn't seal it completely but it got a little more air into that lung, kept him from passing out. He had to have half his lung and a good chunk of his liver taken out. No big deal, livers grow back if you don't booze them to death.

When I woke up, Debbie was sitting there in a bathrobe, holding my hand. Yes, we were talking guilt. Guilt and happiness. She was doing pretty well. Organophosphates are not bioaccumulative. If you survive the dose, they go away and you're back to normal.

The explosion of the mine threw Tom Akers way over to the far side of the railway and they didn't find him until the next day. They did an autopsy, because there were so many possible causes of death, and discovered that he was riddled with cancer. We got in touch with his doctor in Seattle and found out that he'd known of the problem for a couple of months; long enough, I guess, to build up a pretty intense hatred for Alvin Pleshy.

Now we're into the part where we sort out all the legal responsibility. Maybe I'll go to jail, who knows. Basco would have to spend lost of money on lawyers to really nail me, and they just declared bankruptcy.

Which sounds kind of satisfying, but it isn't, because bankruptcy is just another ploy, a way to get out of their union contracts and reorganize the company into a lean, mean, litigating machine. I've bought a lot of BMWs for a lot of corporate lawyers.

On the other hand, they're in huge trouble and eventually they really are going to pay. Dolmacher's evidence was suppressed for a few days but now it's out, and it's the mediapathic goods. The attorney general announced that any corporate execs who participated in the contamination of Dolmacher's body are going to be charged with attempted murder. I hear they have lots of weight machines at the State Penitentiary.

Eventually, Basco's going to eat shit and die. So, when they let me out of the hospital, I picked up a magic marker at an office supply store, went down to the yacht club and drew Basco's logo onto the nose of our new Zodiac. This one was donated by the employees of a software company on Route 128.

Then I went for a spin around the Harbor. On my way out of the club, I blew by a nice fifty-foot yacht that was going out for an afternoon cruise. All the well-dressed people grinned, pointed, raised their glasses. I smiled, gave them the finger, and throttled her up.

ABOUT THE AUTHOR

NEAL STEPHENSON is the author of *The Diamond Age, Snow Crash, Zodiac,* and *The Big U.*